Eternity's Song

Eternity's Song

LeeAnn Pappas

CREATIVE ARTS BOOK COMPANY
Berkeley   California

For information contact:
Creative Arts Book Company
833 Bancroft Way
Berkeley, California 94710

The characters, places, incidents and situations
in this book are imaginary and have no relation
to any person, place or actual happening.

ISBN 088739-471-X
Library of Congress Catalog Number 2002114189

Printed in the United States of America

To T, J and V,
the harmony, melody and rhythm
in my life.
...and to Dad.

Eternity's Song

How long had it been since she'd slept? Forty-eight hours? More? Anna's night with Ian now seemed like a distant memory.

Her rental car pulled up alongside the dock at Balbao. Getting out of the car, she remembered again how much she hated Central America. *If the heat and humidity don't kill me this time, maybe the malaria-carrying mosquitoes will.*

A short, sun-tanned man in a crumpled T-shirt approached her. "Anna, good to see you again. Sorry it's always under these circumstances."

"Marcos, good to see you, too." Marcos Yannis had always been her one-man greeting committee. Unquestionably the best troubleshooter in the shipping industry, he had been her grandfather's trusted first mate for years. There was no impending catastrophe that he couldn't fix.

"We've got a pretty serious situation here."

"What a surprise," she responded. "I thought I was coming to the Panama Canal for a vacation." She immediately regretted her tone of voice. After all, Marcos was just doing his job; it certainly wasn't his fault that her entire life was about to spiral out of control. "I'm sorry," she said, "it was a long trip from London and I'm a little tired. Why don't you brief me?"

"The Xenos was loaded in Peru in a remote open sea port, with a cargo of steel pellets. Apparently, she was loaded incorrectly. There's way too much cargo in the last hold."

"Why didn't the Captain short load the ship? He could've fixed the problem with water and fuel when he got here."

"It was the mother of all stupidities. It was the worst possible port to load large bulk-carriers heading for the Canal. But all excuses aside, what we have now is a vessel that's basically stuck."

"Okay, let's take a look at her." Walking towards the ship, Anna's thoughts once again returned to Ian. How could she have allowed him into her life again? No, why did she ever let him leave in the first place? *I should have stayed in London*, she thought, *Marcos could easily have taken care of this mess.*

"First things first," she said. "Why does this ten million dollar ship look like a pretzel? Do you have the cargo distribution plan and calculations for ballast?"

Anna read over the docking report. "Did anyone notice two thousand tons of ballast water in the starboard tank that could be pumped out? Why don't we start there?"

"Pumping will raise the bow but the stern will get steeper."

Anna knew he was right. "Okay, I've got another idea. Start pumping the ballast tank, while I do some calculations."

After having the tank pumped dry, Marcos approached Anna. "Just like I thought. We raised the bow of the ship. There's a heavy list to port and the stern's getting deeper. I suggest you get your head out of your numbers and come and take a look ... a bit like the Titanic on her way down, right?"

Anna looked up and gasped, "Oh my God." She took a deep breath. "Let's get to work on fixing this thing. Take a look at my numbers. Call the local port agent and arrange to rent the floating crane. We're going to redistribute the cargo to the forward hold."

Marcos glanced down at Anna's calculations and looked back at her with an approving smile. "You've been taught well."

"I was taught by the best my friend ... namely, present company."

Standing on the pier by the ship's stern to oversee the operation, Anna felt the sweat eroding her makeup. Her damp clothes clung to her body. She tried to remember the last time she washed her hair but couldn't. At this moment, she was sure she wouldn't even have recognized herself. Her long black hair was pulled back into a greasy ponytail. Usually glowing, her face was the color of milk toast. She mopped her forehead with a tissue, pausing every other second to shoo the mosquitoes away from her head. She wondered if she smelled quite as bad as Marcos. As if Marcos knew what she was thinking, he turned to her and said, "If you don't mind my asking, what's a nice girl like you doing in a shit-hole like this?"

While she watched the ship's stern rise with each grab-load of the crane, she thought about her grandfather, the great shipping magnate, who had spent his whole life building an empire, the empire he had passed on to her. Now she was about to watch it all slip away. And she thought about her father, who would give his life and soul for her, and how her choice of a husband had crushed him.

As her ship slowly settled to an even keel, a wave of anger and rage swept over her. *Damn it. I can't let this happen. I've got to get it all back: my business, my father's trust ... Ian.* She looked at Marcos. "I don't know."

Marcos looked startled. "Did you say something?"

"You asked me a question a few moments ago, and I answered it. The answer is 'I don't know.'"

"I can handle things from here. You look exhausted. Why don't you go check in to the hotel and get some sleep. It looks like the Xenos will be gliding her way through the Canal in the morning."

"Thanks, Marcos. You're the best. But I'm not going back to the hotel. If you need me, I'll be in London in the morning. It's time that I straightened out a few things back home."

Chapter 1

RICHARD AND SARA, 1962

After singing together only a year, the Casuals had a hit. "I'll Never Let You Go" was the number one single in London. Only the Beatles and the Rolling Stones were more popular. The Casuals had become part of the British invasion.

Guitarist Richard Winters led the group. Critics called his words and music "raw," "untraditional," and "electrifying." His rock songs worked audiences into a frenzy, and then brought them to an icy stillness with his ballads. No matter what he did, crowds responded to his music, his smile, and his evident love of performing.

Richard came from a small working class family on the outskirts of London. He worked hard at school, and even harder after school to help his family make ends meet. He listened to the radio every night before he went to bed, always waiting to hear the latest music coming out of America. His father took note of his passion for music and surprised him with a second-hand guitar for his twelfth birthday.

Richard quickly taught himself to play the blues. He started with the typical 1, 5, 4 progression in 'E' and found himself whispering words as he played. He was surprised at how easy it was. He began writing simple songs that delivered an emotional punch. Friends and family were the first to recognize his talent. By the time he was sixteen, he was playing cover songs at pubs and dance halls with a local band.

His own compositions remained hidden in his room until he met another local musician, Nigel Taylor. Richard and Nigel were emotional polar opposites from the start. Nigel was brooding and introspective and always had a sarcastic quip at the ready. Already a confirmed cynic, he was quick to say, "Everybody is born with a dark side. The only reason people do anything good is to get something in return."

Richard embodied everything Nigel despised. His smile was infectious. Everywhere he went people showered him with affection. But, personality clash not withstanding, their music soared beyond what either could do alone. Along with drummer Christian Aprile and bassist Joseph Olsen, they quickly developed a local following. Within a year, the Casuals were playing large venues in London.

When a talent agent from a local recording company saw their act, he was quick to sign them up. Three songs from their first album climbed to the top of the charts. The critics heralded Richard and Nigel as geniuses and poets. The world did not see the resentment and jealously that slowly boiled beneath their seemingly perfect relationship.

Athens was the final stop of their first European tour. Five major cities in six weeks: Geneva, Paris, Rome, Stockholm, and Athens. For four young men who had never been much farther than the shores of Brighton, this trip was an awakening. Though days passed quickly, the traveling proved tiresome. The glamorous vacation they had anticipated became an endless blur of airports, buses, and hotel rooms. After barely enough time to catch a breath between performances, they'd be off to the next city. They did their only sightseeing through the windows of airplanes and buses.

Nevertheless, they performed every night to sold-out crowds. Police escorts became standard operating procedure. The tour was sure to boost their already soaring record sales. But nothing surpassed the news they heard one morning: the Casuals had hit the American billboard charts with "I'll Never Let You Go" debuting at number five and counting. Fame and fortune were theirs.

The last hotel they would see for awhile was the Athens Palace. Its marble columns and high ceilings reflected its ancient surroundings, but more important, at least to Nigel and Richard, Christian and Joseph, it offered every amenity: swimming pools, room service, and large bathrooms with strong water pressure. It was situated in the heart of Athens, close to Syntagma Square, and from the restaurant on the roof the whole city spread at their feet: the whitewashed houses amidst the winding streets during the day, and atop the Acropolis, the Parthenon blazing in the glow of yellow floodlights at night.

That night would be the last performance of the tour. Nigel was exhausted and chose to spend the afternoon relaxing by the pool. He was glad that the tour was coming to an end, but he didn't relish the thought of returning to London, where, this time of year, it was still damp and chilly. *Just a couple of more albums like this last one and I could retire for life in a place like this.* He began to reminisce about his childhood: growing up in a cold-water one-bedroom flat he shared with his alcoholic mother and two brothers. *Lucky for me Winters came along. Why we sound good together, I'll never know, but he's my meal ticket to ...* He began to doze off.

Jerking awake, he felt a tap on his shoulder and heard the sound of a woman's voice.

"Excuse me sir, you really should get out of the sun. You're burnt to a crisp."

Nigel opened his eyes and couldn't believe his good fortune. Standing over him was the most beautiful young woman he had ever seen. Pretty young groupies were always hanging around backstage and at their hotels, but none of them compared to the woman looking down at him right now.

"Are you all right?" she asked with a look of concern.

Mesmerized by her face and not having heard the part about his burnt flesh, he answered "Yeah ... fine. I'm fine. Why are you asking?"

"If you don't get out of the sun soon, you're going to be hospital-ized tonight."

"Shit. I must've fallen asleep. What time is it?"

"Four o'clock" she answered. "How long have you been out here?"

Nigel couldn't remember. "Don't know. Too long I suppose."

"Well, time to get inside." She turned to leave.

Oh no, he thought. *She's not gonna get away that easily.* He paused and scanned the area. "How about if I move under that umbrella over there. Will I be safe?"

She smiled, "That ought to do nicely." Again, she turned to walk away.

He called after her. "Wait. Will you join me for a drink maybe? I hate to sit alone and if you don't, I'll stay here in the sun and you'll be responsible for my extended stay in the Athens hospital."

"That would be irresponsible of me. All right," she continued still smiling, "lead the way."

They began to walk. She turned to him. The low rays of the late afternoon sun bounced off her cheekbones and illuminated her incred-ible complexion. "My name's Sara, Sara Stavropoulos, and you are?"

Nigel had never believed in fate before, but at this moment, nothing seemed certain.

Nigel was on top of the world. Just a short time ago he could barely get a date on a Saturday night. *Look at me now, having a drink in Athens with the most beautiful woman in Europe.*

Sara Stavropoulos was undeniably beautiful. She was tall and slender. Her long blond hair was pulled back into a French braid that was slowly coming apart to reveal a slight wave. Her eyes were a color Nigel had never seen before: a deep blue-green. He could not stop looking at her intoxicating lips. Perfectly placed high cheekbones brought her loveli-ness into focus.

He let Sara do most of the talking so he could continue to take her all in. A few strategically placed "really's" and "then what's" kept the con-versation flowing. All of a sudden she stopped.

"Are you really listening to me?"

"Are you kidding? Absolutely." And he really was. Nigel knew that men were never quite as focused as when they wanted to get laid. They hang on a woman's every word, acting as if she were actually saying something.

"You were born in New York," he began. "Your father's Greek and he sent you to the American school in Athens so you could discover your heritage. You're a senior in high school and will graduate in two weeks. You're here today because it's about a million degrees and the Athens Palace has the only chilled pool in town."

"I'm impressed." Sara liked Nigel. He was charming, witty, and certainly handsome. But there was something disconnected, something she couldn't put her finger on. "You know, I've been doing most of the talking and you haven't told me anything about yourself yet."

Nigel realized it was getting late and he had to prepare for that night's performance. Hoping to skip the rest of the "getting to know you" pleasantries, he decided to reel her in with his trump card. "I've got to get ready for an engagement, but if you're not doing anything tonight I would love it if you could be my guest—" She cut him off.

"Oh, I'm sorry. I do have plans tonight. My friends and I have tickets to see the Casuals at the Amphitheater. Everyone's talking about how fabulous they are. I haven't heard them yet. Have you?"

Nigel felt delighted in the irony of the moment. He decided to have some fun. "Yes, I think you'll love them." He paused in order to finalize his plan of attack. "Do you have good seats?"

"Fifth row center." She looked down at her watch. "I really should get going. The show starts in a couple of hours. I've enjoyed meeting you. Maybe we'll bump into each other again before you leave."

"Yes, I'm sure we will." Nigel studied her ass as she walked away. *Shit, life just can't get any better than this.*

Sara and her friends arrived at the Amphitheater shortly before showtime. Though it seated only a few hundred, the Amphitheater made up in heritage and beauty what it lacked in size. It was an architectural marvel, made entirely out of marble, situated at the base of the Acropolis where the Parthenon loomed majestically overhead.

As she sat down, a young man approached her.

"Are you Sara Stavropoulos?"

"Yes."

"The Casuals would like you to join them backstage before the concert."

Her interest was peaked and she followed the young man. In the midst of all the chaos, she spotted Nigel who was surrounded by about a dozen frenzied-looking people, poking at his hair, adjusting his tightly fitted T-shirt, and shouting incomprehensible last-minute instructions at his face.

When his eyes caught hers, she waved to him from a distance, but before they could exchange "hellos", someone shouted "five minutes to showtime." Everyone around seemed to jump to life at once. Nigel approached her.

"Surprised to see me here?" he asked breathing heavily from nerves.

"A little."

He cut her off. "Listen, I've got to go. Come back at intermission?"

Before Sara could respond, he was gone. She turned around to leave and bumped head-on into another young man. Her sleeve caught a wire at the neck of his guitar. As she pulled it away, she heard a rip.

"Wait, stay still or it will rip again."

She stopped and watched as he gently detangled her blouse from his guitar. Someone then tapped him on the shoulder. "Two minutes to go, Richard."

He looked up at her and their eyes met. "Sorry about this. Can I offer to buy you another blouse?"

She realized she was staring and quickly looked down at her sleeve. "Oh no. It was totally my fault."

"Then let me buy you dinner after the show tonight." He paused, and almost with a whisper added, "please." Without warning, someone grabbed his arm and began pushing him towards the stage shouting, "Richard, you're on!"

Before he disappeared out the door, he turned around and shouted,

"Meet me at the Athens Palace after the show. Ask for Richard Winters. I'll be waiting for you. What's your name?"

The fans started screaming. He couldn't hear her answer.

Sara never believed in love at first sight but this connection was undeniable. She watched him on stage and knew that she had to find out more about this man. Without hesitating, she headed straight for the Athens Palace after the concert.

When she walked in, she saw Richard sitting in the lobby holding a drink. He looked handsome with his hair, wet with sweat, casually pushed back. He wore a pair of faded dungarees and the same black tight fitting T-shirt that clung to him on stage. His face was soft, not angular, and his large almond-shaped eyes imparted a somewhat sad note to his perfect features. He smiled when he saw her and stood up.

"I wasn't sure you'd come."

"Why wouldn't I? I love going out with total strangers who offer to buy me new blouses."

Sensing Richard knew absolutely nothing about Athens, she chose the restaurant. They took a taxi to the village of Glyfada along the Aegean. They drove through the steep mountainsides paralleling the ocean. Glyfada was a lively town with small cafes lining the docks. Sara headed straight to her favorite restaurant along the water. They sat and listened to the gentle waves of the ocean breaking against the pier and watched as the old fishing boats rocked back and forth to this calming rhythm.

Sara ordered for the two of them without using a menu. She told Richard that it was safer to stick to the traditional Greek food. Using her flawless Greek, she asked the waiter to bring them fresh broiled fish with lemon, a tomato salad, fried potatoes and a bottle of Retsina, the local wine.

They talked for hours about their lives and passions. Her voice was music itself to Richard. As she spoke, he realized that she was his perfect song. She was the definitive chord after an A sharp major, the harmony, rhythm and melody in his life. She was the song he would sing through eternity. Richard Winters was falling in love with this woman sitting across from him.

They took off their shoes and went walking along the nearby beach. They sat down on the sand and once again listened to the sounds of the water.

"How do you write music?" Sara asked him.

"I don't know really, it just comes to me."

"You make it sound so easy."

"It is, when you have the right inspiration."

"Like what?"

"Let's say, on a night like tonight, I look up at the sky and see all these brilliant stars. I'd start a song like this:

Tonight I'll wish on that one
Don't ask, I don't know its name
It doesn't really matter
My wish will always be the same.

That this moment lasts forever
And I'll never have to say good-bye
Because I never want to wonder
Does a heart really cry?

They held hands and watched the sun rise.

The Casuals and their road crew were packing up. It was time to return to London, but Richard had already decided to stay behind in Athens. Sara graduated in two weeks, and he was determined to convince her to continue her studies in London.

He told Nigel on their way down to the lobby in the gilded elevator.

"You're staying in Athens because of a girl you've known for just one night?" Nigel's lack of empathy for "true love" did not surprise Richard.

"Hey, listen," Nigel continued. "I fall in love with a different chick almost every night. You'll get over it in a couple of days. I always do."

"I've noticed," Richard answered. "Look, come with me and meet her. You'll see what I'm talking about. I just can't leave now. She's in the lobby."

When the elevator doors opened, Sara was standing by the front desk. She spotted Richard and began to walk towards him. Nigel's jaw clenched. That was the girl he'd chatted up yesterday. He was hoping he'd see her again, and he didn't hope for things like this very often. She was different, special in some way. And now she was walking toward his partner, the person whose unfailing incorrigible good will and sunny nature irritated him more than anything in this world. How could she have that spineless simp over him? The almighty Richard could do no wrong. He was the darling of the press. The world was mesmerized by his riveting smile, and the pleasure he so evidently took in life. Oh, sure, people liked him too, but not like they did Richard. Mothers wished Richard were their son and their daughters dreamed he was their lover. But Nigel wanted to kill him at that moment. *No, I need him,* he thought. *I can't sell records without that twit.* But the line in the sand had been drawn. *You've won this round, asshole, but the next is mine. Trust me.*

The next week and a half passed quickly. Sara met Richard every day after school. Her familiarity with the city, how she knew her way through tiny back streets that would have confounded many city natives, amazed him. One day she took him to the Plaka, where small tourist shops lined the streets. There, she bartered with the shop owners for souvenirs to take for her friends back in New York.

They spent afternoons sipping lemonade overlooking the Royal Palace and Gardens, and drank Greek coffee in the outdoor cafes around Syntagma Square. In the evenings, they explored nearby villages and spent countless hours walking barefoot on the beaches of the calm Mediterranean.

More quickly than he would have expected, Richard grew accustomed to Retsina wine. One night, after having had a bit too much, he found himself playing the Bouzouki with a local band. Sara couldn't contain her laughter. The site of this pale Brit playing the melody to the Greek sailor dance brought tears of joy to her eyes. At that moment, she knew she loved him. And so did the crowd. They cheered and applauded him, begging him to keep playing. But Richard's eyes were on Sara as she laughed, clapped, and sang the words to the songs. Her love of life, her affection for everyone she met, her generosity of spirit, not to mention her beauty—he felt these as a blessing. He watched her when she got up to dance the Hasapiko. He felt her heart and soul in every measured step. She seemed one with all the people through the ages who had danced these steps to forget the day's hardships, to raise their spirits, and to embrace each other in life.

Richard didn't want this night to end. After the last song, he approached the microphone. "I know you don't understand me," he began, "but I want to thank you all for being such a great audience—and one more thing, Sara Stavropoulos, I can't imagine spending one moment of the rest of my life without you. I love you. 'Se Agapo.'" He paused, then added, "Please, marry me."

Sara stared at the young man holding the microphone, sweat, pouring from his face, his large blue eyes questioning, pleading. She felt herself arise from her chair and had no sense of the hush that filled the room. Drawing near, she put her hand on his arm and said in a low voice that was too strong to be a whisper, "Yes. Of course."

The next day, Richard Winters and Sara Stavropoulos entered a Greek Orthodox church in a nearby village. Not long after, they emerged from a dimly lit chapel as husband and wife.

They spent the first night of their marriage on board the *Beatrice S,* the yacht Sara's father had docked in Piraeus. Only when Richard saw what he initially thought was a luxury ocean liner did he realize the magnitude of her wealth.

"What exactly does your father do in the shipping industry?" he asked her.

"He owns a fleet of ships."

Sara's parents were arriving in two days. The crew had been preparing the yacht for a week. When the chef heard that Sara was on board, with a husband no less, he insisted on preparing all her favorite dishes: fresh fish, crispy spinach pies, and thick pieces of baklava dripping with honey. They ate dinner on the deck and stared out into the sea. Sara thought about what her first night in bed with Richard would be like. She didn't realize how nervous she was until she saw Richard watching her with love, laughter, and concern in his eyes.

"Trust me," he said.

A short time later, she did trust him, as she invited this new person into her body, heart and even her sprit. Filled with him, receiving him, reaching for him, she was complete in a way she had never been. Finally, she was home. Finally, she herself knew the splendor that had always surrounded her.

Lying together in quiet darkness, hearing the water lap against the sides of the boat, she knew their union was unbreakable. *Till death do us part.*

At the first sign of daybreak, the *Beatrice S* sprang to life. Only twenty-four hours to go before Constantine Stavropoulos was on board. The crew both feared and revered him. Constantine Stavropoulos could only be described as larger than life. Though he was literally a big man, well over six feet tall with an extra fifty pounds on his already substantial frame, his life was even bigger. Born in poverty on an island off the coast of Turkey, he began as a deck-hand on the local merchant ships, eventually working his way into the engine rooms as an operator.

He enlisted in the Greek army at the height of World War II and after saving the lives of five of his companymen, returned to his homeland a hero. Shortly thereafter, with the promise of United States citizenship, he enlisted in the American army. While on leave in New York City, he fell in love with a seventeen-year-old American girl named Beatrice, who worked at the bakery where he bought his coffee every morning. With a promise of marriage, he returned to the war where he received a purple heart for his valiant effort at Omaha Beach. He was shot in the chest but managed to survive. He was one of the lucky ones. No one else in his platoon made it to the shore.

Soon after the war, he returned to Greece with his young bride. He opened a small ship-chartering office in the busy port village of Piraeus. Within a few years, the office was thriving. He then mortgaged everything he owned, and with the help of a bank that loaned him the rest of the money, he bought his first ship, an old cargo vessel, but Constantine knew how to keep it full and moving. Soon, he had opened offices in London and New York. His fleet ranged from small container ships carrying lumber and coal to large super-tankers transporting oil from the Saudi Gulf. Constantine's monetary wealth was immeasurable, and so was his love for his only child, Sara.

When Richard and Sara broke the news to him, he stood for a moment in disbelief. Beatrice, who stood nearby, began to cry.

"How could you do this to your mother and me?" he began. He studied Richard. He wanted to reach down the British boy's throat and pull out his heart. "You didn't even have the decency to invite us to your wedding."

"Daddy," Sara said. "We didn't mean to insult you. It was just so sudden. We barely thought about it ourselves. It was just something we had to do at that very moment. Besides, I knew once you met Richard, you'd fall in love with him the way I did." Sara stopped and watched Constantine for a moment. He wasn't listening to her. He was staring at Richard. And although it was probably the lighting, she was sure she saw venom trickling down the sides of his mouth.

From across the room, Richard could feel Constantine's breath on his neck. He stood silent, knowing that anything he might say would just further enrage the older man.

Constantine circled Richard. "I could squeeze that little head of yours with just one hand," he began, "and although that would make me unbelievably happy, my wife and daughter would be very upset with me." He stopped and stared down at Richard. In a low voice, so low that the women could not hear, he said, "So, little English boy, you've put me in a bad position. I'll lose my daughter if I try to break the two of you up. She might even suspect me if you were to have an unfortunate accident. So I'll just wait. I'll wait for her to grow tired of you. I'll wait outside the lawyer's office while you're signing your divorce papers. I'll wait and watch as you and your pathetic music disappear into oblivion."

Richard couldn't swallow. Then, as if the past thirty seconds hadn't occurred, he watched Constantine turn around to his daughter. With a smile he said, "Sara, I'm sorry I acted so poorly. I love you and I support your decision. Richard must be a fine young man, but if for some reason, things don't work out, our door is always open. Now, you say Richard's a musician? Well, I won't believe it until I hear him play my bouzouki."

Richard stood in amazement. *Dr. Jekyll, meet Mr. Hyde.*

At Sara's insistence, they spent the next two weeks of their honeymoon touring the Greek islands with her parents on the *Beatrice S.* She was sure that once Richard got to know her father, he would love him as much as she did. Richard wasn't quite as sure and though he refrained from comment, the thought of spending the next fourteen days with the captain of the *S.S. Psychopath* made him sea-sick before they even left port.

But, as the days went by, he developed a grudging respect for his new father-in-law. He admired his 'take charge' personality and his passion for the sea. If there was a problem in the engine room, Constantine was down there with the crew, getting his hands dirty with the rest of them. He stood at the bridge, even in the roughest weather, telling the others to get some rest while he was the one who probably needed it the most. But, above all, Richard appreciated Constantine's love for his daughter, his wife—the only common thread in their extremely tenuous relationship. Sara was smart, but years of wisdom and experience had made Constantine smarter. Together, they loved to argue about politics and current events. They could spend hours discussing the smallest piece of historical trivia. Richard could sense Constantine's pride in Sara. She, in turn, just glowed in her father's presence.

Although a truce of sorts had been called, Constantine never failed to remind Richard of the dangers liable to beset inexperienced sailors. They fall off of slippery decks and disappear into stormy seas, their arms and legs tangle perilously in ropes, they can accidentally get set on fire in the engine room. The list went on and on.

Richard couldn't wait to get back on to dry ground. When the yacht returned to Piraeus, he and Sara left for London, where he bought a townhouse on Cheyne Walk in Chelsea. Richard's agent kept their marriage quiet, fearing record sales would drop once his fans knew the world's heartthrob had been taken.

Sara enrolled at the University of London and began taking courses in art and art history. Richard went back to work writing music, and soon the Casuals were recording their next album. Within a month, Sara was pregnant. They greeted this unplanned pregnancy with excitement and joy. Although they realized they were young to take on such a huge responsibility, they were thrilled with the idea of bringing their child into the world.

The days passed quickly. Sara remained in school while preparing for the baby's arrival. They decided to take one last vacation to New York before their lives changed change forever. They stayed with Sara's parents in their townhouse on East 68th Street. Although Richard would have preferred a hotel, Constantine would have it no other way. He amused himself by watching his young son-in-law crumble under his constant verbal assaults.

It was in the early hours of daybreak, on a cool summer morning, when Sara went into labor. Richard, Constantine, and Beatrice rushed her to New York Hospital, where she was admitted to the maternity floor. Richard clenched Sara's hand until a nurse made him leave. She looked up at him. He could see that she was scared. "I love you," she said.

"I love you too." And with those last words, he was ushered into the waiting room, where he sat for what seemed to be an eternity. Thirteen hours later, a doctor and nurse walked in, both with somber expressions. The doctor looked at Richard.

"Mr. Winters," he began, "I'm sorry for the news I'm about to tell you. Your wife is dead. We managed to save your baby. You have a daughter."

Richard could not move. Constantine stood up and approached the doctor. "What are you telling me? You've made a mistake. It has to be a mistake."

The doctor looked at Constantine. "I'm sorry sir. Your daughter developed peripartum cardiomyopathy. Her heart muscle weakened during the pregnancy, and she went into congestive heart failure during labor. We had to perform an emergency Cesarean section to rescue the baby. She died shortly after the delivery."

Richard's eyes were filled with tears, but he didn't cry. "Did she have a chance to see the baby?"

"No" the doctor responded. "She was anesthetized."

The nurse approached Richard. "Please, come with me. She's still in the delivery room. You can say good-bye."

Richard entered the silent room. At first he could not bear to approach the bed or to look at Sara. Finally, he gathered up his courage and forced himself to see what he feared would be the worst sight of his life. But there was no horror in the room, only the beauty of his beloved, who looked to be enjoying a tender dream. He took her hand. "I'm sorry," he said, and wept.

After awhile, he sat at her bedside and thought about the short life they'd shared, all the dreams and plans they had for the future. Finally, while still holding her hand he whispered, "My world has changed. This world has changed. You've taken my soul with you, Sara." He bent down and kissed her lips. "I'll love you forever. I promise."

Richard walked down the hall towards the nursery. Peering through the window, he finally spotted an incubator with a card that read, "Winters/Female."

"Hello Winters/Female." He pressed his lips to the glass. "I have so much to tell you about the most beautiful woman who ever walked this earth. Your mother."

On a hot summer morning, on the outskirts of London, Sara's body was laid to rest. The press was in a frenzy, circling the perimeter of the cemetery. No sooner had they discovered that Richard Winters was married, than his wife died, leaving him an infant daughter. What a story. The public would eat it up. Women everywhere would want to console him and mother his baby girl.

The funeral became a zoo. Photographers stepped over one another to get the perfect shot of the little girl being cradled in her grandmother's arms. Reporters hounded anyone who would talk: groundskeepers, limo drivers, even innocent passersby, in hopes of snagging a tabloid headline.

When it was all over, Constantine approached Richard. "So this is how you're going to raise your daughter?" he asked. "Amongst these jackals, these sycophants? They'll never give her a minute's peace. How can a child grow up with no privacy, no security? She won't have a chance. They'll hound her until the day she cracks."

Richard knew Constantine was right. He looked straight into his father-in-law's eyes. At that moment, they were not enemies. They were just two people, two men who had lost the person they each had loved the most in this world. With a vulnerability that earned, if only for the moment, the older man's deep respect, Richard said "What do I do, Constantine? What do I do?"

Constantine looked at Beatrice who was clutching the baby to her chest. "Let us take her home," he said. "She'll be safe with us; we can protect her from all of this. Richard, though your pain is unfathomable at this moment, your life isn't ending today. You'll continue to write music, perform, travel—and that baby will need a stable home."

Beatrice looked up. "Please, Richard" she said, "my own baby just died last week. My arms still remember how she felt. I would sing to her at night and watch the sun rise with her in the morning. Today I wanted to crawl into that coffin with my little Sara. The only thing that stopped me was the thought of my granddaughter—her daughter, and yours, of course." She began to cry.

Constantine looked at his wife and suddenly, his jaw tightened. The truce was over. "I could sue you for custody, Richard, and I might win. I'm sure I could dig up pictures of you with drugs or women, or both. And if that doesn't work, I'll just pay off every judge in every court, for as long as it takes."

He continued talking but Richard stopped listening. He knew Constantine was right. His daughter deserved a stable home. Constantine and Beatrice would protect and care for her when he couldn't. After all, they had raised Sara, and she turned out perfect in every way.

"Stop," he said. "I'll agree on these conditions. First, I am her father, not you. I can see her and take her with me at any time, and I will. Second, you and Beatrice move to London. I want her as close to me as possible." He motioned Constantine to follow him to the crest of a small rise that looked out over the venerable dead. Keeping his voice low and face away from Beatrice, so there was no chance she'd hear him, he said, "Look here, old man. Don't try to fuck me over. I took your daughter away from you. I can take this baby away too. If you try to act on your pathetic threats, you'll never see Anna again, I promise you that. So don't try anything stupid. I'd enjoy watching you cry as she comes running into my arms. That would be the last you'd ever see her."

Chapter 2

ANNA

Constantine and Beatrice Stavropoulos spent every single moment of every waking hour thinking of new ways to make Anna Sara Winters happy. They gave her the best that money could buy: private schools, designer clothes, winter vacations skiing in Zermat, and summers on the Greek islands. But for Anna, nothing could bring her the same sense of joy as her one true passion, her father.

The Casuals continued their reign as the rock and roll kings of the century. Album after album went gold. Each world-wide tour sold out within hours. Despite the adulation and the heady rush of fame, Richard Winters proved to be a dedicated and loving father. Every spare moment he had was spent with his daughter. They had an unbreakable bond: she was his reminder of the woman he still loved and he was her reminder of the mother she had never known.

When Richard wasn't touring, he and Anna spent the weekends together. She cherished those times with her father and spent the week waiting for Friday. He would pick her up in his black Mercedes sports car and take her to his house in Belgravia, where he had allowed her to decorate her own room. Even as a child she had impeccable taste. She loved soft colors and elegant antiques that she and her father would pick up in Notting Hill. The tops of her bureaus and dressers were covered with photographs of the people she loved, Richard, Sara, Constantine and Beatrice. But her favorite picture of all was one she had enlarged to poster-size and tacked behind her door. It was one she had taken of her father, sitting at a piano alone, smiling at her.

Their Saturdays were usually spent taking drives through the countryside, or long walks through London. They loved to observe people in Hyde Park or sit on benches along the Thames and watch the tour boats pass by. In the evenings, Richard would read her stories and sing to her before bedtime. Anna loved the music of her father's voice, and often thought that's how angels must sound. She was comforted knowing that wherever her mother was, she was surrounded by beautiful voices like her father's.

The press cited artistic differences as the reason when they reported the breakup of the musical collaboration of Richard Winters and Nigel Taylor the summer Anna was nine. At the time, Richard and Nigel were on the Fortune 500 list of the wealthiest entertainers in the world. But Richard had grown tired of performing and touring. He had a good ear for new talent and knew how to draw the best out of them. When he did, their music was released on his own S & A Music label. Almost always, his artists went to the top of the charts.

When Richard's days of touring were over, he asked Anna to live with him. Constantine and Beatrice knew that fighting him would be futile so they approached him with just one request: that their granddaughter be allowed to spend two months every summer with them in Greece. Richard had never intended to separate Anna from her grandparents, and knowing how much she loved them, he agreed.

In the summer of 1979, Anna had just turned sixteen. She would begin college in New York in the fall. Naturally inquisitive, she had enjoyed school and worked hard, in large part because it so pleased her father. Without much extra effort, she skipped two grades, though she couldn't understand why adults often made so much of it.

She sat alone on a long white stretch of sand and looked out into the crystal clear waters of Xenos. *Thank God this is the last summer I'll have to spend on this godforsaken island.*

Although Anna loved her grandparents, she preferred to see them in London, where there were things to do. In Greece, the simple became overwhelming. While all of her friends remained in London, she was uprooted and taken back to the same town, on the same island, every year. A dry, barren island within swimming distance to Turkey, it was noteworthy for just one reason: a handful of the world's richest men sprang from this obscure barren rock in the Mediterranean. They all began with menial positions in the shipping industry, and like Constantine, eventually moved into the more lucrative area of ship-owning and fleet-building. Most had moved off of the island early on in their careers, but now, later in life, they relished going back to the motherland every summer to show off all their new toys to one another. And, oh, what a spectacle it was! The docks of the island were filled with the largest, most magnificent yachts in the world—yachts that seemed larger than the towns where these men had grown up, towns where televisions were a rarity and donkeys were still used as beasts of burden.

Every summer Anna became friendly with most of the children of the shipping families. For her, though, it was by necessity, not choice; it was either them, or two months brooding alone. She opted for making the best of things, so she spent the days with her "friends," exploring new beaches and, when she was older, the evenings, at taverns drinking wine and ouzo.

It was a particularly hot day though, and Anna felt like staying close to home. Constantine had rebuilt his childhood home in the town of Amphora. Within a short walking distance was a small crescent-shaped beach surrounded by steep hillsides. One dirt path led to the beach, which was usually frequented only by the local townspeople. That day was different. The beach was busy, almost crowded, and there were many faces she did not recognize. *Now why on earth would tourists want to come to this island,* she thought, *when there are so many more interesting places in the world*—All of a sudden she felt something hit the back of her head. Startled, and without saying a word, she turned around a saw a pink frisbee on the sand besides her. A tall young man began running in her direction.

"Signomi," he said with a thick British accent. "Shit, I'm sorry, I don't speak Greek. Are you Okay? Oh, Christ, do you speak English by any chance? I'm not very good at this thing," he said, pointing to the frisbee. "I've absolutely no control over it." He continued to ramble on with his apologies.

Anna cut him off. "I'm fine," she said, rubbing her head. "It was nothing."

Looking relieved, he stopped short, and took a deep breath. He smiled, displaying a set of beautifully white teeth with razor sharp incisors. "Oh, thank God," he said. "English."

Anna nodded.

Just then, a petite young woman with golden blonde hair that matched the young man's came up to them. She looked at Anna. "I hope you're all right. My apologies for my moron brother. Unfortunately athletic ability never ran in our family."

Anna laughed. "Really, I'm fine." She watched and listened to them as they walked away. The young woman pulled the frisbee out of her brother's hand. "Give me that thing. It's a dangerous weapon in your hands. Now why don't you just go and sit down before you hurt somebody else."

The young man continued to look down at the sand. "Oh, just fuck off, Jackie. I can't take you anymore. Did you ever wonder why you have no friends?"

"Cause I have a moron for a brother and nobody wants to hang around me because you might show up?"

"You're a pain in my ass."

Anna smiled as their voices trailed off. She watched them sit down with two other people. A few moments later, she noticed the same young woman get up and approach a man in a small speedboat that was pulled up close to the shore. After a few moments she yelled back to her group, "He can't understand a word I'm saying."

Anna walked over to her. "Want me to translate something for you?"

Jackie looked surprised but quickly responded, "Yes, please. We want to know how much he wants to take us to the other side of the island. Heard there's a beach there with black sand, but the only way to get there's by boat."

"You're right about that," Anna responded. "That's Sotira Beach." She turned to the man and began negotiating with him. She then turned back to Jackie. "He wants 25 drachmas to take you over."

"Is that good?"

"Yes, but he'll want another 25 to pick you up later."

"Well, my parents will kill us but I think we can scrape it up." Jackie turned to her small party and yelled, "Come on, get your things." She then looked at Anna. "Thanks for your help. Why don't you come along?"

Anna liked the young woman. There was something sweet and sensitive about her face, and she and her brother made her laugh. "Sure, sounds great."

Anna grabbed her things and returned to the boat where the other four had already climbed in. The young man with the frisbee took her hand and helped her on board.

"Hi, I'm Ian," he said. These are my sisters Jacqueline—Jackie—and Phillipa, and that's my brother Joseph. Really, I'm still sorry about that bump on your head."

"Don't mention it. It's nothing. I'm Anna—" Before she could say more, the engine started up. The boat took off with a jerk and within a few seconds was at full throttle making its way across the beach inlet to the other side of the island. Anna stared at the four people in the boat with her, their eyes wide open, drinking in the steep brown mountainsides, the rocky beach formations, and the small towns along the water. They had the same deep inset eyes and golden brown hair. She tried to guess their ages. Joseph was obviously the oldest, maybe nineteen or twenty, and Jackie, the youngest. Sixteen? Ian and Phillipa were in the middle, maybe seventeen and eighteen respectively.

Suddenly, the boat engine stopped. The operator began talking to Anna. The rest looked on and noticed Anna's increasing agitation. She then turned to them.

"You're not going to believe this," she said, "but the boat's running low on petrol and he wants us to get out."

"And go where?" Joseph said, looking around with alarm. "It's all water."

"He wants us to swim to that beach over there." She pointed to a sandy inlet about a quarter of a mile off in the distance. "He said he'll go back to town and fill up the tank and come back for us."

Jackie asked, "Why can't he take us to the beach over there and then go back for petrol?"

"He said the boat's way too heavy, and eating up too much fuel."

Again, with some alarm Joseph asked, "How do we know he's not just going to take our things and leave us here?"

Anna looked at the man. "He knows my family," she said. "He'll be back. You can trust me on this."

Phillipa sighed, "Well, all right, let's go."

One by one, they jumped off of the boat and into the cool water of the inlet. Staying close together, they began to swim towards the shore. There was no rush. The day was theirs to enjoy, so they floated on their backs and watched the birds fly overhead, occasionally rolling over to break some water with a slow side- or breaststroke. An occasional insult between the family members, or a question to Anna broke the silence.

Jackie was the first to approach Anna. "So, tell me, you don't look Greek, so how did you learn to speak it so well?"

"My mother was half Greek, and my grandfather—well, he made me take lessons from the time I was born. Spent a lot of time here too. Almost every summer of my life." Feeling a little winded, she kept her answers short. "So how about you all? Where are you from? Can't place the accent."

Ian swam over to the two of them. "We're from all over England really. My father's job keeps us moving around."

"And what're you doing on this godforsaken island?" Anna asked him.

"Besides swimming you mean?" he answered.

"Yes, of course that's what I mean."

"A friend of my mother's was born here. She invited us to stay in her home for the summer."

Jackie chimed in. "It's got no running water. We take showers by throwing buckets of cold water from the well on each other."

"And the bathroom's in an outhouse," Phillipa added.

"Oh, don't forget the flies," Ian said. "I think there're more flies inside the house than out."

Joseph agreed. "And what's with that disgusting piece of fly paper that mom's friend hangs from the lamp over the dining room table?" he said. "Picture eating breakfast with dead flies dangling in front of you."

They all started laughing and continued swimming. When they finally reached the shore, they stretched out on the sand and rested. The late afternoon sun began to cast a yellow and orange glow over the water.

"How long do you think it will be before the crazy boat-man returns?" Phillipa asked Anna.

"Don't know. Depends on where he's going for the petrol. It could be an hour or two. There's no such thing as time here. He may decide to have an early dinner and take a nap along the way, too. You just never know."

Phillipa looked annoyed. "Great, we don't have any water, food or blankets. So what do we do?"

Jackie answered. "Come on. Things aren't so bad. Anna says that he'll eventually return, and I believe her. So let's make the best of things. I'll think of a game to play." She paused for a few moments. "Okay, we'll sit in a circle. Each one of us will take a turn asking another person a question about movies, books, or music. If the person doesn't know the answer, you get to ask a personal question that must be answered truthfully."

"How will you know it's the truth?" Joseph asked.

"Because the rules are that if we find out you're lying, we'll get to beat the shit out of you," Jackie answered. "Is everyone in? Who wants to go first?"

Joseph sighed. "How could we have let her into this family? Why didn't Mom and Dad just stop with three? Okay, I'll go first. Phil, who directed *A Hard Day's Night*— and get the answer right because there's nothing about your personal life that I want to know."

Phillipa replied, "Something Lester. That's close enough, right?"

"Absolutely," Joseph answered. "Who's next?"

"I'll go next," Ian said. "Jackie, who wrote *The Communist Manifesto*? Was it Groucho, Harpo, or Karl Marx?"

"Oh, you're not taking this seriously at all," she whined. "It was Karl. Now come on, Anna. Help me. You think of something to stump my genius brothers."

"Since you brought up *The Communist Manifesto*, Ian," Anna began, "what did Marx think was the opiate of the masses?"

They all looked surprised. Ian smiled. "I think you're going to be a difficult one to stump. I have absolutely no idea."

"Religion," Anna said. "Marx, for the most part, thought that the masses were ignorant and religion was their opiate. Now I have to think of a personal question to ask you, don't I?" Anna thought for a moment. She felt a little uncomfortable and embarrassed. "All right. What do you think about before you go to sleep at night?"

Ian smiled at her. "Good question, but my thoughts vary depending on the night. Maybe tonight I'll think about you in that cute bathing suit, or maybe without that cute bathing suit."

Anna felt her face flush, and she looked down at the sand. "If you set out to embarrass me, you succeeded."

"Okay, let's keep it moving," Jackie said. "Who goes next?"

The game continued at a slower pace for the next hour. The theme of the personal questions seemed to center around sex and more sex. Anna discovered that Joseph had been sleeping with his girlfriend on a regular basis and Ian had not. Phillipa and Jackie did not have boyfriends and if they did, they would not have sex with them. Joseph fantasized about older women and Jackie, about movie stars. When Anna would miss a question, the group would ask her a relatively easy follow-up like, "Who's your favorite movie star?" or "What are your favorite foods?" It was not until she missed the last question of the game, when they heard the speedboat rounding the corner of the inlet, did she have a chance to say her most personal thought:

"What are you thinking about right now?" Jackie asked.

Without hesitation Anna answered, "I was wishing I had brothers and sisters too."

Chapter 3

LONDON

"Hello, Jackie?"

"Anna? That you?"

The connection between London and New York was terrible, but the sound of Jackie's thick British accent made Anna long for home.

"Finished my last final today and I'll be back in London next week. God, Jackie, I have so much to tell you about."

"Like your letters weren't enough." Jackie laughed. "Think I lived and breathed your entire first year of college with you."

"Oooh, I've just missed you all so much. Can you meet me next week? Maybe Wednesday?"

"Sure, I can swing it. Yes."

"Okay then, four o'clock, at the lounge chairs in Green Park—the ones you see as soon as you get out of the tube station."

"I'll be there. We'll still recognize each other, right?"

"It's only been a year. How much different could we possibly look? Oh—and don't make any other plans. We'll spend the evening together and fill each other in on all the details we missed, right?"

"It's a date." Jackie answered. "Can't wait."

They chatted a few more moments, then Anna hung up the phone. She sat back, lit a cigarette, and stared at the empty walls of her dormitory room. She thought about the last summer on Xenos: exploring new beaches with Jackie, Phillipa, and their brothers, building bonfires in the evenings, and spending nights behind the old lighthouse near the main village. All the years of island hopping aboard her grandfather's yacht didn't compare to the afternoons they'd spent picking fresh figs from village farms and eating them under the trees near the empty dock of the abandoned brick factory. It was under those trees that they would nap after lunch. And, it was under those trees that Anna had fallen in love with these four people who had made her a part of their lives.

The week passed quickly. It was an unusually warm and sunny day in London for the beginning of May. Anna walked slowly along Picadilly, admiring the bright lush grass of Green Park. It was four o'clock as she approached the corner with the tube station. She scanned the crowd looking for Jackie but didn't see her. Suddenly her eyes locked on a familiar-looking young man smiling in her direction. As he walked towards her, she realized it was Ian. He seemed different, but before she had a chance to try to figure out why, she found herself locked in his embrace.

After a moment, he stepped back. "Anna, we've all missed you so much. It's so good to see you."

"You, too. I almost didn't recognize you. You've grown at least a meter." But it wasn't only his height, she thought. His face had become more angular and his eyes more piercing. Even the tone of his voice was different—deeper and more mature. The setting sun behind him, accentuated the gold highlights in his shoulder-length hair. She hadn't spoken to Ian for almost a year, but at that moment it seemed as if only minutes had passed. She felt as if she had known him all her life. She continued to stare at him and suddenly realized she was at a loss for words.

Ian broke the silence. "You look as if you've seen a ghost. I'm not that horrible a sight, am I?"

Horrible? she thought. Not exactly the word she would have used to describe him at that moment. "Uhm, no," she mumbled. "It's just that, well, you've changed so much. I mean, I almost didn't recognize you."

Ian tilted his head sideways. "You said that before. But," he said as he slowly looked her up and down, "I'm not the only one."

Anna felt her face blush. In fact, she knew she had changed quite a bit during that year. Her girlish sixteen-year-old's figure had become that of a maturing woman. She was slightly taller than most of the girls in her class, and her small waist and developed bust line caused her to stand out amongst the other coeds her age. Her face was angular, with high cheekbones and a slightly pointed chin. And her eyes, like her mother's, were large and the color of the bluest waters of the Mediterranean.

Somewhat uncomfortable with Ian's last comment, Anna decided to change the topic. "So," she said in a chipper voice, "where's Jackie? Has she stood me up?"

"No. She said something about a sale at Harrod's. She told me to meet you here in case she was late. Tell me, though, would you have been terribly disappointed if I were her replacement?"

The intimate tone of his question took her by surprise. Before she had time to think, she found herself saying, "No, not at all."

The moment was broken by a high-pitched shout coming from the direction of Buckingham Palace. "Anna, sorry I'm late." They both turned to see Jackie bounding in their direction, her hands loaded with shopping bags from Harrod's.

"Oh, my God, Anna, you look great," Jackie began breathlessly. "Love the long hair, makes you look so much older. Hey, was it always that dark? Looks almost black. Well, whatever you do, don't cut it. Makes you look sexy. So, tell me, have I changed as much as you?"

"You mean aside from the flaming short red hair and the black leather trousers? I don't remember the black nails either. Been listening to the Sex Pistols lately?"

"The London club scene's been great, so I figured when in Rome. But, I've held back from piercing my nose and all."

"Well, the punk rock look suits your personality," Anna said. "I like it on you."

"It's called the lack-of-impulse control look," Ian added. "But I must admit that holding back from piercing her tongue showed an enormous amount of restraint. Meant a lot to her for a moment or two."

Jackie giggled. "Now this is why you love me so much, right?" she said to Ian. Deep down inside you want to loosen up that tight ass and have some fun. You know, do something just for the hell of it. Stop thinking so much."

"Oh God, spare us," Ian said. "Here comes the Jackie Moore philosophy of life—blurt out anything that comes to your head, no matter how inane, and above all never consider the consequences of any action ahead of time. Now what do you say, Anna, wouldn't the world be a better place?"

She gave Jackie an appreciative grin. "I don't know," she said, "but she's right, that's why I love her. So, what do you say we go eat? I'm starving. There's a great cappuccino bar on Picadilly Circus. We can walk, my treat."

With Anna in the middle, the three locked arms and began their walk. Jackie chatted on like an actor engrossed in a soliloquy, while Anna and Ian dutifully listened. They seated themselves at a corner table in the back of the Central Cafe, the hottest of the new cappuccino bars where bad service, loud music, and waiters with attitude were in fashion.

Ian turned to Anna. "So, tell us about New York. You like it?"

Anna blew on her coffee and thought for a moment. "It's nice—no, strange. To be honest, I spent most of my time on the campus so I don't know."

"So much for a specific answer," Ian laughed. "So, did you like the college at least?"

"Well, that was strange too. Being in the city and all, it attracts people from all over. It's a gathering place for the worlds' eccentrics—a place where they all kind of blend in. Their eccentricities don't stand out amongst one another so they feel normal." She paused, took a sip of coffee, and lit a cigarette. "And everybody smokes. That's where I picked up this disgusting habit."

Jackie looked annoyed. "Enough small talk. Any interesting men? I mean, my God, you must have had a thousand guys banging your door down. I want details, if you know what I mean."

"Right," Ian interjected. "Jackie, you see, needs the details because she hasn't had—what's it been, dear sister—one date in over a year now?"

"Oh, fuck you, Ian," Jackie shot back. "It's not like you're Mr. Don Juan over here. Now, just shut up and let Anna talk. I want to hear about her love life. So, go on. Any interesting men?"

Anna looked at the two of them and laughed. *God, how I've missed them*, she thought. "Well," she began, "I'd hardly call any of the guys I met interesting. I was invited to a lot of parties where everyone seemed to know who my father was. The guys always ended up asking me a lot of stupid questions about the Casuals and what it was like growing up with them. Pretty boring stuff really."

"Well, what do you expect from teenage boys?" Jackie said, "that they want to talk about Descartes, Sophocles, and the true meaning of life?"

"Well, it wouldn't hurt for us all to do a little soul-searching once in awhile."

"Soul-searching," Jackie said with surprise. "What the hell are you talking about? All these guys really want to do is get laid, face it. Anna, if it's soul-searching you want, go to a monastery."

Ian stared down at his coffee. "Can we get off of this topic? I feel Jackie's idiotic male-bashing thing getting started here. Anna, tell me about the band you joined. Jackie played me the tape you sent her. Sounded great. What were you playing? Keyboards?"

Anna looked surprised. "Nice of you to remember. But I'm not very good. Have a hard act to follow you know."

"No," Ian was emphatic. "I'm telling you, you're great. You should go into music."

Anna shook her head. "Thanks for the compliment, but no, hard to compete with the world's best. But enough about me. I want to hear about you guys."

Ian shrugged. "Nothing to tell really."

"Bullshit," Jackie wailed. "My moron brother here actually did something unbelievable—he was accepted into the London Academy of Dramatic Arts. He's transferring from Edinburgh in the fall."

Anna grabbed his hand. "That's wonderful. I'm so happy for you! You're going to make a great actor—no, the world's greatest actor. If anyone could command an audience, it's you." Anna had always felt as if Ian had the ability to look into a person's soul. He never just talked to people, he felt every word as well. He made her feel as if she were the only person in the room, the only person that mattered. She knew what it was like not to matter to the people who were talking to her.

With his hand still grasped firmly in hers, she looked into his eyes. "I want to be there, on your opening day, wherever it is. Promise you'll invite me?"

Ian nodded. "Of course—"

But he didn't have time to finish his answer. "Oh, shit," Jackie said. "You're not going to believe who just walked in. Andreas Patras and one of his sidekicks."

"Andreas Patras?" Ian said. "That idiot who drove around Xenos with the Porsche and an entourage?" He began to turn his head.

"Don't look," Anna whispered. "Maybe he won't see us." But it was too late. With an ear-to-ear grin that displayed his large, white, perfectly even teeth, he began heading in their direction.

"Anna, my luv, what a surprise to find you here." He glanced at Jackie and Ian. "Slumming it again, I see?" He bent over and double kissed her.

"Andreas, you always have the right words to say," she shot back.

Some of Anna's earliest memories in life included Andreas Patras. Their respective grandfathers had been childhood friends on Xenos and maintained their summer residences near one another. Every summer since she was an infant, Anna and Andreas were thrown together in a boxing ring masquerading as a play pen. Andreas's idea of amusement included pulling her hair, breaking her toys, beheading her dolls, drowning her stuffed animals and burying her goldfish alive. She found that complaining about him got her nowhere. His parents would reprimand him, and then all hell would break loose. He would start with a silent cry—mouth open but no noise—and then wham, a scream that could break the sound barrier. This was followed by Andreas throwing himself on the floor, legs kicking and arms flailing. His parents would race around trying to console him but to no avail. He would kick and scream until he would vomit. Then, to everyone's horror, he would hold his breath until he turned blue and finally passed out. And what response did this produce from his guilt-ridden parents? Why, more toys and presents for poor little Andreas. Years later, Anna thought that if he only could have included a 360-degree head rotation, he could have landed the leading role in the sequel to the *Exorcist.*

"You all remember my friend Chandon?" Andreas said.

"Of course we do," Anna answered. "How could anyone forget?" Chandon Amarretto was one of Andreas's dutiful ass-kissers. Chandon, however, was different by virtue of being the heir to the alcoholic beverage throne of the same name, although she never knew if it was his first name or last. His French accent with the New York twist amused her, as did his hair style, which was slicked back with so much grease that a toasted marshmallow couldn't stick to it.

"Would you mind, hmm, very much, if we brought chairs to you?" Chandon asked.

"Are you asking us if you could pull up some chairs and join us?" Ian asked. "Because if you are, you'll have to do me a favor first. Just explain to me what kind of accent that is exactly? I mean, didn't you mention last summer that you've been living in London for ten years now? How do you get by without speaking any English, or do you think you're making the ladies swoon with that French bullshit?"

"I sense, how you say, hostility? No? Maybe envy? Then again, what should I care what, how you say, poor dumb-assed hillbilly from mountains thinks?"

"It's '*the* mountains'. You have to remember to use articles, like this, listen: 'you are *the* most arrogant insignificant motherfucker I've ever come across,' etc., etc."

Anna didn't like where the conversation was heading. It was clear that Ian and Chandon didn't particularly get along, so she decided that it was time for the three of them to leave. She stood up. "You know, I'd love for you to join us but actually we were just getting up to leave."

"Sorry to hear that," Andreas said. "How about joining me for dinner tonight instead? A group of us are going out to Annabell's. Your friends are invited too."

"I'll let you know. I'll call you later."

"How could the woman who shared my bed resist my invitation?"

"That was a crib, Andreas. We shared a crib when we were babies."

"You're just splitting hairs." He laughed.

"Those are pretty big hairs to split," Anna answered curtly.

"Crib, bed, sooner or later you know. It's just a matter of time." Andreas turned to Jackie. "You know, our grandfathers have plans for us to marry one day. Wouldn't that be unbelievable? Just think of these two great shipping families merging. We'd be bigger than Onassis. We would rule the world."

"What about love, romance, and all of that?" Jackie asked.

With a big grin, he turned to Anna. "How could she not be in love with me?"

"Because, how you say, you don't look like her father," Chandon interjected.

"What?" Anna said.

"Don't look so surprised, luv," Andreas answered. "Talk amongst the island natives last summer was that you—how should I say this without upsetting you—are very tight with your father, whenever he showed up, of course."

"What he means is you have that Greek myth complex, where you want to have sex with your mother, but in your case, it's your father," Chandon said.

Ian abruptly stood up. His 6 foot 2 frame towered over Chandon. "God, you're such an asshole," he began as he moved closer, "but, before my fist reaches your face, I might as well tell you that it's called the 'Oedipus Complex' and I really have had just about enough of your shithead remarks." Ian grabbed Chandon's collar with one hand and began lifting the other, at which point Andreas reached over and pulled him back.

"Temper, temper," Andreas said while gently removing Ian's hand. "Your family doesn't have enough money to pay the legal bills they'll get after you rearrange my friend's face."

Anna stood up and stared into Ian's eyes. "Don't do it," she said. "He's not worth it. Let's just get out of here." She took Ian and Jackie's hands and began heading towards the door.

Andreas followed, grabbed Anna's arm, and with his perfectly honed sincerest look said, "Call me about tonight, my luv. I'll be waiting."

Anna didn't answer and the three continued to walk. When they reached the sidewalk Ian stopped and looked at her. "How can you be friends with those arrogant pricks?"

"A bad habit I guess," she answered. "You know, they're kind of like cigarettes. You want to give them up but you can never find the right moment. And besides, I've known Andreas all my life, and it makes things even harder."

"So, are you going out with him tonight?" Jackie asked, as she led them down the street.

"Nope. I planned to spend the evening with the two of you."

"Oh, God, Anna. I'm sorry I didn't tell you. We have this family thing tonight back home. You're welcome to come, but it's just my boring relatives from Camden."

Anna's delight in the moment quickly turned to disappointment. "No, thanks anyway. I think I'll pass." She thought for a moment then with a smile added, "but I will take you up on another invitation."

"What's that?" Jackie asked.

"Remember last summer when your parents invited me to stay with you for a couple of weeks this year? They said something about a beach house they'll be renting near Brighton?"

Jackie's eyes opened wide. "Don't tell me you're thinking of coming?"

"If I'm still invited."

"Still invited?" Jackie grabbed her arm, "Of course you're still invited. "This is going to be the best summer ever. Just think of all the new ways we'll figure out to have fun."

The two girls hugged. Anna looked up and saw Ian watching her. When did his eyes get so blue, and shoulders so broad? He smiled at her and she felt the intensity of his stare moving over her body. He had changed so much since last summer. But then again, so did she.

Andreas cancelled his dinner plans in favor of an impromptu party at his apartment. It took him over an hour of begging and pleading, but in the end, and against her better judgment, Anna agreed to go. She had expected to spend the evening with Ian and Jackie, and was feeling lonely. Her father was out late at one of his business dinners, so the idea of a party at Andreas's sounded better than staying home alone.

Andreas's driver picked her up precisely at eight and drove her to the Patras Building, a sixty-story office building. Andreas had turned the penthouse into his own domain. It had all of the luxuries and amenities that every eighteen year old boy would need: four bedrooms and a master suite, a private gym, two Jacuzzis, a sunken living room, and a breathtaking 360 degree view of the greater part of London and the Thames river.

Anna scanned the crowd as she entered. Most of the faces were familiar; Andreas never deviated much from his usual guest list. She had hoped to find someone to have an intelligent conversation with, but, with a sigh of resignation, she realized it was futile. Over the years, she had come to know these people by the nicknames she had secretly given them. The "Wax Museum"—the men and woman who posed along the walls and outside on the balcony. They never said much but they dressed impeccably. The "Party People," who always came equipped with drugs, preferably cocaine, and who hovered around the coffee table in the living room all night. The "Love Dancers," who danced the night away while grinding and rubbing up against each other's privates in the very public living room. And finally, her favorites, the "Extra Appendages," who never left Andreas's side, following him from room to room and hanging on his every word as if he were the Buddha himself. Tonight, the lady appendages sat next to him in the Jacuzzi. They all sipped champagne and secretly prayed to be the next name on his list of weekly love interests.

Anna slowly made her way past the "Wax Museum" to the balcony, where she stood for a few moments to catch a breath of the cool night air. Suddenly, she felt someone's body against her back. From the unmistakable scent of his overpowering aftershave cologne, she knew it was

Andreas. His hands began moving around her waist and she could feel his breath against the back of her neck. With a sudden shudder of revulsion, she turned around to face him.

"I suppose the Jacuzzi wasn't hot enough for you?" she said.

Standing only inches away from her he whispered, "You know snose swomen don't comprare, compare, to you my love. Why don't we go somewhere where we can be alone?"

His breath reeked of alcohol so she turned her head aside. "No, I don't think so. Not tonight, or anytime in my foreseeable life—" She stopped, realizing how abrupt she must have sounded, and added, almost apologetically, "Look, I'm sorry. Maybe my coming here was a mistake. This isn't my crowd and I'm tired."

"No need to apologrize … gize, my darling. I'll drive you home. We'll find time to be alone another night."

"Thanks for the offer, but I'll take a cab."

"Absoslutetely not. No gentleman would allow such a thing. I'm fine, just fine."

"No, I don't think so, Andreas."

"Fine, whatever. Let me at least have my driver take you back."

Anna nodded. "That'll be all right."

"Why don't you wait in front of the building? I'll call down to the lobby and have him bring the car around."

He took her by the waist and led her to the door. He leaned forward and brought his head to hers. "What? No kiss goodsnight?"

She kissed him lightly on the cheek. "Goodsnight."

With a sigh of relief, she walked out the door, took the express elevator to the lobby, and waited outside for Andreas's limo. Within a moment, a red Porsche came to an abrupt halt at her feet. The same tall blond driver who had brought her to the party darted out and opened the passenger side door.

"Where's the limo?" she said as she slid on to the black leather seat.

"Engine problems," he said, as he began to close the door after her. "Mr. Patras told me to use his car." He sprinted to the back of the car, opened the trunk, and took out a brown leather briefcase. Holding it up to her open window he said, "Can you wait here one moment while I take this up to Mr. Patras? He said he needed it right away."

"Sure." Anna sat back, and closed her eyes. She was relieved to be leaving the party but she wasn't exactly thrilled about going home to an empty house. She thought about Jackie and Ian. The night was still young. Maybe she could call them and see if they felt like getting a late drink.

She heard the driver's door open. In an instant, the car took off with a jerk.

It took less than a second for the smell of the overpowering aftershave cologne to permeate the car. She opened her eyes and stared at the driver. It was Andreas.

He flashed her his broadest grin. "Surprise."

"Stop the car and let me out," she demanded in a calm, even tone.

"Not exactly happy to see me, I take it?"

"You heard me, Andreas."

"Yeah, yeah, I heard you. But under one condition."

"No conditions."

"Killjoy. But I don't give a shit what you say anyway. I have the wheel and you're coming with me."

His foot hit the accelerator. Ignoring every STOP sign and red light, he maneuvered through the winding streets of London, eventually finding his way to the nearest motorway. When Anna saw the A-12 East sign, she knew where he was heading, and settled in for the long drive.

Close to forty-five minutes later, Andreas reached his destination: the commercial dockyard in Tilbury. Anna could see the outline of about a dozen cargo ships moored along the various docks. He stopped the car at the end of a long cement pier, got out, and opened the passenger side door.

"Come on," he said. "Get out. I want to show you something."

"I'm sure you do," she said. "But I'm not getting out."

He softened his tone a notch. "Come on," he pleaded. "Just for a second. Then I'll take you right home, promise."

There was no sense in fighting with him. He had the keys. "All right."

She stepped out and looked straight ahead. What stretched out in front of her was no ordinary vessel. It was a supertanker, the Goliath of oil-carrying ships. It spanned the length of four football fields and was capable of hauling over 250,000 tons of oil—enough fuel to heat the entire United States for over three hours.

Anna never got tired of looking at ships. The sheer size of this one amazed her. She loved walking the decks and touching the steely blue metal of the stacks and gangways. The geometric lines of the holds and rails radiated a sense of power and control. She could feel the strength of the structure resonate throughout her body, giving it energy, focus, and life. She took a deep breath of the cool, salty air and turned to Andreas. "She's absolutely magnificent. Do you have a name for her yet?"

"No, but I'm toying with the name 'Anna Sara.' Like it?"

"I'm flattered," she said with a smile, "but I'd write it in chalk if I were you. Don't do anything you can't erase."

Andreas's eyes were glazed over, but underneath the haze, he looked annoyed. "Why's it so hard for you to like me? Women are—what?—like, lined up at my fucking bed, and you—you're always trying to get away."

To her surprise, Anna was swept up with an emotion rarely associated with Andreas: pity. He looked lost and vulnerable. She took his hand, bearing in mind that it could be the drug and alcohol mixture that gave him that faraway look.

"Andreas, I know this is hard for you to understand, but we're two different people," she began. "We have nothing in common. We don't share the same interests. We've been friends for a long time. Why can't we just leave it at that?"

Andreas took his hand away and stared at her. He shook his head and screwed up his face, as if he'd just heard her speaking an entirely different language. "What the fuck??? 'We have nothing in common'? We have everything in common. We grew up in the slame splace, we went to the slame schools, we can both drive that big fucker tanker out there. Jeezus, what the hell else do you want from me?" He stopped and put his hand on her cheek. She didn't say anything.

"Say something, Anna. Tell me you can like me."

"I don't think so, Andreas. I'm sorry."

Andreas looked down. "It's someone else, isn't it?" He looked back into her eyes, his face clearly agitated. "You're in love wis slomeone else? That Ian shithead. I saw the way you were looking at him today." He grabbed her arm. "So, tell me, have you fucked him yet?"

Anna stepped back. "You're a sick and confused person." She jerked her arm back but could not pull free of his grasp. "Let go of me, Andreas," she said. "Your bullying tactics aren't going to make me change my mind."

"Well, maybe this will." Without warning, he pulled her towards him and locked his lips upon hers.

Anna's head was reeling. This was unexpected, even for Andreas. He had never pulled anything like this on her before. They had been alone hundreds of times in the past, and he had never touched her. At that moment, she became all too aware that there was nobody around to help her. The dock was empty and dark. She managed to pull her head aside enough to break free of his mouth. "What the hell are you doing?" she shouted while gasping for air. "Let go of me."

Andreas' grip on her grew stronger and she felt his hands pull up her dress from behind. "That shithead can't make you feel the way I can," he said.

Anna's momentary panic went to rage when she felt his tongue on her neck. There was no way to reason with him. She tried pulling his arms away but couldn't. "Listen to me," she said between clenched teeth. "Let go of me now or you're going regret this."

"Stop fighting me, Anna. I'm a helluva lot bigger than you. Why don't you just enjoy it? You have no choice."

She felt his saliva trickling down her chest beneath her dress, as he continued to lick her neck. She was frantic. He pushed her up against the side of the car. She felt the full weight of his body come up against hers. He fumbled at the back of her dress for a zipper, or buttons. When he realized there weren't any, he ripped it open from the front.

Anna felt her heart racing. "Okay, okay, Andreas," she said, between quick breaths. "Listen, maybe I was wrong."

"Fucking right you was wrong," he said as he pulled down her brassiere straps.

"Wait. Stop what you're doing for a second. I just have to tell you—"

"What?" he asked as he slid his drooling mouth towards her breasts.

"That I was embarrassed to tell you how I really felt about you."

Abruptly, he stopped what he was doing and looked up. "Whad da ya mean?"

It was working.

"So, whad da ya mean?" he repeated impatiently.

"It's just that—well—I've always been in love with you, but, you, being who you are— you know—so handsome and charming, with all these women after you, I just thought—" She lowered her head and stopped.

"Thought what?" Andreas asked with concern. "That I was too good for you? Is slat what you thought?"

Anna nodded. "Yes, I thought you could never love me back, that you'd just grow tired of me."

Andreas pulled away from her and took her head in his hands. "My sweetheart," he said in a soft whisper, "I know, I know how hard it must be. I'd feel the same way if I was in love with me."

What a complete asshole, Anna thought. She put her face to his and softly slid her lips over his cheek. "Thank you," she whispered. "Thank you for understanding."

"So, no more struggling?" he asked as he began to slide his hands under her dress again.

"No," she said, "no more." She softly licked her lips and gently put her mouth to the side of his face again. Then, she opened her mouth, closed her eyes, and bit his face. At the same time, she brought her knee up to meet his groin.

Andreas jumped back, doubled forward in pain, and grabbed his face. "Ohhh, Jeezes," he moaned. "What the fuck? You bitch."

Anna stood back with alarm. She put her hands to her face. She didn't know whether to approach him or to run for her life.

After a few more moments of moaning, Andreas reached into his pocket, pulled out handkerchief, and pressed it against the wound. "My face. Jeezus. I'm bleeding all over the fucking place." He stumbled into his car and pulled down the mirror above the visor. "Crap, oh, shit. It needs stitches." He yelled at Anna. "Get in the fucking car. I need to get to a hospital."

"Are you out of your mind? I'm not getting into the car with you."

"Yeah, right. Whatever. See you around." He put the car in reverse and backed away. Anna was walking towards the Port Captain's office, hoping to find a phone, when she heard the sound of tires shrieking followed by a thunderous crash. She turned around and ran towards Andreas's car. He had backed full-speed into some garbage dumpsters. As she approached, she watched him stagger out and survey the damage.

"Not that I should care, but are you all right?" she asked. "You shouldn't be driving in the first place, you know."

"Whatever. Yeah, shit. I smashed the fender. I'll send you the bill."

Anna walked to the back. "'You'll send me the bill,' you prick," she mumbled. As she bent down to look at the damage, she caught the sight of something, or someone, under the pile of twisted dumpsters.

"Oh, my God," she gasped. "Look under here."

To her horror, she saw a body underneath one of the dumpsters. It was an old man. He didn't move.

"Andreas," she said. "I think you hit him—and I don't think he's breathing. We'd better call for help."

Andreas stared down at the pavement. "Yeah, Okay." His voice sounded mechanical. "Use the phone in my car." He kneeled down and stuck his arm beneath the dumpster. "I think I can reach his arm. Yeah, here it is. I'll check to see if he has a pulse."

Anna ran to the front of the car, reached for the phone, and began dialing. Suddenly, Andreas ripped the phone from the dashboard and slammed the receiver against the wheel. Without giving her a chance to think, he put the car in gear and sped off.

Sweat mixed with the stream of blood from his wound. He wiped his eyes with the sleeve of his shirt and turned to her. "Bitch, you didn't really think I was gonna let you call the police, did you? That guy, just some homeless piece of shit. Maybe he was dead before we got there. Anyway, no one saw us down there, so I'm in the clear."

"No," she screamed. "You can't do that. You just can't leave someone dead like that. Look, we can make an anonymous call."

"Forget it. The guy's not worth it."

"You can't stop me from calling the police when I get home," she shouted.

Andreas hit the accelerator and headed for the nearest hospital. He reached over and pulled her hair so hard her head jerked. "Don't betray me, Anna," he said from between clenched teeth. "I'm warning you. Just forget this ever happened or I'll destroy you and your entire family. Don't think I can't do it." He pushed her head forward and let go of her hair. Her head banged into the dashboard. She looked at Andreas in disbelief. He was a monster—a rapist and a murderer who showed no remorse. She watched him as he continued to glance at his face in the rearview mirror. The sight of him sickened her. She wondered how many women he'd pounded into submission, or how many innocent bystanders he'd trampled to get his way? *Well, not tonight,* she thought. She glared at him and muttered, "You're not going to get away with this tonight, you sick motherfucker—"

Again, Andreas reached over to grab her. This time, his arm slid off the steering wheel. The car swerved and bounced off the shoulder barrier. He struggled too late to get control of the wheel. The car spun around and collided with an oncoming car. Anna heard herself scream before her head hit the passenger side window. The last thing she saw was Andreas's blood-soaked body slumped, behind the steering wheel.

Chapter 4

IAN

Richard Winters and Constantine Stavropoulos stood at the foot of her hospital bed. Anna could hear their voices as they spoke to a third person, who she assumed was a doctor. She tried to open her eyes but the mere effort made her head throb.

The doctor spoke. "Your daughter's going to be fine, Mr. Winters. She was lucky. She's only suffered mild whiplash and some cuts and bruises. We'll be keeping her here overnight for observation, but she'll be ready to go home by tomorrow afternoon."

"Are you sure?" Constantine asked in his most authoritative tone. "She looks terrible. Look at her face: all those bruises and those cuts. Maybe you're overlooking something. Who's the trauma specialist? We should call him in immediately."

"I assure you, Mr. Stavropoulos," the Doctor said, "we've conducted every conceivable test on your granddaughter. With a little rest, she'll be just fine." His beeper went off. "I've got another emergency coming into the ER. I'll check in on her again later."

"Christ, hospitals. They make me sick." Constantine said in disgust.

"And those smug doctors—if it was their granddaughter in that bed I bet there'd be two hundred specialists here by now."

"Take it easy old man. You're gonna to give yourself a heart attack," Richard said as he began to pace the room. "Let's just thank God she's all right. Did you see Andreas? He's got so many wires and tubes in him, he could light up a Christmas tree."

"Yeah, the poor kid."

"Poor kid, my ass. He was shit-faced drunk. Blood alcohol level was off the charts. I just can't understand what Anna was doing in the car with him." The room was quiet for a moment. "Hey Constantine," Richard said in a softer tone, "did you see the bite mark on the kid's face?"

With that comment, the nightmare of the car crash came racing back to her. Anna forced herself to open her eyes. "Dad," she said in a whisper, "I'm sorry."

Both men ran to her side. Richard looked down at her and smiled. "Anna," he said, "you have nothing to be sorry for, except maybe that you scared the living hell out of me." He took her hand. "How do you feel?"

"Like I was hit by a truck," she sighed. "It hurts just to breathe."

"Well, it wasn't a truck," Constantine said as he brushed her hair off her forehead. "It was three cars. You're lucky none of them hit your side, though, Andreas wasn't as lucky."

"Is he going to be all right?"

"He'll pull through," Richard replied. "He was hit pretty hard though. The doctors said something about a concussion, collapsed lung, and some broken ribs. Overall, he looks like shit, lots of cuts and bruises. No doubt he'll get his mail here at the hospital for awhile." He took a deep breath and continued. "Anna, the police are pretty anxious to talk to the two of you. It seems Andreas is in a lot of trouble, drinking and driving and all. They'd like to get a statement from you."

In a flash, Anna saw the face of the old man under the dumpsters. "Dad, there's more to the story than just that."

Constantine and Richard exchanged glances. "We're all ears," Richard said.

The two men stood in disbelief as she painstakingly described every detail of the attempted rape and the subsequent hit and run at the dump-sters. She then told them about Andreas's threats and cold brutality towards her in the car. Although she couldn't remember the crash itself, she described how they fought and how she pulled Andreas away from the steering wheel. When she finished, the room was silent.

Barely able to contain his rage and frustration, Richard once again began to pace the room. "Listen, Anna," he said as he shook his head, trying to comprehend the magnitude of the situation. "What you're telling us, well, this is murder. Hit and run. And you, what he tried to do to you ... I just can't believe it." He stopped short. "He should be put away," he said. "In jail. You have to tell your story to the police."

"What?" Constantine shot back. "Are you crazy? This could destroy his life, not to mention his family's reputation. He made a mistake and he's paid the price, a high price at that. I've known his family for years; they'll straighten him out. Let me talk to them and the boy."

"Where's your bloody ethics, old man?" Richard shouted. "The kid didn't just steal a piece of gum from a candy store. He's a psychopath who should be taken off of the streets before he hurts somebody else. He can't dodge the law just because he's some rich bastard's son. I don't give a shit about the reputation of his family. He tried to rape my daughter, your granddaughter—and let's not forget that there's a dead man under a tombstone of dumpsters down at the pier. Maybe someone should get him out and give him a decent burial."

Anna spoke up. "You two are unbelievable. You'll fight over anything." She looked over at Constantine. "Grandpa, we have to call the police in on this. I'm not out to destroy Andreas's life, but he has to take responsibility for his actions. He has to be held accountable for what he did."

Richard glanced up at Constantine and smiled. "Well, I guess the Win-ters blood wins out, old man. It's just eating you up alive, isn't it?"

Anna gave him a disapproving stare. "Dad, stop it. It's not a contest."

Constantine looked at Richard. "That's right, Dick. Don't be so small."

After spending the night in the hospital, Anna returned with Richard to their home in Belgravia. Richard immediately resumed his usual rou-tine: to the office by seven in the morning and home somewhere between nine and eleven at night. The days dragged by, and Anna began to count the hours before she could meet up with Jackie, Ian, and the rest of the Moore family in Brighton. Besides, two weeks partying with her best friends would help her forget that hideous night.

She had never been to Brighton before but it was just as she had pictured it, a wide stretch of rocky beach filled with local families and tourists trying to get a taste of summer. For many of the British, this was as close to a Mediterranean beach as they'd ever get. Although the weather was usually misty and overcast, umbrellas and blankets crowded the sand, and the ever-present smell of cocoa butter and baby oil wafted through the air.

The greatly anticipated beach house was over a half a mile away. But this minor inconvenience didn't bother Anna in the least. As long as Jackie, Ian, Phillipa, and Joseph were there, the house could have been on Mars.

Richard dropped Anna off shortly after the Moore family had settled in for their two-week stay. Their mother, Angela, looked somewhat embarrassed and apologetic as she met Richard for the first time.

"These aren't quite the accommodations your daughter's used to, I'm afraid," she said as she shook his hand.

Richard fidgeted with his cars keys and glanced around the entranceway. "Oh, no," he said, giving her a bright smile. "The house is lovely. Anna's going to have a wonderful time. I wish I could stay too but my office wouldn't know what to do without me."

"You're being kind, Mr. Winters," Angela said as she self-consciously lowered her eyes.

"It's Richard, just Richard. God, how I hate it when beautiful women like yourself call me Mr. Winters. It's so formal. Really, it makes me feel ancient. I'm not quite there yet, I hope."

Angela was caught off guard by his compliment. The somewhat disheveled appearance of a full-time mother of four teenagers could not hide that she was an attractive woman. She was petite, around five foot two, thin, and had long dark curly hair which framed a perfectly symmetrical heart-shaped face. She put her hands to her face and sighed.

As if enjoying the discomfort he saw in Angela's eyes, Richard shrugged and smiled. "Sorry there, luv," he said. "Didn't mean to make you blush."

Just then, the front door burst open. A tall, middle-aged man with slightly graying auburn hair walked through. He wore a tight-fitting white T shirt and equally tight-fitting worn dungarees. His left hand clung tightly to a bottle of Guinness as he approached Richard, and extended his right.

"Winters, I take it." He wiped his hand on his trousers before grabbing Richard's. "Glad to meet you. I'm Dylan, Dylan Moore."

"Pleasure," Richard said as he flashed one of his infamous smiles. "You've got quite a nice bunch of kids here. They've become like family to Anna."

"Yeah, she's like a third daughter to us. Good thing she doesn't eat too much though. I've got enough mouths to feed as it is."

Richard wasn't sure if Dylan was being serious or if that comment was his way of being funny. In either case, he decided to play it safe. "Maybe I should have offered to pay for her expenses. How thoughtless of me." He reached into his pocket and pulled out his wallet.

Dylan laughed. "Just a joke there. Wouldn't take your money no matter how much you offered. Now put that wallet away."

Richard still wasn't sure.

Dylan continued. "From the way you're holding those keys there, mate, looks like you're ready to go. Why don't you stay and have a beer? We can go outside, smoke a few cigars, and you can show me that fancy car of yours. What's it? A Lambourghini? Never drove one of those before. Mind if I take it for a spin?"

Richard fumbled for words. He didn't want to insult Dylan, but was not about to let someone he'd just met get behind the wheel of his new, eighty thousand dollar car.

Dylan continued. "So, what's one of those cars cost anyway? Ten, twenty thousand?"

Again, Richard searched for words.

"Dylan," Angela interrupted, "I think Richard said something about having to leave right away for a late business meeting."

Richard glanced over to her, and gave her an appreciative smile. "Yes, I'm sorry, Dylan," he said. "Maybe next time. We'll have that beer and go for a drive."

"Yeah, yeah. Sure, whatever."

Richard couldn't be certain, but he could swear he heard Dylan mumble, "You lousy fucking rich prick," as he past him on his way to the kitchen. But, not wanting to make a scene and spoil Anna's vacation with her best friends, he decided not to pursue the issue.

He glanced at his watch and began to walk towards the door. "Well, time for me to head home." Before leaving he turned back and looked at the group of five smiling teenagers. "Have a good time, right?"

Anna spoke for them all. "We'll do our best, Dad."

And in fact, nothing short of pure mayhem and delinquency was on their minds. By the second night, pub and nightclub owners knew them all on a first name basis. No beer went untasted or dance floor untried. They roamed the streets by moonlight, and spent the daylight hours sleeping, moaning, and nursing headaches caused by twelve-inch nails that had been hammered into their skulls. After over a week of guzzling and doing the hustle, they took a break to catch their breath.

It was close to midnight. After tossing in her sheets for nearly an hour, Anna decided to head downstairs, hoping to find someone to help her pass the long hours of the night. From the top of the staircase she saw the glow of the fireplace radiating through a crack in the French doors that separated the living room from the rest of the first floor. Gently, she slid the doors open and saw Ian sitting on the sofa reading a book, using the dim fire as his only source of light. Upon hearing the doors open, he looked up.

"Can't sleep either?" he asked, closing his book.

"No, I fell asleep for awhile, but I was startled awake by a dream."

"A dream, huh? So, tell me, what was it?"

"Just one that I have all the time. Not very interesting really."

"Come on, tell me." He patted the sofa next to him. "Over here, sit. It just so happens I have nothing better to do right now."

"You must be desperate for company then, if you want to hear about my dream, I mean." She lay down on the sofa and put her bare feet on his lap. "So," she sighed, "where do I begin? Well, usually, the dream starts with me—I'm sliding down the side of a steep mountain. I keep looking for something to hold on to, something to stop my fall, but there's nothing, nothing at all. Then, I look up and see my mother at the top. She puts her hand out for me, but I can't reach it. I yell out for her and then I usually wake up."

"Hmm," Ian said as he gently rubbed her toes, "sounds pretty upsetting. I can see why you can't sleep."

"Jackie thinks I should tell it to a shrink."

"The last thing you need is a shrink. You're one of the sanest people I know. Besides, all a shrink will tell you is that you feel scared and alone sometimes and you're looking for help. We all do, but you have the extra burden of not having a mother to hold on to when things get bad."

Anna combed her fingers through her hair, then let it fall slowly back towards her shoulders. "Since when did you get so smart? she said as her blue eyes held his. "Last night you were shit-faced drunk and doing a strip-tease number at the pub, and tonight you're psychoanalyzing my dreams like Sigmund Freud."

Ian shrugged. "It doesn't take a genius to see that you miss having a mother. I can't even imagine what it's like but don't take your dream so seriously. Even Freud said that sometimes a cigar is just a cigar."

"Okay, doctor, tell me. How do I cure my insomnia?" Anna asked.

"Do you really want to know what I think?" he asked as he began to tickle her feet.

"Absolutely," she giggled.

"Okay. Forget what I just said about the cigar. I think the answer to your insomnia is in that dream but you don't see it." Ian stopped what he was doing and became more serious. "When you want to find answers," he said as he looked into her eyes, "or you're feeling scared, you should draw strength from the mountain instead of sliding down it. The mountain's your base of power: it's your father and your grandparents and, of course, your friends. Stop playing the poor little rich girl and use the tools that you have to lift yourself up. When you learn how to do this in your real life, I'll bet the dream will change too."

"Jackie's right. You do think too much."

"You think I'm wrong then?"

"I didn't say that."

"Then what?"

She sat up and faced him. "I just don't see how you could possibly understand my situation. Look at you, you have it all, a great family and—"

"And what? I break out in a cold sweat every night thinking about how I can afford another year of college and you, my God, your grandfather uses my dad's yearly salary as fucking toilet paper." He stopped and shook his head. "Don't you know how much we envy you?"

"Then tell me, Ian," she said, "would you give up your family—no, your mother— for my money?"

There was silence.

"No, of course not," Ian said as he turned away and stared at the fire.

Anna put her hand on his face and gently turned his head back towards her. "I'm sorry. I know you were just trying to help me out." She watched as the shadows of the fire danced across his eyes. After a few moments she realized that she hadn't taken her hand away. Ian put his hand on hers and brought it to his lips. He continued to look into her eyes while he slowly kissed each finger. Anna felt a warm rush overtake her and she knew she wanted to be wrapped in his arms. Her heart began to race and she moved towards him.

"Wait," he whispered. "Not here. I have a better idea."

Within moments, they had grabbed some blankets and were heading down to the beach. They held hands as they walked along the winding streets of Brighton. The night air was cool and still; they took off their shoes once they reached the beach and waded through the calm water of the channel. Anna felt peaceful. She had always loved being with Ian, but this moment was special. She felt connected to him—more than just friends—it was deeper. They spread the blanket out under the pier and sat and listened as the water lapped onto the sand.

Ian leaned over and brushed her hair away from her face. "You're the most beautiful woman that I've ever seen, but you know that, don't you?"

"You were always really good at embarrassing me."

"You don't take compliments well."

Anna felt her cheeks flush and she looked down.

"Don't look away. God, couldn't you sense how much I've wanted to be with you since the moment I saw you in Green Park last month? All I've thought about is this moment, being alone like this."

"You never said anything."

"Neither did you."

Ian reached over and pulled her towards him. Their lips met. Anna's body felt limp and alive all at once. She knew that she had thought of nothing else but this moment too.

Ian continued to kiss her as he began to caress her body. His hands felt strong and warm against her waist. She was certain he could hear her heart pounding as he touched her breasts. She lay back against the blanket and closed her eyes. She felt his hair cascade across her face as he kissed her neck and shoulders.

"Anna?"

"Hmm?"

"Do you want to do more?

"More?

"You know, go on?"

"Oh, I, uhm, I don't know. I think so. Do you?"

Ian laughed. "Do I? You've got to be kidding. I feel like I'm going explode right now."

"I wouldn't want that." She kissed him again. His breathing got heavier. She knew that he was in another world, and she wasn't far behind. As if taking on a mind of its own, her body began moving to the rhythm of his. He removed her panties from beneath her skirt and gently caressed her thighs.

"This is my first time," she said.

Without breaking his stride, Ian answered, "Are you okay with this?"

"Yes, I'm okay with this."

Anna had never experienced anything close to this—the warmth of Ian's touch as he explored her body, the aching and longing her body felt as she pulled him closer to her.

She felt him enter her. He was slow and gentle, being especially careful not to hurt her. She heard him moan several times as he penetrated deeper. She didn't want him to stop.

He thrust deeper and she heard herself gasp. Ian stopped moving and pulled back.

"Are you all right?" he said while taking a deep breath. "Did I hurt you?"

"A little."

"Do you want to stop?"

"I don't think so."

"Sure?"

"Yes."

Once again, Ian penetrated her. His body moved slowly at first. She held her breath waiting for the same sharp pain, but this time it didn't feel quite as bad. Ian's pace quickened as his breath grew heavier. Then, without any warning, he began to pull away from her.

"Oh, God, we have to stop," he said as he continued to breath heavily. "I'm about to lose it and I don't have any birth control."

He rolled alongside her and put his head down near hers. She sat silently and waited for her emotions to recalibrate. The abrupt end of their passionate encounter made her feel as if she had just dropped a thousand feet to earth.

Ian took a deep breath and stroked her hair. "Sorry about that, Anna. Hope it wasn't too terrible for you."

Although this episode wasn't exactly the way she had pictured her first sexual experience, she answered, "No, of course not. It felt wonderful, it really did. I'm sure the next time will be even better."

Ian didn't answer.

His silence annoyed her. He should be telling her how beautiful she is and how incredible she felt. Instead, he just lay there not saying a word. Maybe he was nervous, or self-conscious?

"What's the matter?" she asked him.

"Nothing. But we should go back. I'm not sure what time it is but I think the sun's going to be rising any minute now." He began to get up.

"Wait. I don't want to leave so soon," she said as she pulled him down again. "I want to talk. I'm leaving for New York in a couple of weeks. I don't know when we'll get the chance to be alone like this again."

"I'm sure it will be a long time," he answered.

"It doesn't have to be," she said. "You can visit me, and I'll be home for Christmas—"

Ian cut her off. "Let's be serious. I can't afford to fly off to New York and by the time Christmas comes around, you'll have found someone else."

"What are you saying? I don't want anybody else. I want you."

"God Anna, this turned out all wrong. I shouldn't have let things get out of hand. I really like you. The last thing I want to do is hurt you. I'm sorry, but don't make promises neither one of us will keep."

"What?"

"Look, when you get back to New York, you'll have a line of rich, good-looking guys hanging outside your dorm room. It won't take long before you see that they belong more in your world than I ever will. I don't want to wake up one morning and find a 'Dear John' letter in my mailbox, and believe me, it's going to happen."

"Come on, you know me better than that."

"Do I?"

"I know that I'd never let that happen."

"And I know it will. Let's just be friends. It's safer that way."

"Safer? What does that mean? Why are you so afraid of being hurt? It happens to everyone sooner or later."

"It's different with you. I can't explain it, but it is."

"You know what? You're right. Maybe we don't know each other at all. I certainly didn't know you were so afraid of living."

"I'm not afraid of living. I'm afraid of losing."

"And what happened tonight, I guess my feelings don't count."

"They count. More than you'll ever know. But I said I was sorry for letting the situation get out of control."

Anna stared at him in disbelief. He didn't want to hurt her? Things got out of hand? He's sorry? This couldn't be the same person she had just shared the most intimate moment of her life with.

He stood up and offered her his hand. "Look, I know anything I say now isn't going to help matters, but for what it's worth, I meant what I said before about how I felt about you. The problem is, the closer we get, the more it will hurt in the end."

"Hurt who?"

"Both of us."

"Speak for yourself."

She pushed his hand away and stood up on her own. "So, this is all about you. Poor little Ian. What about me? For someone who thinks so much, you certainly didn't think about how I'd feel."

"I'm just being realistic. I think I'm making it easier on the both of us in the long run."

"So thoughtful of you."

She read him all wrong. They had no emotional bond. They were never meant to be together. "All right, Ian," she said as she looked out into the water, "if that's the way you want it. *Asshole.*"

They walked home in silence. When they reached the house, Ian held the door open for her. She walked past him without so much as even acknowledging his existence. Once back in bed, she thought about him and wished that it all could have ended differently. *But it didn't,* she thought to herself as she stared up at the ceiling, *but someday I'll watch him beg and come crawling back. Make no mistake about that.*

The British Airways terminal at Heathrow was buzzing. The summer over, school was set to resume in less than a week. Anna appreciated Jackie's offer to take her to the airport. Sadly and somewhat reluctantly, they sat together in the first-class lounge, and waited for her flight to New York City to be called.

Anna grabbed Jackie's hand and gave it a light squeeze. "Tell me," she said in a melancholy tone, "why's it when you want time to stand still it flies, and when you want it to fly, the hands on the clock never move?"

"I know what you mean. I've been thinking the same thing. It went by fast, didn't it?"

"She sighed, "Too fast.""

"I never did ask you," Jackie said, "but how did that court case with Andreas go? Did they put him away, or what?"

"Andreas? Be put away? No, I don't think so. His father had some connections in the justice department, so they gave him a year's probation for involuntary manslaughter and then slapped him on the wrist for driving under the influence."

"So, he's back on the streets and up to his old games, I'm sure," Jackie said. "I always knew there was a different set of rules for the 'haves' and the 'have-nots.'" She reached down and grabbed some peanuts from the clear crystal bowl on her end table. "You know, if it were one of my brothers, he'd be locked away for life."

"Your brothers aren't sociopathic. I don't think you have to worry about them being locked away for life." Anna sat silently for a moment, then cleared her throat. "You know Jackie, speaking of your brothers, there's something I haven't told you that I want you to know about."

"Well, blurt it out. What is it?"

"Oh God," Anna said, almost regretting bringing it up in the first place, "how can I say this? Well, I guess there's only one way. Your brother and I had sex one night while we were in Brighton."

Jackie's eyes opened wide and her mouth dropped open. "How disgusting. Don't tell me any more. Which brother? No, I don't want to know."

"Ian."

"Why did you tell me? Please say this is a joke. A momentary lapse in sanity maybe." She closed her eyes and shuddered. "I have to purge this vision from my mind."

"Come on, Jackie. It's not like your brother's Quasimodo."

"Well, I'm still in the denial phase here. I'm sure I'll learn to accept it—you know, like the five stages of death—but I have four more stages to go through. So tell me, are you two an item? Are you in love, or what? If you are, then you've done a great job hiding it. I mean, you two barely said two words to each other the past couple of weeks. I actually thought you had some kind of fight."

"No, we're not in love, and no, we're not an item. We decided that since we live so far apart, it would be best if we didn't commit to each other. I think we're both too young to make any serious commitments anyway."

"Hmm, I'm not so sure I buy that story. I know you better than that. There's something you're not telling me."

"Believe what you want, but that's the story."

"No, that's your story. I'll find out the truth some day. Now, I know I'm going to regret asking you this, but how was it?"

Time to omit a few more details. "Nice, really nice."

Jackie covered her ears. "Okay, enough. I regret the question. There are just some things a sister shouldn't know about her brother." She took her hands down. "In all seriousness, Ian's a good guy. He'd never do anything to hurt you. I'm sure that whatever went on between the two of you meant a lot to him. I'm glad it was a good experience for you, honest I am."

Anna wanted to tell Jackie everything but for some reason, held back. Maybe it was too soon, and besides, the person who had caused her so much humiliation was Jackie's brother.

"Thanks, Jackie. That means a lot to me."

After an intense hug, Anna boarded the plane. She grabbed her pillows and blanket and nested herself in her seat. She stared at the ceiling and thought about what she had said to Jackie. *Too young to make any serious commitments and all, what a load of crap,* she thought. *It will be a cold day in hell before I give him the chance to blow me off like that again.*

Chapter 5

TWO YEARS LATER

Without opening his eyes, Richard knew it was way past his usual waking hour of 6:00 A.M. After the alarm went off several times, he threw the clock across the room. Drinking and screwing until all hours of the night was particularly uncommon for Richard, but the debut party of his hottest new acquisition was an extraordinary event, one that even he couldn't resist. S & A Music had gone over the top for their new pop sensation Amber Stiletto—the 21-year-old platinum blonde whose raw ambition and unleashed sexuality made up for her lack of talent and brains. All of the biggest names in the industry had been there, it was the hottest ticket in town. The alcohol had flowed and enough drugs were acquired to wipe out a few small countries in South America.

Amber expertly worked the crowd, slinking through the club in her skin-tight dress, proudly displaying her perpetually hard nipples and her tight, silicone-injected ass. Her targets were usually the top executive brass of the major labels and studios. Tonight, she was giving them all a view of the new tattoo on the inner part of her right upper thigh. But it was obvious that her attention shifted the moment Richard Winters walked into the room.

Richard, as always, acted as a magnet in a crowd. He was constantly surrounded by six or seven musicians or business types trying to strike up a deal, or just suck up in general. Managing to break free for a moment, he was standing at the bar and waiting for his gin and tonic when Amber pulled up alongside him.

"Wanna do a line? I've got some great coke?" she asked through her plump, silicone enhanced lips.

"Sure. What the hell."

Amber carefully laid out a couple of lines of cocaine on the bar. When Richard reached down to snort his, he felt her hand on his crotch. "You know, Mr. Winters," she said, "I've always wanted to find some way to thank you for giving me a chance. Can you think of any way I can do that?"

Encounters like this weren't unusual for Richard. In fact, he had become quite jaded, but tonight he found himself uncharacteristically aroused by this girl. Maybe it was the lure of all that plastic surgery, or general interest in the survival skills of someone with a cranial vacuum, but whatever it was, he found his dick throbbing and it needed to be thrusting past that tattoo right away.

He grabbed Amber by the waist and led her to the men's room. He closed a stall door behind them and unzipped his pants.

"Wait a minute," Amber said. "Right here? Now? It smells."

"Oh Jeezus Christ," Richard made no effort to hide his irritation. "Do you think this is some kind of game? Do you want to fuck or not?"

Amber took his hand and led it up her dress. She was wet, hot, and waiting for him. "What do you think, lover?" She pulled his hard erection out of his pants and before he knew it, she was down on her knees using her tongue and lips in ways he had never known before. Her stamina amazed. Richard took particular pleasure in seeing just how long she could go without getting a cramp in her jaw. But, knowing the crowd outside the men's room was growing, he let himself lose control and climax. He drew a couple of deep breaths, zipped his pants, and opened the stall door. "God, I need a drink and a cigarette." He stepped out and turned to Amber. "Oh, thanks, luv. You were just great. Maybe I'll catch you again later." He headed to the bar and didn't come up for air until he blacked out and lost consciousness.

With his eyes still closed, Richard lay in bed thinking about the events of the evening. He realized that he had no recollection of anything after the men's room incident with Amber.

His head ached and he wondered who brought him home, undressed him, and put him in his bed. Then, the bathroom door burst open, and Amber walked out in all her buffed splendor. "Oh, you're finally awake, are you?" she squealed. "Here I was just dying of boredom. I didn't know what to do while you slept, so I decided to try your awesome Jacuzzi."

The mystery of how he got home and into bed last night was just solved. Amber slowly walked towards him. She licked her fingers and began rubbing her nipples. She knelt down on the bed next to him. "You know," she said, "I just can't seem to get these things to stand up on me today. Maybe you could help."

Richard rarely allowed women to spend the night at this house. Nothing repulsed him more than waking up next to someone whom he considered a one-time fuck, and Amber was no exception. "What are you doing here?" he asked while reaching for a cigarette.

"You told me to stay."

"I did?" he said. "Now I know I was delirious."

"So are you going to help me with my poor little tits or what?" She pouted her helium infused lips.

"No, but you could make yourself useful by sitting on this."

Amber reached down and stroked Richard's erection. "Anything you say Mr. Win—I guess I should be calling you Richard now."

He took a drag from his cigarette while she climbed on top of him. "No, you can call me Mr. Winters."

To Richard's great relief, it wasn't long before he was shuffling Amber out the front door. He walked to the kitchen and guzzled down two tall glasses of ice water and a handful of aspirin. Then, he walked into the living room, put on Maria Callas in *The Barber of Seville*, and sank into the sofa. He put his head back, closed his eyes, and dozed off. In what seemed to be only moments, he was startled awake by the sound of the doorbell. He waited for the butler to answer it, but then remembered that it was the weekend, George's time off.

Head pounding, he pulled himself off the sofa and headed for the door. The bell continued to ring.

Annoyed, he yanked it open. Standing in front of him was a petite, middle-aged woman with a mass of curly dark hair.

"Sorry," he said, "I'm not buying anything today. Just leave your brochures in the mailbox." He began to close the door.

She held out her hand. "Oh, wait, please, Mr. Winters, I'm Angela Moore, Jackie's mother."

Richard stopped and looked at her. "Yes, of course. I'm sorry. Can't believe I didn't recognize you." The truth was, he had only met her once before and barely took notice of her then. "Please, come in."

"No, I can't. Thank you anyway. I just came by to drop off a few of Anna's things. I've been cleaning out my house recently, now that the kids are all off at college, and I found some of Anna's clothes and jewelry in Jackie's room." She handed him a shopping bag from the Scotch House. "I put them all in here."

"You came all the way from Camden to bring me things Anna would never miss. You really shouldn't have gone to the trouble."

"No, I didn't travel that far." She pointed to the shopping bag. "I work at the Scotch House on Knightsbridge. Tie department. I brought the bag with me to work and walked over after my shift."

"Then you must be tired. Please, come in and have something to drink."

She gave him a bright smile. "Well, actually, it wasn't a very long walk at all, but I could use a glass of water."

He led her to the living room and was walking over to the wet bar when the phone rang. "Wait, one moment while I answer that. It's my butler's day off and I'm expecting a business call."

"On Saturday?"

He laughed. "Tell that to my investors."

He grabbed the phone from behind the bar, balanced it between his ear and shoulder, and began filling two glasses with ice. He watched Angela while he listened to his accountant's high-pitched complaints from New York. She walked over to the stereo in the breakfront and shuffled through some of his albums. She selected one in particular and studied the cover. A navy blue knee-length skirt with a matching double-breasted jacket accentuated her petite frame and small waist. Her long curls were pulled back slightly with a clip, showing off her heart-shaped face and finely arched eyebrows. He wondered why he hadn't noticed how attractive she was the last time they met.

After a few "Hums," he barked out some orders to his accountant and hung up the phone. He approached Angela with two tall glasses of ice water. "You know, it's a beautiful evening. Why don't we take our drinks upstairs? We can sit on my balcony and enjoy the view of the square."

Angela took her glass. "Sounds nice. I wouldn't mind getting off my feet for a few moments."

As they went through the master suite, he noticed her appreciation of the mahogany four-poster bed, turn of the century antique armoire and burgundy and gold Persian area rugs. He led her through the room to the balcony doors and motioned for her to sit on the bench next to him.

"You were right, this is a lovely evening," she said as she sat down and took a sip of her water. "And it's nice to finally get to know you a little better. All the time our daughters have been friends, I don't think we've actually uttered more than a sentence to each other."

"My fault really. I'm always so busy with my business. I never have time to spend with the people who are most important to me, including my own daughter."

"You shouldn't be too hard on yourself. You've done a wonderful job raising her. She's beautiful, sensitive, and smart—"

"Don't be so quick to sanctify me, Mrs. Moore. Those are all qualities she inherited from her mother. Believe me, I had nothing to do with it."

"First off, please call me Angela, and second, your daughter is probably more like you than you think."

Richard laughed. "Oh, God, I hope not." He took a sip of his drink. "You were interested in my album collection downstairs. Which ones did you like?"

"Actually, I was surprised that you had such an impressive opera collection."

"I started getting into it a couple of years ago. But don't tell my colleagues or I'll never hear the end of it."

"You can trust me."

He studied her face. He had never seen such perfectly round eyes with a color bluer and more radiant that a perfect morning sky. "So how did you get so interested in opera?

"From my mother. She was with the Paris Opera before World War II."

"And after?"

"There was no 'after' for most of my family."

"What happened?"

"It's a long story, but not an unfamiliar one to many French Jews. My mother and my grandmother were singers at the Paris Opera, and my grandfather was an artist who owned his own gallery on the Avenue George V. Shortly before the invasion, he heard stories about the fate of the Jews at the hands of the Germans, so he packed up my grandmother and mother and sent them to live with his cousins in England. He stayed behind to help in the war effort."

"And he was killed?"

"Yes, as were all of my relatives who remained in France."

"I'm sorry. I didn't mean to dredge up difficult memories."

"Actually, I wasn't born yet so I have no memory of it at all. What was difficult was growing up with knowledge of the suffering that my relatives experienced. I wish I had memories of them but it was as if their lives were erased. All of their personal belongings were destroyed, and their lifelong accomplishments confiscated. There's almost nothing, nothing left of them at all, not a picture, a letter, or a scrap of paper." She took a deep breath. "You just don't know how lucky you are. You'll live forever through your music. People a hundred years from now will listen to it and feel as if they know a little part of you. You'll touch their hearts and minds then, just as you do now, not to mention your grandchildren and your great-grandchildren. They'll be able to touch and feel you and know where they came from and what their connection to this world is all about."

"That's not my intention when I write."

"No, but it's the reality." She stopped looked over at him. "I'm sorry, I've been rambling on, haven't I? I didn't mean to bore you with my life story."

"Boring is not the word I'd use. So, keep going. You must have been born in England, right?"

"Yes, my mother married a farmer, and we lived in the country. I grew up raising chickens while singing to Verdi and Puccini. I thought it was perfectly normal. I was a teenager before I realized that not everybody could sing all the parts of *La Boheme* in two different languages."

Richard smiled. "So, why didn't you take it up professionally?"

"Because we were poor, and marriage seemed like the right choice at the time."

"And now?"

"What do you mean? In retrospect was it the right thing to do? Should I have given up my children to have a career?"

"I'm just saying that there were other choices you could have made. You could have put off having them—"

"There weren't that many choices for this poor farmer's daughter. I had my elder son, Joseph, before I got married."

"God, I'm such an asshole. I shouldn't be prying. Please, forgive me."

Angela sighed. "That's all right." She stared ahead. "I got a bit self-indulgent. It's not often that I get to sit outside on a beautiful autumn evening and ramble on about myself. I'm usually being hounded for dinner and clean laundry from a husband or a bunch of demanding teenagers." She put down her glass. "Anyway, it's getting late and I have a long train ride to Camden. Next time we meet, I get to ask all the questions."

Richard watched as she stood up. The clip on the back of her head had come loose, and all at once, her hair tumbled forward and covered her cheeks. He wanted to reach up and push it back. At that moment, he realized that he didn't want to stop looking at her.

He had to think of a way to make her stay. "I have season tickets to the Royal Opera. I think they're doing *La Traviata* tonight. Maybe we could get an early dinner somewhere in Covent Garden and walk over to the Opera House?"

She hesitated and sat back down. "The Royal Opera?" she sighed. "I've only seen them on special occasions ... but, I have obligations at home."

Richard sensed she needed only a little prodding. "Look, just call home and tell whoever's there, *your husband of course*, that you had to cover someone's late shift at work."

She sighed again, "Chances like this don't come around very often. All right, but let's keep this between us. I don't think my husband would approve. Especially when he doesn't find dinner on the table."

Just then Richard remembered the face of Dylan Moore. The man in the tight white T-shirt and the bottle of Guinness in his hand, who wanted to take his new Lambourghini for a "spin." "Don't feel so guilty. I'm sure your husband won't mind going down to the local pub for a sandwich or something." He was certain Dylan Moore was no stranger there. "Now come on, before you change your mind. Let's go."

She waited on the balcony while Richard took a quick shower and changed clothes. Then he whisked her downstairs to his waiting limousine. The driver dropped them off at the edge of Covent Garden. They window shopped along King Street as they made their way towards the Central Market. There, they found a small outdoor bistro with a view of the square outside St. Paul's Church. Over sandwiches and beer, they watched the evening street performers entertain the crowd. Tonight a clown was handing out balloons to wide-eyed children, while a mime was trying to figure out how to escape from an invisible box.

After dinner, they walked along Bow Street to the Royal Opera House. They grabbed a quick drink at the Crush Bar, then sat themselves down in their tenth row orchestra seats. A hush fell over the crowd as the program began. But tonight, Richard wasn't interested in the show. From the corner of his eyes he watched Angela, who looked as if she were paralyzed from anticipation. She sat straight up and her hands clenched the armrests at her side. As the show got under-way, she relaxed. She mouthed the words of several arias and closed her eyes for several long stretches. He could sense that she had transported herself onto that stage. When the show was over, she had tears in her eyes. She was the first up for the standing ovation. The force of her "Bravo!" amazed and delighted him.

It was close to eleven when they left the Opera House, but Richard wasn't ready for the evening to end. He convinced Angela to take a walk with him to the river. They walked towards the Waterloo Bridge and rested against the wall of the Embankment Gardens. They talked about politics, art and literature. Aside from having an opinion about everything, Richard was amazed at how well-read she was. Her favorite authors ranged from Plato to Pushkin, and she could recite Shakespearean sonnets as if the words were right in front of her.

Richard couldn't remember when he had enjoyed being with someone this much. Normally, he would engage in pro-forma conversation with a woman to validate her self-esteem, and then get her into bed. But Angela was different. She was smart and beautiful. It was as if she could feel his thoughts, and he could feel hers as well.

He hailed her a taxi well after midnight and watched as it disappeared into the winding streets of London. Then, he started calculating how and when he would see her again.

The next afternoon, he drove over to Knightsbridge and sauntered through the doors of the Scotch House. He breezed his way past the gawking sales people and eventually found his way to the tie department. He quickly spotted Angela and approached her.

Her body stiffened. With a look of surprise she said, "Richard, what are you doing here? Do you need help with a tie?"

Richard kept his voice low. He could see that all the sales people were staring. He picked up the nearest tie from her table display, a green and yellow silk stripe, and handed it to her. "I came by to pick out something for a new navy Armani suit. Think this would go?"

"No," she giggled, "not at all. Now really, why are you here?"

He lowered his voice even more. "Because I wanted to tell you what a great time I had yesterday. And I want to invite you to a dinner party I'm having this Friday night."

She lowered her eyes. "Richard, I had a wonderful time too, but what you're asking—well, it' just not appropriate."

"I knew you would say that, but please listen. I have something important I want to show you. It should arrive by then, and I know you'll love it. Just come by after work. All right? You don't have to stay long."

"All right. I'll stop by after work."

He reached over to her display table again and grabbed two stacks of ties. He handed them to her along with his platinum Visa. "I'm sure I'll find one in here that matches my suit."

She wrapped them up, handed him the shopping bag, and he left the store. Once outside, he felt elated. He began to count the minutes till Friday night.

It was a relatively small gathering for one of Richard's semi-annual dinner parties. Along with hefty bonuses for S & A's top executives came the rare opportunity to mingle with the boss on a personal level. Richard knew how to throw a party and amply rewarded his trusted and loyal staff with pounds of Beluga caviar and gallons of Dom Perignon. This was his one night to show his staff that he wasn't really "the ball-buster" they made him out to be. He made it his personal responsibility to ensure everyone's happiness; he kept the champagne glasses full, and mingled with as much genuine enthusiasm as he could fake.

A chubby middle-aged man put his puffy hand on Richard's shoulder. "Hey, buddy," he snorted in an American accent, "good to see you again. Great party."

A look of confusion swept over Richard's face. *God, I should know this person*, he thought. *Come on, come on. Think, think, think.* Suddenly he blurted out, "Nathan, Nathan Crosby."

"Hey, buddy, I got worried there for a moment. How could you forget your new head of publications?"

Richard thought for a moment. How could he forget? He had hired this man only two months ago—the pit-bull from New York. In that short amount of time, he had restructured and reorganized the entire division. Estimated third quarter earnings were already up by a quarter. The man was good, he was a maverick in his field.

No matter how much Richard detested it, it was time to show some interest in Nathan's life. "So, tell me, how are your wife and children adjusting to London?"

"Just great. That Harrod's—my wife can't get enough ..."

Nathan continued to talk but Richard found himself more interested in staring at the bad hair-transplant on top of his head. He felt another tap on his shoulder.

"Richard, we need to talk."

He turned around. "What's up? You look too serious. You're supposed to be having fun tonight—no business, remember?" He turned back to Nathan. "Have the two of you met yet? Christian Aprile, this is Nathan Crosby, my new publications man. Christian's the head of new talents."

Nathan spoke. "Sure, we've met. Christian here's my man. Can't get enough of listening to that great drumming when I hear those "Casuals" tunes. It's great to see you guys still working together. I mean, why split up a good team? Right buddy?"

Christian turned to Nathan. "This is a bit of a private matter. I hope you don't mind."

"Hey, not a problem. I can take a hint. I'll catch up with you guys later. Oh, by the way, buddy," he said before walking off, "nice pictures of you in *The Sun* last week. You know, the ones of you and that Amber Stiletto. Did you know about the cameras in the john? What the hell, man. You're one lucky S.O.B." His voice trailed off.

When they were alone, Richard spoke. "What an asshole," he mumbled. "If I'd known the cameras were in there, I wouldn't have been fucking her in the toilet." He grinned and turned to Christian. "So, what's up? Were you trying to save me from reaching for a gun and blowing my head off, or do you really have something to tell me?"

Christian stared at Richard from behind a set of brilliant green eyes. He was tall and thin—almost too thin—giving him the look of a man who should be force fed a twelve- ounce steak hourly. His hair was short and dark with bleached white tips moused and gelled into small gravity-defying spikes.

"I saw Nigel today."

Richard's eyes narrowed. "Where?"

"He came to my office."

"And?"

"It seems as if he's been having a lot of financial troubles. He made some bad investments in the stock market, real estate, night clubs, you name it."

"Okay, I'll name it: drugs, alcohol, private planes, yachts, and women. How's that?"

"Look, I think it took a lot of guts for him to come to me today. He's looking for a record deal."

"He can't find one in New York? That's where he's been crawling around lately."

"He said he would rather do business with us. He thinks it would be more 'meaningful.'"

"You mean more lucrative. Putting the names Winters and Taylor on an album cover would send it platinum before it's even released. Look Christian, Nigel and I had problems working together those last couple of years. I'm sorry that things aren't going his way right now, but I don't think I can work with him again."

"You wouldn't have to have any contact with him whatsoever. He'll record his album and I'll produce it. Your paths will never cross, I'll guarantee it."

"God, look at you. He always knew how to push your buttons. He's got you eating out of his hands again."

"If you're questioning my loyalty, you know I'd lie down in front of a moving train for you, Christ, you saved my fucking life more than once. Let me just do the same for someone else. He needs help now, and if you're not willing to do it, let me."

"With my money."

"Fuck you." Christian turned and began to walk away.

"Wait. Okay, but I'm only doing this for you. Do me a favor though and let me hear the demo tape first. I'm not putting my name on any unmitigated shit." Then Richard spotted Angela from the corner of his eye. She was heading towards the bar.

Christian grabbed a glass of champagne from a passing butler and put it in Richard's hand. "Hey, asshole, why don't you go and have a drink with that pretty lady you're staring at."

He laughed. "Am I that obvious?"

"Well, she's certainly got your attention."

Richard maneuvered his way through the crowd and found Angela at the bar waiting for her drink order to be filled. He took her arm. "Put that drink down and come and have some champagne with me outside in the courtyard."

She gave him a soft smile. "Sounds nice."

He took her arm and led her through the glass doors to the garden.

They sat on the bench beneath one of the small Ailanthus trees. He handed her a glass of champagne.

Angela took a sip and looked around. "It's beautiful," she said. "You must spend a lot of time here. The fountains, the birds. It's so tranquil, and the smells, so intoxicating, especially the eucalyptus. It takes my breath away."

"It doesn't take much to take your breath away, then does it?" He lit a cigarette and took a long drag.

"You're mocking me?"

"I would never do that. Trust me."

"I shouldn't be keeping you from your other guests. They're all here to see you."

"You're not keeping me from anything. Being here with you is like a refuge. I'd much rather hear about what takes your breath away than our latest acquisitions and legal battles."

"Why don't you tell me what takes your breath away?"

Richard looked startled. He didn't expect that question.

"The last time we sat outside your house you promised I'd get to ask all the questions next time, right?

"Right, but I thought you'd ask me something a lot simpler, maybe about my life or something."

She shrugged. "Your life? Why, your every movement is chronicled in the tabloids daily, so I'm pretty much caught up on all your current indiscretions. My God, you can't even go to the loo without someone following you in and taking pictures. I often wondered what those photographers expected to find until I saw the pictures of you with Miss Stiletto last week. How you failed to see a cameras in there is beyond me."

Richard squirmed. "I'm sorry you saw those."

"Who didn't?" She took another sip of her drink. "In any case, as for your history, there's not much about that that I don't already know either. You see, I've followed your career since I was a teenager. I was in love with the Casuals. I listened to your albums from the moment I woke up to the time I fell asleep. I read every article I could find about you. I knew your favorite foods, your favorite colors, and what you liked most in women. I had pictures of you on my bedroom wall," she paused and looked over at him, "and it was your face that I'd see in my dreams at night."

Richard took her hand. "Angela."

"Oh God, I can't believe I just said that. Look at me, one sip of alcohol and I'm telling my oldest secrets. You have to understand, I was a child, and you were my fantasy."

"And knowing me now, how do you feel?"

"I don't want to answer that. Besides, you were supposed to be answering all the questions tonight, remember?"

"Okay, then," he said as he put his hands on her face, "do you really want to know what takes my breath away? It's you. You do."

Immediately, she drew back and stood up. "Stop, don't say anymore. This isn't right, I think I should go."

"I won't try to stop you, but do me one favor before you leave."

"What?"

"Come with me upstairs, to my room. Don't look at me like that. I just want to show you something."

"I don't think that would be appropriate."

"Come on, I promise, I won't say another word and I won't touch you again, please."

Reluctantly, she followed him inside. They made their way past the guests and up the stairs to the master suite. "Well," she said, "what is it that you'd—" she stopped before she finished her sentence and walked over to the wall opposite his bed.

"Is this what I think it is?"

"Yes, a painting by Jean Pierre Wagman, your grandfather. 'Two Ladies in a Field.' Judging by your resemblance to them, I assume the younger one is your mother and the older, your grandmother."

Slowly, Angela reached up and touched the painting. All at once, her eyes were filled with tears. Then, she covered her face with her hands and began to weep. Richard walked over and put his arms around her. She stood motionless, crying in his embrace.

With tears still in her eyes, she looked up at him. "How? How did you get this?"

"It wasn't that hard. I had someone research any records of your grandfather's artwork after the war. This one belonged to a Swiss family who bought it from a gallery in Geneva. They were willing to sell it to me, for the right price of course. I had someone pick it up yesterday."

Angela stared at him in disbelief. "Why did you go to all this trouble?"

"For you. I thought it would make you happy."

She stepped back and continued to stare at him. "I don't know what to say, and I don't know what you want. People don't just don't go around doing things like this for no reason."

"But I do have a reason. I just said it. I thought it would make you happy.

"Then I suppose I should say thank you for letting me see it."

"Letting you see it? It's yours. I was going to have it wrapped up and sent to you."

"Richard, really, I can't accept it."

"It's a gift."

"No, I just can't."

"Come on, you don't think I want a painting of your mother and grandmother hanging in my room forever. That would make me a little strange. If there's anything I'd want across from my bed, it would be a picture of you."

Angela smiled. "That would be a little strange too."

Richard touched her face. "No it wouldn't. I don't think there'd be anything more wonderful than seeing your face before I go to sleep at night—and waking up to it in the morning."

Angela looked down and clasped her hands. "I think I'd better go."

"Right, sorry, I promised you downstairs that I wouldn't do that."

"Yes, you did. But I'd still better go."

"Why? What are you so nervous about?"

"I'm not nervous. It's just not appropriate."

"Oh, you're nervous all right. And it's because you have feelings for me. Admit it, there's something between us. We can both feel it."

She shook her head. "I have feelings for you. But not in that way."

"What way?"

"The way you're looking at me right now."

"I don't believe you. I'm not an idiot. It wasn't the champagne that made you say those things in the garden. That was you."

Angela looked up. There were tears in her eyes. "Stop it. You're just playing games with me. How could you have feelings for me? I'm a sales clerk from Camden."

"Why do you make that sound like a bad thing?"

"Because I'm not part of this world of yours—the one downstairs, the one with the champagne and caviar."

"I don't want that world. I want you."

"How could you say that? You can have anyone. Why would you want to complicate your life with someone like me?"

"Because I want to be with you." He leaned over and took her face in his hands. Then, he put his lips to hers.

Angela jerked back. "Don't toy with me, I'm not that easy." She walked over to the door and opened it. "Please don't call me or try to contact me again. I'm married, I have obligations."

"Take a chance Angela," Richard said.

She stopped and looked back at him.

Richard continued. "Let yourself be happy for a change. I'm not out to play games with you. How could I? You're the most unbelievable person I've met in years. Maybe you can't believe that, but I know it's the truth. I love being with you, and I know you feel the same way about me. Trust your feelings, and trust me."

She shook her head. "No," she said, and walked out. She ran down the stairs and out the front door. Richard stood at the top of the staircase and watched her leave. *Damn it. I scared her off.* He had to devise a new game plan to get her back.

"No action tonight with the little lady, hey, buddy?"

He turned so fast that Nathan took a step backwards. "If you ever want to see another paycheck, you fat little prick, you better hope I forget you just said that." He walked down the stairs to the bar. *So much for showing my warm and fuzzy side tonight,* he thought.

Christian approached him. "You look terrible. Are you all right?"

"Tell me something," he said, "do I look untrustworthy?"

Christian laughed. "Well, now that you mention it—"

"Fuck you. You're fired." Richard grabbed a bottle of vodka and headed for his room.

Richard awoke to the sound of his bedroom door bursting open.

"Hey, asshole, get out of bed. It's 2:00 o'clock in the afternoon."

Without opening his eyes, he knew it was Christian. No one else would have enough guts to wake him up, knowing he had a sure-fire hangover, and call him an asshole on top of it.

"Get out of my bloody room. I thought I fired you last night anyway."

Christian threw back the blinds. "You know I never take anything you say seriously. Now, get up. I brought Nigel's demo tape for you to hear."

"The last thing I want right now is to hear that slime-bag's voice." He got up and walked to the bathroom sink and splashed cold water over his face.

Christian yelled over the noise of the water. "Well, you better find time to do it because he's coming over here this evening. He really wants to hear your opinion of his new sound."

Richard walked out of the bathroom and slammed the door behind him. "How could you do this to me? I don't want to see anyone today. Your face is making me nauseous enough as it is."

"Oh, come on, Richard, Nathan told me last night that you got jilted by the woman you couldn't take your eyes off of. It happens to all of us. But if it will make you feel any better, she's been sitting in your living room for about an hour now listening to *Madam Butterfly*. Quite a nice lady I'd say."

"What?" Richard headed straight for the door, then looked over his shoulder. "Hey, asshole, get lost." He bounded down the staircase. The living room was empty. He ran over to the glass doors and looked outside into the courtyard. There, he saw Angela, sitting underneath the Ailanthus tree. He walked outside.

She looked at him. "I'm not sure what I'm doing here," she said softly. "I only know that I want to apologize for what I said last night. I don't think you're a bad person and I don't think you meant to hurt me."

"No, I didn't." He walked over to her. "Would you mind if I sit next to you?"

"No, of course not."

He took her hand. "I meant what I said last night—the way I feel about you. Do you think you could ever feel the same about me?"

She shook her head. "You know I already do. You were right. I'm afraid. I'm afraid I don't know where this is going to take us. You told me to take a chance. That's not something I'm particularly good at. The last time I did, I had a baby nine months later."

"That's not so bad," he smiled. "I love kids."

"Richard, be serious. This is all so new to me."

"I am being serious. And, this is new to me too. I haven't felt this way about anyone for years. I can't tell you where this is going. But wherever it is, we'll go there together. I'm scared too Angela. The last time I took a chance, I lost a piece of my heart."

"I'm so afraid we're going to lose so much more."

"Like what? Our families?"

"When they find out."

"Then let's not say anything for awhile. Let's just enjoy the moment and see where we go. I promise you, I'll never hurt you. Trust me."

She brushed Richard's hair off his face. "What am I getting myself into?"

Richard leaned over and kissed her. This time she returned the kiss. He felt exhilarated. He had forgotten what it was like to be in the arms of someone he actually cared for, to feel alive by her smile, and to melt with her slightest touch. He was falling in love, and he knew it.

"Where do we go from here?" she asked.

"On a ride. A wonderful ride. And we'll take it slow. Savor every single moment—my love.

Richard didn't think it would ever happen, but his heart and body felt alive again.

Autumn quickly turned to winter, then to spring. Richard would have to leave Angela to attend Anna's graduation from Columbia University.

After tossing aside her cap and gown, Anna met Richard at their pre-designated spot on 116th Street and Broadway. When she saw him, she raced into his arms and they both cried, he for the little girl who had grown up and she, for just making it through the last four years in one piece.

Richard had planned a special evening for the two of them: theater, dinner at the Four Seasons, and a buggy ride through Central Park. When the evening ended, they grabbed ice cream bars from a street vendor and walked along the eastern end of the park towards 72nd Street. Several years earlier Richard had purchased a luxury penthouse to serve as his home away from home during his brief visits with his daughter. When they reached the building, neither of them felt ready to end of the evening so they sat on a park bench and watched the bustling city unfold before them. With tears in his eyes, Richard leaned over and hugged Anna.

She rested her head on his chest and sighed. "Oh, please, Dad. You're not going to tell me that you're sad to see your baby growing up, are you?

"Of course I am. That's just what fathers do. But I also want to tell you how sorry I am that I haven't been able to spend a lot of time with you lately."

"That's all right. You've been busy at S & A, and I've been here in New York. There's plenty of time to catch up."

"God, it just all went so fast. Look at you. All grown up. These past couple of years were so important and I should have been there for you. I mean, I was supposed to prepare you for life and all."

"Prepare for what? Don't be so hard on yourself Dad. You did the best you could. Besides, how was your business supposed to survive without you?"

"That's not an excuse. S & A could practically run itself by now. I never needed to spend so much time there."

"Then why did you?"

Richard knew this moment was coming. It was time to tell Anna the truth, or at least part of it. "I suppose I have to tell you this sooner or later. I've been seeing someone for some time now."

Anna could see Richard talking, but the only sound she could hear was the beating of her own heart.

"Dad, tell me you're talking about a therapist."

"I know this is hard for you, but no, she's not a therapist. You know that I haven't had a serious relationship with anyone since your mother, but it's been a long time, too long. I need someone in my life, and I think I've found her."

"Oh."

"Anna, you're my daughter. You're everything to me, but she completes a side of me that I'd forgotten I'd had."

"I feel like I'm losing you. It was okay when I thought you were working, but now that I know there's someone in your life, someone besides me, it's different."

"No one can replace you Anna." He kissed her on the head. "I love you."

Anna saw how hard her father was trying, and decided to give him a chance. "So when do I meet her?"

"It's a little complicated, darling."

"'Complicated?' What do you mean?"

"She's married."

"You're joking." She tried to contain a giggle. "Why, in God's name, would you get yourself involved with a married woman?"

"It's simple. I fell in love."

"Well, then," she said, running her fingers through his hair, "she'll just have to divorce her husband. Let's face it, there's no man in the world that can compete with Richard Winters."

He took her hand. "Thanks darling but things get even more complicated here. She has several children as well."

"You've got your hands full, don't you?" She smiled. "I'm glad she makes you happy, honest I am."

"Thanks, darling," he said. "Maybe we should head in now, okay? I'm getting tired."

"Tired? Did I hear correctly? Richard Winters, the world record holder for the most number of days spent behind an office desk without sleep. What has this woman done to you? When can I meet her? We're going to have to have a long talk."

"Not any time soon."

"I'll be good, I promise."

"You don't know how."

"You raised me."

"That's why I'm afraid. Come on, let's go."

Anna reached out her hand. Richard pulled her to her feet. Arm in arm, they headed for the door.

"By the way," Richard said, "you're grandfather called from Tunisia this morning. The ship's ready to leave next week."

"Great."

"Are you sure you want to do this? S & A Music would love to have a new executive director. I could have your name printed on the door by morning."

"Thanks for the offer, but Grandpa really needs me now. He's getting old and I don't think there's anyone at SeaCorp that he can trust. He wants to start teaching me the ropes. There's no better way to learn than from the bottom up."

"But an oil tanker? I could charter you the Q.E II."

"Well, Dad, whether you like it or not, from this moment on, I'm in the shipping industry, so save the Q.E II for another time. Come on. Don't give me that worried face. Grandpa's going to be with me the whole time. He's missed his days on the sea, and this will give him the chance to feel alive again."

"God help the world if he's going to be navigating."

"No, he's not navigating. I am."

Richard laughed. "Where did you come from? Most young women would be dreaming of traveling Europe after college. Here you are, anxious to swab the decks of an oil tanker."

"I guess I get that sense of adventure from you."

"No, I let you spend too much time with your grandfather. I should have sliced him out of your life early on—he's like a cancerous tumor."

"Now, now. Be nice."

"Why, he's not here."

"That never stopped you before."

Richard opened the door of his apartment and let them both in. "So, is Jackie ready to go, too?"

"How could I commit to a year on the sea without her?"

"I can't even imagine the chaos the two of you are going to cause on that ship. Your grandfather has no idea what he's up against." He smiled. "Maybe this wasn't such a bad idea after all."

Anna kissed him on the cheek. "That thought ought to lull you to sleep tonight. Goodnight Dad."

He watched as she disappeared into her bedroom and then poured himself a cognac. He walked over to the balcony, opened the sliding glass doors, and stepped outside. He thought about the woman he missed so much in London. He wished he could share every part of his life with her. She would have loved watching Anna graduate today. She would have beamed with pride just as he did. *But, it's impossible,* he thought. *Too many people would get hurt. Anna would never get over the shock, and her children—they'd hate me forever.* He thought about the lies and cheating, and hated himself. But he knew he would never go back to the life he had without Angela, a life that less than a year ago had been empty and meaningless.

Chapter 6

THE OCEAN

Anna and Jackie arrived in Hamburg the very morning the ship was scheduled to depart for Beirut. Knowing how late Anna and Jackie could be, Constantine sent his personal car and driver to the airport to collect them. He would tolerate no delays or interruptions. The ship was scheduled to set sail at 1:00 P.M. and it would set sail at 1:00 P.M.

The limousine arrived at the dock shortly before noon. Two men quickly approached the car, grabbed the girls' luggage and began shuffling them up the steep gangway towards the bridge.

"Nothing like cutting it close, eh?"

Hearing the so-familiar voice, Anna stopped short and turned around. Feeling twelve years old again, she threw her dignity aside and ran into his arms.

"Don't try to melt my heart, little one," Constantine said while hugging her. "I told you to get here two days ago."

"I know, I'm sorry. We just had to say good-bye to a lot of people in London. But I promise, from now on, you're the boss: whatever you say, goes."

Constantine tried to look stern. "Just remember you said that. I will not tolerate insubordination on this ship." His eyes were twinkling.

The two girls nodded sheepishly and followed Constantine toward the bridge. "It's been a long time since you've sailed with me, Anna," he said over his shoulder. "Do you remember anything I've taught you?"

"I think so. This is a class T-2 tanker. From the looks of her, she's capable of carrying about 20,000 tons of cargo. Am I right?"

Constantine stopped and turned around. "Yes, and what kind of cargo can she carry?"

"Well, this particular ship looks new, maybe only three or four years old, so she can haul anything from crude oil to grains. By the smell of things, she just discharged some kind of heating oil."

Constantine gave her an approving smile. "Very good. Number 2 heating oil to be exact." He turned around again and continued to walk. "Come on. Let me show you where we're heading, and don't get cocky. You and your friend still have a lot to learn."

They entered the bridge, where three men stood huddled, staring at a stack of maps. Startled, they all looked up.

"Gentlemen," Constantine said, "this is my granddaughter, Anna, and her friend Jackie. They'll be traveling with us for the next few months."

The largest of the three men extended his hand. He was tall and stocky, at least fifty to sixty pounds overweight, and had a black bushy mustache. "Welcome aboard." His grin displayed at least three gold teeth. "I'm Captain Stavros. These are my first and my second mates, Mr. Nick Alexander and Mr. Marcos Yannis. I'm sorry that the accommodations won't be up to your standards, Miss Winters. We've never had a woman on board before, but we'll do everything we can to make your trip as comfortable as possible."

Anna immediately disliked him. She hated to be patronized—and he smelled of alcohol. "Thank you for your concern over my comfort, but if I had wanted to take a luxury cruise, I would have chartered a yacht. We're here to learn the business, so I hope you won't mind when I look over your shoulder."

Stavros looked at his team and raised his eyebrows. "If it's an education the young lady wants, we'll make sure she gets the best. Right men?" What was meant to be a hearty laugh became a rough cough. Finally he hacked up a vile-looking phlegm into a grimy handkerchief. "Come, ladies," he continued, "I'll show you the course we'll be taking."

The girls moved toward the table covered with maps. Jackie leaned over to Anna. "This guy gives me the creeps." she whispered, " I wonder where he keeps his pet parrot and the hook?"

"Mr. Yannis," Constantine said, "what's our heading?"

Marcos Yannis stepped back and made room for Jackie and Anna. "Take a look here." He pointed to a large incomprehensible-looking map filled with thousands of small numbers and lines. "Our trip originated in Beirut." He held what looked like a sharp pair of tweezers over Lebanon. "We transported about 130,000 barrels of heating oil to Hamburg, and now we're going to return to Beirut in ballast, reload, pass through the Suez Canal, and discharge in Bombay."

"What does 'in ballast' mean?'" Jackie asked.

"After discharging the cargo, the ship rises up out of the water, which makes it difficult to navigate through choppy waters or a storm. So, we load her up with sea water to weigh her down. It makes the ride much smoother."

Anna liked Marcos. His eyes and his skin were like her grandfather's. She could see that both men had spent many years on the sea. But Marcos squinted hard behind thick black-rimmed glasses. That gave him the appearance of being either happy or confused; it was hard to tell which.

Marcos continued. "After Bombay, we'll wash out the holds and pick up 20,000 tons of wheat from Galvaston and take it to Stockholm."

Jackie studied the path. "The line you drew plotting our course from the Mediterranean to Texas is curved. Wouldn't it be faster to take a straight path?"

"That is a straight path," Constantine interjected. "If we'd plotted it on a globe, the line would be straight but since we're working with a flat surface, trying to represent a round one, certain compensations have to be made. I'll explain it all to you in detail as we go along."

"My dear girls," Captain Stavros said in his most condescending tone, "navigating a ship is a very technical job. Why worry your pretty little heads about numbers and coordinates?" He looked at the other men for approval. Taking their lack of expression as a sign of agreement, he snorted, coughed and hacked again. "Just relax and enjoy the sights. I'm sure you'll enjoy the shopping when we visit some very exotic ports."

The two girls exchanged glances but before Anna had a chance to respond, Constantine took her arm and quickly ushered her towards the door. "Come on," he said, "let's leave the men to their work now. We'll be pulling out in a few minutes. They'll be plenty of time for more questions later on."

When they left the bridge, Anna turned to her grandfather. "Gramps, how can you tolerate that guy?"

"Who?"

"What do you mean who? The captain, Stavros. He's condescending and he reeks of alcohol. You should fire him. Get somebody else."

"Anna," Constantine responded, "he's a good man, a good captain. As a matter of fact, one of the best. I've known him for years. I can trust him. He's always been loyal, so sometimes you have to overlook certain things. You'll learn, my dear."

Then he showed them to their quarters, where their bags were already waiting. A set of lumpy bunk beds in the corner and a bare ceiling light-bulb failed to brighten what looked like a cell, with its steel gray walls. A small porthole that looked painted shut offered the only potential access to fresh air or sunlight. Jackie looked around and let out a long sigh. "Welcome to hell."

"If you think this is hell," Anna responded, "wait until you've tasted the food."

After a few short days at sea, food was the farthest thing from Jackie's mind. The trip through the English Channel was uncharacteristically calm, when they crossed the Bay of Biscay and entered the North Atlantic, the weather began to change.

Anna stood in the bridge with Captain Stavros and listened to weather forecasts. They were about to hit a major storm, possibly a full-blown gale, within the next twenty-four hours. The Captain ordered every opening and steel door battened down, and proceeded on course.

"Shouldn't we slow down or turn around to avoid the storm?" she asked the Captain with some alarm.

Stavros took a deep breath and rolled his eyes. "So many questions from such a pretty girl. You could drive a man to drink."

"You're doing a fine job of that all by yourself," she murmured.

"Did you say something, Miss Winters?"

"Uhm, no, but I would like you to answer my question. Why aren't we slowing down?"

"Because, my dear, we have a schedule to maintain. Any delay will cost your grandfather thousands of dollars a day. But you needn't worry. In a storm, tankers are unaffected by the shipping seas—the waves that hit the ship's deck. When everything is battened down, like it is now, only a fire or main engine breakdown can sink a tanker. Either one of those could leave the ship paralyzed and a broadside target to the waves."

"What would happen then?"

"It would crack in half."

Anna took a deep breath. "Oh." *Sorry I asked.*

Within an hour, the ship was dead in the midst of the storm. The waves hit with increasing severity, and periodically the entire hull of the tanker was under water. The captain eventually slowed the ship down a few revolutions to ease the impact of the waves. By nightfall, the storm had developed into a full gale.

Constantine joined Stavros and Anna on the bridge. "I don't like the feel of things," he said. "Captain, what's our situation?"

"Forty-foot waves have hit us a number of times on the starboard bow, pushing us parallel to them and into the troughs."

"That's not good," Constantine said as he stared out into the storm. Anna felt her knees weaken. She had never seen her grandfather be less than completely confident.

"What's the matter?" she asked. "Are we in trouble?"

Constantine continued to look out into the night. "I've been through a million storms. No, we're not in trouble, but riding parallel to the waves leaves us very vulnerable—it can weaken the structure." He turned to Stavros. "Our cargo's going to have to wait. Slow us down and change course. Let's mark time and ride this one out till the gale passes over."

Stavros shrugged and carried out his orders. Constantine turned to Anna, "Why don't you go back to your quarters? It's going to be a long night. There's no need for us all to lose sleep. Stavros and I will stay here to keep the helmsman alert. We can't afford the slightest mishap."

There was no need to argue; she knew he was right. She returned to their room only to find Jackie flat out on her bed, holding her stomach and moaning. Anna climbed up to her bunk and looked down at Jackie. "You don't look very well. What's the matter?"

"Can't you tell? I've been sea-sick all day. There's nothing left in me to puke up. Tell someone to make this thing stop rolling."

"They're doing the best they can, but I'm afraid it's going to be bad all night."

Jackie let out a moan. "I'm gonna die, I'm telling you. I'm already delirious. I've been lying here all day in misery. The only thing that kept my mind off of stabbing Captain Mucous in the head was watching the damn bracelet you dropped this morning slide back and forth on the floor. When it finally got stuck under the bed, I went hysterical and started crying."

"Which one of my bracelets?"

"That's not the point. I'm loosing my mind."

"No, you're not." Anna jumped down. "Wait here, I'll go and see if I can find some of those nausea patches somewhere."

She walked out to the corridor and bumped into Marcos. "Miss Winters," he said, "the seas are rough tonight. You would be much safer in your room."

"I know," she said trying to keep her balance with each pitch and roll of the ship, "but Jackie's seasick. Maybe you could tell me if there's any medicine around?"

"I'm pretty sure we exhausted our supplies a while ago. We don't carry much to begin with since most seamen don't get seasick. But the Captain has a new first aid kit in his quarters. There's probably something in there she could use."

"Great, but I can't drag the captain off the bridge now. He would kill me. You know he's not crazy about the fact that we're here to begin with. If I complained about seasickness—well, that would just make his day."

"I see your point. I'm sure he won't mind if we go in and get the kit ourselves."

"Won't his door be locked?"

"Nobody locks doors around here. We have nothing to steal."

"Well, sorry to drag you into this, but lead the way."

Just as Marcos had anticipated, Stavros' door was unlocked. They walked in and scanned the room. Like hers, it was stark and bleak.

"Well, there aren't too many places it could be." Anna said, "You take the closet and I'll take the desk."

Anna began opening the drawers. "Hey, Marcos," she said, "what do you think he'd do if he found us going through his things?"

"I don't know, but I did see him polishing a plank one day."

"And I thought you had no sense of humor."

"Who's joking?"

She laughed and continued her search.

"Hey, I found it," Marcos said. He took the first aid box off a high shelf, took out two propalimine patches, and returned it to its original position. "Okay, let's go."

"Great." She began to close the lower drawer when an envelope caught her attention. "Look at this, Marcos."

Marcos grabbed her arm. "Come on, Miss Winters. It's not polite to look at his personal things."

"No, wait. This is too interesting to pass up. It's from a Swiss bank." She opened the envelope. "Two Swiss bank account numbers in his name. Why do you suppose he'd be hiding money in Switzerland?"

"The account balances are zero. There's no money in them."

"Yet. There's no money in them yet. He's about to come across funds that he doesn't want anyone to know about."

"Put it down. There could be a million reasons why he has accounts there. Let's just get out of here." He led her to the door. "I hope you don't plan on telling Stavros what you found while snooping around in his desk?"

"Do you think I'm crazy? But mark my words, Marcos: he's up to something and whatever it is, it's not legal."

By morning, the storm had passed. Upon crossing the Straits of Gibraltar, Anna and Jackie could go out on deck, where they enjoyed the air, the small islands and the brilliant blue waters of the Mediterranean. But their time to relax was short-lived. Shortly after passing the coast of Cyprus, the crew began to prepare to dock in Beirut.

Although they knew their presence to him was monumentally annoying, Anna and Jackie studied every move that Captain Stavros made. They watched as he filled out the docking reports, listened as he radioed the harbor master, and asked questions as he shouted orders to the helmsman and the engineers.

Once the ship was docked, the cargo holds were reloaded with heating oil. Then the crew began to replenish the diminished supply of fresh fruits, vegetables, and medicines. Marcos stood on the deck with Jackie and Anna and watched as his men negotiated with the local farmers for produce.

"Look at them," he said. "Those idiots will never learn."

"Learn what?" Jackie asked.

"The last time the crew ate fresh produce from Beirut, they were all sick for a week. Trust me. Stick to the frozen stuff we loaded in Germany."

"So why don't you tell them to stop?" Anna asked.

"It's a union thing. Their contract says we have to provide them with fresh fruits and vegetables, so they make it a point to buy them wherever we dock. The part I never get though is why they continue to eat it. I'd rather see them throw it overboard." He sighed. "The union—now that is a subject unto itself. A couple of years ago, I was preparing to dock in Liberia when something went wrong with one of the anchors. I had to quickly summon one of the engineers, who was on break, to the bridge. We were getting dangerously close to land, and the engineer was nowhere in sight. I started shouting for him, when the third mate notified me that, according to the union rules, I had to give him a fifteen-minute notice before he had to report. So there he was, in the galley, drinking his coffee, while the ship was about to plow into the dock ahead."

Anna started to laugh. "Oh, come on, that can't be true."

"Have I ever lied to you?"

"So, what happened?"

"I didn't want to get in trouble with the union, so I fixed the problem myself." He turned and motioned for them to follow him. "Come on. Let's get ready to pull out of here. I only hope they loaded enough Immodium and toilet paper to get us through the upcoming nightmare."

The ship arrived in Port Said and waited outside the harbor to receive a departure time to enter the Suez Canal. Although Anna had transited the Canal in the past with her grandfather, in never ceased to amaze her: one hundred and one miles long (ninety-three man-made,) and only wide enough to accommodate one ship passing at a time. The northbound convoys meet the southbound convoys at two passing points so the departure times must be perfectly coordinated. However, unanticipated delays at the northbound end turned their relatively routine trip into an exhausting wait.

After a twenty-four hour standby, they finally took off. The first half of the journey was smooth and relaxing, but when they reached the first passing point, the local fruits and vegetables started taking their toll on the crew members. One by one, they began dropping like flies. Within hours, the only people left standing were Anna, Jackie, Marcos, Stavros, and one engineer who was allergic to fresh foods. After exhausting all medical supplies in what seemed to be minutes, they quickly decided to cut the trip short at the exit of the Canal and find a doctor in the city of Aden.

Stavros took command of the bridge while Marcos and the engineer were left to handle the anchors and the engine room. As they approached Aden, Stavros slowed the engines. Hoping there was something she could do to help, Anna walked towards the bridge.

"You're not heading where I think you're heading, right?"

She turned around and saw Marcos. "Where else would I be going?"

He took her arm. "Anna, be reasonable. I don't think your presence would be appreciated on the bridge right now. The captain's under a lot of pressure and there's really nothing you can do. Besides, it's going to be another waiting game, I'm afraid. There's a British tanker loaded with gasoline anchored ahead of us. We have to stop here and wait for it to leave before we can dock."

Although disappointed, she nodded. "Okay. I'll just go and make myself a cup of tea or something. See you later." She turned around and headed for the galley. *Hmm, tea,* she thought, *I'll bet the Captain could use some tea too.*

With a hot cup of tea in her hand, she opened the door to the bridge. The room was empty. The autopilot was steering the ship straight ahead. Within seconds, she understood the magnitude of the situation and gasped.

With one foot still in the door she turned around and screamed. "Help! I need some help over here fast."

As if reading her mind, Marcos appeared in front of her. "What the hell's going on? Why aren't we slowing down?" He pushed Anna aside and entered the bridge. "Jeezus Christ. Where's Stavros?"

Anna heart was pounding. "I don't know. I just walked in and found the place like this. But never mind that now. Look over there. The British tanker—we're on a direct collision course and closing in fast."

"That's the one loaded with gasoline—my God, we're both gonna explode." Marcos grabbed her hand and moved her towards the controls. "Quick, we don't have much time." He took the helm. "I'll steer us in and you—just do whatever I say, Okay?"

She nodded. "We're going in too fast. I don't think we have enough time to stop."

"We don't have any choice. Ready?" He turned the wheel hard right. "Reverse the engines."

Anna could feel the sweat dripping down her back. She reached for the controls and eased the engines into reverse. "Got it!" She felt the ship begin to slow. "We're slowing down. We're going to be all right."

"Don't start relaxing yet," Marcos yelled back. "This is a tanker. It doesn't stop on a dime; we're still going in too fast. Drop the main anchor."

Beads of sweat made her eyes sting. She pulled her T-shirt over her face, wiped her eyes, and readjusted her focus. She looked down at the control panel. "The main anchor, the main anchor," she mumbled, "where the hell—" She spotted the big red lever to her right and pulled down on it hard. She heard the clang of the chain roar from the rear of the ship. "Okay," she shouted to Marcos, "it's dropping."

"Put the brake on it."

Gently, she applied pressure to the break lever when, a dozen different warning signals lit up on the control panel. "Marcos, what the hell's happening?"

"We're going too fast. We just burned the brake lining. The chain's running free. Drop the other anchor."

She did, then watched as the British tanker drew closer and closer. "Oh my God, we're not going to make it. Look, the crew on the other tanker: they see us coming, Marcos. They're jumping off. "

"We're gonna make it. Just do what I say. Now gently, again, put the brake on the anchor and—"

"—and what?"

"And pray. That's all we've got left."

Anna took a deep breath. "Come on, come on, please, slow down and turn."

Within seconds, they could feel the ship pulling to the right. The second anchor held together and helped pull the ship parallel to the British tanker—both resting about fifteen feet apart.

Giddy with relief, Anna hugged Marcos and laughed. "You did it, you did it. You're the best."

Marcos stood frozen. "I don't know what the hell just happened. I've been through a hundred close calls before, but this topped them all."

Still panting from her recent rush of adrenaline, Anna asked, "It was Stavros, wasn't it? What do you think happened to him?"

"I don't know. But when I find that son of a bitch, I'm gonna kill him. But first I should find your grandfather." He turned to leave. "By the way Miss Winters, nice piloting. You could be my first mate any time."

They never found out what happened to Captain Stavros. In fact, he was never to be seen again on that journey. When the ship finally arrived in Bombay, Anna received a ship-to-shore call from Andreas.

"My crew enjoyed their little swim in the Red Sea, Anna."

"I didn't know that was your ship, Andreas. If I did, I wouldn't have been so quick to divert the collision."

"Always ready with the quick come-backs. But I'd be more careful if I were you. You wouldn't want your grandfather to be declared incompetent on the seas, now would you?"

"My grandfather wasn't at the helm. If he had been, we never would have gotten into that situation. But rest assured, Andreas. The Captain in charge won't be navigating the high seas any time soon."

"For your sake, I'm glad to hear that, although I must say, that the thought of pressing charges against you and your family was a high point in my otherwise dull week."

"Well, thank you for this brief and uninteresting chat. If there's nothing else—"

"Oh, but there is. I just wanted to let you know that I have a big surprise waiting for you when you get to Texas. Enjoy it, my darling."

He hung up.

Several weeks later, the ship approached the docks in Galvaston, Texas. Anna decided to tell Constantine about the Swiss bank account numbers she found in Stavros's room, and the strange phone call from Andreas.

"It doesn't take a genius to figure out that we were set up in Aden, Grandpa. I think Andreas paid off Stavros to sabotage our ship."

"But it doesn't make sense," he responded. "Why would Patras want to blow up one of his own ships too? Besides, think of all the people who would have died."

"We already know that Andreas doesn't have a conscience, so the loss of a few lives wouldn't bother him in the least. And as for why he would destroy one of his own ships in the process? That's easy. For the insurance money, what else?"

There was a knock on the door. "There's a ship-to-shore call for you coming from Galvaston, Mr. Stavropoulos."

"I'll take it in here."

Anna watched her grandfather as he talked on the phone. His expression became serious. He said almost nothing and was silent as he hung up the phone.

"What's the matter?" she asked. "Is something wrong at home? Is Grandma all right?"

"Calm down. Everything's fine at home. That was a friend of mine, a Port Captain, from Galvaston. He says that we're going to be boarded by the U.S. Drug Enforcement Administration as soon as we dock."

"What for?"

"They say they have evidence that we're smuggling in drugs from Asia."

"That's ridiculous. You've got an impeccable record. And as for the crew, well—you know everybody on this ship, they would never do anything like that either."

"Oh, yeah? How well did we know Stavros? Maybe he planted something, who knows? If they find something, it could ruin us. The government would seize our ships and we'd be shut down. Summon the entire crew to the galley. I want every inch of this place searched. I don't want those DEA guys to find as much as one single poppy seed from a bagel stuck between anyone's teeth."

After an exhausting five-hour search, nothing was found. Anna and Jackie met back in their quarters and began packing their bags

"Do you think this whole drug raid thing is a hoax?" Jackie asked.

"I don't know, but assuming we're not arrested when we arrive, I'm looking forward to spending the next three days in Galveston's best hotel."

"Aren't you just a little nervous? Maybe something was overlooked?"

"I'm very nervous. But, we've searched every inch of this thing. Come on, let's just finish packing." Anna looked down at her wrist. "By the way, my gold bracelet, the one that slid under the bed—did you ever get it out?"

"No, I'll get it now." Jackie reached under the bed. "It's stuck against the wall. Come over here and help slide me under."

Jackie lay down on her back while Anna pushed.

"Oh, my God," Jackie said. "I think I just found what we've been looking for."

Anna crawled under the bed and looked up. Strapped under the mattress were four brick-sized plastic bags filled with a white powder.

"What do you think it is?" Jackie asked. "Opium, heroin, cocaine?"

"I don't know, but let's get it out of here. We're docking in about an hour. We don't have much time."

With the help of Marcos and Constantine, the girls put the bags in a large pillowcase filled with canned goods from the kitchen and threw the whole package overboard. They all sighed with relief as they watched their unwanted contraband sink to the bottom of the ocean.

When they arrived in Galvaston, a dozen crisply suited Federal Agents and their overly zealous barking dogs came on board. They pushed past the crew and headed straight to the owners' quarters. After a few moments, they emerged and began an inch-by-inch search of the rest of the ship. Satisfied that every corner had been examined and every stitch of clothing sniffed, they approached Constantine.

"Our sources must have been mistaken, Mr. Stavropoulos. I'm sorry we wasted your time."

"Maybe you should check out your leads more thoroughly next time," he said.

"You're absolutely right. Again, my sincerest apologies."

The agents collected their dogs and left the ship. Relieved to have just diverted another disaster, Jackie and Anna grabbed their bags and headed for the gangway. On their way down, a young man in a baggy jumpsuit approached them. He was holding a bouquet of red roses.

He looked down at his delivery slip. "You two purdy ladies wouldn't know where I could find a Miss Anna Winters, would ja?"

"That's me." Anna said while taking the flowers out of the man's hands. She reached into the center of bouquet and grabbed the card.

"So who's your secret admirer?" Jackie asked.

"One guess." She read the card out loud.

I hope you enjoy surprises, my darling.—Andreas

"I wonder what else he's got in store for us?" Jackie asked.

"I don't know, but I don't want to stick around here and find out."

They checked into a nearby resort where they had reservations. That evening, Constantine joined them. He also wanted to unwind and take a breath. As glad as Anna was to see him, she felt a sudden rush of sadness. His usual confident stride had given way to a slow shuffle. Although they had spent two months on shipboard, with bracing air and bright sunshine, he looked pale and fragile. She helped him check in and got him settled in his room. They agreed to meet in the lounge for a drink.

"This trip's taken a toll on you, hasn't it?" she asked while sipping a martini.

He looked resigned. "I'm not as young as I used to be."

"Maybe this was too much for you."

"I can never give it up."

"Why don't you go back home to Grandma? I'm sure she's been lonely without you. I know you've been missing her too."

"And leave you here without me? Impossible. Your father and grandmother would kill me."

"Don't worry about me. I've got Jackie and Marcos. But you, maybe you should think about retiring. You've spent your whole life on the sea. It's time to think about the woman you married. Maybe you should make up for the years you were apart."

"Why the sudden urge to get rid of me?"

"I don't want to get rid of you, but I think you're putting off the inevitable. I know you better than you think Gramps. You were always traveling, always on the go. You think you'll die of boredom if you quit, or, worse, have to admit that you're getting old."

"So you think I'm getting old, that I can't handle the sea anymore."

"Grandpa, you'll be clutching the wheel of a ship on your death bed. It will take an army of men to pry it away from you."

"Damn right it will."

"But maybe there's more to life than business. I think you've just forgotten what it's like to be with the person you love. You're not going to be bored if you stop all this. Find something that you and grandma can do together. Travel, take up golf, go fishing.

"You're making me sick."

She got up and wrapped her arms around him. "I love you, Grandpa, and I want you around for a long, long time. So go home and relax. Find a new life with Grandma."

"I guess I could use a little vacation, and I mean little. But as for you continuing this trip without me—it's out of the question. I appreciate your concern little one, but it will take more than an army of men to pry me off that ship." He got up and looked at Anna. "I know I say it all the time, but it's amazing how much you're like your mother. Sometimes I feel it's like she never left. Lucky for you didn't get any of your father's genes."

Anna's frowned. "You certainly know how to spoil a moment, don't you? But you know what? For all the horrible things you say about him, I think deep down inside you admire my dad."

"And how did you come to that conclusion?"

"Because he's the only person who ever stood up to you. You love to make people cower. But he never did, and you respect him for that."

"You know what I think about this idea?"

"What? That it's crazy?"

"No. That it doesn't matter how I feel about him. Because your love more than compensates for my distaste."

Just then, Jackie approached them. She had obviously been crying: her cheeks were tear-stained.

"What's the matter? Why are you crying?" Anna asked.

"I just got a call from Joseph. I have to go home right away." She put her hands over her eyes and started crying again.

Constantine put his arms around her. "Is everybody all right at home? Is someone sick?"

"My father, he's dead."

Chapter 7

RICHARD AND NIGEL

I t was a cold October day. The wind rocked the trees and sent a chill through the people huddled together to say their last farewells to Dylan Moore. Richard Winters stood apart from the mourners. He watched helplessly as the woman he loved wept for her husband of twenty-five years. He knew her tears were for her loss and for the guilt that had tormented her since the day he entered her life.

Constantine held Anna's hand as the casket was lowered into the ground. The children of Dylan and Angela Moore each threw a handful of dirt into his grave. Then they watched as their mother threw in a bouquet of red roses. It was all they could do to contain their tears when she bent down to touch the tombstone, her fingers tracing his name and the year of death. Whispering something meant only for his ears, she kissed her fingertips and put them back on the stone. With that, she stood up and wrapped herself in the arms of her grieving children.

Gusts of cold wind blew in the dark clouds that announced an impending storm. Slowly, the crowd began dispersing, leaving behind the immediate family. The Moores stood frozen, still trying to comprehend what had just changed their lives forever.

After a few moments, Constantine put his hand on Angela's shoulder. "There's a storm coming in, Mrs. Moore. We should all be heading indoors."

She looked up at him with the eyes of a lost child. "Yes, you're right," she said, "and it's only just beginning, isn't it?"

"I've been in the belly of a million storms, Angela, and somehow I've managed to keep from drowning. You will too."

She gave Constantine a hug. "Thank you for all your support. You didn't have to come here today, but I appreciate the fact that you did."

"Of course I had to come. You're part of my family. Now come, it's time to leave here."

The group walked toward the waiting cars. Anna linked arms with Jackie and followed a few paces behind the rest. "I'm so sorry, Jackie. If there's anything I can do—"

"There's nothing you can do, but thanks. I just can't believe it. This is all such a shock."

"Maybe it's a good time for you all to get away for awhile. You need time to be together as a family again. My grandparents have had a chateau in the French countryside for years. They'd like for you to use it. You can go and forget about the outside world. It will be there when you're ready to return."

Jackie gave Anna's hand a gentle squeeze. "Thanks," she said in a melancholy whisper, "and not just for the invitation, but for being the best friend anyone could ever ask for."

"Same here, Jackie. Now, tell me you'll go."

"I can't speak for all of us, but I do know that my brothers and sister would never consider it unless they knew you were going too."

"But this should be a family thing."

"You *are* our family, remember?"

Anna had never felt closer to Jackie than she did at that moment. Deep down she knew they were more than friends. In another life, they would have been connected in some deep way, probably as sisters, but possibly even as two branches of the same tree, or two petals from the same flower.

She looked at Jackie's face. Her eyes seemed sunken and hollow. If ever

Jackie needed her best friend, it was now, and Anna was not about to let her down. "Okay, I'll be there. You can count on me."

The two girls gave each other a gentle hug then split apart. Anna joined Richard and Constantine; the three of them stood in silence and watched as the limousines pulled away.

They climbed into their own waiting car, which sped through the long narrow roads of the English countryside. Constantine and Anna talked of the day's events and reflected on life's uncertainties. Uncharacteristically quiet, Richard watched out the window as the green meadows and pastures blurred by. Although he managed to answer a few questions here and there, his mind was elsewhere. It was back in Camden, in front of the house where Angela's husband had been killed.

Dylan Moore had been hit by a truck. He hadn't seen it coming. He hadn't seen any of it coming. He was an innocent man whose life Richard destroyed. Richard's guilt was overwhelming, but it wasn't for his part in Dylan's death: it was for the sense of release he felt afterward. With Dylan conveniently out of her life, Angela was finally free to be with him.

But there was more. Her children would blame Angela for the accident, and Richard could never let that happen, even if he had to pay the blackmail. So the secrecy and lies continued.

He could remember the exact day it all began, every word, sound and detail that led to this moment: the doorbell ringing, and Nigel. *God, I never should have let him in.*

Christian had warned him that Nigel was on the way over to discuss his demo tape. It was the day he had kissed Angela for the first time.

They had spent the morning together, talking, kissing, touching. They had promised to move slowly with their relationship. It was several days later when they finally made love, but that first day, that first kiss, was more special to Richard. That was the day his life became alive again. Angela made him remember how to laugh, and feel and love.

They spent time in their favorite spot—the balcony of Richard's bedroom. It was a cool day and the sun was shining. They sipped coffee and talked about their lives. Richard wanted to know everything about her, every detail, every second of her past. It was then that the doorbell rang.

"Aren't you going to answer it?" Angela asked.

"No, I know who it is and I don't particularly want to see him right now." He gave her a brilliant smile. "I've got better things to do."

She stood up. "Go on. You might as well. It's getting late and I've got to be going soon."

"Can't you call home and say you're working late?"

She lowered her eyes and sighed. "The lies start so soon, don't they? You know, the gods don't tread lightly on liars and sinners."

He brushed her hair away from her face. "Then I'll be damned to hell, won't I? But I'd rather an eternity there than my time here on earth spent without you."

"Then I suppose we'll be there together." She got up and began to dress. "Go on and open the door. I have to go sooner or later."

Reluctantly, Richard headed towards the door. Hoping Nigel's child-like impatience would get the better of him, he slowly walked down the stairs. He looked out the peephole. To his profound disappointment he saw Nigel waiting there, nervously tapping his foot and puffing heavily on a cigarette.

He opened the door and managed to muster up an insincere grin. "It's been a long time, hasn't it, Nigel?" he said. "You're looking fit, as usual."

'Fit' was the only way Richard knew how to describe Nigel's appearance. He never quite seemed to fit the stereotypical image of the 1960's rock and roll icon: long hair, drug-induced emaciation and black leather outfitting. In fact, he never looked like he belonged on a stage with a guitar at all. If someone were to try and guess, without knowing him, where he was from, most would likely say that he belonged on a Texas oil-field, or a cattle ranch in the Plains.

His hair was ash-blond, carelessly blown to one side, and no matter what time of the year it was, his skin always had a golden-brown glow. He had the confident stride of a man who knew his body made women melt— broad shoulders, a wash-board-like abdomen and tight strong thighs which were always perfectly accentuated by the right pair of skin-tight blue-jeans. All this, of course, was no natural phenomenon. It was a result of hours or grueling workouts at the gym, a strong bottle of peroxide, and the neighborhood "Tan and Go," where he had a lifetime membership.

Nigel breezed past Richard and walked inside. "Yeah, mate, thanks for having me over. Heard you tied on a big one last night. Head's pounding you a bit, eh?"

Only since I saw you at the door. "No, I'm feeling fine, thanks for asking. Come on in. What are you drinking? *at the moment, or snorting, or shooting?"*

Now there was one of life's true mysteries: besides the fact that Nigel should have died of black lung disease years ago, it never ceased to amaze Richard how he could maintain that cowboy stud-like physique while injecting God knows how many chemicals into his body.

"I'll have whatever you're having." Nigel answered. He glanced around the room. "Nice place you have here, mate. Life's been good to you since the break-up."

Richard handed him a double Scotch on the rocks. "That was a long time ago. Seems like another lifetime, doesn't it?"

Nigel walked over to the fireplace and glanced at the pictures on the mantle. "This is a nice shot of us, isn't it? That summer in New York, the first time we played Madison Square Garden. It doesn't seem like a life-time ago, God, I can remember the day this picture was taken. It seems like yesterday."

"Maybe you're right."

"And this, look at this picture of Sara. This must have been taken in Greece, the summer we all met. Strange, I don't remember her hair being so dark."

"That's because it's not Sara. It's our daughter, Anna."

Nigel lifted the picture off the mantle and took a closer look. "My God, I can't believe it. The last time I saw her she was—what? Nine, ten years old? Hard to believe that a shmuck like you could produce a beauty like this." Just then, a movement on the stairway caught his eye. He grinned like a Cheshire cat. "You're just surrounded by beauties, aren't you, mate?"

Richard turned around and saw Angela heading toward the front door. "Wait," he called out to her, "you weren't planning on leaving without saying good-bye were you?"

She paused and turned around. "I didn't want to interrupt anything."

He walked over to the stairway and gave her a long, passionate kiss. "Feel free to interrupt me anytime. I'll see you tomorrow, right?"

"Right." Reluctantly, she turned and walked out the door.

"A beautiful woman, mate, but a little old, wouldn't you say?"

"Old? We're the same age."

"That's what I mean. You haven't been seen with anyone even close to drinking age lately."

"Let's forget about my personal life for the moment. Sit down and tell me what's on your mind." Richard wanted to get this over with.

"I thought Christian already told you. I've just recorded some hot new tracks and I thought I'd give you the first shot at signing me on."

The first shot. Richard knew Nigel was desperate. He had already been turned down by three recording companies in New York and two in London. The word was out that he was broke. But he had made a promise to Christian, and he wasn't about to break it.

"You're right," Richard said. "Christian handed me the tapes last night but, to be honest, I haven't had a chance to listen to them yet."

"No problem. Let's play them now." He walked over to the stereo and inserted a tape. Then he seated himself on the sofa, propped his feet up on the coffee table, and lit a fresh cigarette from the smoldering butt of the old one.

And then it began. The cacophonous sound of what Richard had termed "penis" guitar—riff after riff of whining guitar solos with no melody or rhythm whatsoever, an extension of ego as much as of anatomy.

For the most part, Richard felt, 'penis guitar' should be limited. It had no business dominating a mainstream rock and roll album. And it didn't, because just when he thought it was all over, the lyrics kicked in:

Do you think you have the answers
to the questions in my mind?
Do you want to try to argue about
the cover of The Times?

Truthfully my darling,
It makes no difference to me.
You're not worth my extra effort,
I'd rather watch T.V.

So smart,
You think you're so smart.
I can talk you circles and
tear you apart.

I used to think
I had to take all your crap
But watch out baby,
I'm gonna stab you in the back.

Richard was numb. It was undeniably the worst pile of garbage he had heard in a long time. When it was all over, he struggled to find the right words to say. "A little edgy, wouldn't you say?"

Nigel nodded. "Yeah. Edgy. That's a good thing, right? It's new, fresh. I think it's where the future of rock and roll is heading. Can't you feel it? You know, the raw energy? It cuts you like a knife, realism at its best."

Richard knew that there was no way he could keep his commitment to Christian. The public would never buy it, and more important, he could never lend his name to such crap. He took a long gulp of Scotch and cleared his throat. "Nigel, I have to tell you, I don't think it's going to sell."

"What do you mean? It's great. It's the best sound I've developed since the Casuals."

You've developed since the Casuals? Oh, here we go again. Richard felt a knot beginning to develop in the pit of his stomach. But he wasn't in the mood to relive old confrontations with Nigel so he fumbled to let him down gently. "Look, I'm not saying that it's terrible—*no ghastly would be more like it*— but maybe it could use a little fine tuning or something. Why don't you go back to the drawing board for awhile and work on it? Try adding some music that's slightly more mainstream. I have to think about record sales, remember?"

Nigel fidgeted through his pockets for a cigarette. "Come on. Take a chance. What are you so afraid of? Stop clinging to that old established vanguard. Try expanding your mind. Let loose and show some creative energy."

"I take chances, but they're well calculated ones. How do you think I got to top of the industry?"

"Let's not play games with each other. You know I wouldn't have come to you if you weren't my last chance. I need this deal. Things are bad with me—financially—you know."

"You had a lot of money when we broke up. You should have planned more carefully."

"Yeah, I could have lived off my royalties if you hadn't bought up all the rights."

"I offered you a fair price and you voluntarily sold them to me. No-body put a gun to your head."

"You knew I needed the money." Nigel looked visibly agitated. He reached in his pocket again. "Mind if I light up a joint?"

"Well, yes, actually I do."

"Since when did you get to be so puritanical?"

Richard felt the conversation deteriorating. He knew it was inevitable. With a sigh of resignation, he took off his proverbial white gloves and dug right in. "You know what? Go ahead and smoke. It will make the rest of this conversation more bearable for the both of us."

"What's that supposed to mean?"

"It means that there's no way in hell that I'm going to give you a con-tract for that unbearable crap that you call an album."

Nigel froze. "So that's what you really think? I guess I shouldn't have expected more from someone who—"

"Who what? Go ahead and say it. Who's jealous of your creativity? Jealous of the real genius and brains behind the Casuals? Get a life. I don't give a shit what you thought about us twenty years ago. Go ahead and think you were the musical mastermind, that I would be nothing if it weren't for you. Just get it through your head that I don't care."

Nigel stood up and walked towards him. "Oh, you care. In fact, you care so much that it physically hurts you, doesn't it? But it's not about the music. It's about your Sara, and it will torture you until the day you die, won't it?"

Nigel had gone for the jugular, opening a wound that was still throbbing and raw. "What you said to me that day was a lie. I can never prove it but I know the truth." Richard's jaw was as tight as his fists.

"Then why are your hands shaking? Face it, Richard: she wanted me. You were suffocating her. You never did understand her and I did. She begged me to take her away with me. In fact, I can still feel her body against mine while she pleaded."

Richard grabbed Nigel's collar. "You sick motherfucker. Get out of my house."

"You don't want to believe it but you have to. There's no other way that I'd know where that birthmark was, would I? She came to me one night Richard, remember— when you were at one of your little boy-scout meetings. She begged me to let her in, saying she had made a big mistake. That it was me that she wanted all along. She took off my shirt, then unbuttoned her dress and let it drop to the floor. The heat was intense between us. She told me that I unleashed in her feelings of passion and sensuality that she never felt with you."

Richard's head was throbbing. He couldn't bear hearing any more. He knew it was a lie—Nigel's only defense after years of pent-up jealously and rage—but the birthmark on her upper thigh: how did he know? Did she tell him? But why? He couldn't think any more. His stomach felt sick and he needed to throw up.

Nigel continued. "Look at you, you pathetic slob. You still can't believe your wife wasn't the virtuous little Madonna you thought you married. She was a whore who shared my bed—"

Richard lunged at Nigel and, with both hands, formed a choke hold around his neck. Nigel broke free and began to laugh. "Watch it you loser, or I'll sue you for assault." Moving towards the door, he snarled,

"I'll make this easy on you and leave. Just hope our little discussion doesn't keep you up tonight."

Richard caught his breath. "You're finished in this industry, you prick. I'll see to it that nobody ever answers your calls again. If you think your finances are bad now, just wait. You'll be begging for spare change at Picadilly Circus."

"Nobody ever gets the best of me, Winters. I'll find a way to bounce back. I always do."

"Then I'll find a way to kick you and your little tin cup back into the gutter."

A year passed before Richard heard from Nigel again. His reappearance came as no big surprise, but what he was carrying threw Richard completely off balance.

It was a typically hectic day at his office. In front of him sat two piles of mail: one, of invitations and fan mail, and the other, of unopened contracts and complaints, none of which he'd get to till after five. In addition to never-ending staff and board meetings, interruptions of some kind punctuated his day. His intercom buzzer rang so incessantly that his secretary may well have been sitting on it, and after years of practice, he managed to juggle about three phone calls at a time, even in the bathroom. Nothing got in the way of his manic working habits, except that day.

"Mr. Winters," the smooth voice over the intercom said, "Mr. Nigel Taylor is here to see you."

Richard almost dropped the phone. Whatever it was Nigel wanted to see him about wasn't going to make him happy. "Tell him I can't see him now."

Just then, the door burst open. "I know you're not busy, asshole. So sit back and listen. We've got a few things to talk about."

Richard stood up. "Get out before I call security. We've got absolutely nothing to talk about."

Nigel threw a large manila envelope onto his desk. "Why don't you take a look at that first? Maybe you'll be little more talkative then."

"Fuck you and your envelope and get out of my office."

"Okay, mate. But the pictures inside are pretty good, quite flattering I'd say. Especially the ones of Angela in your bed. Telephoto lenses are amazing. You should keep your drapes drawn more often, you know. But I bet you will from now on."

Richard felt his blood draining from his face. He opened the envelope. Inside were picture after picture of him and Angela in his bedroom. There was no question that they were real, but the question was, what was Nigel planning on doing with them?

"Don't bother ripping them up, mate. Negatives, you know."

"You're the lowest life form known to man, you know that?"

"There's miles to go, Winters. I haven't even gotten close to my lowest point yet."

"So, what do you want? You're going to give these to a tabloid? You think the public hasn't seen me screwing women before? Some of the things in the tabloids make these look tame. Hell, these are in my bedroom, how boring."

"You're bluffing. You think I don't know who the woman is. If this were some slut you picked up in a club, you're right. Nobody would care. But this is the love of your pathetic life—and she's married. And nobody knows, right? Wrong. I know every detail. I've had the two of you followed for some time now. Actually, I started out just following you. You couldn't hold top honors for sainthood forever. I knew you'd slip up somewhere."

"Screw you."

"Please, let me finish. You and your pretty girlfriend developed a nice little pattern. She reports to work at nine sharp. Meets you for lunch at the Ritz, in a suit. She eats you for lunch, wipes her pretty little lips and goes back to work. All so very proper. After work, you take a few romantic walks, maybe screw some more, and always sit out on your balcony. Then you put her in a cab and send her back to her pumpkin patch.

You've probably guessed that I'm after something, right? But what? You just haven't figured it out yet. Oh, you needn't worry about my giving these to a tabloid. That would be too cliché. I have a better plan. I have a messenger parked outside right now. He's waiting for me to tell him whether or not to deliver the pictures to her husband today, or go home."

Richard's eyes narrowed. "What do you want from me?"

"Remember that recording contract you never gave me? I think you should call your lawyer and have it drawn up today. Make it a five-year contract, starting at a million pounds a year. And don't forget the sign-on bonus. Another million will do just fine."

"You're out of your mind. There's no way on earth I'm going to record that album for you. You think I'm going to give you a million pounds a year to produce more of that shit too? Everyone in the industry will know I've been blackmailed."

"Think about what you're saying. You know I'll give those pictures to her husband. And your days of playing house with your girlfriend will be over."

Richard knew that. Nigel was quite prepared to hand over those pictures to Dylan. Either way, Nigel would have won. If Dylan saw them, his relationship with Angela would be exposed. If he didn't, Nigel would get his contract. Richard was trapped, unless....

"You know what, Taylor? Maybe you did me a favor by coming here today. It's time Angela and I told our families about this whole thing. There's no point in trying to keep it a secret much longer. If it wasn't you it would've been some slime-bag on T.V. So, your pictures don't really matter, do they? As a matter of fact, I'll call her now, and we'll do it today."

"The pictures matter, you know they do. Telling her husband about it and having him see her like this are two different things. Besides, she's not ready to tell anybody yet and you know it. She'll collapse at the thought of it. Pick up the phone and call your lawyer, or I'll use it to deliver those pictures."

"No, Taylor, you're not going to win. We're telling her husband today."

"It'll be too late."

"It doesn't matter. You've lost; face it. Now, get the hell out of my office."

Nigel turned around and walked out. Richard looked at his watch. Three o'clock. *She's still at work.* He grabbed the phone and dialed her direct line. "Come on, Angela. Pick up the phone," he mumbled. The phone continued to ring. "Christ, someone's got to be covering her area. Come on, come on." After six or seven more rings he slammed the receiver down. "Shit." He ran to the door and headed straight for the elevator. Over his shoulder, he barked, "Call the Scotch House. Get someone there to tell Angela Moore to call me on my car phone."

He was about half way to the store when the phone rang. It was Angela. "Where've you been? I have to talk to you."

"I'm covering two areas today. What's the matter?"

"I'll tell you after I pick you up. Be outside. I'll be there in about five minutes."

Richard slowed the car just enough to open the passenger side door, pull her in, and be in fourth gear again within a matter of seconds.

"What's going on? You're acting like a lunatic."

When he told her what had just happened, Angela could barely speak. "No," she said. "We can't tell him. I'm not ready."

"We have no choice."

"Then I should tell him alone."

"No, I have to be there with you."

"Why?"

"Because I want him to know how much I love you."

They sat in silence for a few moments. "Is he home?"

"Yes, I think so. He finished a carpentry job early today."

"Then we have to hurry. I don't want Nigel's messenger to get there before we do."

After a few moments his Lambourghini screeched onto Carlyle Street in Camden. Richard swerved to the right to avoid an onrushing car.

Angela gasped. "My God, slow down. You'll get us killed."

Richard maneuvered the car around two large asphalt trucks and a dumpster. "What the hell's going on here? Your street's a bloody mess. Can't even see your house."

Angela pointed to the third house in a row of shingled Victorians. "Over there, the one behind the bulldozers. There was a water main break on our street earlier this week. It's been a mess since."

Richard stopped the car in front of her house. He began to open his door when she grabbed his arm. "Listen, I have to do this alone."

He understood. He leaned over and kissed her. "Okay. I'll go back to my office and wait. Remember, I love you."

The front door creaked open when she let herself in. The house was quiet. "Dylan," she called, "are you home?" No answer. "Dylan? Where are you?" She walked into the kitchen. There he was, slumped over the white Formica table. He held the pictures in his right hand, and a bottle of Scotch in his left. When he looked up, she saw a madman staring at her.

"How could you do this to me?" His eyes were filled with tears, but his face was filled with rage.

"Dylan ... I have to explain—"

"Explain what?" he shouted. "These disgusting pictures of my wife with that piece of shit. Did he pay you? Tell me. Or were you so starstruck that you'd do anything so he'd fuck you?"

She closed her eyes and leaned against the wall. "No, it's not that at all."

He took a long gulp from the bottle. "What then?" He moved closer to her. "You think he loves you? You? Have you taken a look at yourself lately? You're a forty-year-old stupid shopkeeper. That's all you ever were. You were lucky I came along and married you or you'd be a forty-year-old stupid spinster right now."

She put her hands to her face and wept. "Please, Dylan, stop. I know what I did was wrong. But Richard and I want to be together. Maybe it's time that you knew."

The bottle went flying across the room and shattered against the refrigerator. "You fucking whore. After everything I've done for you."

Angela cringed. She had never seen him in this state before. She wasn't sure what he was capable of. But instead of moving towards her, he walked out of the kitchen toward the front door. Again she heard it creak, then Dylan's voice—now it was calm and even-toned.

"I loved you, Angela," he said. "Maybe I couldn't give you all the things he can, but I tried. This was all I knew how to do."

She heard the door close behind him and in that moment, saw flashes of the last twenty years of her life: the birth of their children, the anniversaries, the Christmas trees, and the long days at the beach. They had been good years. She didn't regret any of them. She needed to say good-bye to Dylan the right way. She wanted to tell him that she had loved him and always would. Running to the front door, she pulled it open with a jerk.

"Dylan," she shouted.

He didn't turn. The roar of the street construction swallowed every sound.

This time she screamed. "Dylan!"

By this time, he stood between two small bulldozers. He turned around, a look of hope and fear—and something else she would never know, on his face.

She walked towards him. "Wait, I need to tell you something."

"What is it?" he shouted back.

Before she could speak, one of the trucks moved. The driver shifted forward, then jerked into reverse. The gears ground but instead of stopping, the truck kept jerking backward. The driver couldn't have known what caused the slight bump before he crashed into the other bulldozer. He couldn't have heard the man's gasp, and the woman's scream.

Richard was in his office when Angela's called. He wanted to hold her and console her, but this wasn't the right time. Her whole family would be there. How could this of all turned out so wrong? They couldn't tell the children now, not while they were grieving over their father. He picked up the intercom. "Get me Nigel Taylor on the phone."

Within seconds, his secretary buzzed back. "He's holding on the line for you, Mr. Winters."

"You son of a bitch, I can't believe you did it."

"I told you I would. Did things get a little ugly at home?"

"Dylan Moore is dead. He was hit by a bulldozer on the street outside his own house. So screw your blackmailing efforts, Taylor. It's over."

There was silence on the other end. "That's a real shame, but actually, it doesn't really change much, does it? I mean, it wouldn't be such a great time for her kids to see all those naughty pictures, would it? Mommy giving Richard a blow job the day before daddy gets killed."

"You piece of shit."

"Whatever. Listen, why don't you spare the little lady further pain and suffering, and just give in."

"You've got your contract, Taylor. You can pick it up in the morning."

"Good boy, Richard. You make being me so much fun."

A few days after the funeral, Christian and Richard flew by private jet to the French countryside to join Anna and the rest of the group. Angela had stayed behind in London, promising to meet up with them at some point. She and Richard had agreed that it wouldn't be wise to be seen together for some time. They had spoken to each other only a few times since Dylan's death. Their last conversation hung around Richard's neck like a noose.

"Dylan wasn't a bad person you know," she said. "He did nothing to deserve what I did to him." He tried to console her but it was futile. Her nightmare had just begun and he knew the only way out would be to tell her children the truth. But when?

Anna and the rest of the Moore family had already arrived in Oos, a small, village about two hours south of Paris. Though it had been almost four years since they had been together like this, they recaptured the comfort and ease they had once felt within moments.

Richard invited Christian along to spend time with the family. He needed the support of a close friend, and it never hurt to have a business associate along to kick around new ideas for S & A. The evening Richard arrived, he and Anna a lit a fire in the library, always their favorite room to sit and talk. They loved the dark oak walls with ornate moldings, the soft Persian carpets, the stone fireplace, and, of course, the ebony Steinway in the corner. Richard strummed the acoustic Stratacaster that always went with him when he traveled. Suddenly a knock at the door interrupted their quiet conversation.

"Do you mind if I barge in on you?" Jackie asked. "I'm so depressed. I've been moping about all by myself for hours. I could use some company to get my mind off things, you know?"

"I know," Richard said. "Come in. Tell me what I can do to get you to smile again?" A sad smile played over his features.

Jackie sat down on the sofa next to Anna. "Oh, I don't know," she sighed. "How about playing something for me? Would you do that, Mr. Winters? On the piano?"

"Of course. No, wait. I have a better idea," he answered. "I'll play my guitar and Anna will play the piano." He turned to his daughter. "You still remember how, right?"

A look of annoyance shadowed Anna's downturned face. "Of course, but don't get too technical on me. Keep in simple." She sat down at the keyboard. "Let's start with the blues in G".

Within moments, music resonated through the old walls, filling the entire house with haunting melodies and soothing rhythms. Slowly, everyone else found themselves drawn to the library.

Feeling a bit self-conscious, Anna stopped. "I hate being the only one performing. Why doesn't somebody else give it a go?"

"Because none of us has any talent," Joseph answered.

"That's not true at all." She turned to Ian. "I saw the opening night review of Jane Eyre a couple of months ago. The play stunk, but the critics said you were great."

"So, what do you want?" he asked. "A few lines from Jane Eyre?"

"No," Anna said thoughtfully. "I want something a little grittier."

"Grittier? What does that mean?"

"I know," Jackie interrupted. "How about that new piece you've been rehearsing for God knows how long? The one by that new Swedish play-wright, Wachnusen?"

"Wachtmeister," Ian said.

"That's the one. It sounded pretty gritty to me," Jackie said.

"All right. But I'll need some help. How about it Anna, since this was your idea."

She felt herself cringe. "I don't know the lines."

"When I look your way, all you have to say is, 'Ragnar, don't jump. I'm still alive. The doctor has cured me, and I came back to tell you that I love you.'"

"You're kidding," Anna laughed.

"Hey, this writer won two Tony's last year," Ian said.

"With material like that? Oh well. Sure, I'll give it a go."

"Okay," Ian said. "The stage is set. I'm standing at the edge of a cliff somewhere in Dover. It's raining. I look out to the sea below and say: 'My Wiveka, she's gone. In all the world, in all my life, the only thing real I can feel is this change. The sea of my soul has shifted. The vibrance of the universe has left with her. There's nothing left but me and this place, where I stand….'"

What Anna thought would be an inane soliloquy caught her off guard. The controlled passion in Ian's voice, summoned as if on cue, mesmerized her. He was no longer in that room, he was someplace far away, in another period of time, another state of being. And, he took her there too. She closed her eyes and continued to listen. *God, how could he do this to me again?* When she opened her eyes he was watching her.

"Go ahead and say it," he said.

She realized he was talking to her. "Say what?"

"The next line."

"Right. Sorry. Ragnar, don't jump. I'm still alive. The doctor has cured me and I came back to tell you I love you."

He walked over, touched her chin, and continued his passage. "My angel. If only this were real. In another life, I'll live with your beauty again …"

When he finished, everyone sat in stunned silence, then broke into applause. "I had no idea how talented you were, Ian," Richard said. "The critics are right. We'll be seeing your name in lights soon."

"Ian looked apologetic. "I'm not in it for the fame. I do it mostly because I like the art."

"Then you're smart as well as talented. Fame and notoriety have their good moments, but they come at a very high price. Unfortunately, you can't have one without the other."

"So I've heard," he said. He turned to Anna. "Now that I've done my bit, how about you?"

"I've already played. Let somebody else have the spotlight."

"No, you played with your father. This time, do it alone."

"If you're setting out to embarrass me, you're doing a pretty good job of it." She walked over to the piano. "I haven't written music since my freshman year," she paused and thought for a moment, "but there's a piece I always liked. Let me see if I can remember it."

She sat at the keyboard and played two chords in succession, followed by slow, deliberate, singular notes. The melody was despondent, almost sorrowful. After a few riffs, she stopped and looked up. "Sorry, I can't remember anymore."

"It was beautiful, darling," Richard said. "No lyrics?"

Of course there are words, but I don't think I can bear to sing them here," she thought. "Yes, there are words," she said softly. "It's called The Days of Summer."

"Well, come on then. Let's hear it all," Richard said. "I'll play the rhythm this time."

Richard took up his guitar. Anna felt as if her heart were about to be ripped out of her body. She couldn't believe she had gotten herself into this situation. The last thing she had ever wanted was for Ian to hear this song. But it was too late. Before she knew it, Richard was two riffs into the rhythm and waiting for her to join in on the melody. *Well, here it goes,* she thought.

In the haze of evening
In the heat, I wrote,
But I can't remember why,
I had to escape, from you.

It's been a long time
since that summer,
dreaming past midnight,
singing songs till dawn.
Why was it me who
always forgot the words
to eternity's song?

When she finished, the room was quiet. Christian broke the silence. "A sad song, Anna. Do we dare ask what your inspiration was?"

She glanced at Jackie, then to Ian. "No inspiration really. I just made it up." She stood up. "Now, can I step down and let the true musicians take over? Dad, Christian, please."

Christian headed for the piano. "It's about time you asked," he said as he adjusted his skin-tight leather trousers. "Come on, Winters. We can entertain this crowd with some of our ancient oldies but goodies, right?"

The moment they started playing, Ian walked out of the room. From the window, Anna spotted him sitting alone, on the patio, just outside the library. She followed him.

When he saw her, he gave a look of complete surprise. "What are you doing out here?" he asked.

"I came to talk to you. Why do you look so shocked?"

"Because for the last four years you've done an excellent job of avoiding me completely."

"That's just your imagination."

"No, it's not, you and I both know that. Nice song by the way. Tell me, what *was* your inspiration?"

She felt a chill run through her body and began rubbing her arms with her hands. "Just like I told everybody inside, I made it up, why? You think you had something to do with it?"

He shrugged, "Maybe."

She smiled. "Maybe your head's getting too small for that big fat ego you're developing. You're starting to believe what the critics are saying about you. You better watch it, it's down hill from here you know."

"Thanks for the advice. I'll be sure to quote you and the part about my small head when I'm accepting my Oscar some day."

Anna started to laugh. No matter how much she tried to stay angry with him, she couldn't.

Ian continued. "I sent you an invitation to my opening night. Remember you promised me that you'd stop whatever you were doing and be there? You weren't."

"I know. I'm sorry. I was busy."

"Doing what?"

"I don't remember, but it was important."

"I'm sure it was."

Anna rubbed her hands together. "The night air is chillier than I thought."

"Then come here and dance with me. You can hear the music through the window. It's beautiful and I'll warm you up."

Anna looked at him quizzically. "What are you up to, Ian?" she asked as she moved closer. "You haven't looked at me like this in a long time." She put her arms around his neck and began slowly moving to the faint sounds coming from the library.

"Why do you think I'm scheming something up?" he said as he ran his hands through her hair. "Is it too much to think that I just want to hold you ... and say I'm sorry?"

"For what?"

"For being such an asshole that night. I was wrong. I was a kid and I was stupid. I don't blame you for being angry with me. I just don't want us to be enemies for the rest of our lives."

Anna closed her eyes. She loved the feel of his silky hair against her cheek. She'd waited a long time to hear these words from him.

"We're not enemies."

"No? Then why have we barely spoken in four years?"

"We've spoken."

"Not the way we used to. I miss you, Anna." He leaned forward and put his face against hers.

She stopped dancing and stepped back. "Don't, it's too late. I've been hurt by you once before. Besides, I don't feel the way I used to."

"Oh no? I don't believe what you just said. I felt the truth in your touch a moment ago."

She looked into his eyes, so blue and passionate. She felt herself getting lost in his gaze and pulled herself back. "You're mistaken," she said.

He moved closer and cupped her face in his hands. "No, you're mistaken. You're letting your pride get in the way. Let's not say good-bye again."

She was at a loss for words. With a jerk, she pushed his hands away.

"Why now? Why all of a sudden these feelings for me? I don't get you, Ian. You had your chance four years ago. Now it's too late."

"Don't do this Anna. Can't you just forget what happened back then? We were kids, and kids make mistakes."

"I didn't think it was a mistake. I wanted to make a go of it with you, if you remember. You're the one that blew me off."

"Don't put it that way. I was just scared of so many things—mostly that you'd discover that I was just a nothing, a nobody."

"I never thought that."

"I'm sorry, I know that now. Listen, let's try to get to know each other again. I promise I'll be honest with you. I won't let my insecurities get in the way again."

"I don't know."

"Anna, if we say good-bye tonight, I'm afraid we'll never have another chance to be together. Who knows where our lives will take us tomorrow, or five years from now. Let yourself go and forget your stubborn pride."

"I don't think I can. I don't have the energy for you right now. I poured it all out four years ago.

"Is that what you really feel, or are those just some words you were waiting to say for a long time?"

She smiled and shook her head. "Both. I really feel it and your damn right, I was waiting to say it."

"You want to see me beg?"

She shook her head. "At one point I did, but I don't think it matters now. I think you're right, we don't know where we'll be in the future, but right now, I'm not ready for you. You come with too many uncertainties, and I'm certain I don't want that. We'll always be friends, Ian, but as for tomorrow, or five years from now, we'll both be where we belong: in two different worlds.

Chapter 8

NEW YORK CITY, THREE YEARS LATER

Nigel scanned the crowd. Parties didn't get any better than Cookie Anderson's pre-award night bashes. Her 3,000-square-foot SoHo loft acted as a magnet to all the top names in the industry, admittance was only granted to those on the 'A' list in the world of music and entertainment. And, he was part of that 'A' list. For the first time since the Casuals, his name—Nigel Taylor—was included in the elite list of nominees. The New York City Music Reviewers Circle added his name to the category of the 'Best Solo Guitarist in a Non-Specific or Categorical Genre' (whatever that meant) and he couldn't care less.

Nigel was feeling especially good tonight. Even though sales of Dog Ears were dismally low, a small group of downtown critics had hailed it as "the second coming: the future of rock and roll." That elite group, of course, was swallowed up by the overwhelming majority of critics who felt the same way the record-buying public did: that Nigel's debut album, wasn't worth the damage to the nervous system it caused. But tonight, he was being recognized as the true artist he knew he was. So, in celebration, he downed a few vodka tonics, snorted a couple of lines of coke, and smoked a small joint, just to take the edge off.

"Hello, darling. So glad you could make it tonight. Having a good time? No?"

There she was, Cookie Anderson herself, dressed in her signature black with a neckline plunging so low that a simple sneeze would liberate her nipples. He leaned over and kissed her on both cheeks. "Great party, Cookie. Unparalleled. Love your place too. What do you call it? Extreme minimalist? Amazing what you've managed to do with absolutely nothing."

"Thank you, darling. I think absolutely nothing in a room makes a statement, don't you? You know, emptiness, hollow at the core, makes us all think of our souls. Maybe just makes us all think, no?"

Nigel always got a kick out of how she ended every sentence with "no," even when she meant "yes," which was most of the time. He glanced around the room and wondered where she sat during the day, or slept at night. "Yes, it certainly makes one think," he said. "By the way," he added, "thanks for the good review last month. Not too many critics appreciate great art. Glad to know you're not pressured by the mainstream."

"Don't think it was easy either, darling. My editor wanted to trash it. But, with a little arm twisting, I convinced her to print it. I heard your new double album is coming out next month. If you're counting on a similar review, I'll be counting on a similar performance in my bedroom. Maybe this time, you could practice some of those Latin words on me, no?"

Nigel grinned. "Absolutely. What are friends for, no?" As he turned, he glimpsed a woman with long wavy hair, high cheekbones, and an intoxicating smile. She was engrossed in a conversation with the person next to her, leaning over and laughing with an abandon that made his body weaken. *Sara*, he thought. Why is it that he couldn't get her out of his mind after over twenty years.

Cookie continued. "Just name the time and place, darling."

Nigel lost all interest in his conversation with Cookie. He needed to be alone to collect his composure. "Sure, I'll give you a call," he said. "I'm gonna get another drink. Catch you later, all right?"

"All right, darling, but before you run off, I thought I'd warn you that your ex is on her way here tonight. As a matter of fact, she may already be somewhere in the crowd right now."

Nigel cringed. His ex-wife, Helena de la Cartier, the only bitch from Hell who actually managed to claw her way back to the living. "Thanks for the warning," he said as he felt his flesh crawling. "Doubt she's already here though. The hairs on my arms aren't standing up yet."

"Oh, why the long face, darling?" Cookie leaned strategically forward to let Nigel catch a glimpse of her abundant décolletage. "Let me think of a way to cheer you up, no?"

Nigel stared down at her heaving cleavage. Cookie was in the mood for some action, but tonight wasn't the night, at least not with her. He reached over and tugged at her dress, causing her right nipple to pop out from its flimsy constraint. "Whoops, sorry there, Cooks." he said. "Better go to the loo and pull yourself in. Your tits'll be causing a riot."

He snickered as he walked off, grabbed another vodka tonic, and headed for Cookie's office. Once inside, he closed the door behind him and sat at the desk. He thought about how much the dark haired woman in the crowd resembled Sara. He moaned slightly as he sat back and closed his eyes. Sara: her presence still haunted him. The only woman he ever really loved. He had known from the moment they met, that they were destined to be together.

But Richard got in the way. He ruined it all. The day Richard Winters brought her back to London, Nigel's life turned inside out. He couldn't breathe in the same room with her. He studied her every move, every gesture, every mannerism. He dreamt about her at night and fantasized about her during the day. He thought about what it would be like to hold her and make love to her. He was drowning in a world he had no control over, and it was all Richard's fault. If it weren't for him, Sara would have been his wife. She would still be alive today. He would never have had children with her; that would have meant sharing her with someone else.

He remembered how it tormented him to see her in the arms of the man he hated most in this world, how he felt as if he were going to explode. He had longed tell her how he felt. Maybe she felt the same way and hadn't been able to tell him.

He had bided his time until the night Richard was at one of his Save the Whale meetings, and called. He said he needed a contract that Richard had on his desk. He told her that it was urgent, and that he needed it for a meeting first thing in the morning.

She showed up at his door twenty minutes later. She looked beautiful. Her blonde hair was uncharacteristically loose, falling free to her waist. The blue satin shoulder straps beckoned him to touch them, just to watch them drop past her shoulders. She handed him the envelopes.

"I hope these are the right ones," she said breathlessly.

He took them from her hand. "Why are you breathing so heavily? You didn't run all the way over, did you?"

"You said you needed them quickly."

"I'm glad we don't live on opposite ends of London then, or I would have been responsible for your heart attack. Come on in. Have a drink and cool off."

He held the door open while she walked in. Her wild orchid cologne made him breathe heavily. He almost swooned as she walked past him towards the living room.

"I love your house, Nigel," she said. "It's so you. So comfortable. I'd want to lounge around here all day."

Nigel followed her glance and visualized the two of them on the sofa, her in his arms with his head buried in her long hair. "You're welcome to lounge around here any time you want, Sara." His thoughts quickly returned to the present, and his immediate plan. "Now, what can I get you to drink? How about a cold glass of wine? I just opened a great French Chardonnay."

"Sounds great."

She followed him into the kitchen and stood next to him as he poured. "Tell me, Sara," he said, "what do you do with yourself while your husband's away at all those meetings? You must get quite lonely."

She took a glass from his hand. "Not really. I enjoy being by myself. I get a chance to read, and to write. I like writing, you know. I've even been writing some music lately." She lifted her glass. "What do we drink to, Nigel?"

"Your music, and that I get a chance to hear it some day."

"Okay. Cheers then." She took a sip. "You're right. This is quite good."

He couldn't take his eyes off her. He wanted to reach over and pull her into his arms and feel her silky skin against his. But he had to wait. The timing wasn't right, just yet.

She continued. "You know, I'm glad I came here. We never get a chance to talk, you and I. You and Richard are so close, and I barely know anything about you."

"To be honest, Richard doesn't know much about me either. We're not as close as you think. We just play great music together."

"Who do you share your thoughts with then? A girlfriend?"

"No, don't have one at the moment. Even if I did, I don't think I could share my thoughts with her, or anybody for that matter."

She looked surprised. "Why? Are they so terrible?"

"Yes, they are. Does that scare you?"

"I don't know. Do you think about murder and rape? If that's the case, yes, it does scare me."

Although murder and rape were high on his fantasy hit list for the Winters, he said, "That would make me a monster now, wouldn't it? Come on. Let's go inside and sit down."

They sat on the sofa opposite each other and finished the bottle of wine in record time. Nigel knew his plan was working. His little fly was getting closer to the trap. He poured on the charm. Sara relaxed and laughed at all his jokes. When he reached and touched her several times, and she didn't flinch. She even reciprocated, with an occasional hand on his arm. The time was right. They were both ready.

"So tell me, Sara," he said. "What do you write about when you're alone? Your thoughts, your dreams, what?"

She didn't answer.

He continued. "What *are* your thoughts? That maybe there's a world out there you never got to explore? That someday you'll be suffocated by a bunch of kids and a controlling husband?"

"Stop it, Nigel. You're not being very funny."

"I'm not trying to be. Sometimes you must think that you were too young to get married."

She closed her eyes and, again, didn't answer. He was reading her mind now; the alcohol had gone right to her head. She was confused, and there was no stopping him. "How many men did you sleep with before Richard? None, right? I'll bet you wonder at night what it's like to be in the arms of someone else. You wonder if you made the right choice, that maybe, just maybe, there was someone else out there for you. Someone whose touches would bring you to a point of ecstasy your husband never could."

She turned away. "Please, stop it, Nigel. I can't listen to you anymore."

"Why? Because it's the truth?"

"No," she paused, "not all of it."

"No?"

He reached over and touched the strap of her dress and let it fall. He stroked her shoulder, and then slowly brought his lips to her neck. She didn't resist him. He moved closer. "It's all true, Sara," he whispered. "Let me be the man you've dreamt about. Let yourself go and touch me. I can take you to the places you've only fantasized about." He took her head in his hands and brought her lips to his. He felt her lips trembling, but he didn't stop. Their tongues met—and he knew she wanted him. He unbuttoned her dress and brought it down to her waist. He took her breasts in his hands and couldn't control himself any longer. He needed it all. But the moment he unbuttoned his trousers his whole world came crashing down around him.

She pulled away. "No, Nigel, please stop. I can't do this."

"Don't ask me to stop. Please, Sara, we've gone too far."

"I can't. Just get off of me."

He had gone too fast. He should have taken it slower. Just a few more moments and she wouldn't have pulled away. He had blown the chance he had waited so long for. He would never have another chance like this, just the two of them, alone in his house, without anybody knowing. "Don't toy with me, Sara. We both want this. I can feel it."

"No Nigel. I don't know what got into me. Maybe it was the wine. I don't usually drink this much. It went right to my head."

"It wasn't the wine, and you know it."

"Even if it wasn't, I was wrong in any case. I love Richard. There'll never be anyone else for me."

"You're wrong. You're dead wrong." He held her down and pulled her dress up over her hips. She screamed and began struggling. But he knew she was no match for him. The rest would be effortless he thought. Then, the doorbell rang. It distracted him for a moment. He quickly regained his concentration and began lowering his trousers. The doorbell kept ringing. Then the unthinkable happened. He heard a key opening the door and someone walking in. He got up. Sara quickly sat up and buttoned her dress.

He heard a woman's voice in the hallway. "Oh, Mr. Taylor. Sorry, I didn't know you were here."

It was Elizabeth, his assistant. She was the only other person who had a key to his house.

She continued apologetically. "I had to come by and pick up your mail. I can take care of it tomorrow though. Sorry I interrupted." She turned to leave.

"No, wait," Sara shouted. "Don't go. You can stay and do your work now." Her hands were shaking.

Nigel was numb. He could barely move. It was all over. He had lost her. There was nothing he could do to take back what just happened. "I'm sorry Sara," he whispered. But before he had a chance to finish apologizing, she walked over to him.

"Don't you ever come near me again, you son of a bitch. I'm not going to tell my husband what happened here tonight, I'm just as much to blame as you are, and besides—your partnership is too important to him. But I'm warning you, if you ever come near me again I will tell him. I can promise you that."

She walked out of his house and seven months later she was dead. She was already pregnant then, and didn't know it. Funny thing was, he never saw the birthmark he later taunted Richard with. When she returned to London after her wedding, he had given her a four-leaf clover he found on a photo-shoot, to wish her luck in her marriage. She took it and smiled, "But I already have one just like it," she said, "right here." She touched her upper thigh. "It's my birthmark, a four-leaf clover."

It's too bad that clover never brought her luck, he thought. He glanced at his watch. It was almost midnight. He had been sitting in Cookie's office for almost an hour. It was time to let go of his ghosts and join the living. Just then, the door opened. It was another ghost, no—a nightmare. His ex-wife walked in.

"Helena," he said, "what are you doing stalking this end of town? Don't you know sunrise is in just a few hours? You should run back to your coffin before it's too late."

"Oh, come now, daaahling, look who's talking. I just heard you've been sitting here alone in the dark for almost an hour. Think of me as your savior, the one who's here to rescue you from your creepy solitude."

"My 'savior:' you're anything but that, Helena."

"Oh, put down your boxing gloves and give me a kiss."

He studied her every move as she walked towards him. What was her angle today? Why the sudden intimate tone? Helena de la Cartier had never been anything but a heavy anchor around his neck. She had dragged him down from the day they met. He had been swept away by her exotic beauty: a New York model with almond-shaped eyes, endless legs, and enough cleavage to amuse an entire football team—which she boasted about having done on a number of occasions. They met while she was on a hunt for money, and he, for a trophy to show off to his mates back home. They had absolutely nothing in common except for two things which kept them together for close to ten years: a deep hunger for spending ungodly amounts of money on themselves and an even deeper hunger for long, drawn-out sessions of sado-masochistic sex, often resulting in discreet visits to their nearby doctor or hospital emergency room.

She pressed her lips hard against his. "Come on, daaahling. Let's lock the door. One for old time's sake—what do you say?"

Once again, she pressed her mouth against his. This time, Nigel could feel the force of her teeth grinding into his lower lip. Before she had a chance to draw her first ounce of blood, he pushed her away. "Why don't you tell me what you're after first?"

"Let's talk business later." She picked up her skirt and sat on his lap.

"I'm feeling a bit amorous at the moment. Nobody could ever satisfy me the way you could."

"And God knows you went looking. Even while we were married."

"And you were the pious saint who sat home and baked cookies? Come on, daaahling. Who are you kidding? Neither of us will ever be given awards for fidelity." She put her hand on his crotch. "Come on. Helena needs some attention now."

Nigel was coming down from his drug-induced high, and although a quick fuck with his ex-wife would help take the edge off, another hit of coke would do the same thing. And if he had the choice at the moment, which in fact he did, the coke would be less dangerous. It wouldn't demand anything in return afterwards.

"Put the stapler down, Helena," he said. "I'm not in the mood right now."

She pouted. "Oh, why the party pooper?"

"Because every time since our divorce that we've screwed around I've lost out on something big afterwards. So let's cut the crap and get to whatever it is you came here for."

She got up and put the stapler back on the desk. "Too bad," she said with disappointment. "Now that would've been a toy we'd never tried before. Just when I thought we'd done it all, right?"

"Yeah, and I've got the scars to prove it."

She straightened her posture. "All right, so let's talk business then, daaahling. It's been two years since you've paid me half of what you owed me at the settlement. It's time you paid off the rest."

"You almost wiped me out two years ago."

"You have an eight million dollar contract with S & A, and I almost wiped you out? I don't think so. Maybe it's time my lawyers started digging again."

"They dug me into the ground the last time. You took half of what I made, and the other half went to the government. How could I possibly have anything left?"

Helena's large almond eyes narrowed to slits. "Because that was two years ago and you've had plenty of time to accumulate more. So cough it up or it'll get uglier than the last time."

"Nothing could get uglier than that—the abuse pictures you gave the tabloids? You know I never laid a hand on you, at least not when you didn't want me to. I couldn't believe how low you stooped."

"I learned from the master himself. Besides, what's not to believe? That you were hiding money from me? Money that you owed me. I deserved every dime I got at the settlement. God knows, I had to endure close to ten years of marriage to you. Your average women would have committed suicide."

"Give it up, Helena. I just don't have that kind of money right now."

"But you will. Your new double album is coming out in a couple of months. I'm sure you'll get a lump sum payment for it."

"I have to have something to live on."

"But I come first, and don't you forget it. I'll be expecting a big fat check the day that album comes out, or your reputation will be in the toilet again. Oh, and don't kid yourself. Your last album was the worst piece of shit I'd ever heard. I hope you don't think for a second that I would have let Cookie print her gushing review, if it weren't for her persuasive bedroom performances. Quite satisfying, I'd say. Maybe I should thank you too. I heard you taught her a few new tricks. Actually it was all rather reminiscent of our old antics, with one major accessory missing, of course."

"You know what, Helena? I bow to the master. You have truly become more despicable than I ever thought you could."

She looked satisfied. As she slowly walked toward him, she lifted her skirt to the point where it was obvious that she wore nothing underneath. "Thank you, daaahling," she purred. She sat on his lap and straddled her legs around him. "Now why don't you give Helena that kiss she's been waiting for?"

Looking a little battered and bruised, Nigel emerged from the office close to an hour later.

Someone grabbed his shoulder. "Hey mate, looks like you've been through a war."

It was Christian, a friendly face. It was time to relax and enjoy himself again. "Hey," he joked, "I didn't know assholes were allowed through the door. How did you get yourself an invitation?"

"Richard's been nominated for a couple of things. I'm here to accept the awards for him if he wins."

"So, the boss allowed you to extract your head from his ass then?"

"I wouldn't put it that way, but, I'll be here for a couple days."

"Come on then, I could use another drink, how 'bout you?"

Christian shook his head.

"Still on the wagon, huh? What? Five years now? Don't know how you do it."

Christian pulled up his sleeve. "This is how I do it. I look at these bloody track marks and thank God the drugs and booze didn't kill me."

"Spare me the details. I've heard your story before."

"You just hate knowing it was Richard that found me half-dead in my flat with a needle hanging out of my arm."

"Right, Richard the savior again. Everybody's hero."

"If it weren't for him, I'd be dead. I lost it all after the group broke up. Turning to drugs was the wrong thing to do. But, he was there through it all. At the hospital twenty-four hours a day, and later at rehab. And after all that, he offered me a job. I didn't see anyone else extending their hand to me."

"So what? Look at yourself. You're nothing more than his sidekick, ass-wipe, whatever you want to call it. You just handed over your life to that ass-hole."

"I didn't hand over my life. I may owe him a lot, but he's my friend too. I'd be there to pick up his bloody pieces if he ever needed me to. But you'd be the one to kick him over again, right?"

"You're damn right I would." Suddenly, again, he spotted the woman with the long hair and the riveting smile. His mood changed. "Hey, mate, look over there, in the corner. Who's the woman talking to the short, bald guy? She's absolutely beautiful."

Christian broke into a huge smile. "You don't know who that is?"

Nigel looked surprised. "No, should I?"

"Come on. I'll introduce you."

As they wove their way through the thinning crowd, the woman who had piqued Nigel's attention looked more and more familiar. His palms got sweaty. He could feel his heart pounding against his chest. When they reached her, she turned to face them. Nigel couldn't move. He was paralyzed. He wanted to reach out to her, but his arms wouldn't follow his command.

With the expression of a small child who had just found her favorite toy, she burst out into a brilliant smile and grabbed Christian's hands. "Oh, what a great surprise. I had no idea you'd be here." She put her arms around his waist. "Tell, me," she continued, "what brings you here?"

He stood back and held her shoulders. "Your father," he said. "What else? I'm here to collect more awards for him."

Nigel was in another world. He couldn't believe the words that just came out of Christian's mouth. "Your father," his enemy. The only thing that made Nigel's life worth living was planning and eventually executing Richard's destruction. And look who stood before him at that moment?

Except for her dark hair, she was the image of her mother. But that didn't matter. She wasn't Sara. Nobody could ever take Sara's place. No, this was Richard Winters' only child. And that made her his enemy too. His mind was racing. He knew this chance encounter could benefit him in some way. She could be a useful tool. But how? He watched the gladness on her face as she talked to Christian. One thing was certain: Winters would lay down his life for his daughter.

Christian took her hand. "Anna," he said, "I'd like you to meet somebody. This is Nigel Taylor. You've probably met before though."

She turned to Nigel and looked directly into his eyes. "Yes, of course. I recognized you right away. We met a long time ago. I was only a child, but I still remember."

Her voice was melodic, and her eyes, intoxicating. He was taken aback by her presence. He hadn't expected to feel this way about a person he was determined to use as a means to some gruesome end. He extended his hand. "Yes," he said. "I remember too. You've changed quite a bit since then though."

Anna took his hand and laughed. "I should hope so. It would be rather odd if I were still going around in my pigtails and braces, now wouldn't it?"

Christian laughed. "No, it would just give you even more character than you already have." He glanced around the room. "You're not here alone, are you?"

"No, Jackie's here somewhere."

Just then, a pair of woman's hands covered Christian's eyes from behind. Whispering in his ear, she said, "Guess who?"

Christian twisted around and stepped back. She was tall and slender. Her dark brown hair loosely fell to her shoulders, accentuating her oval face and deep eyes. She was dressed in a black business blazer, a white collared shirt unbuttoned to her brassiere, a short black skirt, and six-inch heels. All of which reflected her perfectly: a serious demeanor, a hint of danger, and a flair for fun. "Jackie? My God, I almost didn't recognize you."

She tilted her head and pouted her full, red lips. "Have I changed that much?"

Christian arched his eyebrow. "Transformed is more like it. You look absolutely beautiful."

Anna leaned over to him. "You can stop drooling now, you know."

Christian looked embarrassed. "I didn't know I was, but some things just can't be helped." Without taking his eyes off of Jackie, he continued. "You know, this party's getting stale. Why don't we all get out of here and go dancing. I know a great new club downtown. What do you say?"

Anna looked at Jackie and shrugged. "Why not?"

Without as much as a single good-bye to the hostess, they headed straight toward the door. Within moments, the four of them were in a taxi, speeding their way through the winding streets of Greenwich Village towards the hottest of the new nightclubs along the waterfront.

At one o'clock in the morning the line outside the door still snaked its way alongside the building. Upon seeing Christian and Nigel get out of the cab, the two linebackers who guarded the door threw open the red velvet ropes and welcomed the four of them in with some gushing words of flattery.

Jackie grabbed Christian's hand and headed for the dance floor. "Now, that's what I call service," she giggled. "I'll have to hang around you more often."

Without hesitation he answered, "Yes, well, we'll just have to work on that, won't we?"

Nigel wasn't in the mood for dancing. He needed a drink, and fast. This whole situation threw him completely off guard. Here he was, alone with Anna Winters, who was charming, beautiful, and, most important, clueless about his relationship with her father. If she had any idea at all, he was certain that she wouldn't be there with him right now. She was relaxed and ready to have fun which was not characteristic of someone who knew that her companion was blackmailing her father for a few million dollars.

The room was vibrating with the movement of people dancing. Anna watched Christian and Jackie on the dance floor. Their bodies moved so close to one another that a sheet of paper couldn't be slipped between them. With a look of amusement she turned to Nigel. "Looks like they're really getting along, right?"

He studied them for a moment. "Why not? Jackie's a beautiful girl, and Christian—well, I guess you could call him a decent guy." He turned to her. "Come on. Let me buy you drink. We can hit the dance floor later."

She followed him through the crowd to the bar. "Just a glass of white wine for me, thanks."

He watched her as she took a sip. Although she had the face of her mother, her expressions and mannerisms were those of her father: the tight grip of her hand against the glass, and the way she squinted when she drank. It was as if Nigel were facing Richard *and* Sara. He threw back two vodka tonics in quick succession and touched her arm. "Tell me something," he said. "Have you seen much of your father lately?"

"What?" she yelled over the music.

"I said—oh, never mind. It's too loud in here." He grabbed her hand. "Let's find somewhere where we can talk."

Still holding her hand, he took her to a staircase that led to the second floor. When they reached the top, they were greeted by another bouncer, who asked to see Nigel's VIP card. Satisfied with his celebrity status, he opened the door. The room was small and intimate, with a large oak bar in the corner. Green velvet sofas and cocktail tables scattered throughout. The crowd was small, with only a few sunglass-clad entertainment-types who sat about smoking cigars while talking on their cell phones.

They sat down on one of the empty sofas. "Much better, don't you think? Nigel asked.

"Well yes," she answered, "if you enjoy breathing in cigar smoke."

So much for lighting up my cigar, he thought.

"So tell me," she continued, "what were you trying to ask me downstairs?"

"I was wondering if you'd seen your father lately."

"No, not at all. I've been so busy here in New York, with business and all, that I've only had the chance to see him on holidays. You probably see him more than I do."

"I doubt that," he answered. "So what kind of business are you in?"

"Shipping, mercantile shipping. I'm running my grandfather's New York office."

Right. How could he have forgotten? Little Anna Winters, heiress to the Stavropoulos shipping fortune. She had gotten it all when her mother died: the trust and an eventual inheritance that possibly outweighed the entire gross national product of Europe. Richard's fortune was pennies compared to her grandfather's. His plan was starting to take form, but it depended on one thing: just how innocent and trusting this girl could be.

"Why New York?" he asked. "Why didn't you want to run an office in London? It must be lonely for you here."

"No, I love it here," she answered brightly. "Besides, I have Jackie. She works in the office with me. If it weren't for her, I probably would be lonely."

"No boyfriend then?"

She shrugged. "No, not at the moment."

Bingo. "I can't believe that a beautiful woman like you doesn't have at least two or three boyfriends."

Her face turned red. "Thanks for the compliment, but no. The right person just hasn't come along."

"So, you believe in fate? That somewhere out there the right person is waiting for you?"

"You don't?"

"I believe in a lot of things—chance encounters, the intensity of a moment, the passion in someone's eyes, and the thrill of a first kiss. But do I believe in that certain someone? That she's out there, waiting for me? The definitive answer to my dreams? I don't think so. Then I'd overlook the everyday moments that make life worth living: like sharing a glance with a lovely stranger, or feeling a connection with someone I've just met in a subway, or even bumping into the daughter of an old friend, the daughter I hadn't seen since she was ten years old."

Anna couldn't help but smile. "So, this is one of those encounters that makes your life worth living then?"

He looked directly into her eyes. "Absolutely."

She studied his face for a moment. "Thank you." She paused a moment, then added in a whisper, "you have very nice eyes, you know."

He reached over and brushed his fingers across her cheek. "Thank *you*," he said. "You do too." He held her gaze a few extra seconds. She didn't look away. *A bit too easy. Not only is she trusting, but uninhibited as well.* But, unlike his catastrophic evening with Sara, this campaign was going to be well thought out. He would plan every detail, rehearse every conceivable conversation. The outcome would be so sweet that even he couldn't believe his own depravity. He could see himself telling Richard Winters the words that would tear his heart out, "I've just married your daughter." He could barely contain himself. He needed to celebrate—some champagne, a joint. No, Anna wouldn't like that. He had to polish up his act, for the time being of course. Just then, his thoughts were interrupted.

"I'm in the mood for some dancing? What do you say?" she asked.

The last thing he felt like doing at the moment was dancing. "Absolutely," he said. "I was just thinking the same thing." He took her arm and led her back down the staircase.

Anna Winters, Anna Taylor—that sounded good. His mind reeled with the possibilities. If he were lucky, the old geezer grandfather would be dead in a couple of years and his financial future would be set forever. And then there was Richard. The thought of revenge was so sweet he could barely contain a spontaneous orgasm.

When they reached the dance floor, the crowd had thinned to a few hard-core party-goers.

"Hey, Nigel, look over there." She pointed to the middle of the floor.

He turned to see Jackie and Christian planted squarely in the center of the room locked in a kiss. "They're getting on better than we thought," he said with a wry smile.

Once again, she looked into his eyes. "Fate? Or the intensity of the moment?"

He had no answer. Fates are written and rewritten every day. Just yesterday she might have been destined to marry a staid corporate chap or lawyer, but today—well, her life's story was being edited. *Anna Winters,* he thought, *your life's about to turn upside down.*

Chapter 9

THE NEXT DAY

Anna stared out the window of her penthouse office at SeaCorp Inc.
What 30 years ago started out as a small back-room operation in
Manhattan's lower East Side had blossomed into a merchant shipping
fleet of over 80 tankers with offices in New York, London, and Athens.
And here she was, barely 25 years old, at the helm of the largest of the
three offices. But, what had sounded like a glamorous position, filled with
international travel and fascinating people, turned out to be a daily survival contest with an undermining staff and treasonous board. She knew
her position and power came too quickly. She had told her grandfather, on
a number of occasions, that she would have preferred to work her way up
the ranks. But, his deep confidence in her business and organizational
skills landed her in the forefront of this deeply entrenched, male-domi-
nated industry. This, of course, bred so much resentment among the rank
and file that "watch your back" had become her daily mantra.

Ready to tackle the days' events, she sat at her desk. Like the rest of
her office, it was clean, and stark. Never anything out of place: personal-
ized note cards in the upper right hand corner, 'in' and 'out' boxes in the

upper left, a pencil holder with freshly sharpened pencils near her name-plate, and a steep stack of 'urgently needed' file folders placed squarely in the center.

With a sigh of resignation, she reached for the first folder just as the intercom rang. She picked up the phone and laughed at Jackie's raspy plea. "I could use about a bottle of aspirin and a tank of coffee. How about you?"

"I was just thinking the same thing. Come on in."

Within seconds, the door opened and Jackie staggered in. She took a seat opposite Anna and propped her feet up on the desk. Anna opened her lower right hand desk drawer. "So, what's it going to be today?" she asked while rummaging through an assortment of bottles and jars.

Jackie closed her eyes and slid her fingers through her hair. "The usual hangover cocktail, thanks."

Anna handed her a bottle of antacids and a few aspirin. "So, are you going to fill me in on all the details now or later?"

Jackie walked over to the wet bar in the corner and poured herself a glass of water. "Where do you want me to start?"

"How about at the part where Nigel and I dropped you and Christian off at his hotel? ... Oh, by the way, I liked the outfit you wore last night. Looks a bit wrinkled today though. Didn't run back to your place for a change of clothes this morning, I take it."

Jackie leaned up against the bar. "Glad to know your hangover hasn't affected your keen observational skills." She raised her glass in the air, said "Cheers mate," drank the entire glass in two long gulps, and clanged it back down on the bar. "So, what do you think happened? We got hot and sweaty, rolled around in the sheets, and fell asleep." She poured herself another glass and giggled. "I could ask the same thing of you. You and Nigel looked pretty cozy there."

Anna shook her head. "He just dropped me off at my apartment and we said good-bye."

"No 'I'll see you' or 'I'll call you tomorrow' or anything like that?"

"No."

"Are you disappointed?"

Anna paused for a moment and sighed. "I don't know."

"Oh, Anna, get in touch with yourself. If you like him, you should call."

The truth was, she wasn't sure how she felt about Nigel. He was charming, and handsome, but with all the alcohol and electricity in the air last night, she was sure she had let herself get a little carried away.

"So, are you going to call him?" Jackie repeated impatiently. "I mean, let's face it. It's not as if you've been seeing anyone recently. As a matter of fact, I can't remember the last time you dated anyone seriously, or even looked at any man with much interest. What's going on? Come on, you tell me everything. I mean, you even told me about your fling with my brother."

Anna shot Jackie a sharp glance.

"Oh," Jackie said as if she'd just uncovered a secret plot to blow up the world, "That's it. It's Ian, isn't it? You're not over him, are you? There was more to your little story than you let on. Maybe it wasn't a mutual break-up all those years ago?"

Anna shifted uncomfortably.

Jackie dug further. "I'm right, aren't I?"

Anna slammed her hands down on her desk. "All right, Jackie. Enough. And no, it wasn't a mutual break-up all those years ago. It was Ian that didn't want to continue our relationship. But that was a long time ago. I'm over it."

"Oh, really?" Jackie said. "I don't believe you."

"It's true," she answered unconvincingly.

"Then prove it."

"How?"

Jackie walked over to the desk, picked up the telephone receiver, and handed it to Anna. "Call Nigel."

Anna felt herself cringe. It wasn't as if she didn't like Nigel, but she wasn't sure that she was ready for a relationship. The problem was, she couldn't figure out what was stopping her. Jackie was right. It had been a long time since she had shown any interest in a man, and no matter how much she hated to admit it, the last man she had any real feelings for was Ian. She couldn't let him control her emotions any longer. It was time to move on.

She grabbed the telephone receiver out of Jackie's hand. "Fine." You want me to prove that I'm over your brother, then I will." She stabbed at the intercom button. "Call the Waldorf Astoria," she barked, "and get me Nigel Taylor on the line." She hung up the phone and looked back at Jackie. "Satisfied?"

"Yes," Jackie answered pensively.

"Now," Anna continued, "are you going to call Christian?"

"Don't have to. He's already called me. We're making plans to see each other in London next weekend."

Anna was taken by surprise. Jackie's eager admirers had never interested her enough to send her packing overseas on the weekends. "So, this is serious then?"

"Oh Anna, don't give me those puppy-dog eyes. I'm not leaving forever. Just a couple of days, that's all." She paused and looked around the room.

"What's the matter?" Anna asked. "I can tell something's bothering you. Is it something about Christian?"

"No," Jackie answered. "It's not him. It's that whole issue with Ian. I didn't know how you felt, and well, there's something I have to tell you. I got a call from home this morning—"

Anna's intercom rang. "Hold that thought," she said. She pushed the button for the speaker phone. Her receptionist's high-pitched twang came over the line. "Miss Winters, Mr. Taylor's not in his room. The receptionist at the Waldorf wants to know if you'd like to leave a message."

Anna felt a mixture of relief and disappointment. "No, no message. I'll try again later."

Her receptionist continued. "I also have Mr. Vlakas on another line. He said it's urgent."

Anna picked up the receiver to the phone and cut off the speaker. She spoke a few moments, put the receiver down, and looked at Jackie. "Straighten up and look professional. That annoying bean-counter from chartering is coming in. Looks like we have some kind of situation going on in Argentina."

The door opened as she was speaking. Anna stood up.

Anna motioned to the empty chair opposite her desk. "Mr. Vlakas, please, come in. Have a seat and fill us in on the problem."

Vlakas sat down and cleared his throat. His disdain at having to report to someone at least 35 years his junior was obvious. "We have a supertanker loaded with about 250,000 barrels of crude oil docked in Buenos Aires. It's scheduled to arrive in South Africa early next week."

"And the problem is?" Anna asked.

"I was just getting to that." Vlakas did not hide an expression of annoyance. "The problem is that she's registered under a Panamanian flag. The port official in Buenos Aires found some obscure Panamanian rule that says that if you're operating a Panamanian ship, a third of the crew must be from that country. He won't let the ship go until we adhere to the rule."

"How many Panamanian nationals do we have on there now?" Anna asked.

"None," he responded almost victoriously.

"So, fly a crew in. How hard could that be?"

"Normally, not hard at all, but, the Panamanian Ship Operators Union is on strike, and their strikes have been known to last weeks, if not months."

Anna put her hand on her forehead and looked down. "You've got to be kidding me. I don't want to think about the money we're losing every minute because of this pin-head bureaucrat." She paused. She knew Vlakas was enjoying this moment. He, and the rest of the office, lived to see her sweat in situations like this. She thought about calling her grandfather and asking him for advice but quickly decided against it. She had insisted that he slow down and take more time off. Even she wanted to, he was vacationing on the island of Xenos where getting an audible telephone call through to his home would require no less than an act of God. Instead, she did the next best thing and asked herself, *now what would he do in a situation like this?* Then it became clear.

She jotted down a list of names and handed them to Vlakas. "Get me the phone numbers of all these people and call me on my car phone in one hour." She turned to Jackie. "Have my secretary book me on the next flight to Buenos Aires. If there isn't one within the next couple of hours, tell her to have the company plane ready at the airport. Oh, and Vlakas, where's Markos Yannis? I want him to meet me there. I may need his help."

Clearly disappointed by her quick response, he answered, "He's already on his way, Miss Winters."

She slapped her hands down on her desk. "Okay. Let's get to work."

By 7:00 A.M. the next day, Anna stood on a bustling shipping dock in Buenos Aires. Unlike New York, Argentina was chilly this time of year and having forgotten to pack a heavy coat, she stood shivering on the pier waiting for Marcos to arrive. After a few moments, she felt a tap on her shoulder.

"You're going to catch your death of cold, Miss Winters."

She blew into her hands and rubbed them together. "Yes, and that would make everyone back in New York just as happy as little clams, right?"

He began to take off his coat. "They'll learn to love you. Everybody does. Besides, they've never seen you handle a ship the way I have. If they did, they'd understand how much you deserve your position." Gently, he put the coat around her shoulders. "Here, put this on until we get inside." He turned around and pointed to a small wooden shack adjacent to the pier. "The port official's waiting for us in his office. His name is Gutierrez. Not a particularly smart guy but has a sixth sense for smelling a good opportunity."

Knowing all too well what he meant by "a good opportunity," she nodded and, holding the coat closed, began to walk. The noise on the dock was beginning to reach its daily crescendo and although she couldn't hear their footsteps, she knew they were walking in unison. In a strange way, this comforted her. Marcos was her rock in this business and although she probably didn't need him in Buenos Aires, she felt safer knowing he was around.

"So tell me, Marcos," she said, "what's your take on this? What's Gutierrez' angle? What does he want from us? Or should I say, how much does he want from us?"

"It didn't take you long to catch on. He probably wants a bribe, a pretty big one. He knows we're losing about ten to twenty thousand dollars a day sitting here. So, he's figuring that we'll pay about anything he wants to let us go."

"That sounds right, but tell me: we're in Buenos Aires all the time. How come we've never seen this guy before?"

"He was transferred from another port." They stopped at the door. "So, what's the plan? Are we going to pay him off?"

Anna gave him a disapproving stare. "You know me better than that. Stavropoulos and Winters don't pay anybody off for anything. If you do, you get a reputation, and, before you know it, all the sleazy underworld wants to get in on the action." She put her hand on his shoulder. "Hey, don't look so worried. Have I ever let you down before?" She pulled a sheet of paper out of her handbag and handed it to him. "I made a list of few things I'll need for this evening. Do your best to get them all, but the most important item is the last one. You'll see, it's the icing on the cake."

Marcos read over the list and started laughing. "No problem, Miss Winters. Maybe it is time I start learning from you."

They knocked on the door of the office but before letting themselves in, Anna took off Marcos' coat and unbuttoned her blouse a few notches. She glanced over at him and shrugged. "You've got to do what you've got to do, right?" They opened the door and stepped in. Captain Gutierrez looked up from behind his small wooden desk.

"Ahhhh, Marcos, I was expecting you," he looked over at Anna, "and who's this beautiful lady you have with you? Your secretary I assume?"

Marcos looked embarrassed. "No, Captain. This is the owner of the ship, Anna Winters."

Gutierrez arched his eyebrow and stood up. He was a short man, maybe 5 foot 5 or 6, with graying hair and a wiry mustache. His silver polyester blazer fit snugly around his sagging waist. Anna couldn't decide whether he reminded her of a South American dictator or an aging druglord.

She extended her hand. "Captain Gutierrez, it's a pleasure to meet you." She lowered her voice a bit. "But I must say, I wasn't expecting to see such a handsome man."

Clearly pleased by Anna's compliment, the Captain took her hand, shook it, and held it a few extra moments.

Trying to hide her revulsion, she leaned toward him. "You know, Captain, this whole issue about the crew not being Panamanian is ridiculous. No one's ever questioned it before. Now, what if I promise that as soon as their strike is over, I'll have them meet up with the ship wherever it's docked?"

He took a deep breath and shook his head. "I'm sorry, Miss Winters. Rules are rules." He paused and looked straight into her eyes. "But perhaps we could talk about some other arrangements tonight, over cocktails?"

Anna's eye caught Marcos'. His smirk made her want to burst out laughing. Trying to contain herself, she looked down and answered, "I'd like nothing better. How about the bar in my hotel, eight o'clock sharp?"

Gutierrez arched his eyebrow again. "I'll see you there."

They walked out of the office. Again, with their stride in unison, Anna turned to Marcos. "You men," she said, "you're all so easy to read. You only think with one part of your body, and it's not your brains."

Still smirking, he answered, "When you're right, you're right."

The cocktail lounge in the Buenos Aires Grand Royal hotel was dark and intimate. Anna sat at a small round table for two alongside a wall of windows overlooking the gardens. She slowly sipped a glass of white wine. From the corner of her eye she spotted Gutierrez heading for her table. *In his best attire*, she thought, his silver polyester blazer accented by an extra-wide paisley tie.

Doing her best to put on a seductive look, she stood up and said, "I hope you don't mind that I took the liberty of ordering us some champagne."

He sat down and loosened his tie a bit. "For what occasion, my dear? We haven't even discussed any, uhm, arrangements."

"We're both adults. Why don't you just tell me what you want?"

"I see you're a woman who likes to take care of business first and maybe play later?" He arched his eyebrow again.

Realizing that his eyebrow arching was his pathetic attempt at being sexy, she said, "Yes, we'll play later. So tell me, how can I get my ship out of here?"

"How about by giving me about 200,000 of your American dollars?"

"That's a bit steep."

"Ah, Miss Winters, or should I say, Anna? That's what you rich Americans call a drop in a bucket."

The waiter brought the champagne and poured two glasses.

Anna took a sip. "Dom Perignon, my favorite. I always drink it on special occasions. You see, Captain, what would you do if I were to tell you that I've been recording this conversation and, a port official soliciting a bribe, well, you get my drift."

Showing absolutely no surprise, Gutierrez shook his head. "Oh, Miss Winters, you disappoint me. You should know better than that. By the time you turn that tape in to the authorities, they arrest me, so on and so forth. It could take months, even years. In the meantime, your ship's still in Buenos Aires waiting for a striking crew from Panama and losing hundreds of thousands of dollars a day. I can see that you're a smart business woman, so why don't you just hand over the money?"

Anna reached under the table and picked up her briefcase. "You're right Captain. Getting you arrested for taking bribes wouldn't get my ship out of here, but it would make me feel a lot better." She opened the briefcase, took out a folded piece of heavy linen, and handed it to him. "Here, unfold it."

"You intrigue me, my dear." He unfolded it and looked up. "I don't understand. What is it?"

"A Liberian flag. I had the ship reregistered this morning. The last I heard, they don't care how many nationals I have on board operating her. So I guess we'll be pulling out in the morning." She stood up and closed her briefcase. "Oh, and Captain, the waiter over there: he's with the Buenos Aires police. I wouldn't try leaving the city limits if I were you."

Gutierrez sat motionless.

Then, in one long swallow, Anna finished her champagne, put the glass down, and arched her eyebrow. "I guess play time is over, Captain."

Word of her victory spread quickly throughout the New York office. Two dozen red roses were delivered to her suite the next morning with a note from the executive staff: "Great job—see you soon."

Not exactly exalting words of gratitude, but a start. Still lounging in

her pajamas, she lay in bed and thought about how she would like to celebrate her victory. She picked up the phone and called Jackie. After
telling her every detail, Anna saw that it was well into the afternoon,
time to pack and head for the airport.

"Okay, I'll see you when I get back."

There was a pause on the other end.

"Hello? Are you there?" Anna asked anxiously.

"Yes, I'm here. Do you remember there was something I had to tell
you before you left?"

"I remember. What is it?"

"It's about Ian. He's getting married. I'm going back to London this
weekend for the wedding."

Silence.

"Anna, did you hear me?"

"Yes, I heard you," she said softly, then added, "I didn't even know he
had a girlfriend."

"Neither did I. Apparently it was all very quick. She'd just joined his
theater group. It was love at first sight, at least that's what I heard.
Listen, I know you have a history with him and all, but you've convinced
me that you're over it. So, why don't you come along?"

Was she kidding? The last thing she wanted to do was watch Ian get
married. "No, I think I'll pass. I have a lot of work to take care of when
I get back."

"All right then. I'll see you next week."

She hung up the phone. Why should Ian's marriage matter to her at all?
It's not as if we were meant to be together or anything. She was over him.
She had convinced Jackie of that. But why couldn't she convince herself?
She wouldn't think about it any more. She threw her suitcase on the bed
and reached for her clothes. She thought about her apartment in New
York. Suddenly she realized that she wasn't relishing the thought of
returning. Everything seemed so empty. She never felt so alone in her life.

She reached for the phone and dialed the airport. Within a matter of
moments she had a flight booked for Athens and a connection to Xenos. No
matter how much she loathed that little island, one of the people who loved
her the most in this world would be there waiting for her: her grandfather.

Anna spent the next few days lounging on her grandfather's yacht and taking long walks along the beach. In the evening, she would drive down to the local market, pick up some fresh fish, and grill it for Constantine and Beatrice. She felt safe, secure, and very loved in the confines of her grandparent's home. Before she knew it, two weeks had gone by, and Constantine and Beatrice began packing to return to their autumn residence in Athens. She knew that her vacation was also over, but she couldn't resist staying a few more days, even if it meant being there without them.

A couple of days later, she saw her grandparents off at the airport. She then drove back to the village alone. The sun was setting behind the mountains. She opened the car windows and let the cool breeze blow through her hair. She drove along the winding roads through the hills and mountains, occasionally looking down to watch the tranquil waters of the Mediterranean lap against the white, sandy shores.

She decided to stop at the market before heading home. She had a craving for fresh fish and earlier in the day had seen the local fishermen bring in an unusually large catch.

In an effort to get ready for the evening dinner crowds, the local cafes had already set up their tables and chairs along the dock. She walked past them to the market, picked out two small fish, and headed back to her car. Suddenly she heard a Greek waiter shouting for someone to help him translate a menu for a tourist. Feeling sorry for the tourist, who had just been referred to as the English moron, she walked over to help.

The tourist sat hidden behind his menu. Anna spoke. "Can I help you order?"

"Yes, that would be greatly appreciated," he answered. He put down his menu and looked up. They both stared for a moment and broke out laughing.

"Oh my God, Nigel, I can't believe it's you." Anna said. "What on earth are you doing on this island?"

"I heard it was a great vacation spot for someone who's trying to avoid crowds," he answered.

"If you want to avoid crowds, it's great, but as for a glamorous vacation spot? I don't think so. There's nothing to do or see here that's of any interest to anyone besides the locals."

"I don't happen to agree with you at all. I'm looking at something absolutely beautiful right now." He stood up and pulled out a chair for her. "Please, sit down and join me for something to eat."

"As much as I'd like to join you, the food here's terrible." She paused for a moment. "I have a better idea. I just bought some things at the market. Why don't you come home with me? I'll cook us up a fabulous dinner."

Without hesitating a moment, Nigel stood up. "Sounds great. Lead the way."

Meeting Nigel on Xenos couldn't have been more opportune for Anna. Although she enjoyed being alone in her grandparent's home, the idea of spending some time with a handsome, charismatic musician seemed much more attractive.

When they reached the house, she hurried into the kitchen and brought out a bottle of her favorite French wine. She then led Nigel down a winding path to a small alcove along the water to her grandfather's private beach.

They sat on the sand and drank the wine. Anna enjoyed listening to the sound of Nigel's voice as he told her stories about his youth, and his earlier days as a musician. She, in turn, told him stories about her childhood days on the island: the unusual cast of characters, the long, summers, and the loneliness that went along with it.

Nigel's voice, mellow and measured, took on a melodic tone that harmonized with the sounds of the softly crashing waves. "It seems strange to me that someone who's so beautiful and fun to be with could be lonely," he whispered. "I'd think you'd have a million friends."

"Friends? I have a lot of friends. But there always seems to be something missing. An emptiness I haven't been able to fill."

He looked deeply into her eyes. "What do you suppose it will take to fill it?"

Anna began to feel a bit drowsy from the wine. She lay back on the sand and stared at the night sky. "Did you ever see so many stars?" she said. "There's no place like this in the world."

Nigel looked down at her. "You're changing the subject." He brushed her hair from her face. "What will it take to fill that emptiness inside you, Anna?" he whispered.

She studied his face. He was beautiful with his strong, chiseled jaw and deep, penetrating green eyes. *God, I could look at him forever."* She thought about his question: what would it take to fill that emptiness? She didn't know. But one thing she did know: at that moment she felt wonderful, wanted and secure with him. She reached up and touched his face.

He held her hand for a moment, then suddenly let it drop. "You know, it's getting late. I should be going back to my hotel now."

That wasn't quite the response she was waiting for. "Wait. We haven't had dinner yet."

"To be honest, I'm not really hungry. But there was something I wanted you to hear before I leave."

"What?"

He grinned. "I need a guitar or a piano."

"Come on then. I've got both at the house."

When they got there, they sat in the backyard patio, where the floodlights illuminated the pool and gardens. Anna handed Nigel her father's guitar. After adjusting the tuning pegs a few notches, he began strumming a soft, slow rhythm.

What a better place
to meet than Paris,
you came to talk
one dark, dark day,
Then suddenly
without a warning,
you got up
and walked away.

I was cold the night
before we met
and you touched upon
my inner soul.

The only one
that's ever reached me,
God, I never wanted
to let you go.

So now Anna,
we met in Paris,
New York, L.A., someplace
far, far away.
Can't you see
I'm crying my heart out.
Please don't get up
and walk away.

Anna felt tears running down her cheeks. "My God," she said, "you wrote that for me? Nobody's ever done that before. Not even my father. It was so beautiful."

"No, Anna," he said. "You're beautiful. The world should be writing songs about you. You make it so easy." He stood up. "Listen, I should be going."

She felt confused. "But why?"

"Because this situation's dangerous. I'm having thoughts I shouldn't be having."

Anna stood up and looked straight into his eyes. "They're probably the same thoughts I'm having." As she leaned close to him, their lips met. He pulled her into his arms and kissed her with a fervor and passion that she'd never felt.

"You know what?" she whispered to him.

"What?" he asked while slowly kissing her neck.

"I think I have the answer to your question now."

"What question?"

"You asked me what it would take to fill that emptiness in me. It's you. I think I've been waiting for you. Does that scare you?"

He stopped kissing her and smiled. "No, Anna. Why would that scare me? I've been in love with you since the moment we met back in New York. Bumping into you here on Xenos was no coincidence. I found out where you were from someone in your office. I had to see you, to be with you. I felt lost when you left. I just wasn't sure how you felt about me. Now I know and I couldn't be happier. I want to be with you, forever. Does that scare *you*?"

She felt both exhilarated and apprehensive. She hardly knew this man, but in the short amount of time she had spent with him, he had made her feel happier than she had felt since—God, who could remember? "No," she said, "I'm not scared."

"Good." He swept her up into his arms and grinned. "Now, show me the way to your bedroom."

Forty-eight hours later, Anna called the local telephone operator to get her a line through to London.

"Hello? Dad?" she said. "I couldn't wait another minute to tell you. I just got married today—and you're going to die when I tell you who it is."

Chapter 10

LONDON, THREE YEARS LATER

The rush-hour traffic along Piccadilly had slowed to a veritable standstill. Richard glanced at the clock on his dashboard. It hadn't even reached 8:00 A.M. and the outside temperature was well over 90 degrees. London was in the midst of a heat spell the likes of which it hadn't experienced since the turn of the century. His car sat motionless alongside Green Park. He watched as the needle of his heat gauge slowly approached the critical mark. He turned off the air conditioner and opened the windows. He felt almost suffocated by the rush of the hot, sticky air and the deafening sounds of angry, honking horns. Realizing that his car hadn't moved an inch in more than twenty minutes, he pulled over to the loading zone of the Ritz Hotel, got out, and lit up a cigarette.

Constantine's contracts can wait. He handed the doorman a large bill and asked him to watch his car. He then made his way over to the park and sat down on one of the green and white striped chairs near the newsstand. He put his head back and felt the hot sun against his face. He tried to remember the last time he had been here but couldn't. Then it came to him. With Anna, over twenty years ago. She was just a baby. *My God,* he thought. *How I miss those times.*

He hadn't spoken to her in maybe three years. He wished he could take back everything he had said that last time but it was too late. The damage was done, and Nigel had won. But how else should he have reacted? What else could he have said? Like a movie on constant rewind, that day played over and over again in his mind.

Anna's telephone call from Xenos had taken him by surprise. His complete shock quickly turned to revulsion and he hung up the phone without uttering a word. It was only at Angela's insistence that he called back and asked to see them both in London immediately. To him, of course, this union was nothing short of grotesque. He knew Nigel's motives, and he also knew that this visit was Nigel's coup—the culmination of his life's sick ambition to see him groveling on his knees. But how could he tell his daughter she was being used as a pawn in a twisted game of revenge?

The doorbell rang. It was time to face them both and he still hadn't a clue as to what he'd say. He opened the door and saw his daughter's face, so innocent and beautiful, and beside her, well—Rodin couldn't have found a better model for the faces on the "Gates of Hell."

"Dad," Anna said, "Your response to our marriage confused me. I thought you'd be happy for me."

"Yes, Richard," Nigel said while taking her hand, "you realize you left your daughter in tears after she hung up. Not a very nice reaction to the happiest day of her life."

Richard controlled his desire to vomit by quickly visualizing some gruesome and hideous torture for his ex-partner. Like watching his skin ooze off in a bathtub filled with acid. Or seeing him clinging to a slippery cliff above large shards of broken glass or a pit of boiling volcanic magma.

"Dad," Anna said impatiently, "now that you've had some time to think, aren't you going to say something nice, like 'congratulations?'"

Richard thought for a moment. He couldn't lie and if he didn't, he would break his daughter's heart. But, this situation was unthinkable. He had to try to make her realize she had made a mistake. The problem was, the mistake was standing next to her and he knew it wasn't going to go away without a fight.

"Anna," he said apologetically, "I must admit, your telephone call took me by surprise. I'm glad that you're happy, but, don't you think your decision was rather quick?"

"Well yes," Nigel grinned. "That's the beauty of love at first sight. You know how it is, Richard. You and your wife were married in what, two weeks?"

Richard glared at him. "Don't compare this to my marriage, you—" he stopped and looked at Anna. He knew what Nigel was up to. He wanted to make him lose control, maybe even take a swipe at him. Nothing would be more repellent to his daughter than watching her father go after the man she loved—or thought she did. He quickly regained his composure. "Look," he continued, "all I'm saying is that I don't think you two really took the time to get to know each other."

"Dad," Anna answered, "we love each other. Nothing else is important."

"Don't be so naïve, darling," Richard said. "A person's past is an indication of how he'll behave in the future. Did Nigel happen to mention that he's been married before? Did he tell you why his wife left him?"

Nigel shook his head. "Richard, please. Dredging up my past isn't going to help your case. Anna knows all about it."

Richard looked at him in disbelief. "Everything? You mean to tell me you told her everything? I find that particularly hard to believe."

"As hard to believe as the fact that you've also told her everything about your life, or did you leave out a few things too?"

"What's that supposed to mean, you son of a bitch?"

"Only that sometimes we may hold back certain information about ourselves, so as to protect the ones we love."

Anna interrupted. "I don't know what the two of you a talking about, but whatever it is, it's got to stop."

"It's never going to stop, Anna," Nigel said. "I don't think your father's ever going to accept me." He turned to Richard. "Come on. What's really eating you? It's not my past marriage. Hell, I'm over forty years old. It would be rather odd if I hadn't been married before." He watched Richard cringe, and smiled with delight. "Oh, there it is, isn't it? You can't bear the thought of your little baby marrying someone who's old enough to be her father?"

Richard glared at Nigel. "Yes, the words 'child molester' did come to mind."

"Oh, so here we are, at the root of the problem," Nigel said. "You're upset that your virtuous daughter is having sex with a man who's almost twenty years older than she is?" He took Anna's hand and smiled. "Well, Richard, if it would make you feel better, you should know that she wasn't quite as virtuous as you thought when we met, although she did have a lot of catching up to do."

There it was, the words that he knew would send Richard flying over the edge. The thought of his beautiful little baby having sex with this grotesque excuse for a man made him want to explode. He looked at Nigel almost pleadingly. "Don't do this, please. You know you've already won. Just let her go."

Nigel took Anna's head in his hands and gave her a long, passionate kiss.

Anna gazed into his eyes. "What was that for?"

"To show your father what true love is all about."

Richard walked over to Nigel and shoved him up against the fireplace. He put his arm under his neck and pinned his head against the fieldstone of the mantel. Then, with a voice that came from somewhere deep within his soul, he heard himself say, "Get away from her, you sick bastard. I'll give you anything you want. Just leave her alone. Name your price."

Anna looked at him with horror. "Dad, what are you doing?"

Still pinned to the mantel Nigel felt the back of his head. He waved his hand at Richard. "Blood, look at that," he said triumphantly. Then he muttered, "you just put the nail in your own coffin, asshole. Say good-bye to her today because it's the last time you'll see your little baby for a long time. She's mine now, and I'll never let her go. There's nothing you can do to buy me out. I just married a fucking gold mine."

Anna raced over to the two of them. "Dad," she cried, "get your hands off him." She pulled them apart and threw her arms around Nigel. "Come on, we'd better get to a hospital. You probably need stitches." She led him to the door, but before she walked out she turned around and faced her father. "I don't think it would be a good idea for you to call me for a long time. What you did here today was unconscionable. I'll call you when I feel I can forgive you."

The hot rays of the morning sun still poured over his face. *When she can forgive me—Christ,* Richard thought to himself, *was I that head-strong when I was her age?* But time had passed quickly, and here he was, three years later and they had not spoken a single word.

Richard glanced down at his watch. It was nearly 10:00 A.M. He had promised Constantine to deliver the contracts before the start of his 9:00 A.M. staff meeting. He thought about the envelope in his car. The last remaining ships that had belonged to his wife were being sold for scrap metal. He had inherited them when she died, and now, like signing off on the last tangible remnant of her life, he was using his signature to say goodbye to her once again. It wasn't a happy time for him, but thinking about how Constantine was by now ranting and raving in his office looking for those papers somehow made him feel a lot better.

He jumped back into his car. Since the rush hour traffic had subsided, he pulled up at the world headquarters of SeaCorp Inc. within twenty minutes. Constantine's staff meeting was still in progress, but formalities and protocol were never Richard's strong point, so he burst in and seated himself in the last empty chair at the conference table.

Richard took off his jacket and whispered to the small, nervous-looking man next to him. "Hey, don't you guys believe in air conditioning? It's hotter than hell in here."

The nervous-looking man, looking even more unstrung than just a second ago, leaned over and whispered, "Sorry, Mr. Winters. The air conditioning went down this morning, but they're working on it."

"Well, well," Constantine said, "I see that my son-in-law can't help but continue to disrupt our meeting. I would appreciate it if you would find it in your heart to stop distracting my staff. There's still a lot of work to finish here."

"Yes, you're right. Sorry," Richard answered. "I just wanted to drop off these contracts. I didn't mean to disrupt anything." He stood up and handed the envelope to Constantine.

"And here I thought this gesture of joining my staff meeting meant that you actually might have taken an interest in your wife and your daughter's business?"

"No," he said as he headed for the door, "I have no interest in it at all."

"Well, if you did, maybe you'd have something to talk to your daughter about, but I guess it's too late for that."

Richard stopped and turned around. "Let's take this conversation into your office."

The staff of SeaCorp squirmed in their seats as they watched the two men go into the adjoining office.

Once inside, Richard slammed the door behind him. He ran his hands through his hair and clenched his fists together. Then, in an explosion of rage, he shouted, "Can't you just give me a break, just one fucking break? I mean, once, just once, I'd like to have a normal conversation with you."

Constantine sat down at his desk. He was sweating heavily. He took off his jacket and loosened his tie. "What do you want from me, Richard? That after all these years I call you "son" and you call me "daddy"? I think you've been smoking too many of those marijuana cigarettes of yours."

"I don't smoke pot. I never smoked pot. You don't even know me. You never even wanted to."

Constantine pulled out a handkerchief and wiped his forehead. "I don't have time for this. I'm a busy man and, at the moment, very tired. Besides, what are you doing here, arguing with me, whining like a little baby about a relationship we'll never have? What's really bothering you is the fact that you haven't spoken to your daughter in over three years. You should be calling her. Maybe she needs you more than you think. You should have tried to understand why she married that man. Maybe your relationship with her had something to do with that."

"What do you mean, 'my relationship'? You raised her, not me. If anyone had anything to do with it, it was you."

Constantine stood up and leaned against his desk. "You arrogant fool. How could you blame me for your problems? Take some responsibility for your actions. You're her father. Maybe if you had spent more time with her …"

"I spent plenty of time with her."

"Then why did she have the need to marry a man almost twice her age?"

"I don't know why," Richard shouted.

"Then it's your responsibility to find out." He held his head for a moment and looked down.

Richard watched Constantine for a moment. He looked much paler than usual. Richard was sure that he could see him swaying from side to side. "Hey, old man," he said. "You don't look good. Why don't you sit down? I'll get you some water."

Richard filled a glass with water from the pitcher on the desk. He handed it to Constantine, who reached for it with both hands. Suddenly, the glass dropped to the floor and Constantine clutched his chest. Within an instant, he fell forward. Richard reached out with both arms to break his fall but they both crashed to the floor.

Richard yelled for help. Within seconds, the door burst open and twenty or more double-breasted suits came flooding in.

"Somebody call an ambulance," Richard shouted. He quickly rolled out from underneath Constantine and turned him on his back. He felt for a pulse, but nothing. He looked at the crowd. "CPR! Does anybody know CPR?"

None of the double-breasted suits said a word. *Oh God*, Richard thought, *it's up to me.* He started talking to himself. "I've read about this. I can do it, I can do it." He pulled Constantine's chin up and pinched his nose. "Two breaths, one, two—now how many chest compressions? Five or fifteen? Fuck it, I'll do fifteen." He put his palms against Constantine's chest and started pumping. "One and two and three and...." He checked for a pulse again. Nothing. He continued through another rotation, and another. After what seemed like an eternity, one of the suits who was kneeling down besides the body said, "I feel a pulse."

Richard immediately stopped what he was doing and sat back. He held Constantine's hand and waited for the paramedics to arrive. He rode with him in the ambulance. It was only after the doctors in the emergency room assured him that his father-in-law was going to be all right, that he allowed himself to feel the pain of what this loss would have meant. Then he cried, harder than he had for the loss of his wife, because this time, what was left of the family he knew he couldn't live without, would truly all have been gone.

Richard clung tightly to his paper cup, occasionally sipping what was left of his cold coffee. The waiting room outside the intensive care unit was empty except for him and Beatrice. He watched her as she sat and read her magazines, and wondered how she managed to keep her composure. He knew very little about her. She was always just a fixture next to Constantine. She never said very much, or maybe she didn't have very much to say. Who knew?

A doctor came out of Constantine's room. "Mr. Winters," he said, "your father-in-law's awake, and he'd like to see you. Please, keep in mind that it's been less than an hour since his angioplasty, so he's a little tired. But overall he's doing fine. He should be ready to go home in a couple of days."

Richard walked in and gave Constantine a smile. "Glad to see you're all right, old man."

"Why did you do it, Richard?" he asked. "You finally had your chance. I could have been out of your life for good. You could have just let me die."

Richard moved closer and knelt down beside the bed. "Why did I do it? That's a ridiculous question. You're my family, and, like it or not, we'll always be stuck with each other. Besides, if you were gone, there would be nobody left whose sole purpose in life was to undermine and emasculate me at every opportunity."

"I hope you don't really think that's all I'm good for."

"No, and I don't mean to make a joke of this whole thing. When you were lying on the floor, not breathing, I felt my whole world crashing down around me. You must realize that, through all the insults and constant name-calling, I respect and admire you more than anyone I've ever met. Look at you, Constantine. Look at the life you've built from nothing. It took guts, courage and a genius that most of us can only dream of."

"And you, Richard: you did the same."

He shook his head.

"Why do you hate yourself so much? Why can't you let yourself be happy? Are you still trying to punish yourself for something that happened so long ago?"

"You can't tell me you still don't hate me for marrying your daughter? That maybe she'd still be alive today if it weren't for me?"

"Is that what you think? No, Richard. Sara was just not meant to be on this earth for a long time. She had a weak heart that nobody knew about. But she left us a precious gift, one that shouldn't be neglected. That's what I'm angry about. Your daughter, Sara's daughter, needs you right now. It's not too late to make up for some of that lost time."

"What do you mean, she needs me? Is Anna unhappy?"

"It's difficult to tell. She doesn't confide in me about her marriage. But something's wrong and she needs someone to talk to."

Just then, the door opened slightly. A beautiful face surrounded by a mass of curly hair peered through. "I know I'm not supposed to be here, but I told the nurse outside that you're my uncle, and she let me in."

Constantine motioned for her to enter. "Angela it's always comforting to see your radiant smile."

Richard stood up and made room for Angela to approach the bed. She took Constantine's hand and glanced at Richard. "I know I shouldn't be here but—"

Again, the door opened. "Grandpa, my God ..." A tear-stained Anna rushed to his bed.

"How could this happen? I told you to slow down. From now on, I'm going to handle everything. I won't allow you to step one foot into that office again."

"It didn't have anything to do with my work load," Constantine said. "I inherited some bad genes from my father. The doctors assured me they cleared it all up. I'll be up and around by tomorrow, promise."

She smiled and put her hand on his cheek. "I love you, Grandpa." Then, as if feeling two sets of eyes penetrating her skull, she turned around. "Dad, Mrs. Moore. This is a surprise."

Richard looked deeply into his daughter's eyes. She aged a lifetime since he last saw her. Something was wrong. He realized that it was time to set aside their differences. Constantine was right. She needed his help.

"Anna," he said, opening his arms to her, "I'm sorry it took this for us to see each other again."

Anna paused, then stared at the two of them. "Me, too," she said. "But I'm glad you're here. I've been wanting to call you, but my pride always got the best of me."

"Me, too," Richard said. "I hope you can forgive me."

Her eyes began to fill with tears. "Forgive you? Oh Dad, there's so much I have to tell you."

It was time to come clean. If he expected his daughter to share her life with him, he had to start by telling her the truth about his. *No more lies,* he thought to himself. *It's time to face the consequences.*

He put two fingers to her lips. "I've never been honest with you, darling. I should tell you something first, and I hope you don't hate me for it."

"No, stop. Don't tell me anything." She glanced at Angela and then looked back at Richard. "Hmm," she said, "don't the two of you make a nice couple? What you said about the woman you were in love with? That she was married and had children? Am I on the right track?"

Richard took Angela's hand, and nodded.

Anna beamed. "This is the best news I've heard in a long time. I'm so happy for you." She engulfed them both in a huge hug.

It had been too long since he felt his daughter's arms around him. He closed his eyes and ran his fingers through her hair. "Oh Anna," he said, "I can't tell you how great that feels, but there's more to the story than you think—"

"It doesn't matter, Dad. I'm just glad you're happy."

"Then it's time for me to explain the whole thing."

"No, Richard," Angela said, her soft eyes becoming serious. "Let me. It's as much my story as it is yours." She took Anna's hand. "Come with me. We'll get some coffee and we can talk."

Anna gave her hand a gentle squeeze. "Yes, I'd like that," she said. She paused at the door. "Dad, Grandpa," she said. "I have to tell you, that as much as I'd like to stay in London indefinitely, I have to leave for New York tomorrow morning."

"Why so soon?" Richard asked.

"Some problem with one of the ships that just came in. After that, I have to fly out to South America again, another strike. Then I think it's off to—"

"We've got the picture. Now, just go with Angela. Your grandfather and I have some business to discuss."

When the door closed behind them, Richard turned to Constantine. "What is she running away from?"

"The question is *who? Who* is she running away from?"

"We know who—and you know what? For a guy who's not particularly smart, he's managed to have me by the balls way too long."

"You've let him. Tell me why Richard. Tell me the secrets you've been keeping all these years, and I'll tell you something right now too. This old heart is beating now for one reason, one reason only, to make sure that your daughter is happy again. And there's only one way *that's* going to happen. When Nigel Taylor is wiped off the face of this earth."

Richard smiled down at his father-in-law. "Glad to see we finally have something in common." He pulled up a chair. "Now, let's talk business."

Chapter 11

THE NEXT DAY

"**O**h, please," Anna said, when she entered her New York apartment, "don't clean up after yourself on my account."

Without as much as even glancing in her direction, Nigel answered, "Don't worry. I wasn't planning to." He lay down on the sofa and lit up a joint. Her trip to London had been short—too short, he thought. He hadn't expected her home so quickly, and he knew, from the tone of her voice on the phone, that something wasn't right.

"If you don't like the way things look around here," he said, "you'd better think about staying somewhere else. I can't be bothered with mundane things like housekeeping when I'm composing."

"Oh, is that what you call the offensive noise you've been producing lately?" She looked around the room. In the two days that she'd been gone, he managed to turn her beautiful Park Avenue penthouse into a garbage dump. "I'll call the housekeeper," she said while picking up empty cartons of Chinese food. "In the meantime, I'd appreciate you doing me a small favor."

"What's that?" he asked while taking in a long drag of his cigarette.

She stared at him in disgust. "Start packing your bags. It's time for you to move out."

Nigel sat straight up. "Whoa, luv," he said. "Why so hostile?" He looked at the joint in his hand. "Okay, okay, I'll put it out. Don't be such a hard-ass."

She looked at him in disbelief. "It's not the dope, you idiot. It's you— it's us—we're over."

"Come on, luv," he said. "What's eating you? We're great together. You know that."

"How can you say that with a straight face? You've been lying to me since the day we met. We never had a relationship. It was all some sick game of revenge to you." She stopped and watched him cringe. "Oh ... what? ... did I shock you? Maybe it's time you knew that I know your whole pathetic story. My father told me everything ... about Angela ... about Dylan's death ... your blackmailing him ... everything."

Nigel was speechless. He tried desperately to think of some sort of rebuttal, but nothing came to mind.

Anna continued. "I can't believe I've been so stupid all these years. I tried to rationalize all your odd behavior, your drugs, the strange music."

She continued talking but Nigel could no longer hear her. He was lost in his own thoughts. How could this have happened? It just couldn't be over. There must be something he could do or say ... but what?

He thought about his life—it was perfect. He had a trusting, workaholic wife and the world's most colossal bank account at his disposal. He had worked long and hard to get to this point. The manipulation, the lies, the blackmail — it wasn't easy. Then there was the marriage to Miss Pollyanna—that took a lot more effort than he had originally thought. Actually, it wasn't Anna herself that was difficult to live with, it was a life devoid of all of his favorite toys—that was the hard part. At first, he didn't miss them. He substituted the dope for a legion of cigarettes and a repository of alcohol, and the rest, well, finding total abstinence intolerable, he discreetly snorted and injected in other people's bathrooms and back offices. But as the months went by, his daily cravings began to return, and this time, with a vengeance. So, it wasn't long before he began to give in, slowly at first, and then, as if trying to make up for lost time, it became part of his daily routine.

To his credit, Anna didn't catch on right away. He was careful to indulge in his habits while she was out of the apartment—which wasn't particularly onerous since she practically lived in her office or at some foreign hotel. But, as time passed, he became sloppy. He began to forget where he would leave the bottles and vials.

It was the prescription pills that she found first. However, at that point, he was still quick on his feet. He explained to her that composing music stimulated him so much that he needed the pills to help him sleep at night. Unfortunately, he also explained, the pills made him sleep so well, that he needed a stimulant to keep him awake during the day.

His flimsy excuses satisfied her curiosity for a while but as the evidence against him continued to accumulate, he just, flat out, ran out of stories. *Christ*, he smirked, *I have to admit, some of those stories were plain genius. Homer himself couldn't have woven more brilliantly executed tales for a sequel to the* Odyssey.

"Excuse me," Anna shouted. "What on earth do you find so funny? I've been standing here for the last half hour calling you every four letter word ever created, and you have the nerve to have a smirk on your face. You are truly the most abhorrent person alive."

"Sorry, luv," he said. "Didn't realize I was smirking."

Anna shuddered. "Listen to me Nigel. I have some business to take care of for the next couple of weeks. After that, I'm going to Venice for Jackie's wedding."

"Oh, right, Venice, yea, that'll be great. Forgot all about Jackie and Christian. The wedding ... we'll take a gondola ride, listen to some romantic music, maybe we could get to know each other again."

"What? You actually think you're coming? Are you on another planet? Get this through your head. We're finished. I'm going to call my lawyer before I leave for Venice and have him draw up the papers. In the meantime, I want you out of here."

Lawyer, divorce. So this was it. It was going to end. There was nothing he could do. She knew the truth and even the richest, most intricately fabricated tale wouldn't satisfy her now. He knew that look of determination on her face and frankly, he was too tired to fight it. Besides, the whole situation was beginning to bore him anyway. It was time to move on. Time to get some alimony, maybe a couple of the apartments and the villa, and find his next target.

He looked straight into her eyes. "I'm not going to fight you Anna, or try to explain anything. It's too late for all that. So, why don't we just cut to the chase. Have your lawyer meet with my lawyer and we can discuss the terms for the alimony and division of property."

"What do you mean division of property and alimony? You don't own anything and I'm not asking you for any money. I just want this over."

"No luv. You don't understand. The alimony would be for me. And as for the property, didn't you ever hear of community property? You know, half of what you earned since we were married would go to me."

"Yes," she sighed in a somewhat defeated tone, "that would be true if we were married in New York," she stopped and grinned, "but we weren't. We were married in Greece where community property isn't even in the vocabulary. And, my darling, since all of the court judges are personal friends of my grandfather, it wouldn't be a good idea for you to sue for alimony. They'd rather throw your pathetic ass in jail than give you a penny of his money."

She disappeared into the bedroom and emerged a moment later holding a suitcase. "You have three weeks to pack your things and get out. I'll be at my father's apartment. You can have my calls forwarded there." She slammed the door behind her.

Nigel sat alone in the living room for a little while. He was amazed at how calm he felt. His bottomless supply of money was about to run out, and, for some strange reason, he didn't flinch. *Maybe it was inevitable,* he thought. *Maybe it was time to move on.* He never did like the fact that it was somebody else's money that he spent so lavishly. He always detested having to ask her permission to buy the big items. Although she rarely ever said "no" to the new homes and cars, he was still somewhat bothered by the fact that she denied him the Euro Disney replica that Michael Jackson tried to sell him for their ranch in Texas —*The bloody kill-joy,* he thought, *I might as well have been living in a monastery.*

He walked over to Anna's desk and rummaged through the drawers. *Now, where would she keep it?* he thought.

Maybe the marriage was over but the Stavropoulos fortune was still fair game—and he deserved part, if not all, of it. But he wouldn't be greedy. A few hundred million would suffice. He worked for it. He put in his time. Three years of marriage to Her Royal Heiress was the definition of punishment itself—living like a monk, starved of the things he needed to foster his creative energy.

He continued to rummage, and, after a few moments, he saw it, under a pile of folders— her private phone book. *All I need is a little help from someone who despises that family as much as I do.* He went directly to the "P's." *Now, what was that little shit-assed Greek kid's name?* He ran his finger down the page, *"Paskos? ... no ... Palakos? ... no ... ahhh ... there it is ... Patras. Andreas Patras. Time to give my new friend a little call.*

Chapter 12

VENICE

It came as no surprise when, a year earlier, Jackie announced that she and Christian were getting married. All their friends knew it long before they did. They had been inseparable from day one. Although sex attracted them to each other, they came, much to their amazed joy, to a deeply spiritual love.

From the day of her announcement, Jackie made it clear that she wanted the actual wedding to take place in Venice. She had always dreamed of walking down the isle of the world's most magnificent basilica, wearing a dress made of the finest Venetian lace, while the man she loved waited for her beneath a domed ceiling adorned by the mosaics of the greatest masters of the 11th century.

Richard insisted that no expense be spared, and as a wedding gift, handed the couple a check with enough zero's on it to cover their wedding plus the next royal coronation in England. Five hundred of their closest friends and relatives were flying in on private jets from all over the world. Once there, they were offered first class accommodations at some of the world's finest hotels and inns.

Jackie arranged for the wedding party and immediate family to stay at what she considered the most elegant hotel in Venice. Originally built in the 15th Century for the reigning Doge, the Avanti Palace was restored and converted into a world-class luxury hotel at the turn of the 20th century. Each room was adorned with frescos and marble columns and the lobby and grand ballroom, where the reception was to take place, had gilded archways, domed ceilings with dazzling chandeliers of Murano glass, and paintings by the Renaissance masters Tintoretto and Veronese. And, because it was situated right on the Grand Canal, every window throughout the Palace had a breathtaking view of the majestic waterways and ornate bridges.

Anna was asked to be Maid of Honor. She got there three days early, before the crowds and inevitable rush of paparazzi. She needed some time to herself, to rest and pull her thoughts together. More important, she needed to talk to Jackie. Her break up with Nigel had caused her more pain than she dared believe. She felt as if something were slowly falling apart from somewhere deep within her soul. She was always so confident in her judgment of people and decisions in life, and this mistake was unraveling the foundation of her spirit. She couldn't understand how it happened. How could something she was so certain of, have gone so wrong?

After their initial day of shopping and taking care of wedding details, they finally sat down to talk. They seated themselves at an outdoor cafe along the embankment of the canal. It was a hot day in August and the sounds of tourists bartering for trinkets from the local merchants could be heard all around them. Over three cups of cappuccino, Anna relived the break-up of her marriage. And, seeing the pain in her friend's eyes, Jackie held her hands from across the table and assured her that the past was over.

"You shouldn't loose faith in your judgment," Jackie said with tears forming in her eyes. "He had set out to deceive you from the start. It wasn't your fault. And besides, I think you were a bit vulnerable at that point. You didn't realize it, but you needed someone in your life. Unfortunately, he was the wrong someone."

Anna took out a tissue from her purse and handed it to Jackie. "Look at you," she said with tears in her eyes too, "these are supposed to be the happiest days of your life and I'm making you cry over my problems."

Jackie patted her eyes with the tissue. "You're right," she said, "and I'll only forgive you on one condition."

"Anything," she answered.

"For the next few days I want you to forget about Nigel, your marriage ... and your business." Her eyes became bright again and she gave Anna a devious smile. "We're going to have a blast, like the old days, just me, you, my brothers and sister ... we're going to get wasted, dance in the streets, and stay up till all hours. Are you with me?"

"Well, just one problem."

"What?

"What about Christian? What are you planning on doing with him?"

Jackie laughed. "Oh, I suppose we'll have to invite him too."

"Okay, then. I'm with you." She paused for a moment and then, in a more somber tone, continued. "Before we hit the bars, there's just one more thing I have to ask you."

"What?"

"I need to know how you feel about my father. I know you must be angry at him for what happened—"

Jackie cut her off. "Let's not ruin the moment by over analyzing my feelings for your father right now. Suffice to say that I'm angry and hurt. My father didn't deserve to be deceived by my mother and your father, but the reality is, people are hurt in relationships every day. Anna, I miss my Dad, and maybe he wouldn't have died if he wasn't drunk and distracted by those pictures and all. But that's only maybe. It was an accident, and accidents just happen."

"Do you think you could ever forgive them?"

"I have no choice. How could I live the rest of my life without forgiving my mother? And as for your father, well, he makes my mother so happy ... happier than I've ever seen her in my entire life. I'm sure I'll learn to appreciate him as time goes by. But I still wish my dad were here though. I wish I at least could have said goodbye."

Anna's eyes welled up with tears. "I'm sorry Jackie. If there's any way I could help, you know you could just ask."

Jackie handed Anna back her tissue and smiled. "There is something you could do to help you know. You could stop talking about this. Let's make a pact to only talk about fun things from this moment on ... like ... uhm ... getting you a new haircut, and maybe a manicure and a new sexy dress from Armani's."

"Are you trying to tell me something?"

"Well, now that you've mentioned it, or I should say I've mentioned it, you could use a little pampering you know. Your eyes look tired and," she reached over the table and touched Anna's head, "when's the last time you brushed your hair? There's this great hairdresser at the hotel, Leonardo, claims to be a direct descendent of Leonardo Da Vinci ..."

"All right," Anna said, "I get the hint. Lead the way."

They paid the bill and walked along the concrete embankment toward the hotel. Jackie glanced at her watch and quickened her pace.

"I just remembered," she said, "Joseph and Ian should be coming in at any moment. Come on, hurry along."

Anna remained silent. She had forgotten about Ian, and his wife. To make matters worse, Jackie had made him her partner for the church service. *How uncomfortable is that going to be?*

"Come on," Jackie said anxiously, "you're falling behind. The rehearsal's at six sharp. I want to get you set up with Leonardo so I can help my brother's unpack."

Yes, Leonardo, Anna thought as she looked at her watch. She had no idea who he was but he had three hours to make her look as if she'd just stepped out of the hottest fashion magazine in Italy.

The cafes along Saint Marks Square were busy with the evening rush of tourists. Anna had underestimated Leonardo's passion for perfection and found that she was falling late for the rehearsal. Upon reaching the vast concrete plaza which outstretched before the basilica, she began running and watched euphorically as the thousands of ubiquitous pigeons made a desperate dash to escape her onrushing footsteps; leaping furiously into the air, leaving nothing behind but a perfectly clear horizontal path in her wake.

The family had already gathered at the main entranceway of Saint Mark's Basilica. Above them loomed the great central spire with the sculpture of the Evangelist Saint Mark and the angels which climb towards him on their way to heaven.

Upon reaching the group, she stopped short and looked at Jackie. "Am I late?" she asked breathlessly?

"Yes, but don't worry. Ian and Joseph aren't here yet."

Beneath the shadow of the arched doorway, Anna spotted Richard. She walked over to hug him when, all of a sudden, she stepped back with some alarm. "Dad, what happened to your arm?"

Richard stood beside Angela with his right arm bound tightly in a multicolored sling. Underneath, was a plaster cast extending from his elbow to his wrist. He shrugged his shoulders and looked down at his injury, "Oh, this? It's just a broken arm. Nothing to worry about. I was in a bit of a boating accident."

"What? You hate boats. What on earth were you doing?"

"Since your grandfather was in the hospital, he asked me to take care of some business for him on Xenos. I was there for a couple of days, got bored, and decided to take one of his speed boats out for a spin. Basically, I hadn't a bloody clue as to what I was doing. So there I was, just driving along and wham ... out of the blue, there was this sand bar. Felt like I hit a bloody wall. It knocked me off my feet and I came crashing down hard on this arm. Anyway, lucky for me I wasn't going too fast. Who knows what could have happened."

"You're right," Anna said while she hugged him, "even the most experienced sailors get caught off guard by uncharted sand bars and often, the result isn't pretty." She patted him on the back, "Please, from now on, just stick to the things you know."

Jackie interrupted. "Here they are, finally."

Anna turned and watched as Joseph and Ian approached the group. It had been a long time since she'd seen him, and for a moment she felt as if all the air in her body had been taken away. She stood there, motionless, watching him get closer. How could he have grown more beautiful?—his deep blue eyes even more penetrating—and the rest of him, his hair, his skin—so soft that she just wanted to reach over and let the palms of her hands glide gently over his face. All at once, she was distracted with the sound of Jackie's voice.

"Come on everybody," she said. "Let's not waste more time. Get inside."

Anna let the others go ahead of her into the basilica. She paused and took a deep breath. She gazed at the mosaic above the door. There, in rich tones of gold, red, and blue, sat Jesus Christ. On his shoulder rested the crucifix on which he was hung.

"Beautiful, isn't it?"

She knew the sound of his voice. Still gazing upward she sighed. "Yes, Ian, it is."

"It's called 'Judgment of the World,'" he said as he took her arm and led her through the door. "Appropriate, don't you think?"

Almost to the point of being ironic. "How do you think you and I would be judged at this moment?"

"I suppose it depends on a lot of things. What we've done in the past, how we live our lives, maybe even what we're thinking as we pass through these doors."

She put her arm around his waist and began to walk. "Then I suppose I won't be seeing much sunlight in the afterlife."

Ian stared straight ahead. "Nor will I, I'm afraid."

After the rehearsal, the group gathered back at the hotel for cocktails on the verandah of the main dining hall. Champagne was flowing freely, and after her second glass, Anna got up the nerve to approach Ian. He was standing alone; up against the wrought iron rail that separated the verandah from the dark waters of the canal. She watched him as his eyes followed a passing gondola.

"You look breathtaking tonight," he said, without looking at her.

"Thank you," she said, although she knew she did. Leonardo had performed wonders; pulling her long dark hair back, away from her face—accentuating her large, oval eyes, and full red lips. But, she didn't stop there. She still had enough time to stop at the nearby boutique and pick up a black, ankle-length silk cocktail dress with matching thin-strapped sandals. She had set out to devastate the crowd tonight, and she did just that. She leaned her back against the rail, and after taking another long sip of her champagne, decided to ask him a question that had been plaguing her all evening. "I was wondering. Isn't your wife going to be here?"

"No, she's not," he said. He paused for a moment, but before Anna had time to respond, he continued, "we're not married anymore. Our divorce was finalized last week."

She didn't know if she felt shocked, elated, or both. "This is a surprise," she said. "I had no idea."

"No? It was in all the tabloids last week. Can't imagine you missed the eloquent headlines: 'Hollywood Hunk Gets Dumped'."

Right. Ian Moore, Hollywood's latest golden-boy. She had almost forgotten about his meteoric rise to the top. "Guess I did," she said, "I'm sorry. I can't believe Jackie didn't mention it either."

"We're all so wrapped up in our own worlds right now that other people's problems don't seem very important."

She saw his eyes soften, and at that moment, she saw him as the seventeen-year-old boy that she met on Xenos ten years ago. She remembered how they forged a friendship that they promised, no matter what, they would never break. "That's not true, Ian. Your problems are very important to me. Tell me: are you all right?"

He nodded. "Yes, I'm all right. It was hard though, as I'm sure you know. I heard you just went through the same thing."

"Actually, mine's not quite over—"

He put his drink down on the ledge of the gate. "Come on. Let's not talk about this here. Let's go take a walk, or a gondola ride, or both."

Anna shrugged. "I'm all yours."

They held hands as they walked slowly along the quiet cobblestone streets of San Polo. Ian explained to Anna that his wife had left him while they were shooting a film together in Los Angeles. The film, originally scheduled for completion in two months, dragged well into four. In the meantime, the Hollywood scene began to gnaw at his sanity. He despised the sycophants and feigned affectations of the Hollywood elite. He became homesick for England and his family, and began to count the days when he could return.

In the meantime, his wife was thriving. She loved the night life, the parties, and the slobbering admirers. She couldn't get enough of the attention from the press and even posed for the paparazzi. She gave interviews to whoever asked: the tabloids, fashion magazines, and television talk shows. The word "overexposure" was nowhere to be found in her vocabulary. To prove her point, she granted *Playboy* a four-page spread for their "Hot Hollywood Babes" issue.

When the film shoot was over, she begged Ian not to return to England. She told him that the only way to succeed in the entertainment industry was to move to Los Angeles. But for him, his career in acting meant more than just staring in big budget Hollywood movies. He still had a passion for the stage and smaller, more meaningful films.

They had reached an impasse, and neither of them would budge. Then, one afternoon, she walked into the house they had rented on Malibu beach, packed her suitcase and left — without as much as one "goodbye." Two days later he was served a letter from her lawyer demanding a divorce. They returned to London the next day and signed the necessary papers. She walked out of their lawyer's office and boarded the next plane for L.A. Only a few days later, he read in a London tabloid that she had married Hollywood insider Zachary Landauer; the five foot tall, bald, mega-producer of Hollywood's last two highest-grossing blockbusters.

"So, does that come close to rivaling your story?" he asked Anna.

She laughed softly. "Quite close," she said, "although my story hasn't hit the tabloids yet."

A comfortable silence fell between them as they locked arms and continued to walk. They could hear their footsteps echoing through the stucco buildings and they listened as the waters of the canal lapped gently against the embankments. They stopped in the middle of a small ornate bridge suspended over the Rio di Palazzo.

Pointing straight ahead, Anna said, "Do you see that bridge over there?"

"Yes," Ian answered. "The baroque one."

His knowledge of art and architecture always amazed her. "It's called the 'Bridge of Sighs'. It once connected the Ducal Palace with the prisons. Prisoners were lead over it before they were to appear in court. It was their last chance to see the water from those three lighted windows above. It was said that, as they passed, the town could hear them sighing for their lost freedom."

"It's all so amazing, isn't it? This place ... such beauty ... it's a testament to the glory of the heavens, don't you think?"

"In what way?"

"In that such beauty could only have been created by Divine Inspiration."

Those words touched her. She knew they came from somewhere deep within him. She loved the way he thought about life; always searching and appreciating its beauty and wonder. In all the time she knew him, material objects never interested him—it was always the people he met, the things he read and the places he saw. And now, now that his career made him rich and famous, and he had all the money in the world at his disposal, the only place he wanted to be was with his family.

She looked at him as the small lighted windows from the palace cast a golden reflection on his face. "Ian," she said hesitantly, "remember when we were teenagers, that night on the beach. Tell me the truth, why didn't you want to try to make it work between us? Do you think we would have been that bad together?"

"Bad? No."

"Then what?"

"I think we had to live our lives and make all our mistakes. Otherwise we never would have known—"

"Known what?"

He turned to her. "Do I have to say it? We never would have known how much we really loved each other."

Anna felt her body weaken. He had said what she was thinking. She wanted to say something, but couldn't.

Gently, Ian held her neck between the palms of his hands. "Maybe I was wrong, Anna. Maybe I never should have let you leave me. I don't know. I was afraid of a lot of things too."

She studied his face and saw the pain in his eyes. "What do you mean?"

"I was afraid that I could never measure up to your father, or give you the things you were used to in life. I was the son of a carpenter for Christ's sake—and you, you lived in another world, one filled with yachts, mansions, private planes. I was afraid you'd just get tired of me."

"Get tired of you? Listening the sound of your voice, feeling you in my arms, watching you smile ..." she sighed, "I don't think I could ever grow tired of you. Maybe you were right back then. Maybe we were too young to commit to each other, but not now. I don't want to waste another moment of my life without you. Don't say no. Come with me, share your life with me."

They brought their lips together, and in one, long passionate kiss, erased all the years they'd been apart. A short while later they were in Ian's bed; their bodies furiously entwined in a mad rush of passion. Anna could feel her body soaring and moving with his and in that instant, knew that all the mistakes she had made in the past were made for a reason: to be here, in Ian's arms, and to know, unequivocally, that he had been her destiny all along.

They fell asleep in each other's arms. In the morning, Anna watched Ian as he slept. She watched his chest rise and fall with every breath he took, and she wished she could close her eyes and become part of his dreams.

She walked to the window and opened the shutters. Sunlight streamed in to fill the room with a gentle orange glow.

"Good morning," she heard Ian say.

She returned to bed and covered herself with the satin sheets. She smiled and ran her fingers through his hair. "It's hardly morning anymore."

Ian took her hand and kissed it. Then, while staring into her eyes, he said, "Thank you, for last night, and for loving me ..."

A knock on the door interrupted them. Ian ignored it until he heard the sound of his mother's voice. He quickly got up, threw on his trousers, and opened the door.

"Darling," Angela said, "I'm sorry to bother you but Richard's been going crazy looking for Anna. She wasn't in her room all night, and since the two of you left early last night, I thought, well," she peered through the door, "maybe you'd know where she is?"

Anna threw on Ian's shirt and came to the door. Without even realizing it, she slipped her arm around Ian's waist. "You can tell my Dad you found me. But, why the sudden panic? It's not the first time I haven't been home all night."

"No," Angela answered, "that's not what he was worried about. It seems as though your office has been trying to reach you all morning. They managed to find your father, and told him it has something to do with that old friend of yours, Andreas Patras. Seems as if he wants to see you in London first thing Monday morning. He said it was urgent."

Anna's face fell. How could that name ruin such a perfect day? "Whatever it is, it can wait," she said. "I don't want to be bothered with business right now. Jackie's wedding is tomorrow, and I have a glorious day in Venice ahead of me. Please tell my Dad I'll ring him later, all right?"

"All right, darling," Angela answered. She looked at the two of them and sighed. "You both look radiant, you know. I'm so happy for you. I've watched you since you were children. I always knew you belonged together. I'm glad you finally figured that out too."

Ian bent over and kissed her on the cheek. "Thanks, Mom. That means a lot to me."

A few moments later, the two of them were alone again. Anna walked back to the window. She stared at the afternoon sky and watched the pigeons fly lazily overhead.

Ian walked up behind her and put his arms around her waist. "Are you all right?" he asked her.

"Yes, I'm just a little concerned about that call from Andreas. Whatever he wants, well—it just can't be good."

Ian kissed her neck. "Come on," he said, "forget about it right now. Let's go get some coffee on the Piazza and then, maybe, a gondola ride that lasts the rest of the afternoon."

"Hmmm," she said as she leaned back into his arms, "that sounds great."

But forgetting about Andreas wasn't going to be easy. A sick feeling had developed in her stomach that wasn't going to go away. Why now?

Why the sudden interest in her? His last attempt to destroy her empire had been a miserable failure. *He must have learned some new tricks and I'd bet even the great Houdini would have hard time figuring them out.*

"Come on," she heard Ian say, "let's get moving."

"All right," she said as she reached for her clothes, which were still strewn all over the floor.

Ian bent down to help her. "You can't stop thinking about it, can you?"

"No, It doesn't make sense. Something's not right. I haven't heard from him in what … five years? So why now? Something's triggered him off, but what?"

"Maybe that's not the question you should be asking," he said as he handed over her shoes. "Maybe it's not *what* triggered him off, it's *who*."

"You're right." She sighed. "It's *who*."

Chapter 13

MONDAY, 9:00 A.M.

Anna stared incredulously at the pencil-thin secretary guarding Andreas' office door. "What do you mean, 'Mr. Patras is running late?' He's the one who demanded a 9:00 A.M. meeting."

Like a pit-bull guarding her owner from rabid hounds, the secretary stood her ground. "Just like I said, Ms. Winters, Mr. Patras is not ready to see you yet. Please, take a seat in the lounge. I'll call you when he's through."

Anna glanced at her watch. It was already past 9:00. *Another one of Andreas' mind games.* Demand a meeting, then keep her waiting.

She slumped on the sofa in the lounge. She felt tired and put her head back, to rest. She thought about the wedding. Jackie had looked radiant, and Christian: in all the years she'd known him, she'd never seen him quite so euphoric. The music didn't stop until 5:00 the next morning. The crowd drank, ate, and danced until the sun began to rise. When she watched her father and Angela hold hands and gaze into each other's eyes like teenagers, she could be happy for them both, because she also finally knew what it was like to love someone.

But Ian, although she knew that every part of her body and soul loved him, and always had, he had hurt her once. *I have to learn to trust him again,* she thought, *and that will just take time. We were just children then.*

"Miss Winters ..."

Startled, Anna looked up. The secretary.

She pointed a bony finger in the direction of the door. "Mr. Patras will see you now," she said.

"How magnanimous of him," Anna mumbled as she followed the officious woman, who pointedly blocked the door before holding it open for her.

With trepidation, Anna approached the big desk. Andreas smiled. It had been a long time since she'd seen those large, even white teeth, and she felt herself shudder with revulsion.

He motioned for her to sit down. "Please Anna, have a seat. I took the liberty of having my secretary bring us some Greek coffee. You look like you could use a little right now."

He was right about that. She was so tired she couldn't remember the last time when she'd gotten more than two consecutive hours of sleep. She reached for the small demitasse cup filled with a black murk her grandfather called 1 percent water and 99 percent caffeine. She swallowed the muddy goo in one long gulp. Then, in the tradition of island fortune tellers, she turned the cup over on the saucer.

Andreas did the same. "My great-grandmother was one of the best fortune-tellers on Xenos. She passed a few of her secrets on to me. Shall I read our fortunes now or later?"

Feeling the caffeine rush enter her veins, Anna straightened and sat taller in her chair. "Please, Andreas. Let's just get on with things. Why don't you tell me what it is you dragged me in here for."

He grabbed her cup. "No, I think you need to learn some patience. Why don't I tell you what your cup says."

Anna watched him as he studied the inside of the cup where the coffee mud had hardened to form small lines on the ceramic.

He looked up and grinned. "The dark mark on the bottom tells me that your heart is heavy. And here," he pointed to the side of the cup, "these three lines show that you're conflicted over something or someone." He put the cup down and folded his hands. "Now tell me, Anna. What are you feeling conflicted over?"

Her eyes narrowed. "You're wasting my time."

"No, no. The cup never lies. I know what it is." He grabbed the morning's issue of the *London Star* and turned to the second page. "Look, it's a picture of you and your hillbilly boyfriend kissing on the verandah of your hotel. The two of you look so nice and cozy, trouble is, I'd say, the last I heard, you were still married to that other idiot, Nigel Taylor. My God, Anna, where are your morals?"

"You make me want to vomit. Morals? Look who's talking. You were lucky to find a good plastic surgeon to put your face back together. I can hardly see the scars from that night on the dock—and that's too bad. They would have been a good reminder of your own irreproachable moral standards, don't you think? Now, let's get down to business. You obviously didn't demand to see me to give me a slap on the wrist for infidelity."

The reminder of the car accident changed Andreas's mood from sarcasm to a serious intensity. He put the newspaper aside and took a file folder from his pencil drawer. "No, I didn't bring you here to talk about your love life. You should probably be talking to a psychiatrist about that anyway." He handed her the folder. "What I have here is hard and fast evidence on your recent drug smuggling endeavors, endeavors that relate to your shipping empire."

"What?" Anna grabbed the folder and began rifling through the pages.

"You'll find it's all there. The Swiss bank account numbers traced to your name, the top secret memorandums from your personal computer, the pictures of your crew unloading the contraband. It goes on and on."

"How did you get all this? This was all planted and you know it. You've been setting me up with someone on the inside of my company."

"I'm shocked that you'd accuse me of such a thing, my darling."

"Don't give me your innocent eyes, Andreas. You've tried this before and you failed, miserably. These documents don't mean anything. I can prove they're all phony. Besides there's nothing here with my signature on it, and even if there were, I'd be able to prove that it was forged."

Andreas sighed. "Do what you like, but the British authorities may see things differently. They'll go to great lengths to prove you wrong. That's what they do. They'll scour every one of your ships, scrutinize every phone call and bill ever produced from every one of your offices. Do you see where I'm going with this? You can't keep track of every staff or crew member you've ever had, and you know as well as I do that they're presented with temptations and opportunities every day, at every port. You see, I'm just providing the authorities with ammunition they need to do what they've always wanted to do to mammoth operations like yours: find illegal activity, fine the company an ungodly amount, and ultimately, shut them down."

Anna listened carefully, but she was already one step ahead. She knew he was right. The government would have a field day with what was in this folder. It would be years before she could prove her innocence, and in that time, something else might turn up, something that she and her grandfather hadn't been aware of. It was time to deal with Andreas—on his terms.

"So now what, Andreas? If you were so intent on seeing me shut down, you would have turned this folder over to the government already. You obviously have something else on your mind."

"You're a smart girl. Of course I have something else on my mind. I don't want to see you shut down. I want you to sell me your company, at a fraction of the cost that is. How about $10 million?"

"That's the cost of one ship. I own more than seventy ships. That's not selling you the company; that's giving you the company."

Andreas shrugged. "Giving, selling, whatever. The point here is, how can I say this gently? Uh, I know: how's 'you're fucked?' 'you don't have a choice?'" His smile broadened. "Let's face it. The last thing you want is to see your aging grandfather being dragged away in handcuffs; humiliated in front of his friends and family. And you, my luv? I'm afraid pinstripes wouldn't suit you either."

Anna shifted in her seat. She needed time to think. There had to be a way out.

Andreas spoke. "You look overwhelmed, my luv. I take it that for the first time in your charmed little life, you may actually be speechless?

Why, just yesterday, the only decision you had to make was, who was going to screw you? The hillbilly or the other loser with the guitar? And now, only 24 hours later, you have to make the biggest decision of your life: would you rather see the inside of a jail cell for twenty years or give away everything you and your grandfather ever worked for?"

Andreas was relentless. "You think you smell victory?" Anna said. "I don't think so. I think it's smoke coming from your head, which is about to explode from the huge ego you've developed."

"Don't say—"

"Don't interrupt me. I'm not finished yet. You went through all this trouble to avenge something that happened so many years ago? A bite on your face? If I'd known the extent of your depravity then, I'd have bitten off your dick instead. That would have made this whole game a lot more interesting." She got up.

Andreas looked annoyed. He hadn't expected this reaction. He called after her: "Anna, give me your decision. You know I don't make idle threats."

She turned around and stared at him. She looked at the folder in his hand. Her whole life was in there: her fortune, her strength, her identity. Andreas waved it in front of her. "You can't bear it, can you?" he said. "You can't bear the fact that I've won. You'd rather eat bread and water with mice and rats for the rest of you life than see me run your operation. Don't do it, Anna. Think about it first. I'll give you a week to come to your senses."

A week. What difference would that make? She would never sell him the ships. *Not on your life, Andreas. Not on your life, and I have one week to figure out just how to bury you for good.*

Chapter 14

PANAMA CANAL

Anna had no sooner stepped out of Andreas's office when her cel-
lular phone rang. She stabbed at the elevator button, then reached
into her purse and pulled out the phone. It was her secretary on the line.

"Miss Winters, sorry to bother you but Mr. Vlakas from chartering is
on the line holding for you. He said it was an emergency."

Another emergency, just what she needed. "Okay, put him on."

The doors to the elevator opened and she stepped in. She pressed the
express button to the lobby and waited for the sound of Vlakas's voice.

"Miss Winters?"

"Yes, Vlakas, I'm on the line. What's the emergency?"

"We got a call from the captain of your ship the Xenos. He's docked at
a port outside the Panama Canal. He said something about the ship not
being able to make it through the canal's restricted draft. Too heavy,
tilting, something like that."

"What do you mean 'something like that?'"

"Sorry, Miss Winters. That's all the information I have."

Anna bit her lip. Was Vlakas deliberately trying to irritate her or had he always been this incompetent? Maybe what she had mistaken for intimidation tactics had been sheer stupidity. She made a mental note to have him transferred to some remote dock in Alaska.

"Vlakas," she said, "tell my secretary to have the company jet ready at Heathrow in an hour."

"What should I tell her the destination is?"

She shook her head in disbelief. *My God, how could I have overlooked his incompetence all these years?* The elevator opened, and she stepped out into the marble lobby. "What kind of ridiculous question is that?" she snapped. "We have a ship stuck in Panama, so let's see: where will my destination be? Panama maybe? Christ, did you forget to put your brain in your head this morning?"

There was silence on the other end. She stepped out into the street and put her hand up to hail a cab. "Vlakas, are you still there?"

There was a pause. "Yes."

"Good, tell my secretary to track down Marcos Yannis. I want him to meet there. And Vlakas. ..."

"Yes?"

"You have a new assignment that will require a little traveling. I'd suggest you run out and buy yourself some new parkas and a heavy blanket. The winters are very long and cold where you'll be going." She hung up the phone.

Just as she had planned, Marcos Yannis met her in Balbao, a remote dock outside the Panama Canal. It was hot, and Anna was tired. She hadn't slept the entire way over. Actually, she couldn't remember the last time she'd slept at all.

Marcos briefed her on the situation. The ship's cargo had been loaded incorrectly, with too much weight distributed to the last holds. She quickly ordered the use of the Canal's floating crane and had the cargo load redistributed to the forward holds.

But, her mind was back in London, in Andreas's office. She replayed the events leading up to this point. Andreas's blackmail. How did he plant all that information? He must have had help, someone from the inside, but who? Vlakas maybe? No, he was too stupid. It had to be somebody else, somebody who had something to gain from watching her empire crumble.

But none of this mattered now. The damage had been done. It was up to her to figure out how to undo it. She had worked too hard to make her mark in this business to let Andreas take her operation away from her. Stavropoulos and Winters had become the leaders in the shipping world. The name Stavropoulos alone had become synonymous with strength, power, and worldwide fortune. Anna knew that the operation wasn't hers to sell or give away. It belonged to her grandfather, and, ultimately, her mother. She had inherited it by default, because of a tragedy that only the gods understood.

And now, because of some petty grievance nursed by a disturbed childhood friend, she could lose it all. She was tempted to ask her grandfather for help, but the stress might further weaken his already ailing heart. No, she had to do this alone. Besides, she knew this business better than anyone else. She had navigated the largest supertankers, overseen the loading and unloading of every conceivable cargo, crunched every number, balanced every book. There was nothing she didn't know. If anyone could find a way around Andreas Patras, it was going to be her.

But her troubles didn't end there. She thought about her apartment in New York. She wondered if Nigel had vacated it yet, but deep down she knew he hadn't. Her lawyers had sent out the divorce papers a week ago, only to receive a small fax in return that read: "Sorry, Mrs. Taylor. Too busy to read the papers. My new sound is hot. Can't wait for you to hear it. Nigel."

She couldn't figure him out. Was he so drugged up that he didn't know she'd demanded a divorce, or was this some kind of delaying tactic; a way to prolong her torment in an already agonizing marriage?

Nigel: he was an enigma to her. He had the capacity to charm and sweet talk his way into her life and then, almost overnight, become a repulsive caricature of the man she thought she had married. He could not desist from taunting her about her gullibility. Her father had been right about him from the start, but she wouldn't listen. She had to do it her way.

However, it was time to rid her life of Nigel. But that wasn't going to be easy. His fax made that perfectly clear. What did he want from her?

Love? Not an option. Money? Most likely. She would have to pay him off. Maybe another contract with S & A, or just a few million dollars. Whatever it would take, though he could prolong the divorce for years. That would put a noose around her neck, making it impossible to feel totally free to be with Ian.

Ian. His name alone made her feel more relaxed. Whatever ambivalence she felt about letting him into her life again was slowly melting away. She thought about him waiting for her back in London, and felt her body stir.

But now it was time to go back and face her adversaries head on. There was no reason for her to be in Panama. Marcos could easily have taken care of this mess without her. She had been running away, but in so doing, she had given herself a chance to think. It was time to clear out the shit in her life, messy as that would be. Andreas and Nigel lived life by their own codes where standards, morals, and ethics didn't apply. If she was going to enter their game, to have any chance of winning at all, she'd have to play by their rules, and maybe adopt some new ones of her own.

It was time to stop giving them the upper hand. She had to take control. Andreas was an annoying pest that needed exterminating, and Nigel—-well she hadn't quite figured out what to do about him.

She told Marcos that she would return to London before the ship was ready to enter the Canal. After all, Andreas had given her only a week to decide whether or not to sell him the company. She had less than six days left to develop a plan and put it into action.

Marcos volunteered to drive her to the airport. The air-conditioning in her rented car had broken down and they rolled down the windows to let in a breeze. The car sped along the curvy, palm-tree lines streets towards the airport. Marcos banged on the dashboard on occasion to see, if by some miracle, he could get some cool air to filter in through the vents.

"Don't bother Marcos," Anna said. "When I told the rental agency that I wanted a car with air-conditioning, I was amazed that they had one at all. I suppose I should have specified that I would have liked the unit to work." She glanced at him and gave him a sarcastic smile.

Marcos grinned. "I'm glad to see you smiling again," he said to her.

"You looked so serious this morning. Like the weight of the world was on your shoulders."

The air streaming into the car was hot and humid. She felt beads of sweat pouring down her neck and into her blouse. She piled her pony-tail on top of her head and wiped the sweat from her neck with a tissue she produced from her pocket. "No, the weight of the world isn't on my shoulders, just the weight of the company."

In an attempt to cool herself off, she stuck her head out the window and closed her eyes. She took a deep breath and pictured herself skiing down a steep snowy trail in Zermat, then ice skating along a frozen pond beneath the icy escarpments of the Matterhorn. Then she felt Marcos's hand tugging at her blouse.

"Put your head back in," he said sternly. "Some truck may come along and slice it right off."

She brought her head in and looked at him with some surprise. "Throw in a few curse words, and yours could have been the voice of my grand-father just then."

He looked straight ahead at the road. "Sometimes I feel that way about you."

"You mean you need to protect me like my grandfather would?"

"Someone has to keep your head from getting sliced off."

She reached over and touched his arm. "Thank you, Marcos. Thank you for helping me keep my head on."

When they reached the airport, Anna got out of the car and pulled her suitcase out of the trunk. Marcos grabbed it out of her hand and began walking towards the gate, where the company Learjet was standing by.

"Marcos, please, you don't have to put me on the plane. I'll be fine from here, really," Anna protested.

He put the suitcase down in front of the gate. "You're right. I'm sorry." He paused. "Before you go, there's something I wanted to tell you but—"

Anna realized that Marcos was dead serious, that whatever he wanted to say was very important to him. "So tell me: what is it?"

He hesitated. "I know this is none of my business, and it's probably of no importance to you but—"

"Tell me."

"Your husband, and Andreas. I just thought it was unusual for them to be seen hanging around together."

Andreas and Nigel hanging around together. They don't even know each other. "What are you talking about?"

He squinted behind his thick, black-rimmed glasses. "I was overseeing an operation in New York last week. You remember, the overloaded iron ore tanker that gave us so many problems? Anyway, one of Patras's ships was docked right next to yours. Seems as if it was having some problems too, big ones. Leaking crude oil all over the bay. Some heavy-duty environmental groups were having a fit. Word was that Patras himself was coming over from London to survey the damage."

"So what does this have to do with Nigel?"

"I'm getting to that. Sure enough, Patras shows up, meets with some officials, shakes some hands, and looks like he's about to leave, when, all of a sudden, a big black limo pulls up alongside his. The driver opened the rear door and, well, I couldn't believe it, but your husband got out. I thought, maybe he was coming to see your ship, but no. He headed straight over to Andreas. They talked for awhile, then he handed him a thick white envelope. Patras opened it, read something, and started laughing. He tossed the envelope into his limo, took out another envelope from the front seat, and handed it to your husband. Then they shook hands and left."

Anna was silent.

He shrugged. "I'm sure what I just told you means absolutely nothing, but, for the life of me, I couldn't figure out why your husband would have any kind of business with Patras. I mean, I'm sure he wasn't acting on your account, or your grandfather's. Something just didn't seem right."

It was all too clear. Nigel was the insider. He was the one who planted incriminating evidence against her. She was surprised that she hadn't thought of him before. He had access to everything: her personal computer in the apartment, her checkbooks, the billing records, her bank accounts—everything. He was too stupid to know how to use all these records himself, but with Andreas's help, they could fabricate any kind of documents they wanted.

And the envelope Andreas gave Nigel? A payoff, obviously. Nigel would do anything for the right price. She wondered who approached whom first, but it didn't matter. They both deserved to be together, maybe even burning in some place hotter than Panama in another life.

She kissed Marcos on both cheeks. She began boarding the jet waiting on the tarmac. She walked up the stairs and heard the sounds of the jet engines roaring to life. Before entering the plane, she turned around and saw Marcos standing on the tarmac, waving goodbye. She smiled, and, pointing to her head, yelled, "Thanks for saving my head again."

He pointed to his ears and mouthed, "I can't hear you."

The engines grew loader so she put her hand to her lips, blew him a kiss, and whispered, "Thank you, my friend."

Once in the plane, Anna took her seat, buckled her belt, and leaned back, to rest. She watched out the window as the jet taxied to the runway and took its place in line behind two jumbo jets also waiting for the signal to depart. She listened for a moment as the captain mumbled something about the flight's course and direction. Then, without realizing it, she had fallen into a deep sleep before the wheels of the plane even left the ground.

What seemed like only moments later, she was awakened by a tap on the shoulder. Her eyes felt so sticky from the dry, recycled air, that she had difficulty opening them. She blinked several times and tried to focus on the person standing over her.

"Miss Winters."

She instantly recognized the voice of the co-pilot. He tapped her on the shoulder again. "Miss Winters," he said, "I brought you some coffee. Looks like you could use some."

She rubbed her eyes and shook her head from side to side. Her eyes came into focus and she saw the co-pilot staring at her with some concern. "We'll be landing in about forty-five minutes. Thought you could use that time to freshen up."

She took the coffee with one hand and glanced at her watch. "Two hours," she said with alarm. "I can't believe I slept so long."

"No, Miss Winters, you've been asleep about fourteen hours. Flight zero, zero niner's getting ready to land at Heathrow in less than an hour."

"What!" She couldn't believe it. She looked at her watch again. "How could that be? When did we re-fuel?"

"Some time ago, fourteen hundred hours to be exact, London time that is." He turned to leave. "We've already started our descent and we're preparing for landing."

She knew she had been tired when she got in the plane, but she hadn't realized just how tired she was. She drank her coffee in three long gulps, reached for her bag and got out a brush and a mirror. As she looked into the mirror she began remembering bits and pieces of the dream she'd been having only moments ago. It was the same one she'd had as a child: falling down a mountain, seeing her mother at the top, trying desperately to claw her way back up to her. But this time, there were more people in the dream. Her father, and Ian, and Jackie, maybe even more. She couldn't remember. The other faces were blurry. Somebody was holding her hand, and they were all talking to one another. Even her mother, she was talking too. But what was she saying? Why couldn't she remember? A garbled voice over the intercom brought her back to reality.

"This is your captain. We'll be landing in approximately five minutes. Please make sure your belt is fastened and seat in its upright position."

Just as quickly as it had come, the dream left. *Oh, what do dreams mean anyway?*

Chapter 15

LONDON

Anna's limousine pulled up in front of her Chelsea townhouse, a three story-brownstone on Chayne Walk, a street known for its expensive dwellings and magnificent views of the Thames.

Sara and Richard lived there all the time they were married. After Sara's death, Richard just walked out, taking nothing with him. So he left the house in the capable hands of his former housekeeper, who took up permanent residence in a small room on the first floor. Anna was well into her teen years before she knew the house even existed. She visited it often. Richard realized that she had somehow bonded with walls and all of its contents, he gave it to her on her eighteenth birthday.

Anna loved how the house made her feel warm, somehow close to her mother. Although she renovated and refurbished it several times, she kept pieces that she knew had a special meaning to her mother. The pictures on the fireplace mantle remained untouched. They were Sara's favorites: Constantine, standing near the first ship he ever owned; Beatrice, holding tightly to her little baby on the day of her christening; and Sara, close to nine months pregnant, standing on the second floor balcony, smiling gently as she watched the children playing in the park across the street.

A bit weary from her long trip, Anna climbed up the steps to the front door. Opening it, she immediately felt comforted by the familiar smell of fresh brewed coffee and cinnamon potpourri.

She could hear the heels of her shoes clicking along the parquet floors as she walked toward the living room. She grabbed a stack of mail from the small wrought-iron credenza in the foyer and kept going.

She called out to her housekeeper. "Abigail, I'm home. I'll join you for some of that coffee if it's ready."

No answer. She entered the living room and, all of a sudden, realized why Abigail hadn't responded. Dozens of small candles burned on every surface, all lighting the room with a magical glow. A familiar voice from inside the kitchen called out to her.

"I hope you don't mind, but I turned off the coffee pot. How about some wine instead?"

Anna rushed to the kitchen and threw back the swinging doors. There, she saw Ian standing near the refrigerator, with two wine glasses in one hand and a bottle of her favorite French Chardonnay in the other.

He shrugged and then said, "I gave Abigail the rest of the day off. I hope it's all right with you?"

Sliding her hand along the granite countertops, she slowly walked towards him. "I think I can get over it."

Ian set the glasses down on the counter and began to pour. "Should I ask you how your trip was now, or can all the business talk wait till later?"

Anna edged even closer to him. She took his free hand and placed it on her waist. Then, she put her face against his cheek and stood still for a moment, feeling the heat of his breath against her ear, then her neck. Ian turned to look at her, grasped her hands in his, and stared into her eyes.

Pulling her close, his breathing grew heavier. "I haven't thought of anything but this moment for two days," he whispered.

Anna locked her lips against his and didn't let go. Taking the full weight of his body and losing her balance slightly, she stumbled back a few steps. She bumped back against the kitchen table; they clumsily reached down to catch themselves.

Ian pulled away. "Oh God, I didn't mean to make you fall. I'm such an asshole. You must be exhausted. Why don't I let you get some rest. I can come back later."

There was no way she was going to let him out of that room, even if she had to barricade the doors herself. She was hungry, and he was going to be the main course. She needed to feel his hands on her body, his tongue on her neck, her skin, and her breasts.

Holding both his hands in a vise-like grip, she answered, "Exhausted? Not really. I just had 14 hours of sleep on the plane. You wouldn't believe how much energy I have right now." She lifted herself on to the kitchen table and wrapped her legs around his waist. "You're not going anywhere."

"I guess I'm all yours then." He pushed her back a little and got up on top of her. He looked down at her for a moment. "You know," he whispered, "I'd planned this romantic evening to take place in the living room, under the glow of candlelight."

Anna wasn't listening. She was too busy concentrating on the tiny buttons on his shirt and the quickest possible strategy for undoing them. After fumbling around with the top one for a couple of seconds, she lost patience and ripped the shirt open, as button by button fell to the floor. "Now that was easy," she said with some satisfaction.

Ian sat up on his knees and removed what was left of his shirt. "Oh, well," he said as he began to unzip his trousers, "I suppose these fluorescent lights and this nice hard table can be just as romantic."

Anna pulled him to her, and there, as if they'd just been released from prison, made love. Time and time again, their bodies exploded in a passionate rage, leaving them aching close to two hours later.

Feeling both weary and exhilarated, they lay on the kitchen table and stared at the copper pots and pans dangling from the iron hooks overhead. Ian broke the silence.

"I don't suppose you know how to use any of those things?"

"What? The pots and pans? No, I'm afraid not. How about you?"

"Sorry, not my territory either."

They sat in silence for another moment. "I take it that you're hungry," she said. "I could try to cook something—no, boil something, that can't be too difficult. I'm sure I can do that. Maybe an egg, or a biscuit. Yes, that's it. I can boil a biscuit."

Ian laughed. "No, please don't boil a biscuit on my account. I know a great Italian restaurant that delivers."

Anna slid off the table and reached for her clothes on the floor. "That's a much better plan." She handed him the phone and headed for the door. "I'll be upstairs running some water for the Jacuzzi. Meet me up there when you're through, and don't forget the wine. We didn't get to it the first time around."

She walked out of the kitchen and past through to the living room, where the dozens of small candles had all but burned out. *Hmm*, she thought as she rubbed a dull ache in her lower back, *Ian was right. This probably would have been a bit more comfortable.*

Once upstairs she headed for the master bathroom. She had recently broken down two walls to expand it to include a sauna, a eucalyptus room, a steam shower, and, or course, a large marble Jacuzzi. She filled it to the top and slowly edged her way in.

Within a few moments, Ian walked in and slipped into the tub alongside her. He put his head back and let the powerful jets massage his throbbing back.

"So," he said as he put his hands behind his neck and stared at the ceiling, "I'd like to hear about your trip, and Patras. How's it going with him?"

Anna knew that the fun part of her day was over. It was time to concentrate on business again. "The trip was uneventful really," she began, "The usual garbage: the ship's too heavy, it's too big, it's leaking cargo, it can't hold enough cargo. And on and on."

"You sound like you've almost had enough. You're not thinking of selling it all to Patras, are you?"

"And what if I were?"

Ian sat up and looked straight into her eyes. "I'd say you were crazy. Nothing brings you more to life than your business. Not even me, I'm afraid."

Anna was silent. She reached for her wine and took a long sip.

"So," Ian pressed on, "tell me you're not selling it. Tell me you have a plan to kick his pathetic ass all over the place."

At that moment, Anna couldn't take her eyes away from Ian's perfect face. Fascinated, she watched large water drops slowly snake along the base of his neck and disappear into the forest of golden brown hair on his chest.

He smiled. "You're not listening to me."

"Yes, of course I'm listening." She was suddenly distracted by the ring he wore on the little finger of his left hand. It was a thin, gold band with a small ruby in the center flanked by two tiny diamonds. She reached over and touched it. "I've never noticed this before," she said. "It's pretty. Where did you get it?"

He held his hand up to give her a closer look. "My mother gave it to me recently. It belonged to my grandfather, who gave it to my grandmother just before she escaped from France. He thought she might need to trade it for food or something. Luckily, she didn't, and she wore it until the day she died. She only had a few things that belonged to him, this being one of them, and a medallion, the Star of David, that my mother gave to Joseph."

"It's beautiful."

Ian took a deep breath and sighed. "Yes, it is, and it means a lot to my family, and to me."

"You're lucky to have it. I have something like that too, a medallion that belonged to my great-grandfather, on my Greek side. He gave it to my great-grandmother, just before Turkish soldiers killed him. She and my grandfather settled on Xenos. Even there, Greek people were in danger because of the Turks.

When I was young, my grandfather made me learn traditional folk dances. In one dance, all the girls stood in a line and held hands. When the lead dancer approached a certain line on the floor, she'd jump over it and leave the stage. The woman of the island would commit suicide before they'd allow themselves to be taken by the Turks. As the women held hands and sang the songs of their island, one by one, as they approached the edge of the cliff, they'd jump to their deaths.

"That's a sad story."

Anna's eyes seemed far away. "Yes, it is," she replied. "And that medallion, my mother wore it until the day she died. It was a gold inscription of an Alpha and an Omega. It symbolizes what binds us all together as humans, that we all have a beginning and an end."

"Why aren't you wearing it?"

"I suppose I should. It's upstairs in the attic, along with a lot of other family heirlooms. Some day I'll dig it out."

The sound of the telephone broke the mood. Anna reached to grab it.

"Leave it," Ian said.

She shook her head. "Can't. I'm waiting for some important business calls."

Just then, the doorbell rang. "Well, that'll be dinner anyway," Ian said. He stood up and reached for a towel. "I'll answer the door. Meet me downstairs when you're through."

Once downstairs, Ian relit the fireplace in the living room and set out Anna's Wedgewood china on the cocktail table in front of the brown Beidermeyer sofa. He put some throw pillows around the table for them to sit on, then lit fresh candles between the dishes.

After her call, Anna threw on her bathrobe and bounded down the staircase towards the living room. "It smells delicious," she said as she watched Ian take carryout containers out of a large brown shopping bag provided by the restaurant. "I see I've discovered yet another one of your unique talents tonight: dialing the right restaurants."

"Well, I see it's either that—or starve around this house," he said. "It's a bit odd that you can navigate a supertanker but can't figure out how to turn on your stove."

"Is that some kind of chauvinist remark?" she asked wryly.

He gave her a disapproving look. "You know me better than that. It's just an observation."

She sank into one of the plump throw pillows and began to help him serve the salad. "So, aren't you going to ask me how the business with Patras is going?"

"You kept changing the subject."

"That's because I didn't know the outcome yet. But the phone call I just got, well, it was some information I needed." She paused for a moment and then looked up with the eyes of a cat that was about to pounce on an unsuspecting mouse. "You see, I have a plan, and it's going to put the nail in Patras's coffin for good."

Ian stopped what he was doing and grinned. "I knew it. I knew you weren't going to sell it to him. Now tell me everything—all the details. Who was on the phone?"

"Well, I can't tell you everything yet, because to be honest, it's a work in progress. But the call was from a detective agency in New York. I had them look up a certain Captain Stavros, who's going to be my poor, unsuspecting messenger boy."

"When did all this come about? Why didn't you tell me earlier?"

"I got the idea just before the plane landed in London. I thought, Why do I always let Patras get the better of me? Why don't I just turn the tables for a change? All I had to do was think like him—and that wasn't too hard, because he's an idiot and anyone can think like an idiot. Anyway, I thought, he always backs me into a corner with phony information, trumped-up pictures, planted evidence. I could do that too: superimpose pictures, forge signatures, but then I thought, no, I'm going to do even better. I'm going to do the real thing. When I'm through with him, he's going believe that his company really has been smuggling, but this time it won't be drugs."

"So, what's up?"

"Time is of the essence. I only have till Monday. So I made some calls on the way from the airport. The detective agency from New York tracked down Captain Stavros. You remember, the one who set up my ship to run into the oil tanker in Aden? Well, I just learned that he's still on Patras' payroll. He'll do anything for money. Then I called Marcos. I asked him to clear out a back office for me in one of the old warehouses outside of Marseilles. That's where the whole deal is going to go down."

"What deal?"

"The arms deal."

"You mean, as in weapons deal? Christ, what are you getting yourself involved with?"

"Nothing. Calm down. It's all a setup."

"Anna," he said with some concern, "arms deals mean arms brokers, and they're very dangerous people. They're not interested in playing games with people like you and me. They're the type of people who sleep with AK-47's under their pillows, have friends named Osama, and encourage young men to strap grenades to their bodies."

Seemingly unfazed, Anna began to eat her salad. "You didn't think I was going to deal with a real arms broker? God, I'm not that stupid."

"Thank God for that."

"No, all I need is someone to act like one. Stavros won't know the difference. Nine times out of ten he's too drunk to remember his own name, let alone the difference between an authentic sleazy weapons broker and a fake. He'll be totally out of his element anyway. He'll just be following Patras' instructions, too nervous to ask any questions. He won't know what the transaction's all about. I wouldn't be nervous if I were you. You'll have nothing to worry about."

"What do you mean me? I'll have nothing to worry about."

"Don't look so surprised. I told you all I need is someone to act like an arms dealer. Isn't that what you do for a living? Act, I mean. This will be a piece of cake for someone of your caliber. What are you making now anyway? Ten or twenty million a picture? This won't be the big budget stuff that you're used to, but it could be the small, more meaningful role you've always wanted, Academy Award winning material.

Ian stared at her in amazement. "And just who will be presenting me with this Academy Award? The Guerrilla Terrorists Association of the Arts and Sciences?"

"Clever retort, but no. Listen, Ian, all you'd have to do is meet with Stavros. He'll hand you a shopping list of assault weapons he received, or thinks he received, from Patras. The rest is easy. Just nod a few times, speak some broken French or English, look sleazy, and tell him you'll have the stuff ready to go in two weeks. And don't forget the payoff — there's always a payoff."

Ian put his hands to his head. "There's always a payoff?" Then, with a sigh, a clear admission of defeat, he said, "Okay, Anna. I know better than to waste my time arguing with you. Just tell me what to do—when, and where. But, I still think this is insane. Nothing concrete links this meeting with Patras. No signatures, no personal correspondence, nothing. All you have is Stavros and a list. That's not enough to convince the authorities, or get Patras to back down."

Anna helped herself to a large portion of linguine. She glanced at Ian's dish. "You haven't touched your food," she said. "It's really good. You should eat, you know."

"I'm not hungry right now. I have a lot on my mind, but don't let me stop you. It seems like the idea of falsifying documents and dealing with terrorists increases your appetite."

She twisted the linguine around her fork with gusto. "You know, when the French try to speak English, 'hungry' sounds like 'angry.' Be sure to remember that when you're in Marseille. You know, a French underground operative trying to speak English to a Greek national. It'll be great."

"No darling. What's going to be great is finding a psychiatrist who can diagnose your poor hallucinatory brain and prescribe about a truck-load of Prozac to bring you back down to earth."

Anna shuffled through the remaining plastic cartons, then glanced around the table. "I hope you didn't forget to order dessert."

"Anna," Ian snapped. "Stop eating and listen to me. Your idea of setting Patras up is a good one. But you need more evidence."

All at once, Anna stopped what she was doing and became serious. "Don't you trust me?" she asked.

Ian froze.

Anna continued. "Because I trust you. I'm trusting you with my business, which is my life. It's my line to my past, and everything I ever was, or will be. I could have hired someone to do this, but I didn't. They'd never understand my passion, or my pain, if I lost it all. But you would. You know me, and you'll be me, when you walk into that room with Stavros."

Ian could see tears in her eyes, and took her hands in his.

"Please, Ian," she went on. "It took me a long time to get to this point, to trust you with my life. Tell me that you believe in me, that you'll do this for me."

Ian wiped her eyes with a paper napkin. "Oh, darling, I didn't mean to make you cry. I already told you I'd do it. You know I'd do anything for you. If it will make you feel better, I'll even strap some sticks of dynamite under my shirt to make the whole thing look even more authentic."

Anna giggled. "I know you're concerned about the evidence, but you'll have to trust me on this one. The arms deal isn't what's going to bring Patras down. Its Stavros. I'd explain it more now, but quite honestly, I'm getting a little tired. Jet lag is getting to me and I'm not thinking very clearly."

She picked herself up off the floor and sat on the sofa. "Here," she said, "sit next to me."

Ian pushed aside his uneaten dinner and sank down into the sofa beside her. She lay down and placed her head on his lap. He looked down at her and stroked her hair. She closed her eyes. "Hmmm," she sighed. "I could stay like this all night."

"Remember when we were teenagers?" she asked him. "We used to sit like this all the time."

"Yes, but then you'd put your feet on my lap, not your head."

"Did you want me to put my head on your lap?"

"Of course."

She sighed with apparent relief. "When did you first realize you were in love with me?"

Ian thought for a moment. "You tell me first."

"You're going to think this is crazy," she said. "Probably the day I met you, when you pulled me up into the little fishing boat? I remember it so clearly: the feel of your hand, looking at your face. Your hair was all wet and falling around your shoulders. Then I saw your eyes and thought, 'My God, I could spend the rest of my life looking at those eyes.'

"I dismissed it all at first, thinking that I was just intoxicated by your appearance, but then, as we got to know each other, it all came together. You liked doing all the things I did, you made me laugh with your silly impressions of my Greek friends, and you made me think about all the things I loved in life." She opened her eyes and looked up at him. "Do you think that's crazy?"

"No," he said. "Well, a little maybe, considering you were only a kid."

She swatted him with a small pillow lying on the floor next to the sofa. "And you? It's your turn."

"It was probably that first summer in London, after you were in that car accident with Patras. I came to visit you that night, while you were in the hospital. You were asleep. I saw you lying there: your face was all bruised and you were hooked up to all these monitors. You looked so helpless, and I felt so angry with myself. I blamed myself because I let you go off with Patras. I knew my feelings weren't those of an overprotective big brother, but those of someone falling deeply in love with you."

"But, you didn't tell me"

"Right. Maybe I should have told your father and grandfather first. They would have taken the news well, don't you think? Just how should I have approached them? 'Excuse me, Mr. Winters and Mr. Stavropoulos, I know I'm a poor country boy, with aspirations of being an actor, and I'll never be able to feed the person you love the most in this world. But I love her too, and all her money means absolutely nothing to me. That's not why I love her—'"

Anna reached up and covered his mouth with her hand. "That'll be quite enough, thank you."

"Tell me, darling, do you think I'd be alive today if I'd had told them anything close to that?"

"Maybe you should have added that our love would pay the rent."

"Right, that would have gone over real well."

"They can be somewhat intimidating I suppose. But they're really pussycats underneath all that barking."

"Barking pussycats. I'd hate to be the poor mouse that gets in their way."

"And now? Are you still afraid of them?"

"No, I can hold my own at this point. Besides, if your father ends up marrying my mother, I'd be his stepson, and he wouldn't do anything too macabre to his own family—I hope." Looking surprised, he continued, "My God, if they get married I'd be screwing around with my stepsister. That's illegal, isn't it?"

Always mischievous when happy, Anna tried to frown, and failed. "I think it would only be illegal if we were related by blood."

They sat in silence for a moment. Then Ian reached for her hand. "Here," he said, as he put his gold ring on her ring finger. "I want to give you something to show how much I love you. Please, wear it. I want you to have it."

Anna began to twist it off. "I can't take this. It belongs to your family. It should stay with you."

"You *are* my family, and I want to give it to the woman I love, just like my grandfather did. Please take it, and wear it forever."

She could see that this gesture symbolized his total commitment to her. She also knew that if she accepted it, there was no turning back.

"You can buy me another ring, one that's not a family heirloom."

She could tell he knew that she was afraid of another disastrous commitment. A different ring, any other ring, would be less binding; she could still get out.

"No, Anna," he said. "I don't want to buy you another one. I want you to take this one."

She looked up at him and tried to picture her life without him. In that instant she couldn't. Richard told her that, when he knew he wanted to spend the rest of his life with her mother, he had heard the perfect song he'd always wanted to write. The notes all fit together ... the harmony, rhythm and melody given to him by heaven. And in that moment, she knew what her father meant. Ian was her song, the song she would sing through eternity.

She put the ring back on her finger. "I love you, Ian," she said. "And I'd be honored to wear this ring forever." She reached up and brought his head down to hers. She felt both elated and secure in his arms. She wasn't alone anymore. She could finally share herself with someone she loved and trusted, with her life. In that moment, she looked forward to the next day, the next week, and the next hundred years. They would conquer every challenge.

Ian held her tightly in his arms, and continued to stroke her hair as they both stared lazily into the blaze of the fireplace. Before she knew it, Anna's eyes began to close. She struggled to keep them open but it was a loosing battle.

"Come on," Ian whispered. "Let's go upstairs. We both need some sleep."

She snuggled up against his arms one last time. "I don't want this evening to end," she said. "It's been so wonderful, and tomorrow it's back to reality."

"Yes," he said. "I have to prepare for the role of a lifetime, and the director's only giving me one take, so there's no room for fuck-ups."

He's right. One take's all we've got. "Ian," she said, "do you think we can? If we make a mistake ..."

"You're fucked, I know. But you hired the best, right? Don't worry."

"I am."

"I know. That's okay."

"Oh God," she sighed.

Chapter 16

PATRAS INDUSTRIES, MONDAY MORNING

Anna stood outside of the world headquarters of Patras Industries, a forty-two-story brick building emblazoned with the name of its owner from the top of the forty-second floor, all the way down to the awning above the main entrance. She glanced at her watch. 8:55 A.M. Her meeting with Patras started in five minutes. She clutched the handle of her briefcase. The envelope with the video tape was in there. She checked and rechecked it a hundred times before she left her townhouse.

She replayed the tape in her mind. Ian's meeting with Stavros. It was perfect. Stavros took the bait. All it had taken was a hand-delivered message with Patras's return address on it. Then, after he confirmed that lump-sum payment had reached his Swiss bank account, he was on his way. And Ian: he was spectacular as the French operative code named Anton. Olivier himself couldn't have done a better job. She couldn't wait to see Andreas's expression when he saw it. But that wasn't the crucial envelope she needed. The evidence that was going to make Andreas fall to his knees was still on its way.

She grabbed her cell phone and dialed the number of the detectives she'd hired in New York. Again, no answer. Either their phones were turned off, or they were out of range. *Christ*, she thought. *What kind of detectives are they? They can't even be reached in an emergency.* At that moment, her precious unwavering confidence in them hit bottom.

She glanced at her watch again. She couldn't wait outside any longer. They knew the meeting started at nine sharp. If they didn't see her outside, they'd know to find her in Patras' office, she hoped.

She rode the familiar express elevator to the penthouse suite. Once again, she was greeted by the overzealous pencil-thin receptionist who, this time, ushered her right into Andreas's office.

"Mr. Patras has been waiting for you," she said breathlessly. She swung open the heavy double doors, and there, at the other end of the room, behind an immense antique oak desk, sat Andreas. Sporting his usual insincere smile, he stood up and stretched out his arms as if to embrace the long-lost friend he hadn't seen since his days at war.

"Ah, my luv," he said as he walked towards her. "You look beautiful today. Well-rested I see. I haven't seen you look this lovely since we were children, when you didn't hate me quite so much."

In truth, she knew she looked exceptionally dazzling that morning. She had spent the entire day before in the capable hands of Frederick, her personal trainer, and Egon, her masseuse. They expertly worked their magic on her, and, before she knew it, her skin regained the luminous glow it had lost somewhere between Venice and the Panama Canal.

It was well into the evening before her 'body personnel' left the townhouse. Her favorite hairdresser arrived as they left. He shampooed, snipped, sprayed, gelled, and teased into the night. He left kissing the crucifix he wore saying his hands were just the tools of the Lord. It was truly He who had performed the miracle which just transpired on Anna's head.

Knowing she'd need an extra boost of confidence, she wore her favorite power-suit: the black Chanel wool. Then, she put on her highest, most uncomfortable Prada heels, grabbed her Vuitton briefcase, and marched out of the house. And now, standing in front of Patras, she felt strong and unstoppable.

As Patras approached her, she stepped back. "What's with the arms, Andreas? You're not planning on hugging me, are you?"

Andreas shrugged. "Why not? For old times sake?"

She maneuvered her way around him and headed to one of the two chairs in front of his desk. "God, take it easy on the hallucinogenics in the morning," she mumbled. Then, with a bright smile, she turned to him and said, "I'd rather not."

"Always the killjoy," he said.

The receptionist stuck her head in through the door. "Mr. Patras," she said, "your coffee's here. Should I bring it in?"

"Absolutely," he answered. "I can't start the day without my cup of Greek coffee. You understand, Anna, or has hanging around that British actor made you forget your heritage already?"

"How can I forget when I have reminders like you?"

The receptionist put the coffee tray down on a cleared portion of Andreas's desk. Just as she had done the previous week, Anna swallowed the entire contents of her cup in two long gulps and turned it over on the porcelain saucer. Andreas followed suit and sat back.

"So," he said, "who's going to read our fortunes this week? Shall I give you the honors, or will you allow me?"

"Please, allow me. But I'll save it for later. I don't think you're going to like what you hear."

"Whatever you want, my luv. I take it we'll talk business now, or would you like to save that for later too?" he said sarcastically.

Anna glanced at her watch. *The envelope,* she thought. *Damn it, why's it taking so long to get here?* Nervous but with apparently resolute confidence, she said, "No, I don't think we should waste anymore time. Let's get down to business."

"All right then," he sneered. "I've been looking forward to this moment all week." He reached around back to his settee and grabbed a large manila folder. "I've had my accountant prepare a check for ten million dollars. It's all yours as long as you sign these preliminary contracts for the bulk of your business. My lawyers and accountants will have to meet with yours of course, but these papers will serve in the interim."

Anna took the check and stared at it for a moment. *Ten million dollars,* she thought. *What a crock of shit.* "So, Andreas," she said, "you thought it would be this easy? That I'd just roll over and hand you my ships?"

Andreas looked clearly irritated. "Come on now, luv. We've gone over this before. It's either this, or the old ball and chain—oh wait, bad expression. You've already got a ball and chain: your husband. Maybe I should have said, it's either this or I'm going to fuck you over for good."

Anna took a deep breath. The battle had begun and she was more than ready for the challenge. This was the moment she'd been waiting for. She'd rehearsed this confrontation all week. She continued to stare at the check and then, in a slow, deliberate motion, she tore it in half.

"I don't think so, Andreas," she said. "You've underestimated me for a long time. My company's clean; it always has been. Your evidence and your documents are all a bunch of crap. I'm not afraid of what the authorities will find, but you? Maybe you should be."

Andreas narrowed his eyes. "You just made a big mistake, my luv." He reached for his intercom and rang his receptionist.

"Yes, Mr. Patras?"

Without taking his eyes off Anna, he said, "Gabrielle, get me Henry Brackett from the DEA on the line immediately. Tell him—"

Anna slammed her hand down on the intercom and cut off the line. "I'd cancel that call if I were you."

"You're out of your league, Anna. Don't play games with me. I gave you a chance to walk out of here with your dignity. Now, you're going to end up walking out in handcuffs, with your face splattered all over the nightly news."

He reached for the phone again. Anna walked around to the side of the desk and tore the cord out of the wall. "Now," she said, "I think it's time you listen to me."

Gabrielle opened the door to the office. "Is everything all right in here, Mr. Patras? We were abruptly cut off."

Andreas looked over at Anna, who continued to hold the ripped telephone cord. "Yes, Gabrielle, everything's all right. You can go."

After the receptionist closed the door behind her, Anna put down the ripped cord and reached for her briefcase. "Smart move, Andreas."

"Well, it looks like you have something on your mind, so let's get to it. I'm a busy man with a busy schedule. I'll give you five minutes to tell me what you have hidden in that briefcase of yours. Then I'm going into another office and placing the call to the DEA on another one of my million phones."

Anna felt her heart racing as she opened her briefcase. She needed to stall for more time, but she knew Andreas was serious. Five minutes was all she had with the other envelope nowhere in sight. She pulled out a video cassette from a large bubble wrapper and dangled it in front of Andreas.

"I take it you want me to see what's on that tape?" he asked sarcastically. He pointed to the breakfront against the oak-paneled wall. "The VCR's in there. Be my guest." He grabbed the remote control from his drawer and pressed a few buttons. The breakfront opened up automatically, displaying a state-of-the-art large-screen television with a built-in video cassette player. "Go ahead," he said, "put it in. But I have to warn you, nothing short of seeing Queen Elizabeth in her underwear is going to impress me."

"I have a feeling you're wrong about that," she said as she approached the breakfront. "You're going to love this. It's going to be an instant classic."

She inserted the tape and hit the play button. The screen jumped to life, displaying a fuzzy black and white picture of the inside of a small wood-paneled office. The camera was mounted high in a corner, giving the room a rounded, fish-eye appearance. The room contained only a small plywood desk to one side, with a flimsy black folding chair facing it. The top of the desk was empty except for an old rotary telephone and a tin ashtray piled high with a mountain of cigarette butts. There were no windows; a bare light bulb dangled from the ceiling provided the little light there was.

Then, a flash of movement and the sound of a drawer opening, then closing. A man emerged. He was tall and slender and wearing a baseball cap with his hair pulled tightly into a ponytail underneath. Disheveled clothes: ripped dungarees and a wrinkled T-shirt with an illegible logo featuring naked women and snakes. The brim of the baseball cap cast an angular shadow across his face, making it difficult to see his features, although a three-day stubble was obvious.

He took a seat at his desk ,with his back facing the camera. He rifled through some papers, and then there was a knock at the door.

"Qu'est-ce que c'est?" he hollered.

No answer. The knocking continued.

"Merde," he got up to open the door. A large, stocky middle-aged man entered and stood at the doorway.

"Qui etes-vous?" the man with the baseball cap snapped.

"Me?" the stocky man replied in a loud voice, "No speak French." He pointed to himself. "I'm Stavros. You're expecting me."

The man with the baseball cap scratched his ear. "Oui, and I'm not fucking deaf eezer," he responded in a heavy French accent.

Andreas hit the pause button on his remote control and the screen froze. "What the hell's going on here?" he asked. "What's Stavros doing with the French guy?"

Anna smiled to herself. She was finally watching Andreas squirm. "Maybe you should watch the whole thing," she said. "It will all become clear in a few moments."

She took the remote out of his hand. "Come on," she said. "The fun's just starting."

She hit the play button, and the screen began to move. Still standing at the doorway, Stavros said, "You Anton?"

"Yes, and you muss be an asshole. Keep your voice down, unless you want everyone in Marseille to hear us." Baseball cap walked to his desk and sat down. "You have zee list from Patras?"

Stavros fumbled through his briefcase and pulled out a sheet of paper. Anton grabbed it out of his hand. He glanced at it, and then said, "Hmmm. Nice equipment. Who's ziz for? Ortega? He's zee only one I know still uses zee Mossberg 12-gauge."

Stavros fidgeted with the buttons on his shirt. "Yeah, the shipment's going to South America. Can you get it all?"

Anton continued to read. "Ah," he said. "Tres bien, the Cobray 9-mm 32 round magazine, fake suppressor—good piece, delivers 1,000 rounds without fail. Two cases, magnifique! And here ... oui. Zee Calico 9mm with zee 50 round mag. Ah, pre ban. Very rare."

"Can you get it?"

"Bien sur, ass-hole. Zat's what I do. Now, do you have zee money?"

"Half now, and half on delivery."

"Where's zee drop?"

"Pier du Pont Nief, next Tuesday, 3:00 A.M. sharp." Stavros put the briefcase on the desk and opened it up. "It's all there. Don't bother counting it."

"Merde. It better be ... or you find a grenade up your fucking ass in zee morning."

Stavros walked out and closed the door behind him. The screen went blank.

The room was silent for a moment. Then, as he continued to stare at the blank screen, Andreas said, "This is interesting, Anna. Not that I'm admitting to any illicit activity in the past, but I never ordered this meeting between Stavros and this Anton guy. So, tell me: how did you 'happen' to come upon this tape?"

"It wasn't that hard," she said. "I had a tip-off from someone in Marseille that you were planning to haul some weapons for this guy Ortega in South America. So I found out who the active brokers in the area were and had their offices wired."

Andreas remained unfazed. "I'm not impressed, my luv. Almost disappointed really. I hope this isn't all you have, because if it is, you're screwed. You know as well as I do that your tape's a bunch of bullshit. I didn't put Stavros up to that. If there was a real arms deal going on, he did it on his own accord, and believe me, I'd find that almost impossible to swallow. He's not the brightest bulb in the box, so to speak. Anyway Anna, the bottom line is that you have nothing—no evidence whatsoever. No personal memos from me to Stavros, no telephone conversations— nothing. You don't even have any weapons. So, as short as it was, your move's over. The game's back in my ballpark and it's my turn again."

Shit, he's gonna do it, she thought. *Damn it. I need that other envelope.*

Andreas got up and walked toward the door. "Now, if you'll excuse me, I have a telephone call to make."

She couldn't let him make that call. "No, wait."

He turned around and grinned. "What? Should I have that check reissued?" he asked through a brazenly cold stare.

She hesitated. How could this happen? She had gone over it a thousand times. There shouldn't have been any mistakes.

"I'm waiting for an answer," he said.

"All ri—" She was cut off by Andreas's receptionist, who was standing at the door.

"Mr. Patras," she said, "there are two men here who insist on seeing Ms. Winters. They said it's urgent."

"Not now, Gabrielle," he snapped.

Anna raced towards the door. "Wait. Let me see what they want."

Without giving Andreas a chance to block her exit, she maneuvered her way around him and approached the two black-suited men in the waiting area. She grabbed a large envelope out of the hand of one of them, and whispered through clenched teeth, "What the hell took you so long?"

"Sorry, Ms. Winters," one of the men offered apologetically. "There was another bomb scare in the subway. Left us stuck in there for awhile."

"Subway? With all the money I paid you, you couldn't take a cab?" She tucked the envelope under her arm, turned around, and strode back into Andreas's office.

"So," Andreas said as he closed the door behind her. "You look like you just got some good news. I'll bet you want to share it with me, right?"

Anna sat back down at the desk. "You're incredibly perceptive and it's amazing how you manage to read me so well."

He shrugged, "When you grow up with someone, it's not that hard."

That comment caught Anna off guard. Her mind raced back to the interminably long summers spent avoiding Andreas, and the brief moments when, in his efforts to impress her, he made her laugh. She looked up at him and smiled.

He looked surprised. "What are you smiling about?"

"You know what I just thought of?" she said.

"Don't hold back."

"The time when you and I got drunk for the first time. You had that party at your father's house on Xenos. We were—what? Fourteen? We took a bottle of Ouzo on the dirt path that lead down to your beach. I don't think I had more than two sips, and my head was spinning, but you—my God, you drank the rest of the bottle."

Andreas laughed. "Remember how sick I got?"

"How could I forget? There we were, just walking, and all of a sudden, you leaned over, threw up all over the place, lost your balance, and went tumbling down the path, through all those thorny bushes. I went running after you; I thought you were dead or something. Then out of nowhere, you appeared, your face scratched and those twigs and prickly branches stuck to your hair and sweater."

"And you showed all the concern of a hyena. My face was a bloody mess, and you stood there laughing."

"But you looked so silly."

"And you know what I thought at that moment? That if that's what it took to make you smile and laugh with me, I'd gladly go through the rest of my life with prickly twigs stuck to my head."

Again, she was taken aback by his response. She had forgotten how much she had once meant to him. Although she hated to admit it, he had once meant a great deal to her as well. Those early days on Xenos were some of the loneliest times of her life. She had no family aside from her grandparents. She felt so isolated and alone—and then there was Andreas. Although he irritated her ninety percent of the time, he never failed to be there at her side when she needed someone to talk to. He was sure to include her in on every party, every beach outing, every gathering, no matter how small and insignificant.

They looked at each other for a moment. Then Anna shook her head and handed him the envelope. "This was supposed to be my moment," she said, "but somehow this victory doesn't feel as sweet as I thought it would."

Andreas opened the envelope and skimmed the first page. His smile gave way to a look of concern. "Where did you get these names?"

"Stavros gave them up."

Andreas looked through the next page, and then the next.

"Are you impressed yet?" she asked.

"I'm getting there," he answered. "So, this was your plan all along then. The deal in Marseille was just a trap for Stavros. Am I right?"

"Yeah, that's right. After he left Anton, he was approached by two men who he thought were agents at Interpol. They told him that they had just recorded the whole deal inside the warehouse office. Stavros said he was just a messenger, that he was just acting on your behalf. Then, in an attempt to save his own ass, he offered them a deal: he'd give you up, along with all your contacts, for immunity from prosecution. Two men accompanied him back to his villa in Zurich and got a hand-written confession, which included, among other things, your involvement in the attempt to sabotage my ship in Aden a few years back. But what should concern you more is that his confession also included a list of the brokers and dealers you've been using for your illegal drugs and weapons operations. Those guys aren't going to be too happy when they find out that you and your man Stavros have been blabbering their names about town, are they? You know, instead of letting this list of names slip out, you might prefer turning yourself into the authorities. Jail may be the safer alternative."

Andreas let the papers fall down to the desk. "Well, well," he said, "I guess you've done it. You've got me by the balls. Funny thing is, I knew all along you could do it. I never expected to win. You'd sooner die before you'd turn your ships over to me."

Anna looked at him curiously. "What do you mean? If you didn't expect to win, why did you do it?"

"Just that. I didn't expect to win. Nothing more," he said nonchalantly. "Now, where do we go from here? You have incriminating evidence on me, and I, on you. So, we can both turn our files over to the authorities and face jail time, or we can shake hands and say good-bye, for now."

"Back up again. What are you saying here? That this was all some sort of game? You wanted to see how far I'd go to save my company?"

"In a way, yes. But unlike the games we played as children, the stakes were much higher this time. Made it a lot more fun, don't you think? The adrenaline rush was better than any narcotic I've ever tried."

"Right. How could I have been so stupid? You outgrew decapitating my Barbie Dolls and roasting my goldfish, so you had to do the next best thing. Blow up my ships and have me arrested for smuggling."

"That's an interesting way of looking at it, I suppose. You see, you've always been my favorite playmate. Nobody's even come close to you. The others are just a bunch of losers. They just crumble at the slightest touch, or worse, cry when I take away all their hard-earned toys. But you," he grinned with delight, "look how far down in the trenches you'll go with me. Believe it or not, I have more fun with you than anyone else in my life."

"So, let me get this straight, you consider me your best friend or something? What the hell's wrong with you? You need to find another way of entertaining yourself. We've grown up. Those days are over."

"We may have grown up, but the games are still the same. They've just graduated to another level."

She stood up to leave. "Well, I'm sorry to disappoint you, but the party's got to end sometime. It's time for you to find another best friend, because if I ever hear or see you again, the names on these papers are going to hit the streets. And I won't feel one bit of remorse for the gruesome end you'll suffer."

Andreas' face fell, like that of a child whose playmate has just been called inside by his mother. He slumped back into his chair. "All right, but one last thing before you go."

"What?"

"Your husband."

"What about him?"

"You should know. He was the insider in my operation. He approached me with this whole scheme, and he took a big payoff for it too."

Anna was unfazed. "Thanks for the info, but I already knew that. But tell me: why the confession?"

"Because I never liked the asshole. Never did know what you saw in him. He always seemed like a sleazy fucker, and he proved it too. Anyway,

I don't want to take up anymore of my time figuring out how to fuck him over, so I thought I'd tell you and you'd do my dirty work for me."

Anna laughed. "And here I thought we'd never have anything in common. This is truly a momentous occasion."

He grinned. "I always thought we'd make a great team someday."

They locked eyes for a moment and they both smiled. "If you need help with him Anna, you can always call."

"No, thanks for the offer. I can handle him myself."

"And the hillbilly?"

"Stay out of it."

"I was just going to say that he looks like a nice guy. Not nicer than me, of course. You missed the boat on that one."

"That would have been a wild ride." She shook her head and walked out the door. Then, she paused and turned around. "Before I go," she said, "there's one last thing I need to know."

"What's that?"

"If this whole blackmail scheme was just a game to you, tell me, would you have called the authorities on me in the end, or was that just a bluff?"

"I don't bluff. You know that. If I did, you wouldn't play as hard as you do. My games are to the death. Like two gladiators going into an arena. Protocol dictates that only one comes out alive."

"But we both came out alive."

"This time. And I know what you're thinking: you have me by the balls. As long as you have that list of contacts, I can't touch you. But people like that don't last long. They're around for a couple of years and then they turn up dead somewhere, like a river, or a flea-bag hotel room with a needle sticking out of their arm. Trust me. When they're all gone, Anna Winters will be open season again."

"Don't forget the confession from Stavros. The drug smuggling and sabotage efforts."

"Yeah, yeah," he said dismissively. "I'm investigated for shit like that all the time. I can populate a small country with the number of lawyers I've got on retainer. By the time some jury finds my guilty of anything, I'll be long dead."

She knew he was right. He'd managed to elude the authorities for years. It was the names on that list that he was most afraid of, and it was only a matter of time before they'd all disappear.

"Okay," she sighed. "I'll see you again some time, when hunting season opens, and don't disappoint me. I'll be waiting, and like you said, protocol dictates that only one of us comes out alive. But think twice before you attack again, because I only play to win. And you've only seen a fraction of what I'm capable of."

Andreas clapped his hands. "Until then, my luv."

Anna turned around and walked out. "Until then, Andreas."

Chapter 17

GOING HOME

Anna stepped outside the lobby doors of Patras Industries. Her eyes strained to adjust to the midmorning sun, and she reached in her bag and brought out a pair of sunglasses. She looked around for a taxi, but after seeing that the traffic along Knightsbridge was at a standstill, she opted for the tube.

She began her walk through the pedestrian-crushing crowds, when all of sudden, she was grabbed from behind by a familiar set of arms. Quickly, she turned around and stared into Ian's face. But, before she had a chance to say anything, she saw Jackie and Christian.

"My God, what are you two doing here? You're supposed to be on your honeymoon."

Jackie looked at her quizzically. "How could we stay away? We heard that you might be in trouble, so we cut things short in Tahiti. Came here, you know, to see if there's anything we can do to help."

Anna put her arms around her and hugged her tight. "There's nothing you can do to help. But I'm so glad you're here. I've missed you terribly."

"Me too," Jackie answered.

"Me too," Christian said as he put his arms around the two of them. Jackie shot back, "We could do without the teasing, thank you."

"So," Ian said as he regained his balance after getting jostled by irate pedestrians, "are you going to keep me in suspense much longer? Tell me, how did it go? Is SeaCorp still in business or not?"

Anna gave him a mischievous look. "For now. Yes. It seems that I still have a job."

The words were barely out of her mouth when Jackie let out a congratulatory scream. "Oh, YES. I knew you could do it. You're unbeatable. We're unbeatable. There's nothing we can't do, right?"

Jackie's expressions of pleasure attracted the attention of the onrushing crowd. A circle of onlookers formed around them, with specific attention being paid to Ian.

"Jackie," Ian said, "keep your enthusiasm a little lower. You're attracting a crowd."

"No, brother," she answered. "*You're* attracting a crowd."

Within seconds, Ian was almost hidden by the papers autograph-seekers thrust out to him. "Please, for my little sister. My great-aunt adored you in Dr. Zhivago. Please ..."

Hoping to ease his way out of the situation, he signed autographs and thanked the crowd for their kind words. But the crowd got bigger and more chaotic. Frenzied fans jostled and clawed their way towards him, flailing anything autograph-worthy in his face, including hands, arms, and exposed breasts. Desperate women dodged their way through the moving cars on Knightsbridge, hoping to catch of glimpse of Hollywood's hottest heartthrob.

Without realizing it, Anna, Christian, and Jackie were edged out of the swarming hive, and found themselves in the middle of the street, causing a massive traffic jam.

Alarmed after losing sight of Ian, Anna shouted to Christian, "He's going to get eaten alive in there. Do something!"

"Don't worry, Anna," he answered. "They're not gonna bloody kill him. All they want is a small piece of him to take home ... some hair, a shred of his jacket, a piece of skin ..."

"Shut up and go get him," Jackie snapped. "That's my brother's hair, and I want it all on his head. We'll find a cab somewhere. You just get him out of there."

Anna and Jackie spotted an elderly couple exiting a taxi across the street. They ran for it, motioning for Christian to follow once he'd rescued Ian. Christian took a deep breath and entered the nest of squealing women. He grabbed Ian's hand and, with all his strength, pulled him towards the waiting taxi. The door was open, and they both dove in head first. But, before the cab had a chance to pull away a petite, young blonde threw herself on the hood of the vehicle, pulled up her sweater, and pressed her rather amazing breasts against the windshield. She screamed something like, "I love you, Ian, I'm yours, please, take me with you—" but someone pulled her off the car and she quickly disappeared into the onrushing crowd.

The taxi driver maneuvered around two stopped cars, crossed over into a contra-flow bus lane, sped through a red light, and eventually found himself wandering aimlessly through London.

He turned to his group of passengers in the back seat, and proudly displaying an assortment of gold and missing teeth, sneered, "So, which one of you gents has the pot of gold in your trousers that all the ladies want?"

With the look of three shell-shocked soldiers, Jackie, Christian, and Anna pointed to Ian.

"That'll be him," Jackie said.

"Well, mate," the cab driver continued, "them's must be some pretty fancy family jewels you got in those pants." He let out a hearty laugh and turned back around. "So, where can I take you?"

Anna glanced at her friends. "My place, right?" They all nodded. "Chelsea then," she said to the driver. "Chayne Walk."

Without hesitating, the driver cut over two lanes of traffic and screeched his way through a right turn. His four passengers sat back in silence and took a collective breath. Then, without warning, Jackie slapped Ian in the back of the head and yelled, "What's the matter with you? You nearly got us all killed back there. Can't you keep your head down or something?"

"I wasn't the one jumping up and down like a circus clown," he shot back.

"Well, Studboy, I can't be expected to keep my enthusiasm in check because of you. You're just not going to be allowed to come out with us again. Right guys? I mean, what? We're going to have to go creeping around restaurants from now on, wearing weird disguises, doing all that ridiculous camouflage shit that you see in tabloid magazines. My God, I'm going to open up the paper one day and see a photograph of myself on the beach, you know, taken with a telephoto lens, and my butt will be hanging out all over the place because they distorted the picture to make me look fatter, and the headline will read something like, 'Ian Moore's Sister, Depressed and Fat Over Brother's Newfound Fame'— "

"Oh, shut up." Ian said. "I can't take you anymore. Your voice grates on my nerves. That asinine bullshit that comes rattling out of your mouth is too much. Trust me, no photographers would ever be interested in you anyway. The pictures would never sell, no matter how fat your ass gets."

"Thanks for the compliment," Jackie said.

"One bit of advice from your new brother-in-law?" Christian added.

"Sure." Ian said.

"Don't get too used to all that screaming. It will all fade one day. Fans are fickle, and so is the press. They love to build you up, just to tear you down."

"You know I don't like any of that attention anyway."

"You say that now, but when it's all gone, you'll miss it."

"Do you?"

"I did at first, and it took awhile to get my head back on straight." He looked at Jackie, "But I know what the important things in life are, and I won't let go."

"Glad to hear that," Jackie said.

"You're a good man Christian," Ian said. "I thought I'd have to pay someone to take my sister off my hands."

Again, Jackie slapped Ian on the back of the head.

"Hey," Anna interrupted, "let's put down the boxing gloves and decide what we're going to do to celebrate my victory over Andreas."

Ian, Christian, and Jackie exchanged glances. "I guess you didn't listen to the messages on your answering machine at home yet," Jackie said.

"No. Why? What's up?"

"Your father put together an impromptu birthday party for my mom tonight. He said it's rare to find us all in the same city at once, so he thought it would be a good idea. You're coming, aren't you?"

"Of course I'm coming."

The taxi pulled up alongside Anna's townhouse. She opened the door and stepped out.

"Aren't any of you coming in with me?" she asked as she peered in through the window. "I thought we could at least have a drink or something to celebrate—"

Jackie cut her off. "No, sorry. Can't. I need the rest of the afternoon to get ready."

"Ian," she continued, "what about you? Are you coming in with me, or do you need time to get ready too?"

"No, sorry, darling," he answered. "I've got to run. I'm meeting my agent in a half hour. Something about a new action thriller with Schwarzenegger. Or a remake of Love Story. I've kind of lost track."

"All right," she shrugged. "Guess I'll see you all tonight then. By the way, is there anything in particular your mom wants for her birthday?"

"Yeah," Jackie said, "that we all forget her age." She pulled the door shut and motioned to the cab driver to move on. "See you later, right?" she shouted out the window.

She blew them all a kiss. "See you there," she answered as the cab screeched around the corner.

Anxious to share her victory with her dad, Anna arrived at his house at 8:00 sharp. He greeted her at the door with a huge hug and a bottle of her favorite champagne.

"I heard you have Patras by the balls?"

She nodded.

"Well, sit down. I want to hear all about it before the rest of the company gets here."

"Where's Angela?"

"Upstairs, getting ready. So I have you all to myself now."

She glanced around the room. Richard always had a flair for throwing a party. He sensed the mood of the crowd and decorated accordingly. Tonight, the guests were family, so the tone had to be intimate. The lights were dim, with the glow of the fireplace and few a small lamps barely illuminating the room. At his mahogany grand piano sat a hired musician who played Angela's favorite selections, Beethoven, Lizst and Mozart.

Anna chatted on endlessly about the details of her meeting with Patras.

"You should have seen him, Dad. When I showed him that list of names. His face fell to the floor."

Richard's face lit up. "I never doubted you could do it."

"But it's not over. I don't think he's ever going to stop. He made that perfectly clear before I left."

"I don't know about that. It sounds as if you might have come to some sort of truce. Believe it or not, we all get older, and we see things differently. Some day, he'll get married, have a bunch of kids, and some old petty vendetta won't seem quite as important."

"I don't think it's a vendetta. It's more of a game."

"Games get boring after a while too. He'll find someone else to play with."

"I hope you're right, Dad."

He laughed. "Me too."

Soon after, the guests began to arrive. Joseph was first. He introduced a tall, slim brunette as his fiancee, Leah. Noticing Anna's surprise, Joseph explained that they had only met a couple of months ago—in law school.

"The whole thing was rather quick," he added while adjusting the hastily made knot of his wrinkled bowtie. "You know, hate to use the old cliché 'love at first sight', but sometimes..."

"Yes," Anna said still somewhat surprised. "But I didn't see her at your sister's wedding just a couple of weeks ago."

Leah's voice was deep, at least two octaves lower the average human's. "Nooo," she crooned. "Couldn't make it. Exaaaams. Not like Joseph. Some of us neeeeeed to study."

Jackie and Christian arrived next, followed by Ian, who showed up with Phillipa. With the group finally assembled, Richard grabbed a glass of champagne and stood in the center of the room.

"If you don't mind," he said as he cleared his throat, "I'd like to say a few words." Richard was a master at taking center stage. No matter how big his audience was, each person always felt as if Richard were maintaining constant eye contact with him or her.

"It's not often that we all get together like this," he continued, " and I appreciate you all taking time out from whatever you're doing to celebrate Angela's birthday with me," he lifted his glass. "So, here's to you, my darling. To many more birthdays together."

The group lifted their glasses in unison and repeated, "Happy birthday."

"Before we all resume our conversations," Richard added, "there's just one more thing I'd like to say." He paused and took a deep breath. "I know it's been hard for you all to accept me, as a friend and as an important part of your mother's life. We had a bit of a rocky start, and I'm sorry for that. I hope we've all managed to move on from there because I want you to know that I truly love you all like a family, like my own family, which I'd like you to become—officially, that is. You see, I didn't think I'd ever again feel the need to be with someone forever ..."

Anna felt her heart begin to race. This was it. She knew what was about to come out of her father's mouth. She felt the palms of her hands grow sweaty. He should have told her first. She had known this time would eventually come, but she wasn't ready. Or was she?

Ian slipped his hand through hers and gave it a gentle squeeze. "Relax," he whispered. "It's not the end of the world. He's not dying."

She managed a faint smile. "Right."

"... so," Richard continued, "I'm sure you've all figured out what I'm about to say." He looked straight into Angela's eyes. "My darling, my love, will you marry me?"

The room was silent. Angela smiled, walked towards him, and they embraced. She whispered something in his ear and they both laughed. Richard reached into his pocket and produced a diamond ring that lit up the room. He put it on her finger and they kissed.

"I take it that's a yes Mom," Jackie shouted out.

Angela looked at her family and with tears in her eyes, answered, "That's a yes."

All at once, the room sprang to life. Everyone moved towards Richard and Angela, and, one by one, embraced them. Anna stood back, not knowing what to do or say. She was happy, but at the same time, reluctant to congratulate them.

She grabbed a glass of champagne from a passing tray and wandered off to the library to be alone. She stood in front of the television. Someone had turned it on during the evening to catch the last few minutes of the World Cup Finals: Argentina vs. Greece. She leaned close to the set and studied the faces of the Greek players. She'd sat in the First Class cabin alongside a few of them during her last flight to Athens. She smiled to herself, when she thought about how the men, not realizing she spoke Greek, wagered amongst themselves that they could get her to join at least one of them in the Mile High Club by the end of the trip. Switching into their pathetic English, each tried to charm her with his athletic prowess and stories of grand victories. In the end, none of the players scored another notch in the proverbial bed post or in that case, the tiny toilet bowl in the sky.

She heard someone enter the room and turned around. It was Ian.

"Since when did you get so interested in football?"

"I'm not," she answered. "I just needed some time to be alone. The whole thing in there, it took me by surprise."

"I know, me too," he said. "But I'm happy for them. You should be too."

"Yes, yes. I'm happy," she said dismissively. "It was just so sudden."

"Sudden? They've been dating for what? Five or six years? Come on, Anna, let go. Your father's mourned long enough. Give him a break."

"But things will change. I won't be the most important person in his life anymore."

"I'm sure he has room enough for more than one person. Your relationship won't change."

"How do you know?"

"You sound like a child. Besides, you're the most important person in my life. Doesn't that count for something?"

"Of course it does."

"Then, let your father be happy. Besides, that's the only way you can truly show him how much you love him."

"Tell me something, Ian, how do you feel about him?"

Ian steadied his gaze upon her. "I'm not sure what you mean."

"Do you resent him in some way, because of what happened to your father?"

"My feelings aren't that simple. My mom's been through a lot. She was young when she got married to my father, and I'm not sure if she was ever truly happy. I can't condemn her for falling in love with your father while she was married. I'm not sure what I'd do if I were in that situation. So, it doesn't matter how I feel about your father. He makes my mom happy, and that's all that's important to me."

"I'm glad."

"Me too. Now, do you want to get back to the party?"

Suddenly, they heard Richard's voice. "Hey, you two. Come join us in the other room. The party's in here ..." his voice trailed off and he walked into the library. He headed straight for the television set. "Hey, look what's on," he said. "Some old clips of the Casuals. You guys have to see some of these old clips of the group. They're a real blast."

The rest of the family moved into the library and stood around the television. "What's this all about?" Christian asked. "What station's digging out these old artifacts?"

"Shhhhh," Jackie said. "Someone's saying something. Quiet down. I want to hear."

"And that, ladies and gentlemen, is how it all began. The Casuals, the legends, the rock and roll icons of the '60s. Tonight, in a rare interview, Stacey Roberts will be talking to the genius behind the band, the man who started in all: Nigel Taylor. In a candid, up-front interview, Nigel's agreed to talk about everything in his life, from the breakup of the band to his recent marriage to the heiress Anna Winters and his upcoming album Guts and Rodents. *It's an interview you won't want to miss. So stay tuned."*

Anna gasped. "Nigel. Oh, my God, what's he up to?"

Richard put his arms around her. "Calm down. He's probably just promoting his new piece-of-shit album. Maybe we should turn it off and resume the party. All right?"

"No way," she answered. "I want to hear what that turd has to say."
She turned up the volume.

Stacey: "So here we are, in Nigel's beautiful New York apartment. I want to thank you for letting my film crew in. You're very gracious."

Nigel: "Not a problem."

Stacey: "So, before we talk about your days with the Casuals, can you tell me a little about your upcoming album?"

Nigel: "Sure, it's called Guts and Rodents. *It's a whole different sound for me, more surrealist—and a bit more spiritual maybe."*

Stacey: "Yes, spiritual. That should be interesting. [Holds up piece of paper] Let me read some of the lyrics. Maybe you could help me interpret the spirituality. 'The larvae of the maggots cover the rotting flesh of disease.'"

Nigel: [Smiles]. That's blatant. The maggots are living, moving entities that represent life, and the rotting flesh is obviously death. It's life superimposed onto death. In other words, it's a symbol of rebirth.

Stacey. "Yes, now it's clear. Can't believe I missed it at all. I see here you've dedicated the album to your wife."

Nigel: "Yes. She was my inspiration."

Stacey: "If you don't mind, I'd like to talk about her next. It's no secret that you married the daughter of your ex-partner, Richard Winters, and that the two of you are separated. Is there any chance of a reconciliation?"

Nigel: "Well, Stacey, to be honest, I hope so. You see, Anna and I are deeply in love, but we had problems having children. I think she somehow felt it was her fault, and she became, you know ... very depressed."

Stacey: "So she packed up and left and went running into the arms of Ian Moore?"

Nigel: "Oh, that [laughs]. God, they're childhood friends. It's not serious. How could it be? Ian's a homosexual."

Stacey: "What?"

Nigel: "Oh, sure. It's no secret. Christ, he's come on to me a number of times."

Stacey: "So, you mean to tell me that Hollywood's latest golden boy, every red-blooded woman's fantasy is gay."

Nigel: "As queer as they come."

Stacey: [Looks into the camera] "Well, you heard it here first. Ladies, dream no more. Ian Moore's just another Hollywood illusion. We have to take a quick break, and a deep breath, but stay tuned. Who knows what new secrets Nigel will reveal to us next."

Nobody moved, or even breathed. The telephone rang, but Richard didn't flinch. He just continued to stare at the television set. Then Ian's cell phone rang. He walked away to answer it.

Christian broke the silence. "What in bloody hell was that all about?"

Richard turned off the television. "I don't know. But I don't think I want to hear anymore. Let's just get on with the party."

Anna put her hands to her face. "My God, Dad, how can you be so cavalier about this? Did you hear what he said? That's gonna kill Ian's career. And me, that thing about wanting to have children with him. How repugnant."

"The spawn from hell," Jackie whispered.

"Listen Anna," Richard said ignoring Jackie's comment, "there's no reason to get hysterical about this. I've been through things like this before. Bad press is nothing new. I'll make some calls tomorrow and we'll do damage control. That's it. End of story. Now let's forget about it."

"No," she said. "How could you just shrug this off?" Her voice began to rise. "He's controlled our lives long enough. Damage control isn't enough, damn it. I want a written apology—and I want it printed in every newspaper in the civilized world."

"Stop it, Anna!" Richard said. "You can't even get him to sign your divorce papers, and you want a written apology as well?"

"Dad ..." She couldn't finish her sentence.

"Trust me. Do this my way. Nigel's not someone you can fuck around with. We've all learned that the hard way. Besides, what he said—it will all go away. Ian's in the business. He has to develop a tough skin if he doesn't already have one. This won't be the last time things will be said about him that aren't true. It goes with the territory. Isn't that right Christian?"

Christian nodded. "I can remember one time ..."

Anna cut him off. "But it's been going on too long. He has to be stopped."

"And he will." Richard said. "But do it my way. Now come on, let's get back to the party." He walked out of the room.

She stood there in disbelief. Then, all at once, she felt the gentle weight of a delicate arm around her shoulders. It was Angela.

"Shhh," Angela whispered. "Don't worry so much. We'll get through this, and Ian—he's tougher than you think. Nobody's going to believe what Nigel said anyway."

"Don't be so sure, Mom," Ian said as he approached them. "That was my agent. She saw the whole fucking thing. She said I can forget about Love Story."

"There'll be other parts, darling," Angela said.

"Right," Ian answered. "Maybe when someone films *The Queens of England* they'll offer me the lead."

"Ian, I'm sorry about this," Anna said. "It's my fault. He wants to hurt me, not you.

Look, I'll do whatever it takes to straighten this whole thing out. I have to talk to him about the divorce anyway. I'll go to New York and try to get him to sign the papers. Maybe I can think of a way to get him to recant his statement too."

Ian shook his head. "I don't think that's a good idea. He's dangerous Anna. He's not Patras, you know. He's not after your business because he wants a hell of a lot more. Like ripping your fucking heart out. I don't want you to be alone with him ... ever again."

"Come on. What can he do to me that he hasn't already done? I'll just go and offer him something he wants, like the New York apartment and a lifetime supply of peyote, and be on my way. It'll be quick and painless. You'll see."

"No. I don't have a good feeling about it."

"Then come with me."

"Can't. My agent said there's still a chance to get the Schwarzenegger movie. Maybe they're casting his sidekick as a British queer. In any case, the director wants to meet with me in LA the day after tomorrow."

"Then I'll do it alone."

"No," Angela said. "I'll go with you. Ian's right. You shouldn't be alone."

Anna liked that idea. She could use the moral support and she could use the time to get to know Angela a little better. "Okay," she said. "It's settled. I'll take your mother as a chaperone. Will that make you feel better?"

Ian sighed. "I don't know. I suppose. But I still don't like it."

"Come on," Anna answered. "What could possibly go wrong?"

Chapter 18

New York City, Three Months Later

Anna watched out the window as her plane made its way to Kennedy Airport. A winter storm was approaching, and a thin layer of snow had already blanketed the streets and building- tops below. Although she and Angela had intended to depart for New York earlier, business in London kept her home longer than she'd anticipated. Before she knew it, Christmas was approaching, and her visions of the new year, without the suffocating ex husband, were not materializing. So, she convinced Angela that although she'd have to spend Christmas without Richard, the holidays were spectacular in New York, and shouldn't be missed. Besides, the shopping was unbeatable.

A waiting limousine driver whisked them from the terminal and skidded his way through the exit ramps only to take his place amongst the largest parking lot in New York City, otherwise known as the Van Wyck Expressway. The two women watched the snow pile up on the hood, while the Classic Rock Station softly played "Ruby Tuesday" in the background.

Anna thought about Ian, and how she wished he could be there with her, instead of his mother. But, despite Nigel's sordid lies, the Schwarzenegger film was becoming a reality. With a little help from S & A's finely tuned public relations machine, Ian Moore was once again on top of the Hollywood hunk list. Some secret source tipped off the editors of *The Star* and *National Tattle Tale* that Ian Moore was involved in an intimate liaison with the blonde rock and roll bombshell Amber Stilleto. Within minutes, both tabloids churned out full color layouts of the sexy duo engaged in full-court X-rated behavior. The fans loved it, once again reassured that their idol was the hot-blooded male stud they fantasized about. Of course, Ian barely knew who Amber Stilleto was, having only bumped into her briefly at a party months ago. He remembered the paparazzi frantically flashing pictures of them together, but he could never have imagined what Richard's PR team could produce with a little help of computer-generated graphics and darkroom techniques.

Within a day of the tabloid spread, Ian was back in action. Luckily for him, the director of the Schwarzenegger film was casting a World War II British counterintelligence agent who runs up against Arnold, who plays an American spy infiltrating the German SS (due to his superior intellect and mastery of languages) and discovers the Brit's true identity.

With little time to prepare for the role, Ian took up immediate residency in a beach house in Malibu. Shooting began for the film. He and Anna maintained constant contact through daily telephone calls and weekend visits, but it wasn't enough. Anna found herself missing him more and more as the days went by, so she arranged for Jackie to replace her at the London office for a couple of months. She would meet up in Malibu with Ian after her business in New York.

After inching its way along the Triboro Bridge and down the FDR Drive, the limousine pulled up alongside Richard's apartment building on Fifth Avenue, where Anna and Angela decided to stay while in New York. Although Anna still maintained her apartment on Park Avenue, she had left it in the incapable hands of Nigel, who had promised to vacate it at some point. What point that was, they weren't sure, and in what condition he left it—well, that was another matter entirely.

The doorman grabbed their bags from the trunk and pulled them into the lobby. He was carrying them towards the elevator when Anna stopped him. She wasn't ready to head indoors yet. "Wait a moment," she told him, "I want to get something from one of the bags." She reached into the largest of her bags, pulled out a pair of snow boots, kicked off her shoes and began putting the boots on.

"I think I'll be going for a little walk first," she said. "Angela, why don't you come? There's no better way to see the city than on a quiet snowy night."

Without hesitating, Angela unzipped her suitcase and rummaged her way to the bottom. "I wouldn't miss it," she said as she pulled out her own boots. "Lead the way."

The two women walked slowly down Fifth Avenue along Central Park. Anna told Angela stories about her college days, how she and her roommates walked along Riverside Park in the snow.

In turn, Angela told stories about her own childhood, growing up in the English countryside, and her first memories of Christmas. She reminisced about her mother, how she'd string popcorn and berries for the tree, and her first real present: a porcelain doll with bright blue eyes and black curly hair that she pretended was her baby sister.

Before they knew it, they found themselves at the crossroads of Fiftieth Street and Fifth Avenue. To their right loomed Rockefeller Center with its giant Christmas tree lit up with thousands of multicolored lights. Anna led Angela past the life-size wooden angels toward the tree.

Angela was mesmerized by it all. "I've never seen anything like this," she said. "Enchanting. That's the right word for it, don't you think?"

Anna glanced at Angela whose eyes had grown as wide as a child's. "That's a perfect word for it." She continued leading her toward the tree and then stopped at the wrought-iron fence surrounding the ice skating rink below.

"Do you skate?"

Angela shook her head and laughed. "No, not me."

"Ever tried?"

"No, not that many opportunities."

Anna thought about her winter vacations in Gsadt and Zermatt, skating beneath the Matterhorn and skiing the highest peaks. Their lives had been so different, yet they were bound by the two people they each most loved in this life: Richard Winters and Ian Moore. She took

Angela's arm. "Come on," she said, "let's rent some skates. I'll teach you what I know, though it's not very much."

Angela shrugged. "Why not?" she said.

Within moments, they were laced up and ready to go. Anna locked her arms around Angela's and together, they stepped out onto the ice. Angela's steps were slow and unsteady, but after a couple of trips around the rink, her strides became more confident. She let go of Anna's arm and took her hand instead.

The air was still, as the snow continued to fall. They skated in silence and listened to the waltzes blaring on the megaphone overhead. A small group of onlookers sang "Twelve Days of Christmas." The two women smiled as they tried to remember all the gifts after number five their true loves gave them. When the song was over, Anna felt the grip on her hand tighten.

"Is something wrong?"

"No," Angela said. "There's nothing wrong. I'm just having so much fun. I wish your father were here too. He would have loved this."

That comment hit a nerve. "I wish he were here too. I don't know why he wouldn't come. Maybe you could help me understand."

Angela skated over to the guard rail and stopped. She looked up at the falling snow. "He didn't want us to come here," she said. "He didn't want you to confront Nigel. He thought it was a bad idea."

"But I have to confront him. The divorce will drag on forever if I don't do something to make him sign the papers."

"Your father said he could've handled everything from London."

"Handled everything? Like what?"

"Paid him off from there."

"I don't want my father to pay him off—"

"No, you want to do it yourself."

"It's more than that Angela," she snapped. "It's not just a payoff. He needs to understand what he's done— the lives he's destroyed and the people he's hurt."

"How do you think you're going to do that? Have a heart to heart talk with him?"

"He doesn't have a heart."

"Right. It's not going to be easy. You can't change someone who's inherently a villain into a saint. The most you can do is get out of his way, so he can't hurt you again."

"So, you think this was a mistake too?"

She sighed. "Yes, I do."

"Then why did you come?"

"Because your father wouldn't, and even though he loves you, he's too headstrong to give in, which I think is wrong too. So, aside from my son, who's too involved in his own career at the moment, that leaves me. You see, someone has to be here to support you, someone who loves you. That's what mothers do, you know. They love and support you even when they don't exactly agree with what you're doing."

"You have a lot of experience in the mother department, don't you?"

"Yes, and I know you're probably thinking you're too old for a stepmom, but nobody's too old to have someone love them."

"You're right. I wouldn't even know what to do with a mother if I had one. It was always just me, my dad and my grandparents." Anna stopped and smiled. "I just thought of something Ian said—that there's always room for one more person to love. Now I know that's true. It's actually very easy to let one more person in."

"Amazing how big our hearts can be when we open them up."

"It is. Just do me one favor though."

"Anything."

"When you're officially my stepmother, don't start telling me to clean my room or anything like that."

They both laughed.

Anna rubbed her hands together and looked around. "Maybe we should get going," she said. "The wind's starting to kick up and we have a long walk home."

Anna woke up the next morning with a burst of energy. The sun was pouring in through her bedroom window and she bounded out of bed ready to tackle the day's big event: inspecting the damage done to her old apartment by her soon-to-be ex.

She checked the time. It was already after 9:00, and she was sure there was a lot to do. Angela was already awake; she could smell the fresh coffee brewing in the kitchen. So, after a quick shower, she headed toward the kitchen to join her.

"Are you ready to work?" she asked Angela, while reaching for a cup.

"What makes you so sure the apartment will be a disaster?"

"I lived with the asshole for two years," she answered. "I know his habits. But don't worry, I have a Swat team of cleaning people coming at noon. I just want to survey the nightmare before they get there. Maybe get things in order."

"Are you sure he's gone?"

"My lawyer assured me he is."

"So when are you planning to see him then, to talk about the divorce and all?"

"Maybe tomorrow. I don't know. The lawyers are talking."

Angela put her cup down and headed to the closet. "Well, let's not waste any more time." She reached for her coat and put it on. "It's gonna be a long day."

The snow was piled high on the curb outside the building, which had already started taking on the grayish hue of asphalt and grime. Knowing that finding a taxi without bald tires on a day like today would be impossible, the two women decided to walk. They trudged and sloshed their way through the banks, and eventually found themselves in front of Anna's Park Avenue skyrise.

They pounded their boots out on the slushy welcome mats and took the express elevator to the penthouse. Not sure what she'd find, Anna hesitated a moment before putting the key in the door. Then, she took a deep breath, turned the safety latch, and opened it up. Immediately, they both stood back from the stench of stale tobacco that rushed to overtake them. In unison, they put their hands up to their noses to block the foul odor but they knew it was futile—and about to get worse. Only a military gas mask would have protected them from impending nausea.

Anna walked in first. Without looking around, she headed straight for the balcony windows; she threw them open and took a deep breath.

"It's okay," she said to Angela. "You can come in now."

"But we'll freeze."

"It's either that or choke."

Anna looked around. It was worse than anything she could have imagined. The room was one giant garbage can. Empty food containers everywhere. Half-filled glasses and cups on every table top. Anything that even resembled a small oval was used as an ashtray. She walked over to her mahogany baby grand piano in the corner. A bottle of gin and two glasses had left their water marks in the wood. Cigarette burns on the white ivory keys. An 'A sharp major' had been used as an ashtray too.

She heard Angela gasp.

"Are you all right?" Anna said.

"Yes," she called back. "It's just been a long time since I've seen roaches, the crawling kind, that is."

Anna walked over to her and stared down at the pizza box being visited by a dozen or so crawling insects. She put her hands to her face and closed her eyes.

"This is too disgusting, Angela," she said. "Let's just get out of here and wait for the cleaning people to do their thing. Maybe I'll call them and have them bring some blow torches or something."

"No, darling. That's not a good idea. We should stay and get things started. You don't want strangers coming into your apartment and finding things like that, do you?" She pointed to the floor.

Anna turned around and looked down. "It's not what I'm thinking." She bent down to get a closer look. "A hypodermic needle. Great. I don't suppose anyone would believe Nigel's diabetic."

"I don't suppose."

Anna looked around the room again. It was going to be a daunting task but the last thing she needed was for strangers to come in and find Nigel's drug paraphernalia strewn all over her apartment. "Okay," she sighed. "We'd better get to work. I'll run out and get a few cleaning supplies, and some rubber gloves." She headed for the door. "I'll be back in a few moments." She looked down and stopped short. Nigel's guitar case was in her way. Frustrated, she kicked it aside. The case knocked against a small end table and sent a large Waterford crystal vase crashing to the floor. Anna leaped back and gasped as the glass shattered all around her.

"Are you all right?" Angela shouted.

Anna looked down and the small shards of glass around her feet. "Shit," she said. "Shit, shit shit shit."

Angela, then coming to see what the problem was, took her by the shoulders and led her to the door. "Get going," she said. "I'll get started here. There must be a broom somewhere, right?"

"In the kitchen." She turned around and slammed the door behind her.

What the fuck was that? Nigel thought as he lay in his bed. *Sounded like a fucking bomb went off.* He didn't open his eyes. He couldn't. It hurt too much to even think about it. He wondered where he was, whether it was night or day. Day, it had to be day. He remembered not having to turn on the bathroom light while he puked into the toilet bowl, but maybe that was yesterday.

Something fuzzy was on his face. That was new. It was usually his mouth that just felt fuzzy. He reached up to scratch it but it moved. It was hair, and it wasn't his. He moved his hand to the left and felt a head. There was somebody in the bed with him, but who? Slowly, he moved his head to the side and opened his eyes. The light made his temples throb. Finally, after a few moments, they focused. *Fuck*, he thought, *it's Amber.* What the fuck was she doing there? *Oh yeah*, he thought, *I fucked her.*

He poked at her arm but she didn't move. Maybe she was dead? To warm. Besides, he could never be so lucky. Now, she would wake up and want to talk over coffee, or something. Maybe try to make plans to see each other again. Christ, women were so needy. When were they ever gonna get it? Men just wanted to get off: fuck and move on. End of story.

He grabbed a pack of cigarettes from the bedside table. He knocked over a bottle of pills—the Quaaludes he and Amber had taken at sunrise. It all started to come back to him.

The party—he had invited, maybe 30 or 40 people, all from the record industry, over to the apartment last night. It was wild. They'd jammed all night, but the coke kept him awake. He needed something to come down but he was out of sleeping pills. So he and Amber popped a few 'Ludes. Amber passed out right away but the pills only made him horny. So he climbed on top of her and went to town. *Nothing like an unconscious fuck,* he thought. *No foreplay, no yapping.*

He heard noises in the living room. Someone from the party maybe? No, it couldn't be. He was sure he had seen everyone leave, but who knew? He turned over the pack of cigarettes on the nightstand and two joints tumbled out. Just the thing he needed to get over the hangover. He lit up, inhaled deeply, and stared at the ceiling. He felt the room moving, or was it the bed; he wasn't sure. His mind started to drift—the 'Ludes hadn't worn off yet, and his skin began to tingle. He thought about Amber, her naked body besides his. He touched her breasts and felt the erection beneath the sheets begin to grow.

He pulled off the sheets and rolled on top of her. He heard a soft moan as his hand slid between her legs. "Shit," he whispered. "Don't do me any favors and wake up now."

Suddenly, he heard it again. In the living room. Who the fuck was it and what the hell were they doing? He rolled off of Amber and put on his trousers. *She'll wait,* he thought. *She's not going anywhere for a while.*

He stumbled out of the bedroom and glanced around. Nobody was there. A delicate-looking woman with black curly hair came out of the kitchen.

"Who the fuck are you?" he asked.

Angela was startled. What was he doing here? Nigel, Christ, he might not have known who she was, but she certainly knew him. They had met before, only briefly, at Richard's house in Belgravia. She didn't know then that he was the monster who would help cause the death of her husband.

She didn't know what to say. He wasn't supposed to be there. She fumbled for words. "I'm sorry. I didn't know you were here."

He walked toward her to get a closer look. "I said, who the fuck are you and how did you get in without a key?"

Angela didn't like the tone of his voice. "I have a key," she said. "It's Anna's key. I'm Angela Moore, her ... father's friend."

Nigel was surprised. "Her father's friend?" he said sarcastically. "What do you mean by that? You're a friend of that prick's? That makes you a prick too, doesn't it?" He moved even closer. "So tell me, Angela, what was that, Moorse? What are you doing here?"

Angela stepped back. She didn't like being in the same room with him. He was clearly drunk, or drugged, or something. "Anna and I came by to straighten up her apartment. You were supposed to have moved out."

"What do you mean? Her aparsement?" He was slurring his words. He shook his head as if to clear out the smoke. "We're not divorced. It's still half mine."

Angela stepped back again but her back hit the wall. She felt a wave of panic. "I'm sorry then," she said, "I'll just get my things and leave." He blocked her exit.

He grabbed her arm. "So you're a friend of Richard's? Huh? Did he send you here to spy on me? Is that it? You're one of his fucking little spies? So, what's he looking for? Answer me."

His grip on her arm tightened and it began to hurt. She tried to pull away but he wouldn't let go. "I'm not a spy. I'm Richard's fiancée—"

She couldn't finish her sentence. Nigel released her arm and pushed her backwards in one motion. "What did you say?" he laughed. "Fiancée?"

Angela felt her body trembling. He was clearly out of his mind. Her eyes locked on the front door. She had to get out, but there was no way around him. Then, all at once, with her back up against the wall, she felt the full weight of his body come up against her. She could feel his breath against her face.

He rubbed his body up against hers, pulled her hair back, and whispered into her ear, "So, what are you so nervous about? Didn't Dick tell you? I have a thing about fucking all the women in his life."

My God, she thought. *This can't be happening.* "Please, please, let go of me." She felt tears welling up in her eyes.

Nigel's dick was throbbing. He couldn't have asked for a better wake-up call. Of all the women to wander into his apartment. Christ, how lucky could he be? Winters' fiancée, and she wasn't a dog either. On the contrary, she was quite beautiful. He put his hand between her legs. *Shit,* he thought, *slacks.*

He heard her scream and he covered her mouth. "Don't do that again," he said, "besides, nobody can hear you anyway." He took his hand away and he heard her scream again. He slapped her face, hard, and she fell to the floor.

He sat on top of her and began to unzip his trousers. "What are you crying about?" he asked her as he moved on to her slacks and panties. "If you don't move, I won't hurt you. Besides," he grinned, "you might even like it."

Angela was paralyzed with fear. She felt warm blood oozing from her mouth, and although she wanted to scream she knew he'd hit her again. She struggled slightly, but he was at least twice her size. She felt herself choking. She couldn't get any air. She was crying so hard she began to hyperventilate. Then, it happened: he was inside her. She felt the pain, then the thrusting. She closed her eyes and prayed for it to end but it seemed like an eternity. He was saying something but she couldn't hear anything but her own soft cries for help. Then he began to yell, but she couldn't make out the words. There was so much noise, because of the other voice. There was another voice in the room. She opened her eyes and, using every ounce of her strength, screamed, "Please! Someone, help me!"

Through her tears, she saw Anna standing behind Nigel—with the hypodermic needle poised at his neck. "Hey, shit-head," she screamed, "I said get the hell away from her."

He turned around. "Fuck off, Anna." he said, "Can't you see I'm in the middle of something?"

She didn't hesitate. She pulled his head back by his hair with one hand, and with the other jammed the empty needle into the side of his neck. Like a wounded animal, he let out a loud groan and jerked his head sideways. He reached back and pulled out the needle, saw the blood dripping from its tip, and threw it across the room in a fit of rage.

"Jeezus, you bitch," he screamed. He moved off of Angela and staggered his way to his knees. "I'm gonna fucking kill you."

Anna knew that she had to act fast. She had to get him now, while he was still off balance. She looked around for another weapon. Then she spotted it: the guitar. She ran across the room, threw open the lid and grabbed the ten-pound Fender electric. With a look of defiance, she held it by its neck and dragged it back across the room.

"Don't move, you son of a bitch," she said in a steady tone, "or I'm gonna enjoy crushing your head in with this thing."

Nigel put up his hands. "Whoa, wait," he pleaded. "Not that. You could bloody kill me with that thing."

"And the problem is?"

"Come on now. You don't want to hurt your old luv, Nigel, now would you?"

"Wrong. I'd enjoy every second of it," she snapped back.

"Okay, okay. But it's not what you think. She was begging for it, then things got a little out of hand—"

Anna gripped the neck of the guitar tighter. "Shut up, don't say another word," she warned. "Just move back and—"

Just then, Anna saw Angela standing behind Nigel, with another of her Waterford vases dangling over his head. Without thinking, she blurted out, "My God, wait—" but it was too late. The vase crashed down on his head. Nigel, along with hundreds of pieces of broken glass, tumbled to the floor.

With a look of total satisfaction, Angela looked over his motionless body. "Begging for it, huh?" she mumbled. She gave him a swift kick to his stomach. He groaned and rolled over to his side. "Too bad. He's still alive."

The two women looked at each other. Anna knew what Angela was thinking. Maybe they should finish him off right then and there. It was self-defense. The police would buy it. The drugs, the rape. All the evidence was there. She looked down at the guitar. It would be so easy.

Anna held the guitar over Nigel's head. "What do you think? Do we do it?"

"I don't know."

"He'd be out of our lives for good. Just give me the word."

"Me?"

"I can't make this decision alone."

"Well, I can't do it for you."

"I know, we'll flip a coin. Heads, he keeps his, tails, it goes. Go get a quarter, I'll stand guard."

They were suddenly interrupted by the sound of a woman's raspy voice.

"Hey you guys, you all partying without me?"

Anna and Angela spun around to see a tall blonde, wearing only a miracle bra and thong underwear. *Christ,* Anna thought. *Amber Stiletto— what the hell's she doing here?*

Amber walked over to Nigel. "Hey, what happened here?" she squealed. "What's my little poopsie doll doing all over the floor?"

The two women glanced at each other again. Anna motioned toward the door. "Let's get out of here," she said. She turned to Amber. "You should call a doctor or an ambulance. There was a little accident. Your poopsie doll accidentally dropped a vase over his own head."

Amber looked perplexed. "How'd he do that? The poor little thing."

Anna grabbed Angela's coat and led her to the door. Within moments they were in a taxi racing back to Richard's apartment. Angela was silent. She stared out the window. Anna put her arms around her and stoked her hair gently.

"I'm all right, Anna," she said softly. "Everything will be just fine."

"No," Anna answered. "This was all my fault. We never should've come."

"Then do me a favor," she said. "Call your father when we get in. Tell him to meet with Nigel. Tell him to give that bastard anything he wants to get him out of our lives. No matter what the cost."

"It's done, Angela," she sighed. "Don't worry. It's done."

Chapter 19

LONDON, TWO DAYS LATER

Anna greeted Richard at the front door of her Chelsea townhouse. He hadn't spoken to her since picking them up at the airport two days earlier. Even then, he barely managed to say a few monosyllabic words in her direction. It had taken all her courage to ask him to come see her. When she opened the door, she saw him look away.

"I'm glad you came," she said with some hesitation. "I think that we really need to talk."

Richard walked in, and, without looking in her direction, shot back, "About what?"

Knowing full well where he was heading, she walked ahead of him and handed him a glass. "What's it gonna be?" she asked. "Scotch or Vodka?"

He studied the glass. "Scotch ... and what kind of shitty little glass is this anyway? Made for a midget? Don't you have anything bigger?"

Failing to control her impulses, Anna snapped back, "Why don't you just take the whole bottle?" She caught herself and stopped before saying any more.

He grabbed the Scotch from behind the bar, cracked open the seal, and belted back two long gulps. "Thanks, that was a good idea."

He walked over to the sofa, sat down, and planted the bottle squarely in front of him on the coffee table. "So," he said, "what do you want to talk about? Let me think. It can't be anything that would have to do with me, so it must be about you, right? Maybe your career, you always want to talk about that. The great, mighty Anna Stavropoulos, or is it Winters? You should've stopped at the un-fucking pronounceable Greek name." He took another drink. "Where was I? Right, we were talking about you. That's what we're always doing, talking about you. So, let's talk then."

She walked toward him and stared at the bottle he was now holding on his lap. "Dad," she said, "this isn't the first drink you've had this morning, is it?"

He let his head fall back, then looked in her direction. "So what?" he said. "Why all of a sudden do you give a shit about me ... unless it affects you, of course. Then you'd care. Christ, the world just revolves around you, you and how you're gonna cure its evils. But you couldn't do it this time, could you? You had to try, even after I told you not to, and now— my God, look what you've done. The only woman I've loved in almost thirty years crying from nightmares about the man who raped her, your husband." He closed his eyes and didn't say another word.

Anna felt as if her heart was in a vise. She knew he was angry with her, but this angry? She didn't dare try to defend herself. There was nothing she could say. He was right. He had warned her not to confront Nigel but she was too stubborn to listen.

She sat next him and stared at his face. He looked fragile and vulnerable, and she knew that, behind all the anger, he was in pain. She searched for the right words but could only whisper, "I'm sorry, Dad. I thought I was doing the right thing."

"The right thing," he repeated. "How could you be so naive? You may have been married to him for a couple of years, but I lived and breathed that piece of scum for over half my life. There are things you don't know, that you shouldn't know...."

More? she thought. *My God, his depravity's endless.* "Like what?"

"I can't tell you. It's too hard for me, and it would be harder on you."

Anna's always strong curiosity was pulsating throughout her body, but she knew her father was in too much pain as it was, so she let the issue drop. "Tell me, Dad, " she said. "Angela, is she all right?"

"Yeah," he answered. "She's all right. She'll make it through all this. I brought my shrink over to see her, probably not the best choice considering I've been seeing him for twenty years and look at me. But what the hell. Maybe he'll do something for her."

"I'd like to go see her, but I'm afraid—"

"That she blames you? She doesn't."

"Only you do."

"No," he shot back. "I just think you were in way over your head this time. You should've left it to me from the start. I told you I was gonna handle it."

"I didn't want my daddy fighting my battles for me. I thought I was a big girl and I could do it myself, but I guess I was wrong."

He shook his head. "No, you weren't wrong. You just went up against somebody a hell of a lot bigger than you." He smiled at her. "But I have to say," he continued, "you did a great job with that needle and the guitar. Angela told me all about it. Too bad you didn't finish him."

She smiled back. "We still think the same in a lot of ways. Don't think it didn't cross my mind. Given another minute or two without Amber Stilleto in the room, who knows what would have happened."

"That was an unfortunate interruption."

"You better believe it was."

"Listen, Anna," Richard said, "sometimes you have to admit that you need help. You can't go through life trying to conquer it all by yourself. That's what I'm here for. Promise me that if things ever get rough again, you'll come to me."

"Don't say any more. Of course I promise."

He put the bottle down and took her in his arms. "I'm sorry for what I said," he whispered.

"I'm sorry for this whole mess, Daddy," she whispered back.

"We'll fix it. Don't worry."

"I know."

After a few moments, Richard got up and headed to the kitchen. "I think I need a tall glass of water and a half a dozen aspirin. Maybe I can ward off this hangover before it begins."

Anna followed him into the kitchen, reached into her medicine pantry, and handed him a bottle of aspirin. "So tell me," she said, "I hate to bring up his name again, but did you talk to Nigel at all?"

Richard filled his glass and sat down on a bar stool behind the counter. "Yeah," he nodded, "I talked to him."

"And?"

"What do you think? I asked him what it would take to get him out of our lives?"

"What did he say?"

"You don't want to know."

"Of course I want to know."

Richard shrugged. "All right, but it's only going to make you sick. He's taking the Park Avenue Apartment, the Villa in Zermatt, your summer home on Xenos—"

"No," she gasped, "not that."

"Quiet. I'm not done yet. All the cars, your yacht, and another three-year recording deal with S & A. And he asked for a little spending money to go along with all this—somewhere between five and six million pounds. He said he'll get back to me with the exact figure."

Anna was stunned. She sat silently for a moment. She was still fixated on the house on Xenos. "The house, and the yacht—those are really Grandpa's. I can't give those away."

"I've already cleared it with him. His lawyers are getting the paperwork ready."

She stamped her foot on the floor. "That bastard belongs in jail, not riding around in my cars and yachts."

"That's not the issue," Richard said. "And, that's not all of it either."

"What? I can't believe there's more."

"I've been saving the best for last. All that I just mentioned, well that's just to get him off my back. It doesn't include signing the divorce papers. He wants another lump sum payment for that."

"How much?"

"Don't know. Said he'll get back to me with that one too."

Anna felt herself begin to boil over. "How could he do this?" she said between clenched teeth. "When he goes through all the money, he'll just come back for more. We'll never get rid of him. Maybe we should turn him in to the police. He should've been arrested back in New York for what he did to Angela. And me? I'll just take him to court and get a judge to finalize the divorce."

Richard gave her a disapproving stare. "Stop it, Anna. If Angela presses charges against him, she'll be dragged through the American courts. It would be a media zoo ... the cameras, clips on the nightly gossip shows, the innuendo. Is that what you want?

"I didn't think of that—"

"No, of course you didn't. And what about you? Take him to court? So he can drag you down with him too? Think of the lies he could come up with, the trumped-up pictures he could produce. Think of what he could say about your relationship with Ian. He's already tried to ruin his career once. Next time maybe he can focus on the fact that he's involved with his future stepsister. That'll go over well with his fans, don't you think?"

"So we're back to square one again? Just pay him off."

"Right. And when he comes back for more, I'll just fucking give it to him."

"I feel like a wimp."

"Let's make a pact to just stay afloat."

"For now."

The doorbell rang.

Clearly irritated, Richard said, "Expecting someone?"

"Grandpa."

"Great. Just who I needed to see to make my day complete."

Anna went to the front door. Richard followed. "What's he want?"

"He's just dropping off something that I asked Grandma to find for me. Don't worry. He's on his way to the office. He's not planning on staying. We can finish our conversation later." She opened the door and gave her grandfather a big hug. Constantine stepped inside and handed

Anna a shoebox. Then, he looked past his granddaughter and shuddered upon seeing Richard.

"Well, this is a surprise. I hadn't expected to see you here." He sniffed the air around him. "Ahh," he continued, "and I see you've been drinking too, a little early, even for a *malaka* like you. Wouldn't you say?"

"Grandpa, behave yourself. And no Greek words in front of my Dad. It's rude."

"Please, Anna," Richard said. "You don't have to defend me. Besides, after all these years of hanging around your grandfather, you don't think I know that he just called me an idiot?"

Constantine smirked. "And I thought you never learned any Greek. It's a proud day for Hellenism indeed."

Anna shook her head. "Oh, here we go again."

"No, no," Constantine said. "I'm through for the day. No more insults. I promise."

"I find that hard to believe, but—whatever Gramps." She looked at the shoebox. "So, what's in here? I only asked Grandma to find me mom's medallion."

"Open it up and find out."

Anna took off the lid and peered in. Inside were two small jewelry boxes and a small red leather-bound book. She looked back up at her grandfather. "What's all this?" she asked.

"One of those small boxes is the medallion you wanted, the Alpha and Omega. In the other is your mother's wedding ring—"

"What?" Richard exclaimed. "What do you mean 'her wedding ring'? She was buried with it on."

"No," Constantine said, with some trepidation, "she wasn't. My wife slipped it off her finger before the casket was closed. She felt that the ring belonged with the living, not the dead."

"She should've asked," Richard said.

"My wife is," Constantine paused, "how can I put this? Let's just say she's not very verbal."

"She never had to be. You always talked enough for the two of you."

Anna held up the red leather-bound book. "And this? What is it?"

"That," Constantine said, "your grandmother found while she was looking for the medallion. It's a journal, your mother's journal. She had it with her while she was in New York, when she died. Your grandmother put it away with all her other things, and only found it a couple days ago. She didn't open it, but she thought you might like to."

Anna was overwhelmed. "Yes," she said, with some hesitation, "I guess I'd like to."

"Anyway," Constantine said as he leaned over and kissed her on the cheek, "I've got to go. Staff meeting in a half hour."

"Christ, old man," Richard said, "not even a heart attack can slow you down."

"No," he answered, "not even that." He turned to leave but stopped short and looked back at Richard. "I know we spoke on the phone the other day about Anna's legal transactions with Taylor, but I don't think I asked you," after a long silence, the older man said, "how's Angela?"

Richard was taken aback by Constantine's concern. "She's fine," he said. "No, I mean she'll be fine. Thank you for asking."

"Good, I'm glad to hear that." Again Constantine paused then continued, "Because I was thinking ... I know how much she likes Xenos. She spent a whole summer there with her kids. That's how you met really, so maybe she'd like it if you got married there? You could do it in August, during the festivals, and use my new house for the reception, or the yacht if she'd like. The church in Nassos is beautiful: we could invite the whole town, just like the weddings I remember as a kid."

Richard and Anna were both speechless. They glanced at each other and didn't say a word.

"Anyway," Constantine continued, "it's only a thought. I'm sure you have plans of your own."

Richard was dumbfounded. He couldn't figure out what was behind the sudden peace offering. He hesitated for a second, then answered, "No, we don't have any other plans at the moment. But I don't get it. Why the offer?"

Constantine smiled. "Would you believe that I'm just a nice guy?"

"No. Try again."

"Well, believe what you want. In any case, I happen to like Angela, and besides, Anna's in love with her son, which makes Angela family."

Anna grabbed Richard's arm. "Dad," she said. "It's a great idea. Angela would love it and we'd have a blast."

"Just what I was thinking, Richard," Constantine said. "We could have a party that would send shock waves across the continents. Why don't you call me later? Let me run a few other thoughts past you. Then you can give me your final answer."

"Sure, why not." Richard closed the door behind Constantine and slowly made his way to the living room. Anna followed and handed him the shoebox as he sat down on the sofa.

"Here, Dad," she said. "These things belong more to you than they do to me."

He opened the small jewelry box containing Sara's wedding ring. He took it out and lifted it towards the open window. The sun streaming in bounced off the chain of diamonds and an array of small white lights sparkled across the walls and ceiling.

He didn't say anything as he tilted the ring back and forth, watching as the little dots bounced and danced across the room.

"It's beautiful," Anna said. "What are you going to do with it?"

He put it back in the box and closed the lid. "Don't know," he said. "Put it away with her other things, I guess." He took out the journal and thumbed through the pages. He remembered how distinctive Sara's handwriting had been. She always used print, never script. Each letter was meticulously drawn; the capitals never exceeded a certain height, and the lower cases were perfectly even. And the 'f's,' like a calculus equation, all had a curve on the top, as well as a countercurve on the bottom.

He continued to riffle through the pages. "I didn't even know she kept this." He stopped and showed Anna a page. "Look here: August 21st, her entry for the day we met."

Anna took the book out of his hands and began to read it out loud. Sara's description of their first meeting was just as he remembered it: their accidental meeting behind the stage at the Athens concert, seeing each other after the show at the Palace Hotel, and spending the rest of the night together eating, walking along the beach, and talking, talking until sunrise.

Richard smiled as Anna read on. He remembered every sight, sound, and smell as if were happening all over again. Then, Anna paused before reading the last few lines:

This is it, I know it's it. I can see the future right now. It's hard to believe that it happened so soon, that at 17 I met the man I'm going to share the rest of my life with. I think he knows it too. Richard Winters, the most beautiful man I've ever met or ever will meet—my love and my life, forever.

Anna looked up to see her father wiping tears from his eyes. "Maybe it's not a good idea to read any more of this," she said as she placed the book on the edge of coffee table. "Why don't you just take it home too."

"That's a good idea. This isn't the best day to be bringing back these memories anyway." He shifted uncomfortably on the sofa. His right leg knocked the journal off the table. It fell to the floor, open and face up. When Richard leaned over to pick it up, he saw the first words on the exposed page: "I don't think Richard should know about this. I don't think I can tell him, not yet." He continued reading only to be interrupted by Anna.

"I thought you were going to put it away."

"In a moment. There's something in here that I have to read right now." He continued to read:

Richard was out and Nigel called. He asked me to bring over some contracts that he said he needed immediately. I went. I shouldn't have but I did. He poured me some wine, and we talked for a while. He was being charming and interesting ... and then, he kissed me. I let it happen for a moment, I don't know why. Maybe I was feeling lonely. Richard is always out doing something, leaving me at home. Anyway, it was mistake. I told Nigel so but he wouldn't listen. A few seconds later he tried to force himself on me. It would have happened if his assistant hadn't let herself in and interrupted him.

The guilt is overwhelming. I love Richard so much. I can't believe the whole thing happened. I don't know what to do, if I should tell him or not. It would tear him apart, and break up the partnership. They need each other to work. I don't want to be the one responsible for the breakup of the group. I'll tell Richard some day. But not now.

Richard sat back and thought about what he had just read. There it was: the truth about what really happened that night. It had tormented him for years, and now, it was finally clear.

Anna took the book out of his hands and glanced at the page. "So," she said, "what was so important that you had to read it right now?"

"Why don't you read it and find out?"

Anna's eyes widened as she began to read the entry. The thought of that loathsome creature making a play for her mother made her skin crawl. She thought about what her father had told her just a few moments ago about Nigel—that there was more to his story, things that she didn't know about. This was it.

She finished reading and looked up at her father. "I can't believe it," she said. "Did you know about this? Is this what you couldn't tell me about?"

Richard was so tired he could barely pull his strength together to answer her question. "It's something like that," he sighed. "You see, I never knew what really happened. Your mother died before she had a chance to tell me. The problem is, I got a whole other version from Nigel, one where your mother didn't refuse him."

"And you believed him?"

"No. Yes. I didn't know what to believe. But it's tormented me for years. You see, the last few years the group was together were, let's just say, difficult. Nigel and I had a lot of creative differences. Basically, we couldn't agree on anything. His music was going one way, and mine, another. We fought all the time and I was just getting tired of the whole thing. After awhile, I couldn't take all the arguing, and I wanted out. That's when it became ugly. He knew his career was gonna to take a dive and he couldn't sell records without me, but instead of trying to work things out, he attacked me with anything he could. He undermined my leadership, tried to get Christian and the others to go with him, and when that didn't work, he went for the jugular. He told me stories about your mother; how she really wanted him, and not me."

"But you must have known he was lying."

"Deep down I did, but then he told me about her birthmark, the one on her hip. I don't know how he would have seen it—"

"You mean the four-leaf clover?"

Richard looked at her in surprise. "Yes, did I tell you about it?"

"No, Christian did."

"What? How did he know about it?"

"After a photo shoot one day, he and Nigel and Mom were walking in a field of grass, when Nigel spotted a four-leafed clover. He picked it and gave it to Mom. She put it up against her hip and said she didn't need it, because she already had one as a birthmark right there. Anyway, a few years ago, Christian brought back a painting from Amsterdam, of a little girl holding a bouquet of clovers. He said it reminded him of Mom and he wanted me to have it. That's when he told me."

"I wish he'd told me the story, about twenty years ago."

She put her arms around him. "I'm sorry, Dad. I'm sorry you had to live with that uncertainty all these years."

"Don't be," he said. "I knew he was lying, and I'd get to the bottom of it one of these days. But it's a good to be free of the ghosts." He stood up, put the journal in the shoebox, and handed it to her. "Here, why don't you keep it?"

"Are you sure?"

"My memories of those days are as clear as if they'd happened yesterday. So you keep it. I could never describe them to you as well as she could. But there is one thing I want." He took out the jewelry box. "If you don't mind, I'd like to keep this. It doesn't belong in a dark box. Your grandmother was right: it belongs with the living."

"Whatever you want." She walked him to the door. "It's been a hell of a morning huh?" she said.

"Yes, and thanks for the invitation. I'll be expecting you to come by the house later. Angela could use the company, and so could I."

"Sure, Dad, I'll be there. See you later." She closed the door and headed toward the stairs. Her head was reeling: Nigel's demands, her grandfather's sudden peace offering, and her mother's journal. *All in the span of about an hour,* she thought. *If I had the strength, I could go for a real stiff drink right now.* She opted for her bed instead of the bar. That's what she needed. Between nightmares about Nigel and jet lag, she could count on one hand the hours of sleep she'd had the past couple of nights.

She sank down into the goose down comforter that was still disheveled from the night before, took the phone off the hook, wrapped the comforter around her, wedged up her pillow under her neck, and closed her eyes. This must be what heaven feels like: all warm and cozy, and safe.

But again her sleep was uneasy. Dreams awakened her, but she somehow couldn't differentiate between her dreams and reality. People were talking to her in her room, but she couldn't answer them. She tried to talk, to wake herself up, but she couldn't open her mouth.

Then she felt someone standing over her. She forced herself to open her eyes. There, to her complete astonishment she saw herself. She knew she was dreaming, but everything seemed so alive. The woman smiled and touched her face with a gentle hand. Anna wanted to reach up and touch the woman but her own hand was paralyzed.

The woman leaned closer to her. "You're so beautiful," she whispered, "and I'm so proud of you. Don't worry about anything. Everything's going to be just fine. You'll see." She leaned even closer and brushed Anna's cheek with her lips.

Using every ounce of strength she could find, Anna cried out, "Mom." Instantly, her sleep was broken and she opened her eyes. There, sitting beside her on the bed was Ian.

"Mom?" he said with some surprise. "Not exactly."

Anna sat up and put her arms around him. "Oh, God," she said, "I was having the weirdest dream. But this is real, right?"

"I hope so." He kissed her on the forehead and looked into her eyes. "Are you all right?" he asked. "It looks like I scared the shit out of you."

"You did."

"Sorry, didn't mean to. I got in from LA this morning. Tried to call, but your phone was off the hook, so I let myself in."

"I'm so glad you did."

"Well, it looks like you've seen a ghost."

"Funny you should say that," she answered. "I don't know. Maybe I did, or maybe it was you."

"Since you called me Mom, I take it your apparition was your mother, so tell me: what did she say?"

Anna lay back on the pillow and closed her eyes. "Something like 'everything's going to be all right.' What do you suppose that means?"

Ian unbuttoned his shirt and slipped under the covers alongside her. "Don't know," he said. "You know, ghosts have their own cryptic way of saying things, like 'redrum' for 'murder,' 'beware of the dark side—'

"That was Yoda from *Star Wars*."

"Well, you know what I mean. I don't know why ghosts never come right out and tell you what they want. They leave you little clues, rattle the chandeliers ... you know."

Anna snuggled back against his chest. "You're a regular riot, aren't you?"

He stroked her hair and kissed her neck. She turned around to face him. "I'm glad you're here."

"So am I," he answered. "And Anna, everything will be just fine. You'll see."

"Hey," she smiled, "that's just what the ghost said. So it was you talking to me while I was sleeping. Wasn't it?"

"Maybe—or maybe your ghost and I just think alike."

Chapter 20

XENOS

From a distance, the island of Xenos can only be described as a barren rock in the Aegean Sea. Like Athena springing from the head of Zeus, its steep brown mountains break through the crystal waters, forming magnificent peaks and valleys, eventually winding their way down to white sandy shores below.

The sun had just begun to rise, when Constantine's yacht began its final approach to the small town of Nassos. Anna was already awake and went out on deck to watch as the small towns and villages came into view. She strolled toward the bow and leaned up against the rail. The morning air was cool and refreshing and gave her a quick boost of energy.

She had been looking forward to this trip for the past eight months. Winter in London was miserable, and spring, barely any better. She needed a vacation, and what better excuse than her father's wedding?

Richard had almost immediately accepted Constantine's invitation to have his wedding on the island. Angela loved the idea and so did the rest of the family. Anna and Jackie spent most of the winter planning, shopping, and buying for the event. Although planning a wedding on a remote island was no small task, no detail or penny was spared.

Their first major obstacle was food. Since sea urchins and figs were the island's only nutritional staples, caterers had to be flown in from London and Athens. Then there was the problem of transportation. Although the island had an airport, the three taxi cabs and assorted donkeys weren't going to be enough for all the guests to get around. So, Anna chartered a car ferry and brought in a few dozen limousines. And finally, the last hurdle: lodging—where were the extra people going to stay? After locating only two hotels with screens and flushing toilets as standard operating devices, she booked them out for the week—and proceeded to hunt for private homes and villas to rent.

Richard had initially wanted to keep the whole event small and intimate, but, as the months went by, the guest list kept getting bigger and bigger. Soon, the lists themselves were producing lists, and before they knew it, over five hundred people were invited. This proved the toughest obstacle of all. There was no reception hall large enough to accommodate this crowd. So, Anna arranged to use the entire town square. She had thousands of white roses and orchids brought in to line the cobblestone square. Hundreds of small bistro and cafe tables were placed beneath the ever-present grape vines and trellises.

As Constantin's yacht approached Nassos, the crew sprang to life. Anna watched as the deckhands began to prepare to drop anchor. Handling a two hundred foot yacht was not an easy job. It required the skill of a full-time engineer, three deckhands, a cook, and a certified master-helmsman—in this case, her grandfather. She looked up at the bridge, where she could see him discussing something with his chief mate. His love of the sea was never more apparent than when he stood at the helm of his ship. Her gaze caught his eye, and he looked down at her and smiled. He blew her a kiss, which she quickly blew back while mouthing the words, "kalimera Pappou." Good morning Grandpa.

Ready for her first cup of coffee, Anna turned around and headed to the rear of the ship. The cook had already prepared a light breakfast on the deck. She poured herself a cup of coffee, from the silver urn on the buffet table, then sat down on one of the lounge chairs nearby. She looked up at the sky and smiled. It was always crisp and blue this time of year—never a small cloud or hint of rain.

Then she saw her father approaching with a mug of coffee clenched tightly in his hands.

"What are you doing up this early?"

He sat down beside her and took a sip from his cup. "You know, the usual. Nausea and I couldn't sleep."

"Nausea?" she said with disbelief. "The ocean's a sheet of glass ... not even a ripple for miles. I think your seasickness is all in your head."

"Maybe, or perhaps being with your grandfather brings on that general nauseating feeling."

"Well, you better get used to it. Grandpa's new house is still under construction, so we'll be living off this boat for the next week. I've noticed the two of you getting along pretty well the past couple of days. I'm not sure what's going on, but I'm glad you two finally found something to talk about."

"That's probably wishful thinking on your part."

"I know what I see."

The calm air was suddenly interrupted by the sound of three loud bells followed by the clanging of the anchor chain.

Anna covered her ears. When it was over she looked at her father. "Anchor's down. We're here."

Richard stood up and leaned against the rail. "Great."

He seemed less than enthusiastic about their arrival. "What's the matter Dad? You're not having second thoughts about the wedding, are you?"

"No, no. Of course not," he answered. "It's just this whole place. It brings back a lot of memories, of you, growing up, and me meeting you here in the summers. It all went by so quickly."

"Come on, Dad. Don't start getting sentimental on me. We're here to have a great time, the party of a lifetime. No time for crap like that. Promise?"

"Sorry, darling," he answered. "You're right. No crap like that. I promise." He paused and took a deep breath. "There's something I've been meaning to tell you but I've been putting it off. I didn't want to spoil your vacation."

"This doesn't sound good. What it is?"

"It's about Nigel."

She cringed. "What is it this time?"

"I asked him to meet me here on the island after the wedding."

"What?"

"Calm down. The asshole contacted me a couple of months ago and gave me his final demand for the divorce papers. I couldn't deal with him at the time. The memories of what happened to Angela and all. Well, they were still too fresh. So I kept putting him off. Then, before I knew it, it was August and the wedding was here."

"And you didn't want to leave on your honeymoon with my divorce still hanging over your head? Is that it?"

"Something like that. So I told him to meet me here the day after the wedding and I'd take care of it."

"Talk about spoiling a party."

"I know, I'm sorry."

"How much does he want?"

"It doesn't matter. The only thing that matters is that it's over."

"It will never be over. He'll just find another reason to come back for more."

Richard stared straight ahead and shook his head. "I said, it doesn't matter. Let's just drop the issue right here, all right?"

Anna knew he wasn't really asking a question, it was more of a demand. So she shrugged, leaned over, and gave him a kiss on the cheek. "Whatever you say. Just as long as I don't have to deal with him. I don't think I could be in the same room with him again and not want to kill him. Scary you know. This time, I think I'd actually do it."

Richard smiled. "Another reason why you should leave that shithead to me. I'll take care of him."

"You'll be careful. Right? I know what I'm capable of doing to him. You're probably ready to do a hell of a lot more."

"Than kill him? I don't think there's anything more I could do than that." He smiled. "No, darling, don't worry. Nobody's going to jail. Trust me."

"I do," she answered. "Now let's stop talking about this. Only fun things from here on, okay? So, what do you say? Should we wake the rest of the gang up, or do we let them sleep the day away?"

"Sleep? Are you crazy?" It was the sound of Jackie's voice coming from the buffet table. "Who in bloody hell can sleep with the clanging anchor? And tell me? Why do they have to ring the bells before they let it fall? So they can give us a practice heart attack before the big one comes?"

"Sorry, Jackie," Anna said. "If the crew had known you were still sleeping, I'm certain they would've used the rubber anchor."

"I see you've already taken your smug pills this morning." Jackie walked over to Richard and gave him a kiss on the cheek. Then, in a childlike voice, she said, "Good morning Daddy. Whoops, I forgot. I can't call you that until the day after tomorrow."

Richard laughed. "You can call me that any time you want, darling."

Barefoot, and still in her pajamas, Angela approached the group. She grabbed Jackie's shoulder, and in her most severe mother tone said, "I heard that, and I want you to start behaving yourself young lady, or there'll be severe consequences to pay."

Jackie lowered her eyes and giggled. "Ooh, what's gonna happen?" she asked. "Is daddy gonna spank me?" Then she rolled her eyes and said, "Can't wait."

"Jackie—" Angela snapped.

Richard cut her off. "Relax, darling," he said. "She's just having fun at our expense."

"Yeah, Mom," she said, "chill out."

Jackie looked out at the landscape. The town of Nassos was stirring to life. She watched as the fisherman prepared their nets and boarded their small wooden boats, ready to take on the morning's catch. Then, she looked down at the water, and from where she stood, she could see clear to the bottom—rock formations, fish and all.

"God it's beautiful," Jackie sighed. "Just like I remember it ... when we all met here, for the first time. I can't wait for my brothers and sister to get here. We can take a small boat out to that beach where that crazy fisherman left us stranded, remember? I've told Christian that story a thousand times. Now I can show it to him."

Anna nodded. "Sounds great. Just as long as you don't make us play that truth or dare game again." She glanced at her watch. "Ian's plane is coming in at noon. I promised I'd meet him at the airport. I'd better start getting dressed."

"Hey," Jackie said, "that's in like five hours. Relax."

"Not now. Living off a yacht in a one-donkey town isn't easy. You'll see. The crew here has to prepare the launch to take me to town, so I can wait an hour to find my limo driver, who's probably heaving somewhere from dysentery. And since I hate traveling around in a limo, he'll have to take me to Grandfather's house to pick up my car. I'll try to start it, but the battery will be dead. Then we'll have to call the only auto repair shop in town, but since there are no phones and no cell sites, we'll have to drive there. When we get there, it'll be closed because of some kind of holiday or a strike, and I'll end up stomping my feet and taking the limo to the airport anyway."

Jackie laughed. "Yup, just like I remember it. Some things never change. You need company to get you through it?"

"No, thanks anyway. I'm used to it. Besides, I haven't seen Ian in a couple of weeks...."

"Not a problem," Jackie said with a smirk. "Just as long as you promise me that lots of naughty things are gonna happen."

Anna laughed and began to walk away, then came back to whisper in Jackie's ear, "Don't worry, it's guaranteed."

Nigel was startled awake by the thud of his plane touching down on the tarmac. He looked at his watch. It was early: 11:00 A.M. He rubbed his eyes and reached for a cigarette. *Thank God for private planes,* he thought. *None of that no smoking bullshit.*

"You moron," he heard a woman say. "Put that thing out. Don't you know it makes me nauseous."

"Shut the fuck up, Helena," he answered. "Don't start hounding me."

As he looked out the window, he wondered whatever possessed him to bring his ex-wife along. They had bumped into each other only last month at another downtown party, this one for the release of his greatest hits album: *Fungus Toes*. She seemed intrigued by his new-found respectability and pleasantly surprised by his sudden influx of money. She circled him like a cat around a fishbowl. When the moment was right, she cornered him in an empty back room and took out of her handbag "instruments" that only the most depraved mind could have thought up. Within moments, he was tied, shackled, and bound to anything that protruded from the walls or floors. Ordinary household products took on a whole new meaning. He was amazed at what she could do with Brillo Pads and a potato peeler, but it was what she did with the spaghetti tongs that really reeled him in. Closer to Nirvana than he'd ever been before, when it was all over, he'd finally discovered the meaning of true love: handcuffs, steel wool and pasta.

The door to the plane opened on the tarmac, and the two of them stepped out.

"Holy crap, daaahling," Helena said. "It's hotter than hell on this island. What's it called again? Cyclops?"

"Xenos."

"Right," she looked around. "So where exactly are we? I'll bet you can't even find this godforsaken piece of shit on the map. Your home better be a palace or I'll tear your balls off."

His irritation was growing, but what else did he expect? "Don't worry, Helena. You won't be disappointed. Besides, I have a surprise waiting for you: your own personal entertainment unit."

She pushed him aside and walked toward the gate. "Good," she said, "so that means I don't have to rely on you."

He followed her inside, where they were greeted by their limousine driver. Within moments they were speeding along the one-lane winding road toward the town of Amphora. Helena put her head back on the seat and closed her eyes.

"Don't you want to see the scenery?" Nigel asked her. "It's quite nice, you know."

"The dirt, rocks, and prickly green things the locals probably call plants? No thanks." She made some kind of jerky hand gesture to the driver. "Can't you blast that air-conditioning a little more?" she yelled. "My hair frizzes in this kind of weather."

Nigel reached into his pocket and pulled out a joint. "This is gonna be a long fucking three days," he mumbled.

"I heard that, you prick," Helena shot back. "And why the fuck did we have to come so early? I thought your meeting with Winters wasn't for another couple of days?"

He took a long drag of the joint. "Right, but everyone in the industry's gonna be here for the wedding. Got an invitation to party with Mick and Ringo tonight. Thought you might like that."

Helena shrugged. "I might. We'll see."

The limo pulled up to Nigel's villa in Amphora. What had belonged to Constantine Stavropoulos only two months ago was now legally his. It was a white stucco mansion surrounded by tall lemon and olive trees. To the right was a swimming pool with a small slate path that led to a private beach.

Helena stepped out of the car and sighed indifferently. "So this is it?"

"Not impressed yet?"

"Not really, daaahling," she said. "I've seen big expensive houses before you know. Helena needs more than that to make her happy."

"Come on in then. Maybe we can find something inside."

Before they had a chance to reach the door, it swung open and out stepped a tall blonde wearing a bustier top and high-cut thong underwear. "Poopsie doll," she squealed. "I've been waiting for you." She glanced over at Helena and smiled. "Who's your pretty friend?"

Nigel turned to Helena and whispered, "Your entertainment. You happy now?"

"Daaahling," she purred, "Helena couldn't be happier."

Anna paced back and forth as Olympic Airlines flight 422 touched down at the Xenos International Airport. It had been two weeks since she'd last seen Ian, what with his filming final scenes for *Rivals at War* in Austria and a stream of crisis that only Anna could resolve. Sometimes she yearned for the time when her staff ignored her. One short weekend in Vienna hadn't been enough.

Anna watched as Ian descended the steep flight of stairs leading to the gate. It was a little after noon. The sun was directly overhead and descending passengers couldn't wait to unbutton ties, roll up sleeves, and open collars.

Ian entered the terminal and immediately fell into her embrace. After a passionate kiss that made onlookers avert their eyes, he stepped back and took a look around. "Hey," he said while unbuttoning his shirt, "where's the bloody air-conditioning?"

Anna looked amused. "What? No 'I'm glad to see you,' or 'I've missed you terribly'?"

He put his hand on the back of her neck and, once again, brought his lips to hers. "Of course I'm glad to see you," he whispered, "but tell me, where's the bloody air-conditioning?"

She shrugged. "Sorry, darling," she said, "there isn't any. Hate to disappoint you, but things haven't changed much since the last time you were here. Consider yourself in the *Twilight Zone*. You've just gone back one hundred years. TVs, no phones, some refrigeration, but definitely no air conditioning."

"Right. All alongside luxury yachts, Lambourghinis, and direct satellite transmissions from Wall Street. It's a weird place."

"And I've actually missed it."

"If I remember correctly, you hated being here when you were younger."

"I know, but it grew on me."

She took his hand and led him to the limo, where the driver had already put Ian's bags in the trunk. "You know, it's not that weird here, Ian," she said as the car moved away from the curb. "It's just different." She sat back and thought for a moment, then said, "Let's not go to the boat just yet. Let me take you somewhere else, somewhere that might help you appreciate this place a little better."

The driver turned to Anna. "Sorry, Ms. Winters, but the only place I know how to get to is the town."

"Not a problem." She pointed him towards a long narrow roadway that scarred the side of a steep mountain. "Just follow that road," she said, "you can't get lost."

She sat back and felt Ian's hand slowly moving up the side of her T-shirt. She closed her eyes while he kissed her ear and listened as he whispered, "I've missed you terribly."

"Me too."

They kissed for what seemed like only moments, when the driver said, "Ms. Winters, we must be here. The road doesn't go any farther."

She looked out the window and spotted what she was looking for: the monastery of Nea Nissi. She led Ian toward the small white-washed structure.

She opened the pale blue door and stepped inside, where the air was musty, as if nobody had visited the building in months. Ian followed close behind her. All of a sudden, he stopped and gasped.

"Jeezus Christ," he said as he looked at the walls. "What the hell is this?" Apprehensive, he moved closer trying to make out the white and gray objects in the glass cases that lined the walls. "Skulls and bones. The walls are lined with human skulls and bones, thousands of them."

"That's right," she said, "they are. From people who died trying to get free from the Turks in 1821." She put her arm around his waist and continued. "This island suffered horribly. More than any other Greek island during that war. Over 25,000 people killed and 50,000 taken into slavery. Then the island was burned, burned to the ground. And this monastery? It was built because after the fires, an icon was found hanging from one of the only remaining trees. The people believed it was God's will that they build a monastery here, collect the bones of those who died and put them in the walls."

"A little gruesome."

"You might say so. But I think it made the survivors stronger and helped them go on."

"You don't think it's creepy in here?"

"Creepy? No. I feel strength. It resonates through the walls. It's the strength of angels and the thousands of heroes who died for their freedom. Don't you feel it?"

Ian shook his head. "Not really. All I can think of is getting the hell out of here. I'm going to be having nightmares for a year." He turned and headed for the door. "Anything else you'd like to show me," he asked, "maybe some graveyards, or the city morgue?"

Anna sighed. "Oh, Ian. And here I was trying to help you love this island the way I do. And all you can do is think about getting out!"

He stepped outside and took in the view. "You don't have to sell me on this place, because it's you. It's a part of your history ... bones, yachts, donkeys, and all."

"It took a while for it to grow on me. Give it a chance. You'll love it too. Promise."

"I take it that means we'll be spending a lot of time here in the future."

"Would that be so bad?"

"No, of course not. We'll spend as much time as you want. Hell, I'll even buy us a Lambourghini, build a garage for our pet donkey and stock up on plenty of sea urchins for those special nights. How's that for proving my love to you."

"I'm satisfied."

"Good. Now, can we go somewhere where I can get out of these clothes? I'm still dressed for the Austrian Alps and I'm sweating like a pig."

"You're right. Let me take you somewhere where you can cool off. We can always resume our history lesson later."

Within moments, the driver had turned the car around and was speeding toward Nassos. Once in the town, Anna directed the driver up a small dirt pathway that finally led to a black wrought-iron gate. She opened the window, punched in a code on the adjacent panel, and watched as the gates swung open. There, beyond the gates, sat her grand-father's new summer villa: a white-brick colonial house, three stories tall, and six wings wide. Ionic columns flanked the doorways, and each room on the upper level had its own balcony.

Ian got out of the car and whistled. "Wow," he said, "it's unbelievable. Bigger than the last one."

"Yeah," Anna answered. "Hard to believe more beautiful too."

"Why'd he give that one up?"

"Nigel."

"Right. Sorry."

"Let's go inside. The finishing touches are being put on it now. It's a bit messy, but you can get changed, and we can grab some towels and go down to the beach."

Ian hauled his suitcase from the trunk and followed her inside. Aside from paint cans, ladders, and a few strategically placed pieces of covered furniture, the house was empty. Anna led Ian up the winding staircase toward what would be her bedroom. The sound of their footsteps bounced off the high arched ceilings and echoed throughout the house.

"Tell me Anna," Ian said as he lugged his suitcase behind him. "Who's all this for? There must be fifteen or twenty bedrooms in this place, and there's only one Constantine. So, who's going to use it all?"

"She sighed. "You know my grandfather. Everything has to be larger than life. That's just him. Besides, we'll use it." She stopped outside one of the bedroom doors and held the knob. "This is my room," she said. "I started decorating it already. I had a few things sent over from London last week."

She opened the door. The balcony door was open, so they both stood back and took in the cool cross-breeze from the ocean. Like the rest of the house, the room was painted white. What furniture there was, was covered with large yellow linen sheets. Anna pulled back the sheets from the bed.

"Beautiful, isn't it?" she said referring to a mahogany four-poster bed that she'd picked up at an antique store outside of London. She sat on the edge and bounced up and down on the mattress. "Perfect," she purred.

Ian took off his shirt and let it fall to the floor. "Mind if I try it too?" he asked as he moved towards her.

"Not at all."

But instead of sitting on the bed, he leaned over her and took her face in his hands. "Let's forget the beach," he whispered.

Their lips met, then their tongues. Anna felt the velvety soft touch of his hands under her T-shirt and against her breasts. He moved behind her and kissed her neck while his hands continued to caress her skin. He pulled her shirt off over her head, then covered her body with hundreds of small kisses that electrified her. She reached down, unbuttoned his trousers, and helped him pull them off. He slid his hand under her skirt and pulled off her panties. A second later she felt him inside her, moving deeper with every thrust. Looking into each other's eyes, they were lost in another world, hidden in another plane—one where it was just the two of them, in love and forever together.

Afterward, they wrapped themselves in the sheets and sat on the balcony to watch the sun set behind the horizon of the tranquil Aegean. Anna rested her head on Ian's shoulder and closed her eyes.

"I didn't think I could ever feel this way," she said. "Thank you, Ian."

"For what? I love you. There's nothing to thank me for."

"For not giving up on me. For sticking by me through this divorce, and all the trouble I caused your mother."

"Don't think about all that now. Let's not spoil the moment."

"But I think about it all the time. I'm just so afraid that Nigel will find another excuse not to sign the divorce papers, that I'll never be free off him."

"Anna," he said, while stroking her hair, "you'll be free of him. Trust me."

"I wish I could have your confidence, but I know him. He'll never let me go—or, I should say, he'll never let my money go."

"You're right, but you forgot one thing. People like him have a tendency to self-destruct. An overdose, a car wreck. I wouldn't be surprised if someday his bones wind up in the walls of that monastery of yours, accidentally, of course."

"What are you saying, or do I want to know?"

He laughed. "All I mean is that he's on a downward spiral, moving faster every day. It'll all catch up to him: his lifestyle, his habits, his self-indulgence. He'll be out of your life sooner than you think. Then we'll be free, to do whatever we want."

"To get married? Do you think about that?"

"Yes, and no. I don't need an official document to feel more bound to you than I do at this moment. I love you so much that sometimes I can't breathe when we're apart. My commitment to you will never come from a ring, or a piece of paper. It's from my heart. It always will be."

"Then we are bound together, because my commitment's from my heart too. But I do want a wedding some day, a great big white one. And lots of kids."

"Lots? Just how many is that?"

"I don't know, five, ten."

"Sorry I asked."

"And I want all the boring days …"

"Boring? I can't imagine any day being boring with you around."

"Yes boring, and stop interrupting me. I want the boring days, as well as well as the fun ones. I want everything. Everything that goes along with spending the rest of your life with someone."

"Then that's what we'll have, my darling: a great big wedding, five or ten kids and lots of boring days."

"She sighed. "Just one problem though."

"Nigel."

"Right."

"I told you, stop thinking about him. His days are numbered."

Chapter 21

THE NEXT DAY

Richard watched as a small crowd began to form around the brownstone cathedral in Nassos. Standing outside the wooden portal, he and Anna greeted their guests and waited patiently for Angela's limousine to arrive. It was close to 7:00 P.M. The sun was setting behind the mountains, and a cool breeze could be felt working its way up the steep inclines.

Anna adjusted Richard's bow tie and straightened his collar. "You're sweating, Dad," she whispered. "Nervous, or just hot?"

"Both, I guess."

"Hey. Hey, buddy," said a voice from behind. "It's me, your right hand man. Remember?"

Richard turned around and found himself staring at the top of a shiny bald head. He desperately tried to remember a name, but drew a blank. In a weak attempt to cover his memory lapse, he enthusiastically extended his hand and said, "Hey, man, of course. Wouldn't think of having a wedding without you here. How's it going?"

The man's face melted in a sigh of relief. "Whew," he said, "for a second there, it looked like you had no idea who I was. But you look great man, really." Then he leaned closer to Richard, and said, "Listen, hate to discuss business with you on your wedding day, but I just got the numbers for the fourth quarter earnings: we're up seventeen percent." Then he winked, nodded, and walked away.

Anna tugged at Richard's arm. "Who was that?"

"I have no idea," he answered, "but my fourth quarter earnings on something are up seventeen percent. So, when do we go inside the church? The guests are getting edgy and so am I."

"That's not the way it's done here. I already told you," Anna answered crisply. "You stand here, outside the church. The limo pulls up there, in front of the pathway, and the bride gets out and walks to you. Then you walk into the church together, and the guests follow."

"Right, right," Richard answered. "Just direct me when the time comes. I'll take your lead. And Anna," he added, "thanks for being my best man."

"Any time, Dad."

He stood silent for a moment and stared into her eyes.

"Oh, no, Dad," she said, "you're not getting sentimental on me again. Not now, please."

"Just indulge me this one last time," he whispered. He reached into his pocket, took her hand, and placed a small round object in it.

She didn't need to look at it. She knew what it was. It was a band of white gold, with two rows of emerald-cut diamonds: her mother's wedding ring.

He leaned forward and continued to whisper. "You wear it someday, Anna. Maybe on your wedding day. I hope you'll be as happy as I was, and am, at this moment."

Anna slipped the ring on her finger and kissed him. "I will, Dad. Promise."

The crowd stood still as Angela's limousine pulled up along the path leading to the church. Richard felt paralyzed. He knew the sweat dripping from his forehead had nothing to do with the heat. It was that spot, that moment—he had been there before. He could feel the hand of his wife in his, Sara's hand. It was warm and soft, like the touch of satin against his skin. He held it tight, for the last time, then opened his palm and let go.

He watched as the limousine driver opened the rear doors. Ian and Joseph stepped out first, then Jackie and Phillipa. The girls turned and fluffed out their mother's dress as she gingerly stepped out of the car. She was a vision, more beautiful that he'd ever seen her, in a strapless gown of white organza that was fitted at the top with embroidered lace and pearls. Her hair was a mass of shoulder-length black curls crowned at the top with a tiara of marquisette and precious stones.

Anna slipped her arm through Richard's and sighed. "She looks beautiful, Dad."

For once in his life, Richard was speechless. All he could do was nod. As she left her children behind and walked towards him, she was radiant, smiling with a spirit that came from deep within her heart. Her short walk seemed to him to take an eternity, and then there she was, in front of him. In that instant, the doors to the church flew open. He took her hand, turned around, and faced the altar.

Without hesitating he lead her down the isle. Anna and rest of the family followed, and behind them, the other guests. The service lasted for over an hour, and when it was all over and vows had been exchanged, the crowd cheered and pelted the newlyweds with uncooked rice and birdseed. Then Richard and Angela led the way to the party. She, in her high heels and gown, and he, in his tuxedo, walked down the winding dirt path to the town square, where the champagne and caviar were already flowing.

Helena burst into Nigel's bedroom. "Get the fuck out of bed, you loser. This party's getting stale. Time to move on."

Without lifting his head from the pillow, he looked up at her and groaned, "Jeezuz, you bitch, can't you find some way of amusing yourself?"

Amber pulled her head away from Nigel's fully erect member and squealed, "Hey, Helena, my Poopsie doll's got a bad headache, and I'm doing all I can to make him feel better. Right, baby?"

Nigel smiled and tapped her on the head. "Thank you, my darling. Just ignore the bad lady and get back to work. The headache is still there."

He closed his eyes while Amber resumed her position. But more than just his head was about to split open. His whole body felt like it was hit by a jackhammer. From the moment he arrived on Xenos, it was one party after another starting when he invited Mick and Ringo and "the gang" to his place. Word spread that his villa was the hottest place to be seen. Before he knew it, they were all there: supermodels, screen idols, business tycoons, and top names in the music industry. Each guest, of course, brought carefully chosen fun and games. Heroin was the choice among the models—that, and a handy spoon to facilitate the purging after a nibble on a lettuce leaf. The business types enjoyed coke. It kept them alert enough to have one eye on the stock market while hitting on all the models, and the movie and rock stars enjoyed an assortment of pills, tobacco, liquor, and crystallized chemicals.

Nigel reveled in playing the gracious host. He showed off his villa as if he'd built it with his own two hands. His guests greeted him with an admiration that he hadn't experienced since his days with the old band. His *Greatest Hits* CD was doing well, and he had all the money in the world to burn. Once again, people liked being around him. That it was "in" to be seen with him gave him a sense of euphoria better than any chemical, needle, or cigarette.

But that didn't stop him from indulging in his old habits anyway. He thought about trying to quit, but the pains of withdrawal became more severe each time he tried. The nausea, shakes, chills, and sweats—they all came on so suddenly. He knew that if could just stick it out a couple of days, it would all be over, but his resolve never lasted that long. It would only be a matter of hours before he'd pull out the syringe, tap on his veins, and shoot the chemicals into his eagerly awaiting blood-stream.

He felt Helena's foot kick the bed. "Hey, did you hear me?" she shouted. "Tell blondie down there to get your dick out of her mouth, and get your ass out of bed. I want to join the rest of the gang for the wedding reception."

"I already told you," he moaned. "We weren't invited."

Helena grabbed Amber's hair and pulled her head away from Nigel's throbbing member. "How could you not be invited?" she screamed. "You're his ex-partner. He'd be nothing without you. You made him what he is today. He owes you big time."

It took him a second to realize that Amber was no longer performing one of her exquisitely executed blow jobs on his now failing erection. "Shit," he said as he looked up, "where'd the fuck she go?"

Helena grabbed his balls. "Listen to me, asshole," she said as she began to tighten her grip, "I'll give you a blow job you'll never forget if you don't get your ass out of this bed right now. Everyone who's anyone is down at that party, and that's where I want to be. Got it?"

Nigel felt sick to his stomach. He had never told Helena about his utter disdain for Richard, or his own experiments with blackmail and revenge, but as the pressure on his testicles increased, he figured now wasn't the best time to make a confession. "Okay, okay," he said. "Let go of my fucking balls and we'll go." He grabbed the bottle of vodka from the nightstand and headed to the bathroom. *What the hell,* he thought. *I'm sure it'll be a real kick-ass event.*

The wedding reception was in full swing. The town square, just yesterday a quiet cobblestone quadrangle by the dock, was now an oasis for the newlyweds. The guests dined on everything from lobster tails to imported caviar and danced under the starlight to the sounds of rock and roll legends, who had volunteered to perform for Richard, who had been an inspiration to so many of them.

Richard and Angela worked the crowd, strolling from table to table to thank each guest. Anna watched her father as he shook hand after hand. Eventually, deciding that he'd done enough PR for the evening, she grabbed him from behind and dragged him to the dance floor.

"Sorry, Angela," she said as she pulled him along, "it's time to start loosening him up." The new wave group Inner Soul had just begun their top 40 ballad "Tears in Stride," and Anna wrapped her arms around her father's waist and began swaying to its gentle rhythm.

Resting her head on his shoulder, she said, "Everything turned out great, didn't it? After all that planning, and worry, nothing went wrong. It's just perfect."

"Right," he answered, stepping back and looking into her eyes. "Perfect, just like you."

A moment later Christian and Jackie waltzed their way alongside them. "Hey, Richard," Christian said, "Elton's going to do some of his old tunes tonight. What a blast. Christ, this party's going down in bloody history. What do you say we join him for a jam session? You still remember the chords to our old stuff, right?"

Richard shook his head. "Not a chance," he said. "My days on stage are over. But don't let me stop you. Go ahead, have a blast."

"Nah," Christian answered, "not the same without you."

Just as Anna felt a tap on her shoulder, she took in the smell of an all-too familiar after-shave cologne. She cringed as she turned to see the man she'd hoped wouldn't be standing there. "Andreas, what on earth …"

"Ahhh, don't look so hostile. This is a party, not business. Come, let's have a momentary truce. Have a dance with me." He looked at Richard. "Do you mind?"

Richard stepped back. "It's up to her."

Anna shook her head. "I must be drunk, because I'm about to say yes. What the hell. Let's dance, but keep your distance."

He put one hand in hers and tentatively put the other against her waist. "Is that okay?"

"That's fine." With over a foot between them, they danced a few minutes, then Anna asked, "So tell me. What brings you here? It couldn't be an invitation."

"Wrong, my luv. Your grandfather invited the whole town. Since I have a house here, one of the largest I might add, I thought it would be fun to come and see you again."

"You always did have a strange idea of what's fun."

"Truce, remember?"

"Sorry, it's hard with you."

His face suddenly took on a serious air. "I have to tell you," he said, "I saw your ex husband hanging around the square this morning. Did you know he was here?"

"Yes, but if you don't mind, I'd rather not talk about him right now."

"Not a problem, but I thought I'd tell you he's pretty much gone out of his mind. Incoherent, you know. Ten o'clock in the morning and I couldn't bloody understand a thing he was saying."

"That pretty much sums up my whole marriage."

Andreas laughed. "We all make mistakes, huh, Anna? I know I have." He looked pensive for a moment, then added, "Anyway, getting back to your ex. I couldn't resist a good business opportunity when I saw one, so I unloaded one of my small speed boats on him. I'd been trying to get rid of it. It had been giving me problems, sticky throttle you know, so I convinced him that no rich islander should be without one."

"So you charged him a king's ransom for a shitty boat?"

"What the hell. The idiot knows nothing about boats. I told him this one could break the sound barrier if he gives it enough throttle. He liked that. Living on the edge and all. But I wouldn't be anywhere near the water when he's powering that thing. Way too dangerous for my tastes."

"And mine."

"He's dangerous all around. Take my advice and stay clear or he might take you down with him."

"I know. It should all be over soon."

"Glad to hear it. And the hillbilly? I see you're still toting him around."

"Hey, no insults. Truce, remember?"

"Sorry, I forgot too. Just do me a favor. When you're through dining on opossum and pork rinds, give me a call. I'm still available."

"Can't imagine why."

The music stopped and they stepped apart. "Thanks for the dance, Anna," Andreas said, bowing graciously. "Maybe later again?"

"Don't think so," she answered, "but you're welcome for this one."

Nigel, Amber, and Helena made their way down the dirt path leading to the town square.

"Now that's a party," Helena said as they approached the crowd.

"Fucking A," Nigel said in agreement, "Winters sure knows how to spend his millions." He scanned the crowd for familiar faces. "Hey," he crowed, "there's Clapton." He turned to Amber and Helena. "Hope you don't mind if I dump the two of you here. Time to talk shop with the big boys."

Helena jabbed him with her elbow. "Fuck off, you loser. If Clapton wants to talk with the big boys, he'll make an appointment to see me."

"Bitch," Nigel mumbled as he rubbed his shoulder, "do whatever you want. I'm going for a drink. Catch you later."

The party continued to roar. As anticipated, Elton John hit the stage and rocked the crowd to the sounds of "Saturday Night" and "Bennie and the Jets." Over an hour later, and well past midnight, he was replaced by the new wave phenom crooner "Miles of Style," who slowed the beat down and gave the exhausted crowd a chance to take a breath.

When the music slowed, Anna and Ian, who had been heading the pack on the dance floor, collapsed into each other's arms and groaned.

"I need to sit down," Anna moaned. "My legs feel like they're burning up."

Ian laughed. "You sound like an old lady. Remember Brighton? We didn't stop dancing until the sun came up."

"That seems like a hundred years ago," she answered wearily. "Now just lead me to a chair." She began to walk off the dance floor but stopped short. "Do you smell that?"

What? he answered.

"The burning rope ... that's pot.'

Ian nodded in agreement.

"Shit," she continued. "The local police will go nuts if they find drugs here. Everyone's been warned. Who could be so stupid?"

"Listen," Ian said, "you go sit down. I'll find out who it is and ask them to put it out. I'm sure it's just some misunderstanding."

"Okay," she said. "But don't make a scene or anything. Keep it quiet."

"I'm the king of discreet, remember?"

Ian followed the scent of the burning rope to a small group huddled around a table near the edge of the dock. As he approached, the silhouette of the man puffing heavily on the joint became all too familiar. *Nigel ... what on earth?* he thought as he got closer. *This has got to be a nightmare.* He tapped him on the shoulder. "Hey, buddy, put the drugs away, then do me a favor: haul your fucking ass out of here before I rearrange your face."

Nigel locked eyes with the man standing only a few inches in front of him. The man's name, or where they had met before, escaped him. Puzzled by the stranger's hostility, he looked down at the joint and shrugged. "Hey mate," he said, "cool off, it's only dope. Here," he said as he handed it to him, "looks like you could use some to get whatever bug you have up your ass out."

"I said, put it away and leave."

Nigel laughed. "Who's the fucking narc over here?"

Ian realized that Nigel had no idea who he was, but before he had a chance to reintroduce himself, a high-pitched squeal coming from somewhere in the crowd distracted him. "Ian, it's me. Amber. Remember? We met a club in LA a few months ago."

As if hit over the head with a bucket of ice water, Nigel immediately sobered. "Ian Moore," he blurted out. "What a blast." How lucky could he be? The fun was just about to start. He had wondered who'd be the first to spot him. The cream of the crop would have been Richard of course, but Ian? Well, he had enough ammunition stored to start another world war. He put his hand on Ian's shoulder and grinned. "So, mate, glad you came by. I've been meaning to ask you. Just how *is* your mother? Has she gotten over me yet?"

"What did you just say?"

"You heard me mate. You're mother, does she still see me in her dreams?"

Ian couldn't believe what he'd just heard. Nigel obviously wanted a fight, a physical one at that. He wanted to see the cameras flashing as the two of them went for each other's throats. Nigel would play the victim, of course, as Ian, the jealous lover, pummeled him to the ground. Nigel would find a way to get the press to see it his way. He always did. Ian clenched his fists in rage but kept them still at his side.

"Listen to me, you fucker," he said in an even tone. "I don't know what you're up to, but take my advice and get the hell out of here. Or I'll drag you out myself."

"Sorry, no can do."

"I don't think you heard me. Move out or I'll do it myself."

Nigel remained unfazed. "Come on, mate," he said. "One swing, right here, on my face. Don't you just want to do it? I probably won't feel anyway. Won't remember it either."

Of course he wanted to do it. But it wasn't the time or the place. He leaned closer and lowered his voice. "Yeah," he said, "I'm gonna do it. I'm gonna smash your fucking skull in till you choke on your own blood. But not here. Now, I'm gonna call those big security guys over there and we're gonna escort your pathetic ass out of here."

Nigel paused to savor the moment. He knew Ian wouldn't be able to control himself much longer. But what would it take? What words should he use to watch Ian fly over the edge?

Nigel leaned in a little closer. "I'll tell you what, mate," he said in a low voice, "I'll go quietly if you just tell me one thing?"

"What's that?" Ian asked, knowing quite well he wouldn't like what he was about to hear.

"I'd just like to know, has Anna screamed my name in bed yet? She used to do that, or am I confusing her with your mother?"

That was it. The gloves were off. "You scum bag," Ian mumbled. Then, using all his force, he shoved Nigel back onto the cocktail table behind him. All the glasses and dishes crashed onto the cement. The crowd around the table grew silent as they watched Ian pull Nigel up by the shirt collar. "That was just the beginning," he said as he pulled his arm back and clenched his hand into a tight fist. But, just as he was about to bear his knuckles down onto Nigel's smirking face, someone behind him pulled is arm back.

"Ian, that's enough."

It was Richard. Ian felt a rush of adrenaline, took a couple of deep breaths, and locked eyes with Nigel. "You're a dead man," he whispered. "Remember that." Reluctantly, he let go of Nigel's collar and stepped away.

Richard approached Nigel. The two of them studied each other as a small crowd began to form around them. Neither spoke as the tension continued to mount.

The music stopped. Miles of Style had finished his session. He crooned his thanks into the microphone, then spotting what he thought was a sentimental moment between old friends, he grabbed the microphone again and said, "Whoa, ladies and gents. An unprecedented moment indeed. Richard Winters and Nigel Taylor, together again. Let's give them a round of applause. Maybe we can get them to join us on stage for a jam session? What da ya say?"

The crowd went crazy with cheers and applause. A chant rang out: "Ca-su-als ... Ca-su-als ..." Richard reined in his rage. He knew everyone was watching them. Nigel grinned and shrugged. "What do you say, mate?" he said. "Can't disappoint your adoring fans."

"Don't do it, Nigel," Richard said. "Just walk away."

"Or what?"

"Or I'll see you in hell."

Nigel turned and walked towards the stage. "I'll see you there anyway, mate," he shouted without looking back.

He jumped up on stage and grabbed the mike from Miles. "Thanks, mate," he said as he stared into the crowd. The cheering and chanting continued for a few moments. After subduing the crowd with his thanks, Nigel put on his sincerest face and continued. "Feels like I just won another Grammy." He grinned. "But seriously, this is some night, right?" He put his hand on his heart and looked over at Richard. "My oldest and dearest friend, getting married, again. Well, the memories don't stop. We've done so much together, and shared so much. Right Richard?"

Nigel continued to ramble on as Richard looked on in horror. What had started out as the most perfect night in his life was now ending in catastrophe. Christian raced over to him and began whispering something in his ear, but he couldn't hear him. At that moment, there was no one else in the square. It was just him and Nigel. His was the only voice he could hear and it needed to be eliminated. Slowly, as if on autopilot, he began walking toward the stage. The voice continued to ring in his ear:

"I have to tell you, that I was disappointed that I wasn't asked to be best man, but what the heck? Maybe next time around ..."

Richard continued to push his way through the crowd. His rage was endless. Nothing short of death would do and he didn't care how many people looked on. Ian and Christian grabbed him from behind, but he twisted out of their grip and kept going.

"Well, well. I can't believe it. Here he is, the genius himself. What's it gonna be, Richard? Wanna jam? Maybe "I'll Never Let You Go?" Now who wrote that? Was that me or you? What the hell, what does it all matter now? We're just all one big happy family anyway, me and my father-in-law ..."

Richard walked up the stairs leading to the stage platform. The crowd went wild. The cheers and applause started all over again. As Richard grew closer, Nigel stretched out his arms as if to embrace him. Richard knew Nigel was mocking him, he wanted to see him explode as the crowd watched in horror. He continued to walk. What was it going be? Fall into Nigel's trap, or reel it all in and control the situation?

Before he knew it, he was there, face to face with Nigel, standing only inches apart. He took a deep breath. *What's it gonna be?* he thought. *Control or rage?* The crowd quieted as the two men stared at each other. Then, throwing his adversary completely off guard, Richard let out a brilliant smile, stretched his arms out, and gave Nigel a bear hug with enough force to break a few ribs.

The guests went crazy. The chant started all over again. "Ca-su-als ... Ca-su-als ..." Richard grabbed the microphone from Nigel's hand and turned it off. Then, with one arm still around Nigel's waist, he turned, faced the crowd and waved. Following suit, Nigel did the same. Then, still beaming at the crowd, Richard leaned over to Nigel and whispered, "You're a fucking dead man, Taylor."

Still waving to the crowd, Nigel turned to Richard and answered, "Not if I get you first, asshole."

Chapter 22

THE DIVORCE PAPERS

The wedding reception was an overwhelming success. After his encounter with Nigel, Richard led Angela to a small launch waiting beside the dock and together they sailed back to Constantine's yacht. The crowd loved it: the romance, the drama. It was all unparalleled. The guests lined up on the dock and waved goodbye as their host and hostess disappeared into the distance.

To Richard, though, leaving the party at that moment was a sheer act of survival. It was his way of salvaging the night, his way of protecting Angela from nightmares that were sure to visit her again. But the sight of Nigel triggered her memories of the New York apartment, and although she and Richard both smiled as they waved goodbye, once out of eyesight, her tears began to flow. They didn't stop until daybreak. He held her all night, and whispered reassuring words, but deep down he knew that nothing was going to be all right until Nigel Taylor was out of their lives for good.

He heard a soft knock at the door. Trying not to wake Angela, who had fallen asleep in his arms only moments before, he slipped out of bed and opened the door a crack. It was Constantine.

"How is she?" he whispered with concern.

Richard shrugged. "Don't know," he said. "It was bad, really bad. Didn't think she'd ever stop crying ... finally fell asleep a few minutes ago."

"Should we call a doctor?"

"No," Richard answered sharply. "I don't want to call any attention to the situation. Let's just get this day over with and get the hell out of here."

Constantine nodded in agreement. "The rest of the family's out on the deck having coffee. They're anxious to talk to you. You up to it?"

Richard glanced at his watch and shrugged. "Sure," he said. "I have a few minutes before the next party starts."

The two men continued to talk as they headed for the deck. When they arrived Richard looked around and realized that all eyes were on him. Ian, Joseph, Jackie, and Phillipa stopped what they were doing and stared in his direction. He knew they wanted answers.

But he was tired. He hadn't slept the entire night and the last thing he needed was an inquisition. He looked up at the sky and squinted. The sun was almost directly overhead, and he felt small drops of sweat beginning to form on his neck. Still wearing his tuxedo shirt from the night before, he unbuttoned the two top buttons while his mind raced for the right words to comfort her children.

Anna handed him a cup of coffee and whispered, "Are you okay?"

He shook off the coffee and sat down on a deck chair. "I'm fine," he whispered back. He ran his hands through his hair and looked at the group. Again, his mind began to race.

Jackie broke the silence. "So," she blurted out, "tell us. Just what the hell was that all about last night? You should've belted him, flat out. Right then and there. That piece of shit doesn't deserve to be breathing, let alone you hugging him in front of people." She stood up and began to pace. "Ian did the right thing. You should've let him finish, but you held him back." She stopped dead in her tracks and pointed her finger at him. "You," she continued, "you always hold back. You want to control the situation but you can't. You never could. Now look at my mother. Look what he managed to do."

Jackie's rage stunned Richard. He felt defenseless, and at a loss for words. "I'm sorry you feel that way Jackie," he said, "but I—"

Christian interrupted him. "Don't apologize, Richard," he said. "You did the right thing. The last thing any of us needed last night was another confrontation. The bloody press would've loved it."

Jackie looked at him with rage. "Hey," she yelled. "You're supposed to be on my side. Me, over here, the wife, remember?"

Ian stood up and walked over to his sister. "Sit down and shut up, Jackie," he said. "Richard was right. I should've been the one to control my temper. I just played into that asshole's hands." He grabbed Jackie by the shoulders and sat her down. "Question now is," he continued, "where do we go from here?"

Jackie waved her arms in the air as if she were shooing away flies. "Get away from me, you traitor," she said to Ian. Then, looking back at Richard, she continued, "Step-dad here thinks that all he has to do is pay the asshole off again, and he'll just go away. Right? Wrong. Where's that gotten us before? Hmmm, let me think …" she said, as she put her finger to her temple. "Oh yeah, a dead father, and a mother who's been raped."

"Shut up, Jackie," Ian shouted. "You're way out of line."

"That's all right," Richard whispered. "Maybe I deserved that."

"Maybe you did," Jackie shot back.

"Then what's the alternative?" he said.

"Huh?" For once Jackie was speechless.

"Tell me. Can anyone tell me, what's the alternative?"

"Kill him," Jackie replied.

"What?" Anna said.

"Kill him," she repeated. "Hire someone and have him killed. A contract, a hit man, all that kind of stuff. You have a lot of connections, I'm sure you can find someone."

"Yes, I have connections in entertainment and shipping. Not mafia hit-men." Anna said.

"You're just not trying."

"You're crazy," Anna said. "You've seen *The Godfather* one too many times. No matter how much we'd all love to see Nigel blown away, this is the real world, and in the real Don Corleone won't save your ass from going to jail for murder."

"Then I'll do it," Jackie said sharply. "Since you're all such a bunch of wimps, I'll get a gun and do it myself."

Ian looked at Christian pleadingly. "Can we please get something and stuff it in her mouth? Like a sock? Just anything?" He walked back to his sister and put his hand over her mouth. "Can't you see? What you're saying isn't helpful at all. We're all in this together." Looking at Richard, he said, "And we're not a pack of murderers. Right?"

Richard didn't answer. He just shook his head from side to side.

"Then," Ian continued, "the only thing left to do is to let Richard do what he came here for. Meet with the shit-head, pay him off for the divorce papers, and be on our way. Hopefully, it'll appease him for awhile. In the mean time, if we're lucky, he'll turn up dead from some an overdose or a car accident, and we'll be rid of him for good."

Jackie plied Ian's hand off her mouth. "That's it? That's the plan? Pay him off again and pray?"

"Do you have anything better ... besides shooting him, that is?"

"Bunch of wimps," she mumbled. "But no."

"Then it's settled."

"Right," Richard said as he stood up. "It's settled." He looked at his watch. "It's almost time. The meeting's at 1:00 o'clock. I don't have too much time."

"So where are you going?" Anna asked.

"You didn't think I'd meet him here, on the yacht, did you? I don't want him anywhere near you and Angela."

"So where then?"

Richard looked out at the bay. "Over there." He pointed to a small inlet about a half mile away. "I'm taking the launch out. Taylor's going to meet me there. He's got a boat. We agreed to it last night."

"That's strange. Why not the dock?"

"Too many photographers and nosy people around. I want this done as quietly as possible." He turned and walked away. "I've got to get going. It's time."

"Wait," Anna shouted as she ran up behind him. "I'm going with you."

Richard stopped short and turned around. "The hell you are."

"Hey, those are my divorce papers he's delivering. I think I have the right to be there."

"No, you don't," Richard said, "This is my party. It's been a long time since I've been alone with that shithead, and believe me, I'm looking forward to it."

Anna looked at her father with a sense of concern. Something seemed different, but she couldn't figure out what. "Dad, I—"

"Stop it, Anna," he said. "It's not negotiable. Stay here, I'm taking care of it this time, for the last time."

Shit, Anna didn't like the sound of that. Her father was up to something. Maybe it was the look in his eyes, or that fact that she couldn't read his eyes at all, but something was very wrong. "Okay, Dad. You're right. I'll stay here."

Richard was surprised by how quickly Anna came around. "Fine. Tell your grandfather to have the crew prepared to leave in about an hour. It shouldn't take much longer than that."

He walked back to his state room to get the pay-off money. He stood over the bed and watched Angela as she slept. She was still in her wedding gown. He took off her shoes and adjusted her pillows. Then, pushing some curls away from her face, he leaned down and kissed her on the cheek. She sighed heavily but didn't wake up. "Everything's going to be alright," he whispered. "I promise."

He went to his suitcase and pulled out an envelope. Inside was a check from S & A Music made out to Nigel Taylor for the amount of 5 million pounds. *Son of a bitch*, he thought as he walked out, *let's see if you make it this far.*

He glanced at his watch again. Only 10 minutes left. He couldn't be late. He picked up his pace and walked to the waiting launch. He was going down the rope stairs when he heard Constantine shouting out his name. He looked up.

"Richard."

"I hear you. What is it?"

"A warning. Just got a report on the bridge. Some storms a couple of weeks ago, out at sea. The ocean floor may have shifted. Remember what I've told you. Slow and careful. Right?"

Richard nodded. "Right." He turned around and jumped on to the launch.

"Welcome aboard," he heard Anna say.

Quickly, he turned around and saw her emerge from beneath the rear seats. "What the hell?" he blurted out. "Get out. I don't have time for this."

"Too bad," she said. "If you want to get rid of me, you'll have to throw me overboard."

"Don't think I won't," he said as he moved towards her. "You can swim, right?"

Yikes. She didn't think he was actually going to do it, but she clung on the rear seats. "I'll put up a fight."

"Christ," he said as he put his hands to his head in disgust. "How did you ever get to be such a pain in the ass?"

She shrugged.

He turned and walked to the wheel. "Come on. Sit over here, next to me. Let's get going. Fighting with you is just gonna hold me up and I don't want to be late."

Anna sat next to her father and watched as he turned the ignition key and slowly inched up the throttle. The boat bolted into motion, then took off in the direction of the inlet. The wind felt wonderful against her face, and she sat back and relaxed as the mountains and hilltops went by in the distance.

"You look comfortable behind the wheel." Anna said.

"You think so?"

"Yes. It looks like you're even enjoying it. Can it possibly be you're taking an interest in boats?"

Richard smiled. "It's not so bad really. I can see the attraction. If I could only get rid of this nausea though."

As he approached the inlet, Richard slowed the engine and peered over the boat into the water.

Anna followed the direction of his eyes into the water. "What's the matter? Did you drop something in?"

He didn't answer.

"Dad," she said louder, "did you lose something?"

This time Richard heard her voice and looked up. "No," he said, without looking in her direction. "Everything's fine. Just looking at the ocean. Beautiful, isn't it?"

For someone who was usually so in control of a situation, her father's sudden lack of focus scared her. His new interest in marine splendor was puzzling. She couldn't figure out what was on his mind. She looked at him and smiled. "Yeah, just beautiful. So, is this where we sit and wait for Nigel?"

"This is it," he said as he looked around. "This is the spot."

Nigel was startled awake by the sound of his clock-radio. The volume was set at full blast, and he quickly grabbed a pillow to cover his head, but the music managed to seep through the feathers and silk anyway:

I woke up this morning and saw that you were gone,
Now I'm staring at the ceiling and wondering what went wrong ...

"Jeezus," he mumbled, "who wrote that shit?" He kept listening.

I'll never let you go is what I told you,
I'll never let you go, now let me hold you..
You're eyes are in my mind
Now I'm alone all the time
Crushed and broken
My thoughts are spoken,
Alone, now I'm alone ...

"Why's that sound so familiar?" he thought. "Oh yeah, I wrote it."

He took the pillow off his head and looked at the clock. Alarm clocks weren't part of his daily routine, but this day was different. He and Winters had decided to meet precisely at 1:00, and this wasn't a meeting he was about to miss. By the end of the day, he'd be 5 million pounds richer, all for the price of his signature on a piece of paper.

He lifted his head off the pillow. His stomach turned over; the inevitable hangover and ensuing vomiting. He couldn't escape it, but what did he expect? The drugs and alcohol he consumed last night would have killed the average man, and a few large farm animals. But, it had been a blast, and well worth it. The confrontation with Ian was spectacular, and Winters, well … even though he didn't fall into line, today was another day.

"Daahling," Helena said as she sashayed into the room. "What a party. You were … oh, how can I say … magnifique." She walked over to the radio and turned down the volume.

I'll never let you go is what I told you …

Helena cringed. "God, maybe I should just turn that awful shit off." She reached for the control button.

Nigel swatted her hand. "Hey," he said. "I wrote that awful shit. My first big hit with the Casuals, a classic you know."

"Whatever." She threw open the windows and let the sun stream into the room. The spikes of her six-inch heels clanked along the floor as she slithered her way towards him.

She adjusted the straps of her leopard-skin leotard, leaned over, and let her enormous breasts fall into his face. "My, my," she purred, "I can't tell you what a turn on you were last night. They all want a piece of you … Clapton. Even Bono—you know he told me you were his idol—wants you on his next CD."

She licked her full red lips and planted them firmly on his. Then she thrust her tongue far enough down his throat to pull out his tonsils, then withdrew it slowly. She smiled and said, "You know what did it all for you?" she didn't wait for an answer. "You know why everyone loves you now? It was that moment on stage with Winters. It was brilliant. The world loves him, and now you."

Nigel pushed her away. "Fuck off, Helena," he said. "The world loves me because of me, not him."

She looked surprised. "Don't kid yourself, daahling. I mean, your albums may be selling well, but that's not why Bono's dying to sing with you all of a sudden. Face it. They're all hoping you'll bring Winters along. But what the hell? Just enjoy it. I know I do."

As Nigel sat up, he started to shiver and a familiar wave of nausea hit him. It had been some time since his last hit of smack.

Helena patted him on the head. "Poor baby," she said with absolutely no sympathy. "You look a little pale. Why don't I just leave you to your needle now. I have some things to do. But," she said as she put her tongue in his ear, "keep up the good work. It makes Helena very happy to see you so popular. So don't blow it with your rabbi, Winters that is."

Nigel quickly searched the room for his cache of drugs. It was already a quarter past 12. He didn't have much time to waste. After finding what he was looking for in the nightstand, he quickly located a vein that hadn't been abused to mutilation, injected himself with the heroin, and proceeded to shower. *This shit's taking over my life,* he thought as he stood under to hot water. *It's time to get off, just as soon as I get my money …*

In a few minutes he was dressed and on his way down to his dock. It was hot and he could feel his heart pounding, something didn't feel right. Was it the smack? Too much? Too little? He didn't have time to sit around and figure it out. He heard Helena call to him but he didn't stop.

"Hey," she shouted. "Where you off to?"

Nigel was breathing heavily as he wiped the sweat from his forehead. "I have a meeting with Winters. See ya in a few."

"That's my daahling," Helena yelled back. "Give him a big kiss for me."

Nigel jumped into his speed boat and looked over the control panel. He had only driven one of these things twice before, and he was sober both times. He looked for the ignition. There had to be a key somewhere. There it was, right under the wheel. He turned it to the right and heard the twin engines roar to life. He unhooked the rope on the starboard side and reached for the throttle. He thrust it upward and heard the engine stall. *Patras, that scum-bag. Sold me a piece of shit.*

He turned the ignition key again. This time the engines started right up. He applied some gentle pressure to the throttle and let the boat slowly pick up some speed and move away from the dock. He looked out over the bay and searched for the meeting point. There it was, to the right and in the distance, the inlet where Winters was waiting. He pushed up the throttle full speed and stood up over the windshield to feel the wind and water on his face. All at once he felt powerful and energized. He loved the speed, the feel of the boat as it bumped up against one small wave after another.

"This is the life," he said to himself. "I should just stay here. Screw the rest of the world. Shit, that's what they want to do to me anyway. They all just want a piece of me, my money really—and I've got a shit-load of that." He found himself singing out loud: "I woke up this morning and saw that you were gone ... That song wasn't so bad, quite catchy really."

He continued to sing while the boat raced ahead. But after a few moments, he began to feel dizzy, and the familiar sense of nausea returned. He sat down and stared into the distance. *Fucking Winters, couldn't meet on dry land and make it easier.*

Easier, but why should Winters make it easier? He was his enemy, and always would be. He thought about what Helena said: the world loved him because of Richard. What a crock of shit. The world loved him because he was a genius. It had nothing to do with that prick. The only thing Winters was good for was his money, and that was about to dry out. When he handed over the divorce papers, his endless supply would be cut off. Maybe he shouldn't do it. Maybe he should just take the money and tell Winters he'd put the papers in the mail. That would really get his ass. *Right,* he thought as he reached for the papers, *I can't let him off this easy. He still owes me.* Opening the manila envelope, he took out the papers. Then, one by one, he let them fly into the ocean.

He spotted Richard's boat in the distance. He couldn't wait to see the expression on his face when he tells him the divorce has been postponed. "Poor Anna," he drooled, "she'll just have to cry in the arms of that little queer Moore a bit longer." His boat raced on as he continued to sing:

Yee ha baby
I'll never let you go is what I told you
Fuck you, Winters, now I'm gonna screw you
I'm a fucking genius
You have a little penis

"Christ," he laughed to himself, "I crack myself up."

Richard and Anna didn't say anything as they watched Nigel approach. His boat jumped up and down in the water as it sped full-throttle across the bay.

"Hey," Anna said. "He's going a little fast, don't you think?"

Seemingly unfazed, Richard answered, "He'll slow down, I'm sure."

But Nigel had no intention of slowing down. Exhilarated by his new rendition of his classic hit, he zigzagged his boat from side to side and shouted into the air, "Hey Winters, I have a new song for you to hear." He shouted out a few bars and watched for a response. But Richard's boat was too far away. There was no way he could hear him. "I know what'll get his ass," he murmured to himself. "We'll play a little game. Chicken." He steered directly to Richard's broad-side and continued at full speed. "Who's gonna move first, Winters? Me or you?"

Nigel's boat was closing in on Richard and Anna fast.

"Dad," Anna shouted, "get the engine started. I don't like the looks of things."

Richard didn't move.

"Did you hear me?"

He stared straight ahead. "Come on, fucker," he whispered. "I know what you're doing. You want to play games? You're gonna lose."

Anna's heart began to race. "Dad," she screamed. "This isn't the time to play games. His boat's heading right for us." She reached for the key.

Richard pushed her hand aside, grabbed the key, and threw it overboard. He stared back in Nigel's direction. "Come on, fucker," he said again. "Just keep coming."

"Dad," Anna screamed as she shook him by the shoulders, "you're crazy. This isn't a game to him. He wants to kill you. He's not going to slow down. He doesn't care about his own life."

"He'll slow down," Richard answered "Trust me."

"Look at him," Nigel laughed, "not moving. He thinks I'll turn away. I'll show him. I'll show him who the real man is, and always was." He stuck his head up over the windshield and shouted into the wind, "You're a dead man, Winters."

The roar of the engine was too loud. Richard didn't hear him. The boat was close now. A hundred yards away, maybe less. He felt Anna tug at his shirt. He looked back at her and saw tears in her eyes.

"I'm not gonna let you die, Dad. Not over him," she said as she continued to pull. "We're getting off right now."

"Sit down Anna," he shouted.

"No!"

He couldn't let her get in the way. He had waited for this moment for years: when it would be just the two of them, him and Nigel. The end was too close; it was only a matter of seconds. He picked Anna up by the waist and threw her into the water. She screamed.

"Swim to the shore and keep your head down," he yelled, then added softly, "I've got things to finish up over here."

"Nooo!" She wailed as she clung to the side of the boat. "I'm not leaving you." She looked out and knew they had only seconds left. Nigel's boat was less than fifty yards away, and it wasn't turning.

Nigel was euphoric. "YAHOO sucker, you're a dead man. Oh, baby, I'll never let you go is what I told you. You're a prick and a hard-ass and your daughter's a shrew. Shit, that doesn't rhyme …"

Richard didn't move. "Come on," he said softly, "don't stop now. Keep it coming."

Just then, Nigel spotted someone in the water. Who was it? He squinted as he tried to get a better look. She looked familiar. All at once he realized who it was. It was Sara, his Sara, but what was she doing there? *I'm hallucinating. It can't be. Why now?* He hadn't thought of her for a long time. Maybe she was angry. Maybe she hadn't been dead all this time. That's it. This was no hallucination. She was here, waiting for him. It all made sense to him now. Where else would she be but in Greece, where they'd first met. When was that? Oh, yeah, only last week. "I'll Never Let You Go" had just hit number one on the American billboards. That's why he heard it this morning.

He put his hand on the throttle to slow the boat down. *I'll be right there darling.* But the throttle didn't move. It's stuck. What the hell?" He pulled harder but nothing happened. Suddenly he felt the boat hit a bump that knocked him off his feet. He fell backwards to the floor. He was reaching for the back of his head when he felt another bump. But this time, everything went crashing all around him. Dazed and disoriented, he sat up and watched as his boat flipped backwards like a movie in slow motion. He felt the water crashing in all around him. It was warm, almost comforting, as it hit his skin. He was no longer in the boat. He had been thrown clear and now he was floating, but was it up or down? He needed to take a breath. Yeah, take a breath. He opened his eyes. Shit, they stung. He needed that breath. Just one. The bubbles, follow the bubbles. They were going up.

He kicked his feet furiously a few times. Within seconds, his head broke through the surface of the water. He gasped in some air, then hacked up seawater. Realizing his strength couldn't keep him afloat much longer, he looked around for something to grab on to. The boat was still floating, so he swam alongside it and grabbed the shattered propeller. He took a few deep breaths and looked around. He was safe. Then he remembered Sara. *Shit,* he thought, *that wasn't Sara. It was probably Anna.* How could he have been so stupid? Then it hit him. It was all some sort of set up. Winters had planted something in the water for his boat to crash into. Why else would he just be sitting there, not moving? Well, it didn't work. He was still alive and now Winters was gonna pay. Instead of five million pounds, it was gonna be ten. And fuck the divorce papers, they'll never see the light of day.

His stream of thought was suddenly broken by the smell of something coming from the engine. *Shit,* he thought, *petrol. Probably leaked into the water. Take me a bloody week to get that smell off my skin.* "Winters," he shouted, "you're a fucking dead man. You're never gonna get away from me. You'll see me in your nightmares. I *am* your nightmare. Oh, I'll never let you go, you fucking maggot. Oh, I'll never let you go, you shitty faggot. Hey, not a bad rhyme—"

The explosion was heard throughout the island. Severed electrical chords from the engine erupted into a cascade of sparks, igniting the gas that had spilled from the ruptured tank. The boat flew out of the water and burst into a fireball of gas and smoke. Instantly, it shattered into a thousand little pieces and showered the inlet with shards of glass and broken wood. The explosion would go down in the history books of Xenos: when legendary musician Nigel Taylor suffered an unfortunate, and untimely, death.

Anna and Richard watched as the local police gathered up the rubble and pulled it to shore. Anna was in shock. It all happened so quickly. Only seconds after Richard threw her in the water, Nigel's boat flipped over and exploded. But why? What did he hit? She needed some answers.

The local dock was in a frenzy. The fishermen had joined in on the salvage effort and the townspeople gathered around to witness the discovery of the body.

A short balding man approached them and handed Anna a blanket. From his uniform, Anna guessed he was either part of the local police department or the town's auto-body repair man. He smiled at her graciously and said, "Kiria Winters?"

"Ne," she said while pulling the blanket around her shoulders.

"Eime Capitaneos Georgiou," he said while fidgeting with his belt buckle.

Police, Anna thought, then cut him off, "English, please, if you can. My father doesn't speak Greek.

Georgiou nodded and cleared his throat. "Yez, of course, madam." His accent was almost incomprehensible. "There are sema questions I hev for you and yoora fadder."

"My who? My fadder?"

Annoyed, Georgious shot back, "Sou patera."

"Oh, my father," Anna said, "Of course. Go on, but I have to tell you, we already explained what we saw to another officer. We were planning to meet Mr. Taylor out on the bay and his boat hit something, flipped over, and exploded. That's all we know."

The police officer stared at Richard and again, fidgeted with his belt. "Did yooa know, Mr. Winters, zat yoora boat was behind a dandzerasa sandbar?"

A sandbar? Anna thought. *That's what it was.* How could she have missed it?

"No," Richard answered nonchalantly, "I didn't."

Anna quickly glanced over at him. She might have missed the sand bar in all her anticipation, but how could he? He was staring right down into the water practically the entire time. She'd even asked him what he was looking for. Suddenly Anna heard her grandfather's voice coming from somewhere behind her.

"Ahhh." Constantine said with a broad smile, "there he is. My old friend Georgiou." He put his arms around the police officer and gave him a bear hug. "Bravo. Superb job you and your men are doing. I'll be sure to let my good friend Panos know about it. What's he now? Head constable of the police?"

Clearly pleased with the praise from his childhood friend, Georgiou let out a huge grin and pumped Constantine's hand. "Goot to see you too, old fren." He stopped and said with some hesitation, "and yes, Panos, he how you say head constable, I appreciate dat." He looked back at Richard, and nervously added, "But just a few questions I need to—"

"Ahhhh," Constantine said, "what questions? My son-in-law here already told you the story. And as for that sandbar," he said taking Georgiou by the shoulder, "between you and me, my son-in-law wouldn't recognize one if it shot out of the water and bit him in the ass."

Clearly enjoying the brotherly discourse, Georgiou let out a hearty laugh. But Anna didn't see the joke. She knew her father could recognize sandbars, all too well as a matter of fact. He'd come upon one only a couple of years ago, right in the same area. When it knocked him off his feet, he broke his arm and he went to Jackie's wedding wearing a cast. She looked over at him while Constantine and Georgiou continued to snicker. What had he been up to all this time? It couldn't be what she was thinking. Her father could never be so devious.

Georgiou extended his hand to Richard and Anna. "I think my business here is, how you say ... finished. Thank you for yoora time."

"I take it your investigation is over?" Constantine said.

"I see it was all sama terrible accident."

"Yes, you're a very perceptive man, Georgiou," Constantine said. "I always admired you for that, since the time we were children. A terrible accident. That's exactly what it was. The sea floor changes all the time. Inexperienced sailors don't stand a chance."

Anna looked at her grandfather in disbelief. Those were the words he used just before she and Richard left on the launch. He had said something about storms out at sea possibly changing the local floor patterns. He warned her father to be slow and careful. Did he know about the sandbar too? Was he warning her father because he was afraid it had shifted? And why all the compliments and camaraderie with Georgiou? He never even mentioned this guy before and all of sudden, he's his long-lost friend. It was clear that her grandfather was protecting her father. But why? Were they in on this together?

All of a sudden, they heard shouts coming from a fishing boat pulling up to the dock. "To vrikame, to vrikame," a voice boomed over the bustling crowd.

"What's going on?" Richard asked.

"They found it," Anna said softly. "They found the body." This wasn't a moment she'd been savoring. For all the trouble Nigel Taylor had put her and her family through, still she'd been married to him. She stood back as the crowd huddled around the boat. She saw men and women wince, as the body was lifted onto the dock.

"Poor bastard," she heard a man behind her say. Realizing the tone was all-too familiar, she turned around.

"Andreas," she said, "what are you doing here?"

"Heard the explosion. We all did. The poor bastard didn't have a chance."

"What do you mean, poor bastard? Why the sudden sympathy? I didn't think there'd be any love lost between the two of you."

"There isn't. Just thought, what a way to go. All mangled like that."

"I know what you mean."

"And just think what flashed before his eyes before he went. Hell, if the explosion didn't kill him, his life story did."

"Patras!" It was Georgiou calling to him from the fishing boat. "Ola eine antaxi. Teliosame."

"Okay," Andreas shouted back. "Thanks."

"What's finished?" Anna asked. "What's Georgiou talking about?"

"Part of his investigation. He found out I had sold the boat to Taylor just yesterday. Wanted to know if it was operating all right."

"What did you tell him?"

"What else? That it was perfect, of course."

But it wasn't perfect. He had just told her at the wedding that he'd sold Nigel a faulty boat. He was hiding it from the police. Did he deliberately sell Nigel something that he knew would kill him?

"Andreas," she said with some hesitation, "maybe you should tell the police—"

Constantine cut her off. "Andreas," he said, as he approached them, "tragedy, what a tragedy." The two men shook their heads in anguish. "Come," Constantine said as he took Andreas by the arm. "I have some business to discuss with you. I know a nice new taverna in Ambelos ..." He put an arm around Andreas's shoulder. Their voices trailed off as they walked away.

Lunch! How could her grandfather feel like eating at a time like this? And what's with the cozy new relationship with Andreas? *I'm in the twilight zone,* she thought. *What's going on here?*

Anna watched as Nigel's charred remains were placed in a body bag and whisked off by ambulance to the nearby morgue.

The press, in the meantime, had swooped down on the scene. Cameras were clicking, tape-recorders rewinding and notepads being jotted on, all to document the most gruesome celebrity death of the century. Every press hound was there, trying to sniff out the best picture: the one that would sell for five or ten grand to the sleaziest tabloid. They looked for the burnt remains, but were too late. Then they spotted the next best thing. The grieving widow, shivering, covered with a blanket, alone on the dock.

They converged on Anna like a swarm of locusts. Microphones and cameras were shoved into her face. She swatted them away as she tried to free herself from the pack. But it didn't work. They were shouting at her from all angles. She began to feel disoriented. "Please," she heard herself say, "just leave me alone."

Her head was reeling, and she began to feel faint. This was all too much to bear. Suddenly, someone grabbed her hand and began pulling her away.

A voice rang out over the melee. "Get the cameras out of her face and give her some room."

Ian. He continued to pull her towards him while shoving the paparazzi back. Before she knew it, she found herself at the foot of the dock stepping into her launch. Ian started up the engine and the boat took off towards Constantine's yacht.

"Are you all right?"

She shook her head. "Yes, no, I don't know. Everything happened so fast." She took the seat next to his, reached over to the ignition, and turned the engine off. "I need a few minutes to calm down."

"Sure, of course."

"I have to talk to you before we get on board. There are some things I have to straighten out."

"Like what?"

"I know you're going to think I'm crazy, and paranoid, but I think there was some kind of conspiracy going to kill Nigel."

Ian laughed. "Conspiracy? What the hell are you talking about. Just who was conspiring?"

"Don't laugh. I think it was my father and my grandfather, and maybe even Andreas.

"Oh, Anna—"

She continued. "I think my Dad knew the sandbar was there and he positioned his boat so that Nigel would crash into it. I think my grandfather knew, maybe it was even his idea. And Andreas—well, he sold Nigel the boat. He told me it had a sticky throttle. I don't think Nigel could've slowed down even if he wanted to."

"I know you're under a lot of stress, and this whole things been very traumatic, but it was an accident. Nobody could've planned for Nigel to crash into a sandbar at full speed."

"Maybe not, but they certainly could help stack the deck against him."

"That's what you think?"

"I don't know what to think."

They both sat silently for a moment, then Ian spoke. "Listen, Anna," he said, "even if what you're saying is true, what would you do about it? Turn them all into the police? Put them on trial? None of this can be proven, not even about the boat. It's in about a zillion pieces, and besides that, it's your father and grandfather we're talking about. Do you really want to accuse them of this? Why don't you just look at it this way: the asshole's dead. He was gonna kill himself one way or another. It was only a matter of time, I told you."

Anna looked at him curiously. "Yes," she sighed, "you did tell me that before, all too often."

Ian shook his head and smiled. "So, I'm part of your conspiracy, then? You think I knew this was going to happen?"

"I don't know," she said wearily, "but you have been a little too confident for some time now that Nigel was gonna bite it soon."

"Just intuition. I call what I see. If a man's standing at the top of a mountain and sees two trains coming from opposite directions on the same track, he knows they're eventually going to crash. Does that make him the killer? Or is he calling what he sees?"

"He's calling what he sees, just as long as he's not the one who put them on the same track, right?"

"So you think we all conspired to put Nigel on the same track as the sandbar?"

"Look at me and tell me you didn't."

Ian looked at Anna and smiled. "We were all just calling the inevitable, my darling."

"You didn't answer the question."

Ian stared into her eyes. "Then ask another question. Ask yourself if it matters. Does it really matter to you how that piece of shit died? Because if it does, then go ahead and ask me that same question again."

Anna shook her head. Truth was, it didn't matter. She was glad he was dead and out of their lives. Ian was right. It was going to happen one way or another. And whether he was helped along a little by the people she loved most in this life ... well, maybe that was okay. But did her acceptance of this make her a killer too? If conspiracy was in fact, a reality, her silence made her part of their team. Could she live with that? She thought for a moment, then smiled to herself. Well, if there was ever a team she would be proud to be a part of, it would be that one: Stavropoulos, Winters, Patras, and Moore. Who would have thought they'd ever get together and all agree on anything? *Well, better on the inside of that foursome than on the outs,* she thought. They didn't play small games, losing was never an option, and she knew she belonged with them.

At that moment, she vowed to herself that she would never ask that question again. It didn't matter if Nigel's death was or wasn't an accident. She was part of a fine team, and, like the rest, she always played to win.

She leaned over and kissed Ian passionately. "I love you," she said, "and it doesn't matter."

He took her head in his hands. "So no more questions then?"

"No, no more questions, never." She smiled. "It's over, all over."

Epilogue

The rain fell heavily on the small turn-of-the-century chapel on the outskirts of Manchester. Anna and Richard sat silently and listened as Nigel's childhood pastor mumbled some supposedly heartfelt words of solace to the crowd. It was obvious that the pastor knew his subject only by reputation; otherwise, words like "generous," "sincere," and "modest" wouldn't have been part of his sermon.

But it didn't matter. In as much as the pastor didn't know his subject, he didn't know his audience either. Of the 250 or more people stuffed into the small chapel, 240 were from the press and the other ten consisted of a couple of distant relatives hoping for some kind of inheritance, Anna and her father, and the dynamic duo themselves, Helena and Amber.

Anna knew this day was destined for disaster. She didn't really want to be there in the first place, but her father insisted that they keep up appearances to the end. The press never knew about his rivalry with his ex partner or about her imminent divorce. There was no need to let the world know about it now.

When the service was over, Amber let out a scream that seemed to shake the dust off the rafters. "My poor poopsie-doll," she wailed. She then put her hand to her head, sighed, and fell to the floor. The photographers swooped down on her like a bunch of hungry maggots.

Anna turned to her father. "This is our chance to sneak out of here unscathed."

Richard grabbed her hand. "Let's go before anyone notices." The rain subsided as they exited the rear door.

But the press never lets anyone slip by. They were there, waiting like ravenous vultures, to flash their bulbs on Anna and Richard as they tried to escape the chapel.

"Ms. Winters! Ms. Winters! Over here ... just one question."

Anna stopped running and looked toward the man who had been shouting. He was an eager-looking young boy whose wide eyes and innocent smile made Anna think that this was probably his big break in the business. "Okay, just one question. Then you'll let us go, right?"

The crowd quieted down. "Yes, all right." The young man looked down at his note card, and hesitated.

"Oh, go on, mate," Richard said impatiently, "we don't have all day."

"Okay, okay," the boy said nervously. "Ms. Winters," he began, "did you know your late husband's last album's gone triple platinum since his death?"

"I'm quite aware of that."

"Can you tell us just where are the proceeds going? You're his sole survivor. What are you planning on doing with the money?"

Anna tried to suppress a smile. It was all so ironic. All the money and assets Nigel left were hers to begin with. But this, the album: that was his. It was the first real money he'd made since the Casuals, and he didn't live to enjoy it.

"Well," she said hoping nobody would notice the twinkle in her eye, "my husband always wanted to start a foundation for drug and alcohol rehabilitation. It was an issue close to his heart. So, I'll be donating all the profits of his last album to the new Nigel Taylor Home for Recovering Addicts. He would've wanted it that way."

The press was silent. It was obvious they appreciated her generosity.

"Now, if you'll excuse us," Richard said as he pushed his way to the waiting limousine.

"Ms. Winters, Ms. Winters …"

"I said no more—" She stopped short. It was the pastor running after her.

"Here," he said, as he handed her a brightly colored enamel urn. "You forgot this."

Anna looked down and cringed. *Oh,* she thought, *the ashes.* She thanked the pastor and took the urn from his hand. Then, next to Richard in the back seat of the limo, she handed it to him. "Here," she said, "you hold it. Gives me the creeps."

A short while later their limousine pulled up outside of Richard's home in Belgravia. The rest of the family was there, waiting to hear the details of the memorial before it hit the tabloids.

They were greeted at the door by Ian, who immediately stood back in alarm upon seeing the urn in Richard's hands. "What the hell are you planning on doing with that thing?"

"Don't know," Richard said as he walked past him toward the living room. "I haven't given it much thought yet." He placed the urn in the center of the coffee table and stood back. "I could use a scotch," he said as he looked around. They were all there, his family: Angela and her children, Christian, even Constantine and Beatrice. He couldn't remember ever feeling so alive, and so loved. "What do you say? A round for everyone?"

"Sure," Christian answered. "Club soda for me, but I'll pour for the rest."

Richard followed him behind the bar and lit up a cigarette from a pack hidden behind the bottles.

"Hey, I thought you gave those up?" Angela said as she put her arms around him and kissed him on the cheek.

"I did," he answered, "but this seems like a moment to have one. You know, a scotch and a cigarette, to celebrate."

"Sounds good to me," Christian said as he reached for the pack.

"Me, too," Ian answered as he grabbed the lighter.

Within moments, the room was enveloped in a cloud of smoke while the group sat down on the sofas and sipped their scotch. No sooner had

Anna started her impersonation of the fainting Miss Stiletto than the doorbell rang.

Constantine stood up. "That'll be Andreas," he said as he walked to the door.

"What?" Jackie shouted. "What's with him? Wasn't he the enemy just a short time ago? Now he's like ... part of the family. Maybe we should adopt him."

Nobody answered. Anna continued to sip her scotch as she watched Andreas and Constantine enter the living room. "So, what's this all about, Grandpa?" she asked. "Why the new cozy relationship with Andreas?"

"Ah, Anna, good to see you too," Andreas said. "But you needn't worry. I'm just here on business. Your grandfather and I have been talking about some new ventures."

Anna looked puzzled. "New ventures?" she asked. "Like what?"

"Well, my dear," Constantine said as he poured himself another scotch, "I've been thinking of selling off my ships."

"What?" Anna asked with alarm.

"Don't look so startled, Anna," Constantine said. "This industry: well, I believe its heyday is over. Most big oil companies have their own fleets, and the same's true of the cargo business. Let's face it, we're entering the Nineties, and private fleets like mine will be dinosaurs. It's best we get out while we're still ahead."

"Then, what will you do Grandpa? What's this new business venture with Andreas?" Anna was nothing if not persistent.

"Computers," Andreas shot back with a devious smile. "That's where the money'll be. Software, chips, telecommunications. I've been doing a lot of research. We'll get in now on the ground floor, make some money and pull out in a couple of years."

"So, I guess there'll be no retirement plans for you in the near future." Richard said to Constantine.

"Not while these legs can still move," he answered. "So, Anna, what do you say? Join us?"

"I don't know," Anna said. "It's all so sudden."

"Before you make any decisions, darling," Richard said, "maybe you should think about joining me at S & A. I've always had an office waiting, and besides, maybe we could collaborate on a CD. I've been writing music again," he glanced at Angela, "thanks to my new inspiration."

"Oh, I don't know." She sighed. "Thanks for the offer, but I need some time to think." She looked around the room and saw the faces of all the people she loved. Then, her eyes met Ian's. She remembered the seventeen-year-old boy who helped her onto that fishing boat in Xenos. Who would have known how that one event would have changed her life forever. She had never believed in fate, but when she looked into his eyes that day, her destiny was laid out before her. She hadn't let anything get in her way.

She looked down at the urn on the table and smiled. "Hey," she said, "you know, I don't want to think about my career or business right now. How about we all go out and get something to eat?"

"Now that's an idea," Richard said. "It's on me."

"Just one last thing," Anna said. "Hold on." She took a long drag of her cigarette, opened the urn, and slowly squashed the butt into the thick gray ashes.

Richard looked delighted. "And here I was wondering whether we had enough ashtrays in the house for all these cigarettes," he said as he inhaled deeply and stuffed his butt into the urn too.

"Right," Ian said as he tossed his cigarette into the urn. "Why dirty anything else in the house when this'll do so nicely?"

One by one, the rest of the group followed suit. When the ritual was completed, they all headed to the door.

Anna stood back and grabbed her father's arm. "So, just what are you planning on doing with that urn?" she whispered.

Richard smiled. "I was just about to leave a note to the housekeeper to have her take it out with the rest of the trash."

Anna gave him an appreciative grin. Then, she kissed him lightly on the cheek and stepped aside to let the new Mrs. Winters take her husband's arm. Ian put his arm around Anna, as the others fell in behind, and together they stepped out into the cool spring night.

LEEANN PAPPAS is an adjunct professor of geography in Long Island. Prior to that she worked for the City of New York as a Deputy Assistant Commissioner of Transportation.

Ms. Pappas grew up in New Jersey and Manhattan. As the daughter of a Greek shipping captain, Ms. Pappas traveled the world with her family as a child. These trips, along with her father's stories of actual events at sea, were the inspiration for this book.

LeeAnn is a graduate of Barnard College and Columbia University. She and her husband Tom currently live in New York where they are raising their two daughters.